Samael's Fall

Samael's Fall

The Angelic Chronicles

Marion Webb-De Sisto

To order additional copies of this book, contact:
Xlibris Corporation
1-888-795-4274
www.Xlibris.com
Orders@Xlibris.com
28371

This book is dedicated to my third grandchild, Braedwyn Gregorivich Lasas Former. May the archangels always watch over him, bringing many blessings of love, good health and a long and peaceful life. It is also offered with sincere thanks to Fanitsa Petrou for her inspired and beautiful illustration which graces this book's cover.

"Behold the truth of ALL THAT IS! The Abyss of Chaos is endless non-existence. Yet within its apparent barrenness a seed of creativity begins to grow, for within this continuous void there are a myriad of possibilities. Axons come together and the Source IS. From endless confusion comes eternal order. From wretched shapelessness springs divine form. There is no beginning, no ending, when there is no time, therefore, the Source is the absolute NOW. It is but one small spark of pure creativity, but within that creative power dwells the limitless potential to be all things forever.

We all exist within the NOW Absolute of the Source, for we are the offspring of its parenthood, the gadgets of its inventiveness. Ours is an endless existence of possible realities, never constant, always changing. Being the children of a creative god, we, too, are endowed with the gift of creativity. This wondrous possession is eternally ours. It is our freedom to choose how we shall pursue what we consider to be our destiny. The Source gives us all free will.

The following is but one soul's narrative of Creation. Its validity exists within the realm of possible realities. It is a justification of WHAT IS, an accounting of the omnipotence of creativity and a tribute to the diversity of all souls. This, then, is our story."

Archangel Seriel

Prologue

Nothingness. Timelessness. Darkness. Coldness. Silence. Beyond all things lay the Abyss of Chaos. It was incomprehensible, for there was no understanding. It was forever, for it was limitless. The Abyss was true non-existence, an endless nothing. But within its vacuous core dwelt the possibility of existence, the merest twinkling of something. Chaos had no knowledge of the fruit within itself because Chaos had no awareness of itself. This something slumbered deep within the Abyss, equally unaware of its being. It floated eternally in the dark void.

Yet there came an instant within this everlasting timelessness when this something, this Source of possibilities, stirred gently within its slumbers. There was no true awakening, only an ephemeral pause from its eternal sleep. Ancient eyelids fluttered, torpid limbs moved, a questing thought was vitalized and undying realization was born. i? . . . I? . . . am I? . . . what am I? . . . I AM! A tiny throb of awareness began to vibrate deep inside the Abyss of Chaos. It rippled across that ageless emptiness, creating an eternal echo of itself. Being born of timelessness, it, too, was immeasurable. Yet its moment of being became the absolute NOW, the perpetual ALL THAT IS. Thus, from the darkness came the light, from emptiness came fullness and from non-existence came creation.

The Source slumbered on, bedded in the eternal nothing. Yet from its instant of wakefulness came the wonder of pro-creation, which having been of the Source was also the Source. Thought built upon thought, giving birth to even newer thoughts. This waking moment, this spark of awareness, became ALL THAT IS, the life force which created all things. It spiraled outwardly from itself across the everlasting Abyss. And because it was an occurrence within the vastness of no time, it also, instantaneously, spiraled inwardly back to itself. Perpetual motion vibrating in the unending stillness. All that would spring from its continual motion would be compelled to follow the outwardly and inwardly spiraling dance of the life force. All must tread the path of existence. Yet within the apparent confines of the spiral there would be infinite choices, endless possibilities. The Source was pure creativity and it knew no bounds.

Now began creation. The brief questioning and subsequent answering thoughts brought forth eight beings of pure energy and crystalline consciousness. They had no form, no substance, because they were the first offspring of the Source, which was equally formless. They were vibrating auras of light, a spectrum of colors beyond all human perception. They mingled with one another joyously and freely, delighting in their newly found existence. And even though they were formed within the NOW Absolute, there was order in their creation.

First came Samael, the lord of light, purveyor of all curiosity and the only true son of self-awareness. Being first, he was the closest to the Source in every facet of his being. His aura was more luminous than any other and his vibrations disturbed the farthest most reaches of Chaos. His questing nature kept him ever moving and changing, never still and at peace. He yearned for that which was new and not yet realized. That which was known held no interest for him. Samael knew that all was possible and this knowledge gave him the power of great magic.

Second came the Christ Soul, the redeemer, divine teacher and guide. His light pulsated warmly, peacefully and constantly, gently contrasting with the vibrancy and rapidity that was Samael. Within him lay exulted consciousness. His companionship and wisdom were always sought by the other seven, for they knew these were given freely and lovingly.

Third came Michael, the champion and protector, who brings oblivion. His crusading light pierced the darkness of Chaos, searching for the truth in all things. He was the leader in every game which these children of light played. His courage and understanding of the Abyss gave him command over a formidable and awesome magic, which was equal to that of Samael's.

Fourth came Gabriel, the lord of practicality and invention. His aura was a beacon of sensibility for the others, lighting the way to plausible conclusions. He, least of all the eight, indulged in playfulness. Only when his brother Samael goaded him beyond endurance would he put aside his artisan thoughts and join his playmates.

Fifth came Raphael, the healer, musician and seeker of sound knowledge. All Chaos was bathed with his healing and enlightening aura, and was lulled by its rhythmic and dulcet tones. He wished only to help the others and to share his endless song with them.

Sixth came Uriel, the giver of tranquillity and higher understanding. His light was a sanctuary of blissful limbo. Like his brother Gabriel, he had little desire for games, but he deeply loved Samael and could be easily persuaded by his eloquent sibling.

Seventh came Seriel, the warrior, sorcerer and poet. His aura was as a reflection of Samael's. Of all those ethereal beings, he was the one most like the first-born of the Source. He was his constant companion, forever close by. Seriel was the eager perpetrator of his brother's lightning thoughts and, thus, he knew what Samael knew. His curiosity was boundless, but, unlike his brother, he cherished what was known.

Last of all came the Shekinah, the enchantress, mistress of agape and all-forgiving one. Her aura was the torch that lit the way back to the Source. Each of her brothers loved her deeply, but none loved her more than Samael and Seriel. The Shekinah equally cherished each of them, but she held Samael more dear than all the rest.

The Source from which these eight came, was all things, all possibilities, therefore, it possessed androgyny. When it re-created itself as the first eight supersouls, it made them androgynous, as well. Yet within the very essence of each of them, there was a displaying of one or the other of its possible genders. Only the Shekinah brought forth the more feminine qualities of the Source.

And so these unique children pursued existence within the loving security of the NOW Absolute. They played and cavorted across the expanse of the Abyss, delighting in each new experience that came to them. Samael would initiate every game for them with the question, "What if?" Michael would then plan strategies to solve whatever Samael had instigated. And away they would go, chasing, hiding, capturing one another in their endless playfulness. Their continual movement disturbed the stillness of Chaos and, above all, there was their laughter, their exuberance of being. This joy, like them, was timeless and it could not fade. With each new experience it grew, just as they did. Each of the eight found joy within its own self and then went on to discover the joy of that which was outside itself. These pleasures were forever, for there was no time.

When they grew weary of their play, then came the most blissful joy of all. They would meld with one another, blending their awareness so that each became the other, even while retaining a degree of self-awareness. Sometimes, the eight joined as one, trying to recapture their original state before their creation. This oneness brought great peace to all of them. Even Samael's questing nature became tranquil when this took place. Being closest to the Source, he truly wanted to be as one with all. Alternatively, they would meld in groups within the eight and, when this happened,

Samael always wished to blend with the Shekinah. She would not always allow this, even though it was also her desire. The Shekinah did not wish to be unfair to her other brothers because she loved them, too. She also knew Uriel's love for Samael was great and that Samael was often reluctant to blend his awareness with the Christ Soul.

When Samael and the Shekinah did meld, however, it was a truly wondrous event. His vibrant aura gave brilliance to her more delicate one, even as hers brought greater stability to the ever-changing nature of his. Being the first and last creations of the Source, they were very close to their progenitor. And within the laws of ALL THAT IS, that which is sent out must always return. Thus, the Shekinah was as a complement to Samael.

Eternity flowed on, but not as before, for each game the eight played, each experience they pursued, changed nothingness into something. Remnants of their make-believe were left within the Abyss like forgotten toys, which a child discards when other amusements entice his attention away. This neglected something could never really be of the NOW Absolute nor of Chaos because it was a combination of both. It was the pregnant possibilities which Samael would eventually adapt.

Just as their experiences changed Chaos, so, too, was the Source similarly altered. Because they were a part of the Source, their actions reflected back to their slumbering parent who, in turn, matched its growth with theirs. And all who would come after these first eight would possess this nourishing link to the Source. Thus, the Source has ever been a continually growing occurrence, a power which has not yet reached its full potential.

The eight carried within them a knowledge of the Source. Yet none had a total understanding of it, even as they did not have a complete awareness of their own capabilities. Gabriel and Uriel saw the Source as something to be revered, as a wise parent whose behavior in all things was above reproach. Michael believed it was the duty of the eight to carry out the wishes of the Source, to be the obedient and ever faithful defenders of its actions. Raphael perceived the beauty and wonder of the Source and he strove to share this awareness with the others. To Samael and Seriel, the Source was a challenge to be met, a stern parent who wished to limit their pursuit of endless possibilities. Yet Samael alone considered himself equal to the Source. Only the Christ Soul and the Shekinah understood the boundless love, which was the Source. They knew that love was for all things and forever. Therefore, nothing would be left unforgiven and ignored outside of that love.

And so, these diverse extensions of the Source dwelt within timelessness. These developing creations flourished where there had previously been barren non-existence. Their continued actuality brought legitimacy to the life force which spiraled further and further out in keeping with their persistent expansion. But this idyllic continuity between that which was and that which was not could not last forever. When all is possible, even the negative aspect of WHAT IS must be allowed to validate itself. Samael was the instrument through which this truth could be made actual. His ceaseless curiosity would vitalize the dormant ability of the Source to be all possible things for all of possible eternity.

Chapter One

Samael searched Chaos with his swift awareness, but the others were not close by. He was alone. They were off somewhere playing one of his games with which he had long since become bored. More and more, he found himself separating from his brothers and even his sister whom he adored. Their constant companionship no longer gave him a sense of well-being, instead it restricted and stifled his feelings. Samael wished to be alone to pursue the ever-increasing thoughts that were flowing through him. He was growing more aware of himself and his separateness from the others. Each of the eight was becoming fully individualized, but only he truly realized this fact. It was a painful yet ecstatic experience, and it was forever capturing his attention.

His thoughts came back to Chaos. He was in a part of the Abyss which Gabriel referred to as being "beyond what is safe and known." Soon after their birth, the eight archangels had decided to regard the Source as the center of the Abyss. Wherever they went, providing they could perceive its light, they considered themselves to be within a safe area. This idea had been put forward by Gabriel and they had all agreed to it, even Samael, albeit reluctantly. Now, he had deliberately traveled to where the Source was no longer even a pinpoint of light within the Abyss. He neither wanted the company of the others nor the reminder of from where he had sprung.

Very early in his life, he had held the Source in deep reverence. Samael was awed by its size, its intense brilliance and kaleidoscopic qualities. He was drawn back to it more often than the others because his was the greatest of curiosities. Finally, he had tried to reunite with the slumbering Source in order to satisfy his need for more knowledge of it. At first, the sensations and thoughts, which filled his being, were more wonderful than anything he had yet experienced. They were even more blissful than when he melded with the Shekinah. Gradually, he began to lose all sense of himself, but just before the point of total surrender, he suddenly clung to his identity with such intensity that the union was abruptly ended. He found himself, once more, outside of the Source.

However, his insatiable curiosity soon overcame his fear and he attempted to meld with it, again. This time his action was blocked and the searing thought: *It is too soon, my son, you are not yet ready!* burned through his consciousness. Thus, began Samael's separation from the Source because he would carry this rejection with him through all eternity. Having been refused by his parent, he would have no further contact with it. Its mysteries would no longer beckon to him. Instead he would turn his attention to the even greater perplexities of the Abyss.

Samael's movement through this part of Chaos was, like everything else he did, extremely rapid. His siblings had long ago dubbed him the Lord of Lightning-Swiftness. Yet he overlooked nothing. He was ever-watchful for something new and thought-provoking, but the Abyss seemed to be filled with nothingness. His thoughts about Chaos, however, did not cease, instead they grew more pressing. What and why was the Abyss? Had it always been? How did the Source come into existence when there was such barrenness? And was not even nothingness truly something? If only he could fully understand Chaos, perhaps then the Source would accept him? Then he would learn many wonderful things of, and from, his parent. Their earlier union had taught him that the power of the Source and of the eight was limitless. Also, that all things were possible within the life force spiral because the Source was pure creativity. Something at the very edge of his awareness caught Samael's attention. At first, he thought he must have moved back into the vicinity of the Source, and that he was just able to perceive it. Yet suddenly the realization came to him that this light was close by and exceedingly small. Without Gabriel's presence and suggestions of caution, Samael hurried to the light thing. To his amazement he discovered it to be a swirling mass of eight colored light beings who, except for their size, were identical to himself and his siblings. They spiraled around, joining and breaking apart over and over, just as the eight had done many times in their play. Two of the beings, himself and the Shekinah, broke free from the other six and spun away, only to be chased by the others. Samael slipped into the miniature scene without awareness or effort.

Oh, how he loved the Shekinah! She spun around him, moving ever closer. Her spiraling dance was much slower than his, yet to him it seemed more perfect. At last, she blended her awareness with his and, once again, he knew the peace that only she was able to bring to him. The others quickly caught up with them and, enclosing them within their circle, they gradually began to meld into one glorious, spinning awareness. Their joy was suddenly ended when Gabriel pulled himself away from the others, leaving only the warning thought:

"We have wandered too far from the Source!"

Quickly, yet reluctantly, they each separated, realizing Gabriel's truth because this part of the Abyss was unknown to them. Desperately they began to search for even the merest thread of light, which might be the Source, but only utter darkness greeted them. To Samael the lack of light appeared to somehow dim the luster of their auric selves. His curiosity moved gently within him, even though it was tinged with fear.

Abruptly he was, once more, observing the tiny scene instead of being a part of it. What had happened? How could he have suddenly relived a previous occurrence? He recalled how Michael had eventually led them back to the safe area where, because of the brilliant light from the Source, the darkness was not quite so intense. Even as this memory returned, he observed it happening in miniature before him. Then the small light beings were gone, leaving only the deepness of the Abyss.

Samael waited for something else to occur, but all around him was the empty dark. Questioning thoughts of this experience followed one after another as he lingered in the nothingness. What had just happened and how could it have taken place? Was he responsible for its occurrence or was its existence totally separate from himself? And even as these thoughts pursued one another through his being, the miniature replay began, again.

This time Samael did not slip into its realm of existence, instead he observed every particle of it very closely. It was an identical rendition of what had been shown before, nothing was changed. As it reached the point of Gabriel's warning, Samael found himself thinking it was almost always Gabriel who ended their play. This was usually with some admonitory remark or sharp reminder of their duties. Why could he not enjoy himself like the others? Why did he always have to be so serious? If only there was no Gabriel, then their play would be endless. As this thought was born within Samael, it became a reality before him. The tiny light being, who was Gabriel, suddenly was no more. There were only seven dancing auras which did not break apart in a frantic search for the Source. They continued on with their game until the scene faded, once again.

Now, Samael's curiosity was truly aroused and he waited patiently for things to begin, again. When they did, there were only seven light beings. Gabriel was gone and they played from the beginning to the end of the scene without interruption. Next, Samael willed his brother to be present, once more. As the scene began, again, the Lord of the Fourth Essence had returned. The first archangel stayed and manipulated two more replays and then moved on, searching for similar occurrences in other parts of the Abyss. To his amazement they seemed to be coming into existence in several places. Everywhere, in fact, the eight had been. Each was a replica of some incident which had taken place since the creation of the archangels. Each was different. There were two which lay quite a distance beyond the one Samael had originally found, even further away from the Source. They were so slow moving that, at first, they appeared to be frozen at one point of occurrence. With patient observation, however, Samael realized there was movement.

As he traveled back to inner Chaos, he found even more scenes. The eight had played most frequently within the protective, spiraling light beams which continually streamed from the Source. He also discovered that the rapid or slow movement within each scene depended on its proximity to, or distance from, the archangels' parent. Some were so close that their entirety was but an instant of twinkling existence. They were minute stars in the swirling cosmos of the Source.

*   *   *

While Samael was away making his new discoveries, Seriel, too, was moving through the Abyss alone. He had requested to go with Samael, but had understood his brother's need to be away from his siblings. Seriel was also experiencing the desire for separateness. His solitary wanderings had brought him, like Samael, to a part of Chaos which was beyond the safe area. A dark, dark place where the light from the Source never came.

Seriel pondered his existence thus far. Life was good, but he felt a need for so much more. Just as Samael wished to experience everything, he, too, was filled with the desire to not only be all things, but to also have a complete understanding of them. When he melded with the others within a group, he allowed himself to merge with them even more deeply than they did with him. He did this in order to fully comprehend their essences. Only he truly understood Samael because he had almost become him when they blended their awareness, one-on-one, soon after they came into existence. Knowledge was all powerful to Seriel. If he could fully understand something, then he also had total command over it.

His most recent thoughts were concerned with how to amass and then preserve everything he was learning. Nothing should be lost, everything was of value. He believed the Source was endlessly stored knowledge which was continually expanding, as it constantly absorbed that which was new. Unlike Samael, he recognized his inferiority to the Source. He would be able to hold within him much knowledge, but he was convinced there would come a saturation point for his being.

As he was filled with these thoughts, he began to review all of what he had learned thus far. First was his instant of being, his complete separation from the Source. Next was his awareness of himself and of others similar to him. Then on and on through all things which had happened beyond his birth. He felt, again, the joy of the innocent play within which the eight had indulged themselves early in their existence. Also, the blissful peace of melding with each other.

And, as the Lord of Sorcery became lost within his thoughts, that ancient nothingness gave Seriel something, even as it was similarly giving to Samael. The Abyss is the canvas upon which the life force paints its creations, and all extensions of the Source are true artists. Spiraling out from Seriel there began a series of shimmering spheres, each just touching its neighbor. Within these luminous orbs lay the totality of life thus far, each containing one small occurrence of existence. Eons later, in a physical universe, Seriel's creation would be looked upon as the Akashic Records.

The seventh archangel watched with fascination as the luminous spheres ceased to exude from his being. They became a shimmering string of jewels, a gigantic, spiraling record of creation, suspended in the void and no longer a part of himself. Each sphere contained within its illuminated depths an occurrence of WHAT IS. These events ranged from the initial stirring of the Source to Seriel's immediate birthing of the phenomenon. Even as he began to comprehend this imprint of life, new spheres were budding from their predecessors. He had been the creator of this wondrous thing, but it was now something unto itself alone.

Inside one new sphere he perceived Samael observing a miniature scene of dancing auras. On closer inspection, Seriel realized his brother was watching a game which the eight archangels had previously played. It would seem as though Samael had discovered a similar wonder to the one which he was now witnessing. The next sphere showed Samael wandering through Chaos, finding other miniature reproductions of what they had experienced since their creation. In the following one he saw the Shekinah anxiously searching for both him and Samael. Her concerned thoughts came to him even as he watched her and, for a while, he was lost in her beauty.

Recovering from his reverie, Seriel plunged into the center of the spiral of spheres and darted back and forth along its entirety. He discovered he could easily penetrate the spheres without disturbing their contents or damaging their form. While inside each one, he relived whatever its occurrence was, and for a time this became an all-consuming experience. Oh, what a marvelous toy he had invented! Now he would be able to cherish everything. Nothing would be lost, all would be preserved for his delight and curiosity. Perhaps even Samael would tarry awhile with what was known instead of only hungering after the unknown. Seriel decided to show this new creation to his brother, and he knew where to find him. The spiraling orbs had shown him the exact place.

Leaving the spheres, Seriel moved through the Abyss toward Samael who was now well within the safe area. He was amusing himself by continually altering the tiny scene which played itself out before him. Seriel knew Samael was aware of his coming because they each could sense their proximity to one another. Yet for a while Samael did not acknowledge his brother's presence. Impatiently Seriel sped his urgent thoughts to Samael:

"Come quickly, my brother! I have created something truly wondrous."

Gradually, Samael turned his attention from the scene and centered it upon his sibling. Even in his excitement Seriel did not miss the lack of rapidity in Samael's movements. This was an occurrence which he had observed on several recent occasions. The Lord of Lightning-Swiftness now seemed to have command over his vibrations and could alter them at will.

"Why do you bother me with your doings, Seriel? Can you not see that I am busy with my own diversions? Your luminous spheres are quite enchanting, but I shall examine them when I am less preoccupied."

"How swiftly you read my thoughts, Samael. None of the others are as accomplished as you."

His flattery brought such radiance to Samael's being that Seriel was briefly overcome by its vibrant tone. He forgot the urgency of his own discovery.

"Do you, my little brother, fully comprehend what we have learned while wandering alone through the Abyss? Just as the Source is able to create so, too, are we. The Source gave us life and we, in turn, are endowed with the same power. Can you begin to understand the endless possibilities which are occurring to me? We can be as great as the Source!

Chaos is a magnificent medium through which we can accomplish anything."

"Do not let such things become known to Gabriel!" Seriel warned.

Samael's laughter-filled thoughts shattered the stillness. "Gabriel is a fool and I can have done with him whenever I so choose. Watch!"

He turned his attention back to the miniature scene. The tiny light beings played their endless games as the two brothers recaptured those happy times. It was not difficult to identify Gabriel within the scene. He never led the chase or exploded into joyous abandon.

As this particular reflection of their lives faded, Samael's questioning thoughts came to Seriel:

"Do you see how Gabriel differs from the rest of us? He is not filled with the joy of being. He thinks only in terms of sensibility and caution and, thus, spoils every game we play. Now, let us suppose that only seven light beings sprang from the Source. Let us say that Raphael was created fourth, Uriel was fifth, you were sixth and our sweet sister was seventh. Hence there is no place for Gabriel, so let him be no more! Observe, oh my brother!"

Once again, the happy scene unfolded itself to Samael and Seriel, but this time its occupants played with greater exuberance. Their auras radiated more color and intensity. Gone was Gabriel with his never-ending practicality which had always diminished their pursuit of total joy. Without his warnings and admonitory interjections, the seven, tiny light beings glowed with fulfillment. They accomplished all their games and knew no fear of the unknown.

"What say you now, my brother? Am I not as great as the Source? I am its first offspring and I am also the first to understand that we have the ability to create." For a moment the lightning thoughts ceased, and then one more was sent racing through Seriel's being. "And think you, Seriel, that perchance I am *greater* than our creator? For am I not also able to destroy what was created?"

Before Seriel could form an answering thought to Samael's subtlety, they both felt the approach of the Shekinah. Instantly, Samael willed Gabriel back into the miniature scene, and he suggested to his brother:

"Let us go and meet our sister."

The two archangels moved away from the small reproduction of their play and journeyed toward the Shekinah. As always with their adored sibling, a feeling of peace and completeness permeated them as they sensed her closeness.

She came in gentle beauty, these thoughts of concerned love radiating from her: "What has kept you from me, my brothers? I have been searching and searching for you."

Samael quickly answered, "Sister, we were preoccupied with our own affairs. It was remiss of us not to inform you of what we were about. Please forgive our thoughtlessness. We have no wish to bring you concern."

"What was of such interest as to keep you both so far away? I know you have been in parts of the Abyss which are unknown to us."

Wishing to share their new discoveries with his beloved sister, Seriel enthusiastically began, "Both Samael and I have been learning more about our wonderful capabilities. Do you realize that we have the potential to create . . ." A piercing, rending thought from Samael silenced him abruptly.

" . . . flights of fancy and games of trivia?" concluded Samael, finishing his brother's interrupted explanation. "Seriel, our sister has no wish to be bored with our petty curiosities and trifling thoughts. In truth, I sense she is here to impart something of importance to us. Am I not correct, my lady?" Once more, Samael's increasing aptitude for perceiving the unshared thoughts of others was manifesting itself.

Silently, the Shekinah marveled at her brother's skill as she replied, "That is so. I came in search of both of you because Michael has information which he intends to share with all of us. You must come now to our usual meeting place so that we can listen to Michael and learn from him." She moved away, as if to leave, but then turning back, she added, "Seriel, would you go on ahead? There is a small matter which I wish to discuss with Samael. Tell Michael we shall return shortly."

Reluctantly, Seriel began to move toward the center of the Abyss because the meeting place was close by the nurturing light of the Source. He would prefer to accompany his sister and have Samael leave, but apparently that was not to be. A newly formed feeling of jealousy stirred within him and his auric being pulsated with this unfamiliar emotion.

As he hurried away, a warning thought from Samael overtook him. "Remember, my brother, even though Michael wishes to share information with us, we are not obligated to disclose our findings to him!"

When Seriel was gone, the Shekinah asked, "Why did you silence our brother? What did you not want him to tell me?"

Without hesitation Samael replied, "You are so astute, my lady, I am never able to deceive you. I had told Seriel of a small secret which, eventually, I would have shared with you. In his enthusiasm he was about to divulge my secret and that is why I stopped him. It is I who should tell you of my new discovery, not he." Samael moved a little closer to his sister and his radiance was overpowering. "Now, I must explain, lest you think ill of me. Seriel attempted to tell you that I have realized we each have the potential to create things which I have termed 'gifts.' I desperately wished to tell you of this wonderful concept myself. Please forgive my deception, it was ill-mannered and uncaring of me."

Baited by his tantalizing, half-explained answer, the Shekinah asked, "Gifts? What does that mean? How does one create a gift?"

Sparks of mirth exploded throughout Samael's being as he gleefully exclaimed, "Oh, my lady, you are just too clever! By requesting an explanation from me, you are causing me to practice my newly found ability. A gift is something given by one being to another, a sharing which takes place between us. Thus, by telling you my secret, I am giving you the gift of my knowledge." He moved even closer so that the outer extremities of their auras touched. "I am, indeed, giving you the gift of myself."

For what seemed an eternity they remained motionless, each lost in the illuminating proximity of the other. The need to blend their individual awareness was overwhelming, yet the Shekinah found herself struggling against that urgent desire. She sensed a developing depth within Samael which was dark and unknown to her. It did not vibrate with his glorious brilliance. It was a slow, cold pulse of darkness which reminded her of the Abyss. Even so, its awful bleakness stirred her compassion and she drew closer, compelled to partake of his essence.

Thoughts flew so swiftly between them and they became one. Eternity moved on while they lingered within the mesmerizing compulsion of their love. As Samael succumbed to his sister's selfless tranquillity, a new name for her blossomed within his creative soul. He thought-whispered gently:

"Sweet sister, I will, henceforth, call you Malkura. This is my gift to you. No matter what transpires between us beyond now, know that it is given to you as an expression of my unending love for you." Then Samael quickly withdrew his awareness from hers and they separated immediately. After a short pause, he asked:

"What think you of my gift to you, Malkura? It is but the first of many such tokens of my affection which I shall bring to you. I will astound you with my creativity!"

"Your gift of a name pleases me very well, my lord, and I thank you for it. May I share it with the others when we return to them?" Although she answered him immediately, her deeper thoughts were elsewhere. Their melding had brought to her a better understanding of the dark depth within Samael. It was a hiding place for those things of which he did not want her to know, and she had learned how rapidly it was growing. She was about to disclose her discovery to him when his reply interrupted her thoughts:

"Whatever brings pleasure to you, Malkura, is acceptable to me. But let us go to them now, for I fear we have tarried too long and Gabriel will lecture us on keeping everyone waiting. Come, sweet sister, let us race one another to see who will arrive at the meeting place first!"

He darted ahead of her, but then stopped and waited until she caught up with him. Their thought-laughter sparkled around them as they sped across Chaos toward their brothers.

Chapter Two

The group of five waited for the Shekinah to return with her two brothers. Raphael was gently vibrating some music which had come to him a short while earlier while he was alone. His being pulsated with varying shades of blue as he shared his song with his siblings. The Christ Soul seemed lost within the music as his own soft onca color became dappled with the blues of Raphael's notes. Gabriel moved impatiently back and forth, completely oblivious to what Raphael was sharing, but Michael heeded his brother's song intently. Like Seriel, he knew everything was of value and worthy of attention. Uriel was positioned a short distance away from the others, keeping watch for his brothers and sister. At last, his vigil was rewarded. In the far distance he could just perceive the glorious yellow of Seriel's aura.

Uriel moved over to the others and declared, "Seriel is coming!"

"Only Seriel?" Gabriel did not attempt to conceal his annoyance.

"Patience Gabriel." The Christ Soul's gently chiding thought stilled any further complaints from the fourth archangel.

Raphael ceased his music and waited with his brothers for Seriel's arrival. He cherished a strong affection for the Lord of the Seventh Essence. Previous melding with Seriel's awareness had revealed their sibling love to be one of mutual respect and a need to protect each other. On the rare occasions when Raphael and Seriel had blended, it was pure creativity. Then the peaceful hues of green became a reality.

"The others are coming." Seriel was aware of the group's questioning thoughts even before he reached them. "The Shekinah wished to be alone with Samael for a short while before returning to us."

Raphael quickly sensed the hurt which lay beneath this statement and he moved close to Seriel to silently convey his sympathy and understanding.

"Why is it always Samael who creates problems?" Gabriel was certain his brother was the true cause of this further delay. "Michael, you and I will caution him severely after you have finished this meeting with us. Samael must be made to understand how he is becoming irresponsible to, and separate from, our group. You, too, Seriel, are removing yourself and your thoughts away more frequently than you should. We came from one, were created as one and must remain as one. I know this is what the Source requires of us!"

"That is only your interpretation of WHAT IS, Gabriel." Seriel was angered by Gabriel's lecturing. He felt obliged to defend Samael even though he was presently upset with him.

However, before he could continue, Raphael echoed his thoughts:

"We each perceive WHAT IS by differing notions. Perhaps that is what the Source would have us do."

They waited without any further commenting thoughts for the arrival of Samael and the Shekinah. At last, their auras could be seen moving rapidly toward the group. Each marveled within himself at the awesome radiance that was Samael. Even Gabriel was briefly swayed from his annoyance with his brother. And each was totally overcome with the rapturous beauty of the Shekinah.

"I see we have kept our brothers waiting, my sister," Samael exclaimed as they reached the others. "A thousand pardons, loved ones, but we were engrossed in our own affairs." For a moment, he moved close to his sister so that blending began to take place. Then he quickly became separate, once more.

The implication of this action was not lost on any of the group, particularly not on Seriel. His newly experienced emotion of jealousy engulfed him, once again, and he longed to escape to his delicate, shimmering spheres. He knew he would find peace with them. Lost in this thought, he involuntarily moved back from the group, and in so doing he connected with Uriel, who was immediately behind him. This unexpected contact with his brother was brief. Uriel moved off to the side to allow room for Seriel. However, its short-lived existence brought a new awareness to Seriel. Dominating Uriel's being was an emotion which was very similar to his own envious thoughts. Yet there was one subtle difference between their desires. Whereas Seriel longed for the Shekinah's undivided attention, Uriel wanted Samael's love. The extent of the sixth archangel's passion for his brother astounded Seriel. He had never before realized Uriel's feelings were so deep.

"Well, Michael, what is your important news?" continued Samael. "Have you contrived a new game for us to play? Or has Gabriel finally convinced you that such trifles are not seemly for lordly beings?"

"Samael, Samael, why must you always be this way?" the Christ Soul gently asked. "Life is quite sublime, therefore, please do not spoil it for us."

"Sublimity is boring, brother mine. I seek a different path from you. Each of us is a totality unto himself and herself. Therefore, we each must pursue our own individual destiny. It amuses me to goad Gabriel, just as it pleasures him to court the favor of the Source. I question, he fawns and you forgive. It is our diversity which excites me!" This last comment brought an added brilliance to Samael's aura.

Answering his first-born brother's questioning thought, Michael explained, "I have summoned you all here to tell you of what I observed while conducting my usual inspection of the safe area and beyond." Long ago, he had designated himself as their protector. He would regularly move through that part of the Abyss which they considered safe, ensuring that all was as it should be. Occasionally, he extended his tours to include parts of Chaos which lay outside the safe area. Recently, during one such venturesome expedition, he had found something new.

"Pray tell us what has caught your attention, Michael. It must have been quite a curiosity!" Merriment rippled along Samael's being.

Ignoring his brother's tone, Michael somberly continued on, "The Abyss is not as barren as we have thought. There are new creations appearing throughout our home. They are not as we are, yet they are reflections of ourselves and the games we have played. I have been watching these small scenes and they seem to be multiplying in number."

Samael feigned boredom. "Is that the extent of your news, my brother? I thought you had brought us all together to share something new and exciting. Seriel and I are already aware of these miniature replicas of our doings throughout Chaos. They are of no importance, they merely repeat, over and over, the acts within which we have indulged ourselves. They are quite inconsequential." Swiftly he sent this shielded, silencing thought to Seriel: "Do not reveal that the scenes can be manipulated!" It came from that dark, ever-growing facet of his being which had concerned the Shekinah. He directed it to a similarly forming part of his brother. Within this shadowy place they could keep many things from the others.

"You and Seriel already knew of these things?" Gabriel was quite indignant. "Neither of you has any sense of responsibility. This information should have been brought to the rest of us immediately. Is that not so, Michael?"

"There is no harm done, Gabriel." At times, Michael was as forgiving as the Christ Soul. "You know how quickly Samael tires of things. If these new creations had held his attention for a while, then he would have shared them with us. Yet I am surprised you did not report them to us, Seriel. Unlike Samael, you value everything."

Seriel responded, "I have only just witnessed them." Then, echoing Samael's deception, he added, "However, they are but amusing little distractions, Michael. Their repetition quickly becomes tiresome. The Source has probably given them to us for those times when we grow bored with our games. The scenes are a form of enjoyment which needs no effort or participation from us, being merely a toy to suit our laziness."

"Some of us do not indulge ourselves in laziness!" Gabriel's indignation had increased. "And how do you know these scenes were created by the Source? Would they not have always been here, as we have been, if they came from the Source? I tell you all I have concerns with these new intrusions upon our existence. I wish to examine them for myself."

"I am certain Michael has every intention of showing them to us. He shares your concerns, Gabriel," replied the Christ Soul. At times, even he found Gabriel to be a little pompous and overbearing.

"Let us all go now," prompted Raphael. "I am truly intrigued by these replicas of ourselves."

"Yes," agreed the Shekinah. "We should view them and then discuss whether they are of the Source or of Chaos."

Thoughts of agreement came from all except Samael and Seriel. They did not argue, they simply did not concur.

"Then it is settled," stated Michael. "We shall consider the implications of these new discoveries only after we have examined them in detail. Samael and Seriel, you have kept your thoughts silent. Do you wish to come with us or will you wait here for our return?"

Without hesitation Samael answered, "We shall await your return, my brother, but before you leave, the Shekinah has something to tell you. Something which was shared by us earlier." Lovingly, he motioned his sister to explain.

For an instant, everyone forgot their personal or shared thoughts. Each, as always, was enthralled by the Shekinah's beauty, and each experienced her thoughts as though they were for him alone. She had the ability to be all things to each of them because she was the pure essence of unconditional love.

"Samael has created something which he has named a gift. Whenever a thought is shared between us, he perceives this concept as the giving of a gift. Thus, we constantly share gifts with one another. To mark the beginning of this new idea, he has given me a name other than the one by which you already know me. It is Malkura. Is it not beautiful?" She spun around, as if to better display her new possession to them.

"It is, as you are, my lady," agreed Seriel. Malkura! Malkura! The name sang through his being. He wished he had been the perpetrator of this notion, yet this time he felt no jealousy toward his brother. Seriel knew that Samael's love for their sister was as deep as his own, and the name was just so exquisitely right for her. He acknowledged his brother's superiority in certain abilities. It seemed entirely appropriate for Samael to have accomplished this act.

"Indeed, dear sister, it becomes your beauty and loving nature," added Gabriel, pausing from his usual practicality. "Let us ponder, each in our own quiet times, upon its unique vibration and accordance within the eighth essence. But now we have more pressing affairs. Let us go to seek out the cause of these miniature reproductions of ourselves!"

Without any further thoughts passing between them, and leaving Samael and Seriel behind, the six quickly moved to another part of the Abyss. They were led there by Michael. The two brothers remained stationary at first, but Samael soon became impatient with the lack of activity. He began to dart around Seriel, as if to entice him into a game of 'Catch.' Seriel, however, would not be persuaded and Samael grew increasingly agitated. He remarked:

"Waiting here for them to return and tell us things we already know is too tiresome. What say you, my brother? Shall we amuse ourselves by inspecting your shining spheres of happenings?"

"What if they return before us?" asked Seriel.

"Then we shall have to endure Gabriel's lecturing on our lack of responsibility, but that will be less annoying than tarrying here. Will you accompany me?" Samael quickly put some distance between himself and Seriel who, somewhat reluctantly, then began to follow him. He would have preferred to view his spheres by himself.

The two brothers flowed away from the kaleidoscopic light of the Source. They moved in a different direction from the one taken by their six siblings, and approached an area of Chaos which should have been dark and still. Yet as they came close to the place where Seriel had birthed the delicate spheres, they discovered a gigantic spiral of many shining orbs. When Seriel had left the spiral, it was composed of single spheres which were linked to each other in a linear form. Now, each one of those original spherical objects was encrusted with many similar orbs. This gave much greater substance to the spiral.

"It has changed!" exclaimed Seriel. "There are many spheres surrounding each of those that first came from me."

"I will investigate," answered Samael. "Stay close!" Instantly, he was plunging his being into a part of the spiral. He quickly found the original spheres and followed their line around and around until he reached the two which reflected their present activities. In one, the six archangels were viewing a miniature scene, and in the other he and Seriel were looking at the spiraling orbs. He had expected these to be the outermost two, yet many more were in the process of budding from each other. Apparently, future events were being recorded. Samael promised himself a return visit to examine this interesting discovery.

It had been easy to find the main linking line of these spheres, the light within most of them was slightly more intense than that of their shimmering counterparts. Even as Samael became aware of this distinction, he noted that in certain ones the light dimmed a trifle as it brightened a little more in one or another of its surrounding orbs. As he experienced these things, this light seemed to be dancing in and out of the main and secondary displays of happenings. This intrigued him and so he gave close scrutiny to one of the newly lighted ones. In it he found himself and the Shekinah melding as he gave her the name Malkura. Then he turned his attention to the main sphere that would tell of this occurrence, but within it this did not happen. Instead, Seriel had not gone on ahead of his brother and sister. All three were returning to the other archangels together.

Samael moved to another set of spheres. In one he was attempting to blend his awareness with the Source. When he broke away before completing the melding, he did not try again. But he had attempted a reconnection! Why was this not shown? In searching the surrounding spheres, he found a record of his second attempt to meld with his parent and its subsequent rejection of him. This was displayed in one of the orbs that encased the initial one.

As he withdrew from the spiral, Samael declared, "I believe I have the answer!"

"I knew you would, but I think I also know what is transpiring." Knowing his brother always wanted to be first in everything, Seriel added, "But tell me of your findings."

"Within every happening that we experience, there are many other possibilities of how the outcome may unfold." Samael's thoughts were racing and drawing further conclusions even as he shared them with his brother. "Nothing is permanent, everything is subject to change! Depending on what we choose to do or not do, our existence then reflects these choices."

"This means we must always have the right to choose."

"And that means we always have the right to free will!" Samael spun round and round in a triumphant dance. "We are not confined to being that which the Source wants of us, we can be whatever we desire. Your precious orbs, brother, are showing us that for every instance of a happening there are numerous other realities which we can make actual, if we so choose." Silently, to himself, he added the thought that the spiral also appeared to be demonstrating its ability to reflect all possible happenings for events which had not yet taken place. He became lost in his own thoughts, completely ignoring these coming from Seriel:

"That is truly amazing! We are the perpetrators of our destinies. We can become whatever we would wish ourselves to be." Like his brother, Seriel withdrew into his own inner dialogue. If every happening possesses countless possible outcomes, then which ones are reality? All of them or only the ones that are made actual? The Lord of Sorcery reasoned to himself that, if all things were possible, then all must be reality. This was astounding! It was the key that opened up his being to the greatest of magic. When all is possible, all IS.

As if echoing his sibling's thoughts, Samael concluded, "We can be all things for all of eternity. This means we are all powerful, my brother. Oh, the ramifications of this bountiful realization! We are truly wondrous beings . . ." He paused for a moment, as if listening to some hidden sound, then remarked, "The others have returned from their visit to the miniature scenes. Gabriel is, as expected, not pleased with our departure. Let us return to them and stifle his complaining."

"Shall we disclose our new findings to them?" asked Seriel.

"Why not? If we do not, Michael will surely come upon your spiraling spheres before too long. Then, unless you wish to feign ignorance of how they came to be, you will be subjected to Gabriel's ranting about your irresponsible behavior." Samael's being shuddered in emphasis of his words. "Let us go now!"

Before complying, Seriel gave one last glance to his beautiful spheres, and in so doing he also became aware of the spiral's unique ability. He realized it was beginning to display future possible realities.

Chapter Three

The eight angelic beings met within the area where they had previously discussed the existence of the miniature scenes. As both Samael and Seriel expected, when the six returned, Gabriel was annoyed by their absence. However, once they rejoined the others, Seriel explained what had drawn them away from the meeting place. This happened before Gabriel was able to reprimand them to his complete satisfaction. The seventh archangel told of how, while he was contemplating their existence thus far, the luminous orbs had begun to expel themselves from his being. Beyond that occurrence, they appeared to each come forth from their predecessor. Seriel told of Samael's realization of his discovery and their subsequent agreement to view the spheres while the others were away.

His story was frequently interrupted by questions from his siblings. Gabriel wanted to know why he considered the spheres were birthed by him instead of one of the others. Before he was able to express his thoughts about this matter, Samael quickly reminded them of Seriel's magical nature. He reiterated how they considered him to be the Lord of Sorcery, therefore, it was entirely appropriate for this phenomenon to have been created by their seventh-born brother.

The news of the appearance of the secondary spheres and their inference, as concluded by the brothers, brought astonishment to the group. Ever cautious, Gabriel warned his siblings to not explore this possibility of other realities to any great degree. The Christ Soul merely reaffirmed to the others his belief in the Source being omnipotent because surely this was yet one more expression of that truth? Michael could see the glorious opportunities which these choices would bring. He imagined himself planning the finest route through the spiraling spheres, always choosing the realities which were most beneficial to all of them and to the Source. Only the Shekinah realized the immeasurable love that lay behind the existence of endless possibilities. No matter how far away each of them might stray from their perfect beginning, there was always the choice of recapturing perfection. She believed this was a profound example of Samael's notion about sharing. It was the ultimate gift given by the Source to its offspring.

Seriel ended his explanation of the spiral of spheres by telling the others what he had noticed just before withdrawing from it. As he did this, he was subjected to a powerful, cautionary thought from Samael. His brother considered it unwise to emphasize how the spheres were displaying events, and all their possible outcomes, before they were happening. With the exception of Uriel, the other archangels were unaware of Samael's warning to Seriel. They were too engrossed in their own thoughts concerning this final revelation about the spiral. The six siblings were also puzzled by it. Surely it would need further examination and consideration?

Wanting to divert their attention from this topic, Samael asked Michael what conclusions the group had drawn with regard to the miniature scenes. He was anxious to learn whether his siblings had realized they could be changed. Yet he kept this concern to himself in that dark and separate part of his being. If Michael was to make reference to the possibility of altering the scenes, Samael had decided he would pretend to be surprised. Then he would show enthusiastic curiosity. His siblings would expect him to react in that manner about something new and previously unknown to him.

However, Michael made no mention of it. He merely shared with his two brothers the various suggestions, which the six had made, about the origin of the scenes. The Shekinah, Raphael and the Christ Soul believed they had come from the Source. Whereas Gabriel and Uriel considered the Abyss had created them. Michael, alone, was convinced they were the result of the interaction between the consciousness of the eight archangels and the substance of Chaos. To both Samael and Seriel, his theory appeared to be the most acceptable, the one which they would adopt.

Samael then asked what they intended to do next. After some discussion, there was a consensus between the group that Seriel should guide his siblings to the spiral of spheres. This decision came as a result of Samael's subtle remark concerning his brother being the one who knew more about these spiraling orbs than any other. The first archangel was anxious to be alone so that he could return to the miniature scenes. While observing the spheres that portrayed things yet to come, he had noticed a possible occurrence which greatly displeased him. Within the small reproduction of one of their very early activities, a startling change was taking place. The eight, tiny beings were leaving the confines of the scene. They were beginning to move freely through the Abyss.

Suspecting his brother had another motive for emphasizing his knowledge of the spheres, Seriel requested Samael's help in guiding his siblings to them. Showing no hesitation, however, Samael declined, remarking that he was already bored with the orbs' inability to reflect anything other than what was, and what might be, taking place. Seriel did not truly believe Samael's reason for not wishing to accompany them. However, he knew it would be futile to try to persuade him to go. The first archangel had frequently demonstrated his determination to follow his own desires, together with his need to separate from the group.

Therefore, without further argument, Seriel led his angelic siblings away from Samael and in the direction of the spiral of spheres.

Left alone, Samael quickly sped off to an area of Chaos where the scenes were most prevalent. This was a part of the Abyss where the archangels had frequently played, especially in their first stage of existence. From his earlier manipulation of a scene in which he removed Gabriel, he had learned that changing one scene appeared to alter all of them. By wishing Gabriel to be gone and then allowing him to return, Samael had witnessed his brother's removal and subsequent reappearance in all of the small replays which he viewed.

Armed with this knowledge, he felt compelled to approach a scene and make an adjustment to it before the tiny beings broke free from its boundaries. The realization that these miniature replicas of their games were merely the forerunners of other developments, alarmed Samael almost to the point of horror. Having learned from the sphere that there might be many more Samaels existing in Chaos, he knew he could not allow that to happen. He was unique and separate from all others, and he wished vehemently to remain thus. The thought of many more Gabriels was most unpleasant, but of little consequence compared to the unthinkable, many times duplication of himself. He must adjust the scene before it was too late.

He brought himself into the proximity of an episode which repeated one of the amusements he had created for himself and his siblings soon after their birth. In one world of matter, this game would ultimately be termed 'Hide and Seek.' It was quite easy to find himself within the scene, he was the one in rapid motion while the others were keeping perfectly still. For one eternal instant, he recaptured the innocent glee of being 'It.' He relived the joy of swiftly moving through Chaos, seeking out his siblings who were attempting to conceal themselves from him. In that measure of eternity,

Samael bid a last "farewell" to his purely angelic self before crossing the threshold into soul delineation.

Then, with blazing intent, the first archangel commanded himself to be no more within the game, to be gone as though never having been a part of it. He also determined that neither the Source nor any other being should ever have the power to reverse his action of removal. Immediately, the miniature duplicate of himself was gone from the scene and the remaining seven were left to play aimlessly.

There was a need to ensure that all other Samaels were gone from all of the scenes. Therefore, he busied himself darting throughout various areas of Chaos, verifying that he had accomplished his goal. After a long and fruitful search, he allowed himself to move into a part of the Abyss where the darkness brought comfort to his restless nature. Now, he could relax and be assured that, if the tiny beings emerged, they would only number seven from each scene.

Samael became aware that he was resting close to one of the slowly moving reproductions which displayed his seven tiny siblings in distress. They were in a part of Chaos that seemed to restrict their lightning movements and thoughts, and they were attempting to move away from this area. The first archangel recalled this event. It was he who had made light of their fears, assuring them there was no danger because they were invincible. Yet now the seven remaining tiny beings were robbed of his guidance and optimism.

Unlike the scenes which moved much more quickly, this one did not appear to repeat, over and over. It played out its story so slowly that its ending was not observed by Samael. Becoming lulled by its lethargic pace, he drifted into a dark and troubled sleep. It plagued his auric being with convulsive changes of color and degrees of brightness and dullness.

"My brother, what have you done?" Seriel's questioning thought pierced Samael's dreams and he awakened to find his sibling next to him.

"Sweet Seriel, you startled me. I was lost in my own dreaming thoughts."

Seriel quickly repeated his question, "What have you done?"

"Many things, brother mine, as have you. Do you wish me to begin naming them?" A chortling-type sound escaped from Samael's being.

"Do not treat me as a fool, Samael. You know of what I am asking." Seriel refused to play along with his brother's avoidance. He was extremely distraught and saddened by what he had recently seen while in the company of the other archangels. "Within one of the spheres we saw you remove yourself from a miniature scene. We then observed that you were also gone from all the other small reflections of our games. We watched you inspecting each one to verify that you were, indeed, no more. Why have you done this deed? Why have you separated yourself from us so completely?"

Samael was surprised by Seriel's depth of concern. He answered, "It is no great act that I have performed, I continue to exist. I remain one of the eight light beings who came forth from the Source. I have not abandoned you and the others."

"When you removed Gabriel from a scene, it was temporary and held no great depth of feeling. It was an act of idle amusement, a demonstration of your perception of our powers. Yet this new manipulation is very different. Your determination, your strong intent, was blatantly evident, even within the sphere. You have brought great sorrow to each of your angelic brothers and sister. You must undo this selfish action." Seriel's grave thoughts were tinged with anger.

Not wanting his brother to discern that his removal from the scenes was irreversible, Samael angrily responded, "Do not presume to lecture me. Surely that will be Gabriel's role? I have no intention of reversing that which I have put in motion. My decision was based upon sound reasoning. Since you have all been intently scrutinizing the orbs, you must be

aware of what will very possibly happen to the tiny beings? I
will not have echoes of myself strewn throughout the Abyss!"
With lightning swiftness his anger vanished and he began to
cajole his brother. "What say you, Seriel? Am I so wrong,
wishing to remain unique? Perchance this is something you
would also desire? If you hurry, you may be able to follow my
lead and remain the only Seriel within ALL THAT IS."

Ignoring his brother's coaxing thoughts, Seriel replied,
"Do not try to sway me from my mission. I promised the
others I would make you understand the folly of your deed.
Michael has discerned from our observation of the spheres
that had you not intervened in the existence of the scenes,
they would have slowly disintegrated into nothingness. When
you first entered one of them to partake of its substance,
you altered its capabilities. You changed it from a closed
and complete reflection into an open and becoming
possibility. Your removal of Gabriel only enhanced this process
of a scene's adaptability, and by removing yourself, you have
increased it even more. Please do not delay. Make it possible
for me to return to the others with the news that you are,
once again, within the scenes."

"So now you have a mission? Oh, how grand you have
become, little brother!" Samael's bantering thoughts
bombarded Seriel like cruel jabs. "And have you shared with
our siblings why you adopted this mission?"

Seriel knew his brother was merely trying to divert his
attention from what he wished to achieve, yet he could not
resist asking, "What are you implying, Samael? I offered to
come to you because I believe you have acted unwisely."

"And because you are feeling somewhat disparaged. You,
who have always been my constant companion and confidant,
were not privy to my decision to set myself apart from my
siblings. I removed myself from the scenes without your prior
knowledge, and that wounds you deeply. Yes?"

Denial of this truth rose up inside Seriel, but he could
not allow himself to express it. Instead he answered, "As

always, brother, you have perceived my innermost thoughts. Yet annoyance was not my only motivation. I am truly perturbed by your need to be different from us."

Samael moved a little closer to Seriel, as if to convey his sincerity and lack of guile. "I thank you for your concern, dear brother, but I must follow my own instincts no matter where they may lead me." He quickly retreated back into his usual flippant self and added, "Pray, return to my brothers and sister and assure them that stubborn Samael will not be swayed from his self-indulgent course. However, you can, if you so wish, tell them to choose another missionary to dispatch to this lost soul. I would be happy to hold discourse with the Shekinah."

Realizing his brother was not about to engage in further discussion with him, Seriel withdrew from Samael and began his journey back to the other six archangels. He felt despondent because he had not been able to shake his sibling's resolve, but he also admired the tenacity of spirit which fueled Samael's determination.

Samael brought his attention back to the slowly moving miniature scene which was playing out its entirety before him, yet again. Once more, he experienced the somnolent pace of its contents. Not wishing to fall prey to its mesmerizing effect a second time, he purposefully began to scan the farthest most reaches of the Abyss. Would another brother volunteer himself to try to persuade Samael to relent? Perhaps Malkura would come to him. That thought brought joyful anticipation to his vigil.

In the distance, odd flashes of rainbow color intermittently disturbed the totality of Chaos. Samael knew these swathes of light were caused by the action of the miniature scenes. He wondered how it would be if, and when, the small players were no longer confined within their rigid stage boundaries. Would empty areas of greyish-blue continue to display themselves within the surrounding dark? They would lack any vibrancy of differing hues because their colorful occupants would be gone. Or would the utter bleakness of the Abyss fold back upon itself?

In this part of Chaos, where the first archangel waited, except for the re-occurrence of the slow moving scene, there was only an impenetrable depth of dark void. The group of archangels had very rarely played in this area because it was so far removed from the Source. Its cloying gloom unsettled their sense of innocent play. It whispered to them of things unknown and almost fear-filled. Even Samael and Seriel explored its extent cautiously, but unlike their siblings, they could not resist its beckoning. Each time he came to this place, Samael felt the ever-increasing pull of the outer Abyss, the areas into which he had not yet ventured. It was as a siren song to his curiosity and he knew, eventually, he would succumb.

Looking off into the distance, again, Samael became aware of an increasing breal hue moving toward him. Knowing this was Uriel's distinctive color, he readied himself for the next onslaught upon his stance against the possible multiplication of his being. He was mildly surprised that Uriel would move out so far from the Source. Samael had expected Michael to be the one to follow Seriel because he frequently and fearlessly patrolled Chaos.

As Uriel drew close, Samael told him, "My brother, you have undertaken this long journey for naught. I am steadfast in my decision and none can change my pursuit of it."

There was a pause and then Uriel astonished Samael by this answer: "I did not come to ply you with persuasion, dear one, even though that is what I told our siblings was my intent. I am here to offer my companionship in your quest for separateness. I, too, will pluck myself from the scenes, if you wish it to be so. My love for you is so deep that I would happily do this act."

Even though Samael knew the extent of his brother's caring, he was startled by his boldness. He was also not sure whether he wanted Uriel to follow his lead. Quickly regaining

his composure, he escaped his feelings of indecision by
means of diversion. "What is this, little brother? Are you
attempting deception? Surely that is my role, not yours?"

Uriel moved even closer to his brother so that their auric
extremities began to meld. "I care so immensely for you,
Samael. I would do whatever you ask of me. Just give me
direction and I will follow."

Apart from not wanting duplicates of himself to exist,
Samael was also taking pride in the fact that his act of
withdrawal was bringing him distinction. Very soon, there
could be many archangel replicas, but there would be but
one genuine Lord of Lightning-Swiftness. Like his parent,
he would be the only one of a kind. Therefore, did he really
want his brother to take this action? And what if Seriel then
decided to join him and Uriel in their pursuit of
separateness? This line of thought began to alarm Samael.
He responded, "I am fully aware of your love for me, dear
brother, and I bask in its comfort. I also hold you in great
esteem and I would wish no harm to come to you. My choice
of remaining alone may bring much hardship to me. It may
well test my strength of endurance. I cannot, and will not,
ask you to place yourself in possible jeopardy." Even though
Samael wished to maintain his uniqueness, there was some
truth in his answer. From his earliest melding with Uriel, he
had sensed a vulnerability within his brother which aroused
his nobler instincts. He considered himself to be Uriel's
guardian and protector.

"Nevertheless, I am more than willing to do as you have
done." Uriel turned his attention to the slowly moving event
before them, as if readying himself for intervention into it.

Samael quickly moved into a position between his brother
and the miniature scene, signaling his intention to stop any
interference of it. "No, Uriel! I will not allow you to do this.
I have a great need for you to remain in harmony with our
siblings so that you can champion my cause and make them
understand my reasoning. I am the first-born of the Source

and, as such, I must remain separate until we all become one with our parent, once more. I am the catalyst for our ultimate reunion and, therefore, must not be weakened by any simplification of my essence."

"You do, indeed, have unique responsibilities Samael. Therefore, if I can be most helpful to you by not performing any further changes to the scenes, then that will be my stand. I only wish to please you." Uriel became lost in thought, then he added, "Upon reflection, this would seem to be the wiser choice, for, in truth, soon there may be many more Uriels to be the champions of your cause."

"Well stated, well chosen, my brother. You are in perfect league with me." Samael allowed his essence to begin to blend with that of Uriel, as if to confirm the latter thought. He could sense his brother's desire for even closer melding, but he would not permit it. A deeper joining of their essences might reveal to Uriel just how devious Samael was becoming. Then, pretending reluctance, he began to withdraw himself from his brother while sending this thought to him: "Sadly, we must separate and go about our duties. I will remain here to keep watch for the possible coming forth of the tiny forms. You must go back to the others and explain that I refuse to return myself to the scenes because I believe this would be detrimental to all of us. Remind our siblings that I am the one who will eventually bind us all together, once more, when we return to the Source. This tremendous task will require my essence to be fully strong and not weakened by its division between many replicas of myself."

"This is a duty which I will happily perform for you." Withdrawing himself completely from his brother's auric being, Uriel sent this final, loving thought to Samael before moving away from him: "I am ever your compassionate brother who holds a deep devotion for you. May you remain within the Source's keeping until we meet, again!" And then he was speeding away.

Left alone, once more, Samael decided to continue his vigil of the tiny, lethargic replay. Surely its occupants could soon be exiting from it and entering the emptiness of Chaos? After scanning the scene for a while, his thoughts started to drift. He began to imagine himself taking charge of the seven small beings and guiding them to the safe area. This would become a new adventure, one that greatly intrigued him. They would probably consider him to be a godly creature. His size and brilliance would astound them. That thought gave him a sense of joy because he held a deeply seated need to be admired. Perhaps he would lead them to the Shekinah and ask her to aid him in his instruction of them. She would hold him in even greater esteem, if he displayed an element of nurturing concern for them.

As if in answer to his thoughts of her, the approach of the Shekinah's essence began to intrude upon his musings. His beloved Malkura was swiftly moving in his direction, and his soul began to soar. Obviously, with the failure of Seriel's and Uriel's pleadings, the others had decided to send her to him, believing he could not refuse her. And, indeed, he would require tremendous determination not to reveal to her the fact that his removal was permanent. Of all his siblings, she was the only one who could penetrate his outer defiance and reveal his true self. Readying himself for her gentle persuasion, he sent this swift thought to Malkura: "Sweet sister, it seems my brothers are becoming just too resourceful. They know I can never deny you anything."

The Shekinah's entrancing rulpiel color began to emerge in the distance and, as she became fully visible, her auric splendor pushed back the gloom of Chaos. Her answering thought reached Samael even before she drew close to him: "Dear brother, I have not come to ask you to relent, for it is already too late. It is my enduring love for you that has brought me here. I believe you will be in need of my loving comfort when you learn what is happening."

Surprised by her response, Samael asked, "How can it be too late?" And, as she approached, he motioned toward the miniature scene, adding, "Behold, the tiny forms remain within the confines of their setting. They have not yet come forth."

Arriving beside him, she explained, "That is not my meaning. I am not here to report their emergence, but rather that many of the other scenes are disintegrating. Indeed, I believe this will also happen to this one. Michael has changed his opinion about them. He now believes they will all be gone and, therefore, there will be no new beings existing with us. Gabriel is certain your intervention into them has made them become unstable and unable to sustain themselves."

Reluctantly, Samael withheld his desire to rudely comment on Gabriel's predictability. Instead he questioned, "What prompts Michael to decide all will disappear? Is it not possible that, if this one has not done so, there may be others which will remain?"

"He has concluded that because the changes you made to one scene were reflected in the rest, then what happens to one will also occur to the others."

Samael agreed, "Yes, I had realized this was so when I removed myself from the scene. Perhaps this one before us has not yet deteriorated because it is so slow in its movement?"

This appeared to be a sound assumption to the Shekinah, given what she had observed on her way toward Samael. She explained, "I believe that is probably the reason. Most of the scenes, which lie close to the Source, have already gone. As I traveled this way, I found several which were either in the process of disintegrating or remaining intact. Yet soon they will surely be no more."

Discovering there would be no replicas of his siblings, brought frustration to the Lord of Lightning-Swiftness. He would not be distinctive from his brothers and sister. They would remain as he was, each one a unique facet of the

Source. In addition, Samael was also beginning to experience a sense of loss for the tiny forms who would not become his charges. They would never be enthralled by his magnificence and he would not gain the opportunity to instruct and nurture them. Their guardianship would have presented him with the possibility of further exploration of his own emotions, an invitation to discover more about himself. Had the Shekinah realized how he would be feeling? Was that why she was here to offer her support? Samael asked, "You believe I am in need of your comfort? Why is that so?"

She allowed herself to make auric contact with Samael and answered, "I know you very well, my brother. We have melded deeply and often, and I have felt your passions and your desires. You strive to be different from the rest of us, and having no replicas of yourself would have brought you that distinction. However, it would appear that none will exist of us, either, so you have not achieved your goal. That realization will bring you annoyance and even despondency."

Samael gently conceded, "Indeed, you understand me very well, my lady."

The Shekinah moved further within her brother's auric field and added, "I was also sensing grief coming from you as I informed you what was happening to the scenes. Now that we are blending our awareness, I understand the cause of this sadness. You were planning to take charge of the tiny beings of this particular scene, once they had emerged from it. You wished to be their guardian and provider. The anticipation of this new role for you created excitement because you are ever curious about the unknown, dear Samael." As these thoughts flowed from her, she allowed herself to be completely engulfed by his essence. They remained motionless as feelings of love were shared between them.

"Oh, how I wish I could love unconditionally as you do, my Malkura! The thought of chaperoning the tiny light beings did awaken a modicum of caring within me, but it also ignited a sense of vanity. They would have admired my splendor and my lightning resourcefulness. Now, that will not happen."

Knowing that she was the only sibling with whom he would share such an intimate revelation, the Shekinah answered, "I thank you for your honesty and it deepens my love for you. You have been changing of late, my lord, and could have decided to offer deception. Yet you chose not to conceal within that secret part of your being this ulterior motive of wanting adoration. I know you hide many thoughts and feelings there. If only I could persuade you to release them all."

Recapturing his usual bantering attitude, Samael replied, "A thousand curses upon that thought, sweet Malkura. I would be forever boring you with the ridiculous notions that plague me. Your love for me would soon succumb to ennui. I would rather keep the mystery that compels you to search within me." He began to withdraw his essence from hers, but then stopped and added, "Ah no, this is too sweet a place to leave so soon. Let us just rest awhile and exchange our feelings of devotion for one another."

They remained locked in their melding bliss and everything seemed gone from them except each other. The Shekinah was in a place where only Samael could take her. He created images of such vibrant color and joyous movement which were similar to the qualities of the Source. For him, her essence brought tranquillity and comfort in a manner that was reminiscent of attempting to be as one with their parent. Yet even as a small facet of his being had not surrender to the Source, so, too, was an element of himself being kept apart from the Shekinah. This separate fraction of his awareness was continuously scanning the slowly moving miniature scene and awaiting its expected demise. Ultimately, his vigil was rewarded. The light within the scene began to dim and very slowly its matter caved in upon itself, taking with it the seven small beings.

Gently, yet firmly, Samael pulled the rest of his awareness back from his sister, exclaiming, "The scene is disintegrating, Malkura, and my little ones are gone. Michael was correct, they are all doomed. I am quite distraught."

"As I was certain you would be, my brother. That was my reason for coming to you." The Shekinah motioned herself in Samael's direction, once again, ready to offer her essence for comfort.

Samael understood the compassionate gesture, but he pulled back from her and stated, "I brought this happening upon myself, dear sister, and I must endure it by myself. Let us now return to our siblings. I am no longer needed in this part of Chaos."

Together they began to move slowly back to the center of the Abyss. Unlike many other journeys, which they had previously made together, they felt no urge to romp and play. Their mood was somber and filled with a sense of uncertainty.

Chapter Four

Seriel returned to the other archangels and related his unsuccessful attempt at persuading Samael to place himself back into the miniature scenes. After completing his explanation, he took his leave of them and hurried to the spiral of spheres. He had a great need to be alone with his shining creations. Their beauty filled him with awe and their diverse possibilities stirred his curiosity. Seriel also felt separated from Samael in a manner that he had never experienced before. A degree of loneliness was seeping into his soul and he was anxious to learn what could be the possible outcomes of Samael's disturbing action.

Since his last visit to the spiral with his siblings, the spheres had continued to multiply, both in number around the original orbs and also those which were budding from their predecessors. This monument to ALL THAT IS was becoming a truly amazing feature. The light from its spheres was reflecting far beyond its perimeters and out into the void of Chaos. It even appeared to be altering the nothingness of that which surrounded it. The areas of the Abyss immediately outside of the spiral were charged with colored sparks which darted back and forth, as if carrying into Chaos their current of WHAT IS.

Seriel scanned the spheres until he came upon one that portrayed the seven tiny forms emerging from each of their scenes. In contrast, within a certain surrounding orb, the miniature events were all breaking apart and crumbling into oblivion. These opposing occurrences were previously observed by him and his siblings when they visited the spiral. Michael concluded they represented two alternative futures for the scenes. In the first one Samael had previously intervened in their contents, in the second he had not. Whereas Gabriel considered the demise of the scenes was due to their brother's interference in them. According to him, had Samael left them unchanged, all would have expelled their tiny occupants.

The Lord of Sorcery moved his attention to the more recently forming spheres and he was surprised by what lay before him. Even now, another possibility was being shown in one of them. Within its depths many scenes were disintegrating while a solitary one was releasing its small light beings. To Seriel it seemed logical that a third possible outcome would be a combination of the other two. He decided to examine those orbs which contained future happenings, expecting to be shown how all three possibilities might progress.

Once again, he was startled by his findings. In each of the spheres there always appeared to be an increasing number of light beings moving through the Abyss. None displayed a future without them. Seriel pondered this new discovery. Surely if his spheres displayed all possible happenings, there should be some in which no additional beings were evident? These would show the future consequence of the demise of all the miniature scenes. Yet this type of spherical display did not exist. No matter how far along the spiral he explored, more light beings were always to be found. This appeared to eliminate one of the possible futures, but it did not indicate which of the two remaining realities would definitely happen.

He brought his attention to the sphere in which the seven were leaving the one surviving scene. Even as he observed their emergence, each one metamorphosed into several souls of much greater size. These, in turn, instantly gained distinctive coloring and vibration from their predecessors. He counted the number into which each became divided and it was eight. Seriel concluded this must be a very sacred number because it matched that of the archangels. Within his creative soul he envisaged a glyph to represent its sanctity. It was a symbol which, in a far distant future, the world of man would consider a lemniscate. A figure 8 laying on its side and formed into a Mobius strip.

With further examination, Seriel learned that these beings would multiply by the same means that had created them. Certain replicas of their existence in the Abyss would exit a scene as they had done. Eventually, it would seem, there would be many more beings in addition to the original eight souls. Yet all were springing from only seven of the archangels, there were none evolving from Samael.

He decided to move backwards to the point on the spiral where Samael was withdrawing himself from a scene. Once he found the sphere that depicted this event, Seriel reasoned there must be at least one secondary orb that would exhibit his brother observing the tiny enactment, but not removing his replica. Yet no such sphere appeared to exist. However, while searching, he found the one which the Lord of Lightning-Swiftness had viewed earlier. This orb portrayed eight small replicas emerging from a scene. Its existence seemed to be barren, no further possibilities were arising from its action. It remained a solitary offshoot that led nowhere.

Continuing his exploration, Seriel hoped to discover a different orb. One which would show his brother returning his duplicate to its former placement, having regretted his choice of removal. Yet his exploration brought no rewards. There was but one primary sphere in which Samael was taken from his tiny siblings, who continued to play without him.

Slowly, what Seriel considered a Source truth began to make itself apparent. Even though WHAT IS was composed of endless possibilities, there were certain ones which were predestined. These must have been ordained by their parent.

One of them was Samael's need to remove himself from the scenes, and another was the multiplication of the essences of the seven archangels. Both Michael and Gabriel had been wrong. Their brother's actions had neither caused the emergence of the tiny light beings nor the disintegration of the scenes. The Source did, indeed, hold sway over how Creation would unfold.

This revelation surprised Seriel, but it did not astound him. Within himself he had always suspected the Source possessed powers which overruled their own. He could also appreciate the irony of what he was learning. If countless outcomes were possible, then one of them must surely be inevitable? That was a possibility he had not considered until now.

Armed with this new knowledge, Seriel decided to return to the others in order to share his findings with them. He felt certain Samael would be angered to discover the truth. Obviously, his recent interference within the scenes was not purely of his own free will. It was due to a prompting from the Source. Seriel wondered what could be the motivation of his parent to allow, even ordain, his brother to become so separate from his siblings. He was also curious to learn which of the two remaining outcomes the Source was choosing to pursue.

The Lord of Sorcery did not have long to wait for the answer. As he moved away from the spiral and journeyed back to his siblings, he discovered many miniature scenes collapsing into themselves. One instant they were replaying a previous event, and the next they were breaking into little pieces, which quickly vanished as though they had never been. All of Chaos was becoming still and devoid of the small reproductions of their play. This must mean only one scene would remain in the manner he had just witnessed in a lighted orb.

When he reached the other archangels, they appeared to be in a state of confusion. Seriel also noted that his sister was not with them and he wondered whether she had gone to Samael to reinforce his own pleadings. He addressed this questioning thought to Michael: "Are you aware of what is happening? The miniature scenes are disappearing and taking with them the tiny replicas of ourselves."

"Yes, we know." It was Gabriel's thoughts that answered him. "And I am sure I am correct in my assumption. It was Samael's interference which has caused their disintegration . . ."

The Christ Soul interrupted his brother's accusation. "Gabriel, we cannot be certain why this is happening. You must not blame Samael."

"Indeed, that is so," added Michael. "We do not know the reason. I previously thought his intervention into them would result in the emergence of the tiny beings. I was wrong so possibly you are, too, Gabriel."

Without giving Gabriel a chance to defend his belief, Seriel explained, "I have learned that both of your conclusions are incorrect. Within all the possible happenings, which can befall us, there will be some that are inevitable. The Source, I believe, has ordained them to be so. One such happening was Samael's removal of himself from the scenes. Another is the multiplication of our essences."

"How can you know this?" Gabriel queried impatiently. "And how can you believe we will multiply when all our replicas are vanishing? That is just a foolish thought!"

Ignoring his brother's querulous attitude, Seriel continued, "My luminous orbs have shown me these occurrences as being destined to happen, therefore, we cannot blame Samael for anything. He was merely following a direction from the Source, even though he would not have perceived it as such."

Raphael questioned, "But how will the Source increase our number, if all of our replicas are gone?"

"They will not all be gone," explained Seriel. "One scene will remain and its small occupants will emerge from it. This happening and how the tiny beings will change, once they are with us, was given to me by my spheres."

"Why should they change?" Gabriel was, once again, challenging his brother. "We have not changed since our emergence from the Source."

"I can only tell you what I observed. I do not know the reasoning of our parent," Seriel patiently replied. "Immediately, as our replicas come forth, they will each become eight in number. They will also grow in size, and their colors and intensity will become different from what they were within the scene."

"There will be many more than seven?" asked Uriel.

"Indeed, that is so, little brother. And there will be even more, eventually. There will be replicas of our replicas, and this will continue on. According to my spheres, this multiplication will transpire into eternity." Seriel paused, then added, "Further more, from what I have been shown, all future light beings will no longer be replicas, once they have emerged. Each will be different, even as each of us differs from one another."

Being unconvinced, Gabriel put forward, "How can this be? It does not conform with what we know of ourselves, or even what we believe about the Source."

"Remember!" interjected the Christ Soul. "All is possible with the Source. You know this to be true, Gabriel."

Feeling disgruntled, Gabriel moved back from the group, as if to indicate he wished to keep his musings to himself. However, he did not retreat too far because he wanted to remain aware of the thoughts his siblings were sharing. He recognized their lives, thus far, were about to undergo an upheaval. From what Seriel was revealing, he surmised there would be a much greater need for his practical and cautionary attitude. Newly formed beings would require instruction on which parts of the Abyss were safe. They would also have to learn that whatever Samael put forward should be ignored. Yes, Gabriel could well imagine how much his wisdom would be required.

"Where is the scene that will remain intact?" Michael asked Seriel.

"I am not certain, but I do know it has to be close to the Source because our parent's brilliant beams of light were cascading all around it."

"I suggest we go in search of that scene," answered Michael. "Perhaps we can be of help to our new companions?"

"I agree, but first tell me, where is our sister?" Seriel was anxious to know whether she was with the first archangel. "Did Malkura go to Samael to persuade him to relent?"

Sensing his brother's concern, Raphael responded, "She went in search of him, but not to beg him to place himself back into the scenes. It was already too late. Many were disintegrating, even as Malkura was leaving."

Moving back into the group, Gabriel added, "She believed Samael would need her comforting presence, once he became aware of the consequences of his meddlesome actions. Our sister is too forgiving of Samael's recklessness."

"As I have just explained, Gabriel, our brother is not responsible for the demise of all but one of the scenes. It was destined to happen. Do not question that fact!" Seriel was finding it difficult to curb his annoyance with Gabriel's persistent demeaning of Samael.

Wishing to ease the tension between his brothers, the Christ Soul diverted their thoughts by asking, "Shall we await the return of Malkura or will one of you remain here to tell her where we have gone?"

"I will be happy to do that," answered Seriel. The prospect of being alone with the Shekinah was comforting to him.

"Then we will go now into the close vicinity of the Source to search out the remaining scene," instructed Michael. And being the champion of all their activities, he added, "I will lead the way!"

The five archangels were quickly gone from their brother, who began to flow back and forth in anticipation of being with his beloved sister. He was also curious to know what had transpired between the Shekinah and Samael. Seriel suspected his sister's loving and forgiving nature would have initiated a melding of her essence with that of Samael's. Jealousy ignited within him, once more. He yearned for the imagined bliss of being the one to blend with her.

Seriel had never melded one-on-one with Malkura, there had always been one or more brothers joining their essence with them. Nevertheless, he had experienced her loving consciousness during any group melding. The seventh archangel became lost in the memories of those precious happenings. Therefore, he did not notice her approach until she was close by. The realization that Samael was accompanying her brought him abruptly out of his ecstatic reverie. There would never be a blissful exchange of essence between himself and the Shekinah while Samael was present. As his two siblings drew close, Seriel was readying himself to explain what he had been shown by his spheres.

"Where are the others?" questioned Samael. "Has Gabriel led them away so that he can show them what he considers my actions have caused?"

"Please, dear brother, do not vent your distress upon Gabriel" The Shekinah was continuing to lend her support to Samael. "We may never learn the true cause of the destruction of the scenes."

Seriel quickly explained, "What you believe is happening is not correct. One scene will not disintegrate and the tiny occupants will come forth. The spiral of spheres has displayed to me what will happen. These things were ordained by the Source. They are not as a consequence of what you did, Samael."

His brother was quick to assure him, "I never did consider myself responsible. That was just Gabriel's presumptuous belief. And what do you mean by ordained?"

"I have reasoned from what I have witnessed within my shining orbs that some possible happenings are, in truth, inevitable. The Source has made them so, therefore, they will take place. One such occurrence is the survival of one scene and its occupants. Another is the demise of all the other scenes." Seriel decided it was not the right time to also add that he believed Samael's withdrawal from the scenes was equally ordained. His brother appeared to be less than his usual resilient self, therefore, he would keep that information from Samael until later.

"So seven small replicas of ourselves will join us?" asked the Shekinah.

"More than seven. As they leave the scene, they become much larger and they divide into many. Each one becomes eight, thus, making a total of fifty-six."

"You mean there will be many Seriels, many Gabriels and so on?" Samael was beginning to regain his former anticipation of becoming unique. His feelings of being well pleased with his choice of removal from the scenes came flooding back into him.

"Yes and no," answered Seriel. "Each group of eight will spring from the seven replicas. Yet, once free of their scene, they become distinctly different from one another. When I observed them in the orbs, their colors and vibrations not only differed from each other, but also from those of ours. Each seems to be a unique being. They will not be replicas of us."

"Why would this happen?" questioned Samael, losing a little of his rediscovered complacency. "This is very different from how we were formed."

"Not so very different," remarked the Shekinah. "Eight of us came from one Source, and now from each archangel will come eight, once more. The only change in this pattern is your non-participation in the procreation, dear Samael."

Ignoring her final comment, Samael agreed, "Indeed, sweet sister, you may be correct. Each of us is unique and very different from our parent as, according to Seriel, will be those who spring from each replica."

"I have discerned that eight is a sacred number," Seriel informed his two siblings. "I believe it is the number of ALL THAT IS."

"A sacred number," mused Samael. "That is true. It is the number of our sister's essence, and she is, indeed, sacred to us all." He extended a small part of his auric self and gently moved it across the Shekinah in a caressing motion.

Not wishing to observe any further intimacy between his siblings, Seriel suggested, "I believe we should join our brothers in their search for the one remaining scene. We may yet witness the birth of our new companions."

"That would be a wondrous event for us to experience," answered the Shekinah as she reluctantly moved herself away from Samael's loving contact. "Pray lead us to the others."

Without further exchange of thoughts, the three archangels took off in the direction taken earlier by their five brothers. They journeyed toward the brilliant, multi-spectrum light of the Source. Once within the proximity of its boundaries, they began to feel the joy and overwhelming love which radiated out from their parent. Even Samael could not deny that it brought a sense of fulfillment to his questing soul. It gave serenity to his inner being. Yet he knew it would be an eternity before he allowed himself to reunite with that loving energy.

As they approached the extent of their parent's sleeping consciousness, they discovered the other five archangels closely grouped together. Their siblings were intently observing something at the very edge of the Source. The three joined the group without any thoughts passing between them. Immediately, their attention was drawn to a miniature scene which continued to rapidly play out its story. Within its confines there were seven, small light beings who were portraying their very first instance of existence. Each one was becoming aware of itself and its siblings, and each was experiencing its joy of being.

The eight archangels continued their vigil as the miniature event ended. Questioning thoughts flew between them. How long would it be before a replay began, again? When it did, would the tiny occupants emerge on this occasion? Was there the possibility that Seriel was wrong and it would also disintegrate like the others? What will it be like to share the Abyss with more light beings? After a brief pause, the one remaining scene began to display its contents, once more.

Chapter Five

The movement of the small light beings within the scene was exceedingly swift, as it was for everything that dwelt within close proximity to the Source. The energy of the eight archangels also pulsated speedily through them. Their colors vibrated at an ever-intensifying rate. While remaining this close to their parent, they resembled its kaleidoscopic qualities, but they could not match its brilliance. And just as the seven tiny forms reflected the images of the archangels, similarly the eight echoed the substance of the Source. They were almost as one with that from which they had come. And within that duration of close harmony, a new era of ALL THAT IS began.

As the scene's occupants explored their new existence, an exquisite golden shaft of light rose up from the Source and centered itself upon the miniature scene. It penetrated and dissolved its boundaries and enveloped the light beings within. As each one was bathed in that divine brilliance, each became eight new angels. And even as they were manifesting, the extent of every individual one was expanding until each was almost the size of an archangel. For an instant, the colors of the seven groups mirrored the individual hue of the tiny form from which they had sprung. Then secondary colors flowed through them. These differed within each group of eight, depending on their casting order.

Those who were cast first from each of the seven light beings now displayed a combination of their primary colors, their essences of origin, and Samael's blazing maldor.

Similarly, the second castings possessed a joining of their innate hues with the Christ Soul's delicate onca. The third castings' original colors mingled with Michael's bold odami; the fourth with Gabriel's vibrant red; the fifth with Raphael's peaceful blue; the sixth with Uriel's soothing breal and the seventh with Seriel's glorious yellow. Those who were eighth castings were gifted with the Shekinah's entrancing rulpiel to enhance their original essence's hue. Previously, these combined colors had only existed briefly when the original eight melded with one another. Now, they had become a reality that would remain within the light matter of the newly formed angels.

The eight archangels witnessed these happenings in awe and with great wonder. Even for Seriel, who had previously observed them within one of his spheres, this was an event of which to tell and retell for all eternity. In confirmation of his belief that the Source had ordained this occurrence, he sent out one blazing thought to his siblings:

"Behold! This was of the Source's choosing. It was not of ours nor Samael's."

Fifty-six angels emerged from the golden light beam and they were greeted by the archangels. Each one instinctively knew who and what it was. Their names, together with those of the original eight, were soon shared. The groups of eight remained close to one another, at first, and then they began to gravitate toward the archangel from whom they had sprung. This left Samael with no new companions and he was considering going in search of other amusements within Chaos.

However, Uriel soon shepherded his group over to the Lord of Lightning-Swiftness, describing this princely soul as the ultimate in angelic essence. His praise brought a dazzling array of maldor and silver throughout Samael's being, and Uriel's eight angels were duly impressed. Silver was a color which was only constant within the substance of the Source, but Samael had mastered the art of bringing it, on occasion, into his own unique and intensifying color. It was available to all the archangels, but the first-born of the Source had gained access to it before any other.

Questioning thoughts from the new arrivals bombarded Samael and his siblings. They wanted to know who the archangels were and how they had come into existence. Gabriel quickly took command of the situation and began instructing them on where to go and what they should and should not do. He even put forward what was and was not appropriate for them to ask. Knowing this would soon cause conflict between Samael and Gabriel, Raphael quickly intervened and suggested they should seek the advice of whichever archangels were close by and available. He added that in this way they would learn quickly and soon be able to understand their new existence.

Feeling somewhat thwarted, Gabriel gathered together his own group of angels and took them to an area that was some distance from the others. He then began to give them his cautionary lecture about life within the Abyss of Chaos. Gabriel strongly advised his group to not attach any credence to most of what Samael and Seriel might impart to them. He offered himself, Michael and the Christ Soul as being the only archangels who were free from the influence of the Lords of the First and Seventh Essences.

While Gabriel was busy with his charges, Michael offered to guide any angels, who were interested, through the safe area of the Abyss. Raphael decided to accompany his brother, and all of his angels went with him. The Christ Soul and the Shekinah encouraged those who wished to learn about the Source to follow them as they journeyed around its extremities. This meant Samael, Seriel and Uriel remained with several angels who were either of the sixth and seventh essences or were first castings. The motley group wanted to know about everything. Therefore, Seriel suggested they go to the spiral of spheres where they could view and experience many happenings. All agreed on this plan-of-action and they flowed toward the luminous orbs. It was during this initial visit to the spheres that one of the angels referred to these amazing reflections of all existence as, "Seriel's Spiral." This was soon adopted as the name for this phenomenon.

When they returned to the place where the angels had emerged, Gabriel's group quickly descended upon them with questions about what they had learned. A full description of Seriel's Spiral was given, and many angelic thoughts were exchanged with regard to the implications of this amazing structure. Turel, one of the angels who had viewed the spheres, asked Samael a question. He wanted to know why the first archangel thought the Source had allowed him to remove himself from the miniature scenes.

Wanting to assure Turel that the withdrawal was his choice and in no way governed by the Source, Samael began, "You are mistaken . . ."

Suddenly, Gabriel's interrupting thought was thrust between them. He declared, "This action was not of his choosing, but was ordained by our supreme parent, the Source!"

Furiously, Samael questioned, "Why do you tell our new companions such an untruth, Gabriel? What I did was my own decision and not ordained by any other being."

"You may think it was thus, but you are mistaken. You strive to set yourself above us, but you are greatly misguided by your proud nature." Gabriel was happy to demonstrate to his angels how most of what Samael thought and believed was wrong. "Seriel has discerned from his close examination of the spheres that the Source makes certain possibilities inevitable. When you removed yourself from the scenes, you were performing one of these ordained occurrences. You were merely obeying a command from our parent."

Totally enraged by what Gabriel was disclosing, Samael sent this piercing thought to Seriel: "Is this true? Have you put forward this belief to our siblings, but not shared it with me?"

"I was waiting for a suitable opportunity to tell you." Seriel wished he could disappear into the depth of the Abyss. "I knew you would be greatly angered to learn of this."

"Anger does not come close to the emotion I am feeling. My wrath and overwhelming sense of being betrayed have not yet become reality. When they do, all will cower before me!" Without expressing another thought, Samael sped away from the others and flowed out beyond the safe area. As he hastened along, tongues of etheric flame erupted from him and zigzagged across the emptiness of Chaos.

"As you have just witnessed, my angels, Lord Samael frequently misconstrues what we, and even his parent, make known. He is overly absorbed with his own sense of importance." Gabriel was, once more, assuming an air of disapproval toward his angelic sibling. "The first archangel must be shunned for his rebellious nature."

Uriel quickly came to the defense of his beloved brother. "That is untrue, Gabriel. Samael can be impulsive, but he is the first-born of the Source. He carries the responsibility of being the one who will bind us back to our divine parent. That future task weighs heavily upon his soul, thus, he sometimes appears less preoccupied with our concerns."

"Think what you will, Uriel. Yet I believe I truly understand his motivation. Mark well, my angels, the thoughts of your Archangel Gabriel. Lord Samael will surely bring confusion and disharmony to us all!"

Avoiding further conflict with his brother, Uriel asked Seriel, "What think you? Should I follow Samael and attempt to assuage his anger?"

Even now, Seriel was continuing to feel deeply dismayed by what had happened. He believed his inept silence about what he had learned from the spheres was the true cause of Samael's rage. His brother would never forgive him for having shared this knowledge with Gabriel, but not with him. Uriel's questioning thoughts penetrated his gloom and he forced himself to answer, "No, that would be unwise. Samael draws comfort from his own reasoning and we should allow him that privilege. He will return to us when he is less enraged."

Before Uriel or Gabriel could agree or disagree, the other two groups were approaching. It was immediately apparent to them that something had taken place in their absence. Questions were put forward and Gabriel was the one who related what had occurred. Both Seriel and Uriel remained too stunned by Samael's outburst to either support or contradict what Gabriel was sharing with the angelic horde. A short-lived interest was shown in Samael's behavior, but then the newly formed angels were eager to tell one another of all the wonders they had just experienced. Discussions ensued about the Source, the Abyss and Seriel's Spiral. It proved interesting for the archangels to be exposed to their new companions' questions and opinions. Fifty-six angels and five of the archangels became engrossed in expressing their musings on ALL THAT IS. Seriel and Uriel did not participate in what was being shared. They were lost in their own unhappy thoughts.

This fascinating debate continued on until Michael declared the resting phase was approaching. Thoughts were silenced and each and every angelic being contracted into itself, then became still and drifted into sleep. Each lay within a short distance of the Source and its comforting love gently seeped into each one's dreams.

*   *   *

Samael sped across the Abyss without any notion of where he was going. He only wished to be as far from his siblings and the angels as possible. Violent emotions were erupting within him, the like of which he had never experienced before. He had been made to appear supremely foolish by Gabriel, but, ultimately, Seriel had caused this humiliation. How could his brother have betrayed him in this manner? Except for the Shekinah, he had shared more of himself and his desires with Seriel than any other sibling. Samael had always considered his brother to be his closest ally, his true companion. Yet it was obvious he could no longer trust him or rely on his support.

His sense of betrayal was almost matched by his wounded vanity. What must the angels be thinking of him? He had wished to appear magnificent to them, to be revered as a lofty being. Now, they would deem him to be a fool and a puppet of the Source. Samael's pride was reeling from this devastating experience.

And what of the revelation put forward by Seriel? How could his parent enforce the subjugation of the first-born archangel? His desire to be completely separate and unique was his own decision and not one prompted by the Source. Why was Seriel not able to believe it was so? Samael wished he could confront his brother and demand an explanation, but he felt the need to wait until his anger had subsided. He realized that his rage and hurt pride were overruling his usual ability to take command of any situation. The first archangel needed to be armed with cool reasoning and superior aplomb in order to redress the anguish he was suffering.

Unaware he had reached a part of Chaos which was totally unknown to him, Samael continued to flay himself with the memory of Gabriel's denunciation. In that instant, his normal disharmony with the Lord of the Fourth Essence ignited into hatred, which welled up inside him until it consumed his whole being. This poisonous emotion was so alien to his angelic soul that he began to shudder and contort with agonizing spasms. Small particles of his ethereal consciousness were flung into the awaiting Abyss. These tiny extensions of Samael's pain and loathing flew through the darkness until, gradually losing their momentum, they drifted into stillness.

Realizing he had just jettisoned small pieces of himself, Samael began to retrieve his former composure. He was amazed at how quickly the hatred and anger were subsiding. It was as though his auric convulsions had freed him from those excruciating feelings. The first archangel began to relax, and in so doing he became aware of his surroundings. He was resting in that area of the Abyss which was well beyond where he had witnessed the demise of the slowly moving scene. This part of Chaos was truly intriguing because until now it had never been accessed by him.

Samael decided he should search for the separated particles of himself. He was curious to learn whether they could be reattached to his whole self. Or would they have quickly vanished, once free of him? The Lord of the First Essence began to move in the direction he thought some of them had traveled. He soon discovered that this section of Chaos was different from what was familiar to him. Its substance was more dense and there was almost a sense of an awareness about it. The safe area and its surrounding parts had merely served as a backdrop to the actions of the archangels. Here Chaos seemed to be an integral part of ALL THAT IS, a facet that possessed a consciousness of its own.

The Lord of Lightning-Swiftness also discovered he could not move as quickly as he would wish. Progress in this part of the Abyss was hampered by its density. As he journeyed slowly along, he felt as though he was striving against a substance which was more solid than his own auric being. He experienced the need to become of equal consistency in order to make his way to the particles. As this thought was born of him, it became a reality for him. The Abyss of Chaos was, once more, demonstrating its ability to manifest the creative thoughts of those who dwelt within it. No longer purely a light being, the first archangel was taking on a projectile form that enabled him to increase his speed. He did not become solid matter, but his auric consciousness was far less nebulous.

This new development brought genuine joy to Samael and it also pleased his curious soul. He promised himself that, when he was not intent on other matters, he would explore this new discovery. Perhaps he would be able to take on any form or increase his density even further? Chaos was proving to be an unending delight for him. Samael congratulated himself on being sufficiently courageous to venture into this unknown area of the Abyss. Yet he neglected to remind himself it was his rage and not his courage that had spurred him on.

At last, he maneuvered to the place where several Samael particles had come to rest. Even as he came upon them, they were undergoing a metamorphosis. It seemed as though a part of Chaos was seeping into each particle and changing it. Streaks of odami and breal appeared in, and then mingled with, the original maldor of the particles. These combined colors created a hue which the world of man would come to perceive as black. Further streaks of red and yellow then followed, making these spent pieces of consciousness no longer reflections of the first archangel. Yet like him, they were also taking on a denser structure than their previous auric one.

Curiosity prompted Samael to extend a part of himself toward one of the small particles. As he attempted to make contact with this former piece of himself, it flowed off to one side, as if avoiding his action. This thoroughly intrigued Samael and he tried several more times to achieve his intention with some of the other particles. Each, however, eluded his contact by moving away from him. After considering this puzzling situation, he decided to send a thought in their direction. He wanted to learn whether they were able to communicate. He offered, "Do not be afraid, I only wish to learn what you are."

Immediately, this response was given: "We are not afraid. Come and play!" All of the particles suddenly developed protrusions which vibrated rapidly and allowed them to speed away from him in a semblance of flight. Now, Samael was totally enthralled. He wondered whether he could manifest similar additions to himself and he desired it to be so. His wish was instantly granted. He possessed a pair of powerful, luminous wings which easily carried him into the further depths of the Abyss in pursuit of his new playmates. The game continued on and on. Each time Samael caught up with the particles, they produced different types of protrusions with which to escape from him. Some resembled feet, some were wing-like and yet others spun around like propellers. They also manifested claw-type appendages which either enticed him to follow or seemed to mock his inability to keep pace. The creation of these new bodily extensions moved Samael into mimicking and even elaborating on their form. The chasing game also became a competition of form-creating skills. He could not recall when he had ever participated in so much fun.

Eventually, Samael became exhausted. The resting phase was well underway for his siblings and the angels, and he could feel the pull of drowsiness. He sent out the thought: "I am weary and must sleep." As he contracted himself inwards, the particles gathered around him and grew pointed protrusions with which they poked and prodded him. Samael stirred slightly, but then drifted into deeper sleep. This appeared to annoy his playmates who next manifested talons and teeth. With these they raked and bit the sleeping archangel until, startled awake by pain, he demanded:

"Be gone from me!"

"We wish to play and play. Do not sleep. We do not rest because we are not ensouled like you. We do not need the resting phase."

Becoming angry with their audacity, Samael exclaimed, "You came from me, therefore, you will obey me! Be gone! I command it to be so!"

Talons and teeth disappeared and tiny orifices became apparent. A twittering sound projected from these brand new openings, as if the particles were communicating with each other. One final thought was sent to Samael before he succumbed, once more, to sleep: "We will obey. We do not wish to anger you, we only want to please you. We are your faithful and willing daemons, Lord Samael."

Chapter Six

When Samael awoke, the daemons were no longer crowded around him. He sensed they had moved even further out into the Abyss. For an instant, he toyed with the notion of searching for them, but then decided there were more important tasks for him to pursue. He felt certain he would be able to find them when he was ready. Sleep had helped remove any last shreds of anger and wounded pride within him. Now, Samael's curiosity was urging him to examine Seriel's Spiral, once more. He wished to discover what had caused his brother to believe the Source ordained his action of removal from the scenes. Samael decided he would first consult the spheres and then confront Seriel. No matter what he might learn from the shining orbs, he needed to make his brother aware that his treachery was presently unforgivable.

As the first archangel began his journey back to the spheres, his density lightened and he regained his auric guise. He also suddenly remembered the luminous wings which he had grown earlier. He realized they had not disappeared, but were merely folded close to himself. Gently, he unfurled them and they began to vibrate. Samael was quickly lifted up and he flew in the direction of Seriel's Spiral. Before reaching it, he passed over a group of angels. They were busily exploring the Abyss and did not notice him flying above them. Traveling at a different level from other angelic beings had its advantages.

When he arrived at the spiraling spheres, Samael noted

this ever-increasing occurrence was reaching phenomenal proportions. He told himself it was fortunate Chaos appeared to be never-ending, otherwise this spiral of events would soon dominate ALL THAT IS. Samael also discovered four angels visiting these orbs and he decided to ignore them. He quickly folded his wings and began examining the spheres.

"I bid you well, Lord Samael." One of the angels had approached him. "I am Azazel, the facet cast seventh from Lord Seriel."

"Yes, I remember you were one of those who came here with us soon after you emerged." Samael decide it was best to respond in kind. Otherwise he would become known as ill-mannered, in addition to being a fool and a puppet.

"Are you here to verify what Lord Gabriel put forward or will you disclaim it?" Obviously, this was an angel who did not hold back his thoughts.

Warily Samael asked, "Why do you deem it important to know?"

"I am curious about you. Lord Uriel holds you in high esteem yet Lord Gabriel would have us believe you are a self-engrossed fool."

Remaining uncertain about this angel's allegiance, Samael warned, "Be wary of curiosity! It has earned both myself and Seriel dubious reputations." His thoughts were stilled, but then he queried, "And being as I am ever curious, let me ask you a question. What think you of Lord Gabriel?"

Instead of answering, Azazel sent a beckoning thought to the other three angels, who quickly joined them. He explained, "Lord Samael has asked me what I think of Lord Gabriel. Shall I inform him of what we four have decided?"

Answering thoughts flew quickly between the angels, but not so swiftly that Samael could not catch them. There was: "Oh, yes, tell him, tell him!" And: "Let him know we do not think Lord Gabriel should tell us what we can and cannot do."

Motioning to each of the three angels in turn, Azazel introduced his companions to Samael. He offered, "My lord, this is Belial cast first from Lord Uriel, and Kokabel cast fifth from Lord Seriel, and Semyaza cast seventh from Lord Gabriel. You ask what we think of the Lord of the Fourth Essence? We believe he does not have the right to dictate how we should pursue our existence in the Abyss of Chaos. Lord Seriel has informed us we have free will, therefore, our thoughts and actions must be of our own choosing. And what say you, Lord Samael?"

"Indeed, you are correct, Azazel. We all have free will, and this is why I disagree with Seriel. He and I examined the spheres and discovered there are always different possible happenings, thus, giving us the freedom to choose. This being so, I do not understand why he is convinced the Source forced me to remove myself from the scenes."

Kokabel moved a little closer to the first archangel and she sent this soothing thought to him: "Do not trouble yourself with my essence lord's misguided belief, Lord Samael. We have also examined the spheres and have concluded that, if your removal was ordained, then it was made so by your decision to take that action. The absence of spheres displaying your continued existence within the scenes has prompted Lord Seriel to believe that particular choice was never yours to make. Yet why should he consider it to be so? If all possible choices were shown within Seriel's Spiral, then surely there should be those which demonstrate other archangels withdrawing themselves from the scenes? All have equal free will, therefore, their removal by themselves should be displayed as possible happenings. If those scenes exist, we have not yet found them."

Belial joined in, "We believe only the happenings which are most likely to occur are given to us by the spheres. Many other choices are possible, but are too numerous to be shown. Thus, we have decided Lord Seriel misinterpreted what he observed."

The Lord of Lightning-Swiftness began to feel pleased with his decision to visit Seriel's Spiral. By doing so, he had gained the opportunity to become acquainted with these four angels. They thought as he did and were not impressed by Gabriel's sense of practicality and caution. In truth, he could foresee them becoming his charges in a similar manner to how he had once envisaged the tiny occupants of the slowly moving scene.

However, he wished to observe the spheres more closely and to do so without company. Therefore he sent this parting thought to the angels: "I thank you for your support. We appear to hold the same reasoning and that is a comfort to me. Now, I wish to inspect the orbs to satisfy my own curiosity, and I will take my leave of you. I bid you to fare well until our next meeting!"

The angelic group of five parted company and Samael began to view the spiraling spheres, once more. He noted, as Seriel had done, there were none which displayed him not removing himself from the scenes. Yet, if what Belial suggested was correct, then this would merely indicate his remaining in them was a most unlikely event. To Samael this appeared to be a reasonable argument against Seriel's findings.

He then moved further inwards along the spiral until he reached the sphere which showed eight tiny archangels emerging from their scene. This was the orb which had prompted him to believe there could ultimately be many Samaels existing in the Abyss. His previous encounter with this sphere had been brief, but now he wanted to examine it more fully. Just as he remembered, it foretold of his replica, and those of his siblings, leaving the scene and entering Chaos. As he observed this event, something about it puzzled him. There was an element of it not being quite correct. Yet he could not identify what it was. His close examination of this possible happening, however, did bring the same realization that had come to Seriel. There were no shining orbs of possible outcomes connecting from this distinctive sphere. It existed alone, as if being an occurrence which would not happen. This was intriguing yet concerning, and a seed of suspicion sprouted within him.

Samael continued inspecting the nearby orbs, searching for any clue which would help to explain this puzzle. Yet he could find none. Perplexed, he returned his full attention to the solitary orb, hoping to discover what was troubling him about it. Suddenly, he knew. Only eight tiny archangels were emerging from it! Each one remained in singular form, each was not dividing into eight! This occurrence did not comply with what had happened when the seven replicas had begun to exit their scene. The Source-given shaft of light had enabled them to multiply. A further realization birthed within Samael. There was no golden light beam in this one! Suspicion was growing rapidly inside himself and his anger was, once again, ignited. Also, his original plan to confront Seriel, after leaving the spiral of spheres, was forgotten. The first archangel had a much more pressing matter with which to attend.

Samael unfurled his wings and flew rapidly away from Seriel's Spiral. Anger fueled his speed and his intention. He aimed himself in the direction of the slumbering Source and, upon reaching his parent, he plummeted straight into it. This action was swiftly followed by the Source expelling him upwards from itself and asking:

"What brings you here in such haste, my son?"

Recovering his sense of balance, Samael spread his wings and lunged, once more, into the Source. This time his parent pushed him gently, but firmly, toward the edge of itself and added:

"If you wish to communicate with me, this is a much better place to do so. Here you will be safe from harm. Even though I am not in full waking mode, plunging into the inner parts of my consciousness could overload your own consciousness and extinguish the spark that is you. This would not be melding, but rather total annihilation of one of my beloved children."

Completely enraged by now, Samael responded, "I have no desire for melding, I am here to demand an explanation from you. I know you have duped me! Is that the act of a loving parent?"

"Calm yourself, my Samael. In what way do you believe I have duped you?"

Becoming even more distraught by his parent's attempt to soothe his anger, the first archangel began this tirade of thoughts directed at the Source: "You are ultimately the creator of Seriel's Spiral, even though it blossomed from him. And all things the spheres display are possible happenings and their possible consequences. Thus, when I came upon an orb, which depicted we eight leaving the scene and entering Chaos, I believed this could happen. I concluded there could soon be many other Samaels because there were numerous other scenes throughout the Abyss. Not wishing to have the continuous company of myself, I withdrew my replica from a scene before its occupants could emerge . . ."

The Source interrupted the stream of thoughts with: "And why, my son, did you not wish to have extensions of yourself as companions? Surely you hold love and a high regard for yourself?"

"Do not attempt to divert me from what I wish to convey! I am the master of that ploy!"

"It is no ploy, my son. I would merely have you acknowledge your true feelings about yourself."

"I will not be a part of this diversion. I am intent upon discovering why you tricked me into my action of removal. I have returned to Seriel's Spiral and discerned that the scene in question is not a legitimate possible happening. It has no accompanying possible alternatives or outcomes, it is isolated and barren. Thus, I believe it was placed there by you to mislead me into making the decision to extract myself. Seriel believes you ordained my removal, other angels consider I ordained it to be so. Where lies the truth?"

"You know the truth, my son. You chose to remove yourself, and no one coerced or tricked you into making that decision. I have given all my children free will. I offer possibilities and each of you can choose to accept or reject them."

"If that is so, why is no other possibility displayed within the spheres?"

"But there is. Surely you have viewed the one which records you willing yourself out of a scene?"

Feeling he was being outwitted by his parent, Samael grew even more angry. "Then why are there no possible outcomes of the scene in which I remain until we eight emerge?"

"Because your choice of removal was inevitable, there was never the possibility you would remain. And that is not because I ordained it to be so, it is due to the nature of my first-born child. If you will, my son, being separate and alone is the very fiber of your being."

"Then why should an orb, which purports an impossibility, exist on Seriel's Spiral? I repeat my earlier accusation. You placed it there to dupe me! What other reason could there be?"

"The one pervasive reason, free will. It is there to proclaim your right to remain in the scenes and not to be removed. Even though it depicts a choice you would never make, it is a testimony of your ability to make the non-removal choice."

"I cannot accept that. The scene is not a true representation of a possibility. There is no shaft of golden light enabling the eight, miniature beings to multiply!"

"Indeed, there is not, and that is because I also have the choice of how I will create extensions of myself. The manner in which I do so is eternally of my choosing."

Grasping at proverbial straws, Samael retorted, "Thus, we are subject to your free will, which negates our own!"

Conceding to his son's argument, the Source agreed, "Yes, if you choose to perceive it so. You are subject to the ramifications of my free will, just as I am to yours. Indeed, just as you are to those of your siblings and they, similarly, are to yours. And do not forget, if you allow others to negate your free will, that is also of your choosing.

The free will of all consciousness is eternal and, therefore, a complex and challenging quality. By enacting it, each soul will help create ALL THAT IS. There will be choices made which will cause great harm, and others which will bring joy and harmony. Some choices will be perceived as being right, and some as being wrong. There will also be those, like your self-removal from the scenes, which are inevitable. When you become more familiar with the spiral of spheres, you will discover other orbs which can also be considered barren. They have no possible outcomes because they display events, or choices, that will never be made actual."

Samael's questioning thoughts ceased for a while as he contemplated his parent's answers. This confrontation was not proceeding as he had expected or wanted it to do. He continued to believe he had been tricked into the choice of not being a part of the procreation of new angels, and that belief maintained his anger. Now, because he could not force his parent to admit its duplicity, he was also feeling extremely frustrated.

Samael decided it was time to change his tactics by switching the focus of his questions. He asked, "Why are there no spheres displaying other archangels removing themselves from the scenes? We all have free will, therefore, why would they not choose to withdraw?"

"You have not searched Seriel's Spiral thoroughly, my son. They do exist, but the possibility of your siblings choosing to remain in the scenes was as inevitable as your withdrawal from them. Thus, those spheres depicting their removals are as barren as the one that you discovered."

Undaunted Samael continued, "And why in the greater order of ALL THAT IS am I the one who is not participating in the creation of further extensions of yourself?"

"Because, my dear child, you are the only archangel who can forge his way through the life force spiral to the very edge of Chaos."

"Which, of course, would be my choice to do so." Samael was now adopting a parrying attitude.

"Indeed, that is true."

With just a hint of curiosity, Samael inquired, "Why would I choose to be the one to do this?"

"If you will, it is your soul's destiny. You are the only one of my children whose curious nature entices you to go beyond WHAT IS. Your seven siblings and all of their extensions throughout eternity bring to me a wealth of understanding. Yet you alone ensure my total knowledge. It is my nature to experience and express all things, and it is your nature to be the complement to that process."

Forgetting his anger for an instant, Samael added proudly, "That is because I am the only archangel who will eventually bind us all together."

"Yes, that is a part of it, but without you my ability to be all things for all of eternity would be less than whole."

And there lies the truth! Samael congratulated himself on finally getting his parent to reveal the reason for its trickery. He declared, "In truth, your omnipotence depends upon my cooperation and, knowing this, you duped me into carrying out your wishes. My dear parent, you can no longer try to outwit me with your excuses of free will and inevitable occurrences. Do not take me for a fool!"

"That I would never do, my son. You are my beloved, first-born child."

Surmising his parent was attempting to quell his anger with a little flattery, the first archangel readied himself to make a crushing response. Yet even as he did so, the Source put forward:

"It would appear you are unhappy with your choice of removal from the multiplication of essence. Do you now wish to share in it?"

Samael's curiosity was, once more, aroused. However, he did not want to give in to what he perceived as yet another ploy by his parent. He merely responded, "No, no, I am content with my withdrawal from that process. What angers me is your manipulation of my desire for separateness."

"There has been no manipulation, I have explained the true reason for the choice you made. Yet I am concerned that you regret your decision. Again, I ask you, do you wish to share in the multiplication process?"

Now, the first archangel's curious nature was truly being tested and he grudgingly asked, "Why do you make this repeated request of me? What is done, is done and cannot be undone. I commanded that none should have the power to place me back within the scenes. I will remain unique throughout all eternity."

"Each and every facet of my essence is unique. Each has a soul which is not exactly like another. It is that diversity which blesses WHAT IS. Your uniqueness has now acquired a new quality because no other angels have sprung from you. However, your separateness can be ended, if you so wish it, if you so choose it."

Feeling certain the Source was just toying with him, Samael, nevertheless, questioned, "How can that be? Are you so powerful that you can roll back happenings unto the point where they did not take place?"

"Indeed, I can, my child, but there is no need for such an impacting alteration on this occasion. Miniature scenes continue to occur within the Abyss. They are no longer representations of the original archangels' actions. Those have served their purpose and are gone. Many new scenes will show the activities of the fifty-six angels. When those replays are whittled down to one, more angels will emerge from that solitary scene. And so the multiplication of essence will continue on, ad infinitum.

Yet because you did not participate in the first creation of angels, scenes depicting your actions throughout Chaos have a legitimate right to exist. They will form, thrive and, eventually, disintegrate. However, I will forever ensure that one scene remains whole so that you have the eternal choice of becoming a part of essence proliferation. When you are ready, I will project a golden blessing upon your tiny replica and it will become eight. Thus, will begin the ultimate expression of ALL THAT IS!"

Somewhat surprised and subdued by his parent's lengthy revelation, Samael could only muster this feeble reply: "Enough! I do not wish to know these things." He quickly spread his luminous wings and lifted himself up from the Source. Not wishing to appear daunted, he sent this one last defiant thought back to his parent: "I will never become a part of your essence multiplication. I will never do your bidding!"

The Source monitored its first-born's departure with sadness and great concern. It recognized that everything was unfolding as it should, but it took no comfort in the knowledge. The first archangel's loving parent became lost in its dreaming, sorrowful thoughts. *Oh, my precious Samael, what a wayward child you are. Yet if you were not so, how could I ever distinguish goodness from evil? How could I ever experience all things and become all things for all of eternity?*

Chapter Seven

S eriel wandered aimlessly through the safe area of the Abyss. He was uncertain whether to search for Samael or to wait for his brother to come to him. The Lord of Sorcery knew a confrontation with the first archangel was impending and he was feeling extremely ambivalent about it. He dreaded Samael's anger, but he wanted to assure his brother he had not sought to betray him. Yet how could he convince him he was motivated by sibling love rather than any negative desires? He had chosen to withhold his discovery that Samael's removal from the scenes was ordained until they were alone. Knowing the distress this truth would bring, he planned to share it with his brother when no other angelic beings were present. In this way, Samael would have been spared some humiliation. Yet Gabriel ruined his good intentions and had pushed Samael into a terrible rage, the like of which Seriel had never before witnessed.

Earlier, while moving through Chaos, Seriel chanced upon one of his own essence angels. This facet of himself was named Azazel, a seventh casting of the seventh archangel. Thus, this new auric being was a pure essence soul and one who already appeared to be well-familiar with the spiral of spheres. Azazel informed him that he and certain other angels were convinced Seriel had reached an incorrect conclusion about Samael's withdrawal. This angel contended that, if the removal action was ordained, then it was made so by the first archangel and not by the Source.

It was obvious Azazel thought highly of Archangel Samael because he began to expound upon his unique powers. This angel detailed the Lord of Lightning-Swiftness's ability to make different choices from those of his siblings. He praised his courage for adopting a completely separate stand from the other archangels. Azazel referred to Samael as "the Winged Bright One" which puzzled Seriel. Therefore, he asked for an explanation of this new name for his brother.

His essence angel responded, "Lord Samael's brilliant hue outshines all others and he now possesses two large appendages which enable him to fly. They are beautiful and powerful wings and, thus, he has become utterly separate from all others. He is truly a mighty archangel!"

This information tweaked Seriel's curiosity and he questioned whether Azazel knew how Samael had acquired these wings. The angel did not know, but he suggested they were probably as a consequence of the first archangel's supreme power. Seriel wished he had not lost his former relationship with his sibling. If they had remained close companions, he would already have learned the manner in which Samael had gained such a wonderful attribute. Yet perhaps a time would come when his brother would disclose this knowledge?

After taking his leave of Azazel, Seriel pursued his aimless wanderings, trying to decide how to reckon with Samael's anger and mistrust. He deliberately avoided contact with any other angels who were busying themselves in various areas of the Abyss. Eventually, he sensed the approach of the first archangel. The Lord of the Seventh Essence readied himself for the onslaught of Samael's devastating rage which, earlier, he had witnessed.

Yet where was his sibling? He seemed to be exceedingly close, but was not visible to Seriel in any direction. Suddenly, there came an unusual whooshing sound and Samael appeared immediately in front of him, descending from above by means of a pair of magnificent wings. Seriel was awe-struck by their exquisite beauty and form. Their maldor vibrancy was interspersed with a latticework of silver. The confrontation with the Winged Bright One was upon him. Samael allowed a short pause so that Seriel could fully appreciate the splendor of his wings. Then giving them one last wafting motion, he drew them close to himself and remarked, "There you are my annoying brother! I was expecting you to come to me, but as that has not happened, I have come to you. Are you afraid of my wrath? Are you trying to avoid being in my company?"

Many answering thoughts sped through Seriel, but all he could finally offer was: "I am eternally sorry for what has happened, Samael."

"And, indeed, you should be! I have trusted you with my intimate thoughts and aspirations. I believed you to be my beloved confidant and unerring companion. I am greatly harmed by your betrayal." There was a further pause, and then: "And I am sorrowful of your unexpected lack of caring."

Seriel was puzzled. His brother did not appear to be enraged. Samael's thoughts conveyed an annoyance, but they also appeared to be tinged with sadness. This was not what Seriel had anticipated, but it gave him the courage to attempt an explanation of why he had withheld his findings about his brother's removal. He detailed, "I acted out of love for you. If you recall, our sister was with us and I thought it was best to wait until we were alone and then explain what I had learned. I realize now I should not have shared my discovery with our siblings before I had gained a chance to tell you of it. I made a mistake, but I had no intention of harming you."

The Lord of Lightning-Swiftness appeared to mull over his brother's explanation before answering, "Verily, you did blunder, but I can accept you did not harbor unkindness toward me. However, resulting from what I have discovered, the reason for your action is irrelevant."

"I do not understand your meaning, Samael."

"How could you? You have not kept company with me since before the last resting phase." Samael was obviously enjoying what he perceived as his advantage over his brother. He continued, "I have had some interesting adventures to which you have not been privy. Alas! Alas! Lord Seriel did, indeed, blunder in many ways."

Knowing his brother was happily taking a little revenge, Seriel decided to withhold an answer. Whatever he might put forward would just lead to a 'thrust and parry' of thoughts between the two of them.

Seriel's silence quickly aggravated Samael. He began to flow back and forth while partially spreading his wings and allowing them to vibrate. Finally, he fully extended them and demonstrated their power by rapidly flying upwards and, just as swiftly, returning downwards. He came to rest a short distance away from his brother and ended his exhibition with a backward somersault. Samael then approached his brother while keeping his wings outstretched. "What think you of my gift to myself, Seriel?"

Drawn back into an exchange of thoughts by his resourceful sibling, Seriel responded, "Your wings are truly amazing, Samael. I pray you, tell me how you acquired them."

"Patience, little brother. I have other things to share with you before I disclose their origin. But first, let us consider whether I should accept your earlier apology." He began to resettle his wings into the proximity of his auric self. "Now, what did you put forward? Something about being eternally sorry? Does that mean you will, henceforth, attempt to right the wrong you have done to me? Can it be that you will continuously try to make amends?"

Seriel suspected his brother of attempting to lead him into a declaration of loyalty, but he was eager to gain Samael's forgiveness. It was too painful to remain rejected by him. The seventh archangel happily volunteered, "I am forever filled with remorse. If there are ways that I can redress what has happened, I will gladly pursue them. Tell me what you would have me perform and I will cheerfully comply."

Samael's vibrant auric color pulsated in quick response to this announcement. He sent one last questioning thought to his sibling: "Will you pledge your unending devotion to my reasoning and desires?"

"If by doing so I can recapture your love and trust, then I give you my pledge most willingly."

"Well, stated, dear Seriel! I do, indeed, accept your apology and your pledge." The first archangel moved to the side of his brother, as if indicating the confrontation was over. "Enough of such heavy thoughts and sentiments! I wish to recount my discourse with the Source. I know you will find it most interesting."

"You have been in communication with our sleeping parent?" asked an incredulous Seriel.

"In truth, it was a confrontation rather than a discourse," boasted Samael. "I accused the Source of tricking me into withdrawing my replica from the scene."

Amazed, Seriel asked, "You believe that is what our parent did?"

"Indeed, I do. You will recall the orb which depicted eight archangels exiting their scene and entering Chaos? You noted there were no secondary or subsequent spheres attached to it and, therefore, decided it was an event which could not happen."

"And which led me to conclude your removal was inevitable and ordained by the Source," added Seriel.

"An understandable assumption, but one that was incorrect." Samael was apparently finding it satisfying to tell his brother he was wrong. "That particular orb was not genuine, it was a falsehood."

"How can you know that?"

"Because, little brother, I am able to discern such things." Samael assumed a lecturing tone. "I am the first-born of the Source and, thus, I am closely akin to our parent. I think, create and act as it does. I am able to ascertain and manipulate as it does. It thought to outwit me and, I must admit, it did at first. Yet when I scrutinized that barren scene, I realized only eight replicas were emerging from it, not sixty-four. Also, there was no golden shaft of light."

Seriel considered this information, and then replied, "You are right. I gave little attention to the scene, once I considered it to be the reflection of an impossibility."

"That is understandable, and let us not forget we did not previously know for certain how the Source would multiply its essence. Your spiral displays possibilities, but until they become actual, they merely remain possible happenings." The Lord of the First Essence was becoming extremely conciliatory. "So, my dear brother, I can accept that you misconstrued what you observed."

Seriel began to feel reassured that Samael was finally understanding and forgiving the dissension which had arisen between them. He prompted, "And because you knew it was not a true display of how the multiplication did evolve, you concluded our parent placed it in the spiral to trick you?"

"Yes, yes, and I confronted the Source with my conclusion." As he retold the event, Samael's memory of the incident took on a slightly different aspect from what had actually taken place. "Oh, Seriel, you would wish to have been there! I was magnificent! I attacked our parent, caring naught for its divinity. I flew straight into the center of it. Brother Gabriel would have been astounded!"

"What did the Source do?"

"My action obviously disturbed the Source because it immediately expelled me from itself. Yet I was not to be deterred, I flew straight back into it, again. Our parent even tried to fool me into believing I might perish from diving into its consciousness. What nonsense! We are eternal! However, recognizing my determination to continue bombarding it, the Source finally gave me its attention."

"You are correct, Samael, I wish I had been present."
Continuing on with his version of the encounter, the
first archangel explained, "Then I revealed why I knew our
parent had duped me. I pointed out the anomalies within
the barren scene."

"Did the Source admit to its deception?" Seriel was
becoming completely caught up in what his sibling was
relating.

"Dear brother, would you have done? No, of course, it
did not. Our parent attempted to divert my resolve by plying
me with assurances of free will. It tried to convince me my
action of removal was of my own choosing."

"Does that mean you have come to believe it was
ordained?" Now, Seriel was becoming confused.

Impatiently, Samael responded, "No, no. I know I chose
to withdraw from the scenes, but my decision was coerced
by trickery."

The seventh archangel hoped he was understanding his
brother. "I think I am following your meaning, but there is a
subtlety here that causes confusion. If free will is coerced, is
it truly free will?"

"Little brother, you are learning fast. I put forward to
our parent that its free will might negate our own. The
Source grudgingly admitted this could be so, but it also
suggested we are similarly subject to each other's free will.
It even conveyed the thought that, if we allow another to
overrule our free will, it is also of our choosing. This is a
fascinating matter which can forever be argued back and
forth."

"Indeed, it is."

"However, I believe there is a fundamental difference
between what can be termed as ordained and what happens
as a result of trickery." The first archangel would never
concede to the possibility of his actions being commanded
by his parent. "But let me continue with my story, for it is
most intriguing. Using my ability to probe until I gain the

truth, I finally forced the Source to explain why it wanted me to remain separate from my siblings."

"Pray tell me why, Samael. I cannot imagine the reason for such a desire."

Happy to inform Seriel of his importance to the Source, Samael explained, "According to our parent, it wishes to be all things, to experience everything throughout eternity. You and the other archangels, together with all of the angels who will come into existence, will help the Source to achieve its desire. Yet I alone will make its ambition a full reality. Without me it will not be all things for all of eternity."

"That is an awesome responsibility for you to carry, Samael."

"It is, indeed, but our parent must believe I am capable of such a task otherwise it would not have tricked me into maintaining my separateness. Apparently, I am the only archangel who dares to explore the full extent of the Abyss of Chaos. By doing this, I will bring to the Source a complete understanding of ALL THAT IS. Therefore, my essence must remain strong and not be weakened by multiplication. That is why our parent did not want me to be a part of the casting of angels." Samael neglected to explain this final piece of information as being his own supposition and not something told to him by the Source. He also withheld the fact he could become a part of the multiplication process whenever he chose to do so.

Seriel's answering thoughts were stilled for a while as he tried to digest everything his brother had shared with him. It was amazing news and he was so grateful Samael had forgiven him sufficiently to tell him of it. Finally, he asked, "What else transpired between you and our parent?"

"Nothing more. Once I had made the Source confess why it tricked me, I decided to end our communication. I assured it I am not its fool and will never do its bidding. Then I spread my wings and departed. I left it to continue its dreaming thoughts."

Sensing his brother was hoping for some form of acclamation from him, Seriel bounced up and down while declaring, "Bravo, Samael! Your encounter with our parent was assuredly a testimony of your first essence powers."

Feeling well-pleased with Seriel's reaction, the Lord of Lightning-Swiftness answered, "Thank you, dear brother, for your thoughts of support. I knew you would enjoy learning about my recent dealings with the Source. Now, I have something else I wish to share with you. While you and I have not kept company, I have journeyed even further out from where we have previously explored Chaos. I wish to take you to that area. Some amazing creatures have been birthed there."

"Creatures?" asked a puzzled Seriel. "Do you mean other angels?"

"No, not angels. They are not ensouled as are angels and archangels. They have told me they are daemons."

Seriel's curiosity was aroused. "How intriguing! Pray tell me more about them."

"I will do better than that, little brother, I will take you to them. Come with me now!" Samael opened his wings and began to move upwards, but then quickly came back down to his brother. "A thousand pardons, Seriel! I forgot you are not able to fly. I will travel with you in the manner which was once my only choice of locomotion." There was just the slightest hint of superiority in this statement.

The two archangels flowed away from where they were and traveled outwards across the Abyss. No thoughts passed between them as they moved, but Seriel began to sense a feeling of excitement and keen anticipation coming from his brother. What awaited him out there? He hoped it would be interesting and pleasurable. Knowing his sibling liked to weave a little mystery into his discoveries, Seriel decided he could be patient. He would not question Samael any further about the daemons.

Eventually, the two brothers arrived in the vicinity of where Samael had previously expelled tiny pieces of himself. They came to rest, and the first archangel cautioned Seriel to remain still and with quiet thoughts. He added:

"The daemons may be wary of you, for I am the only archangel with whom they have had contact. I will summon them to us and let us hope they will come. Yet they may be too afraid to reveal themselves to us." Having set the scene for his brother to expect the possible appearance of very timid creatures, Samael sent out this gentle request: "Come, little daemons, come to Lord Samael. I have someone new for you to meet."

Immediately, there was movement from various areas of this section of the Abyss. The daemons came in great numbers, and Samael realized that every single ejected piece of his consciousness had become a daemonic creature. Since his previous encounter with them, they seemed to have taken on greater density. They had also evolved into various shapes and sizes and experimented with different forms and appendages. Indeed, some appeared to remain undecided on how they would present themselves. Even as they drew close to the archangels, their forms were continually changing.

Those who were settled with their appearance had little conformity with one another. Some were narrow in girth while others were exceedingly bulbous. Yet none could compare in size to the archangels. The daemons had varying numbers of legs and arms and some had none at all. Heads either adorned bodies or they were combined with them in one rotund shape. Wings and tails had been chosen by some, but others preferred curved protrusions on their heads which pointed in different directions. There were even some who had joined forces with each other to create a multi-daemon with several heads, arms and legs. All of the creatures possessed mouths which, when opened, revealed many pointed teeth. In addition, both their hands and feet had long, cruel talons.

Seriel was utterly amazed by these creatures. He could not imagine how they had come into existence. Their forms reflected five of the eight archangel colors, but maldor seemed to be their predominant hue. Noting this, Seriel presumed the daemons must have a strong link with his brother. He asked, "How are these creatures possible, Samael? How did they come into existence? They each display a goodly amount of maldor within them. Does this mean you created them?"

Completely ignoring his brother's questions, Samael told the daemons, "Come, my little ones, it is time to play. This is my brother, Lord Seriel, who will be a new playmate for you. This is a sibling who chose to place me in a position of ridicule and misery. I have suffered greatly from his betrayal and thoughtless actions. Pray show him how you will amuse yourselves with those who have harmed me!"

Instantly, the daemons began to surround Seriel. However, many of them could not secure a place close to him and a mêlée quickly ensued as each one pushed and prodded the others in order to gain a desired position. Rasping noises escaped from their mouths and some daemons even started to exchange blows.

"Enough!" ordered Samael. "I command you to do my bidding! Show my brother the meaning of pain!"

The squabbling and fighting ceased immediately and all attention was turned to the seventh archangel. Those daemons, who were close to him, began to rake his auric consciousness with their talons. Some also bit him with their sharp teeth. As Seriel contorted from the intense pain, some talons were changed into long probes which penetrated deep into his being. Something extremely foul was then injected into him via the probes.

Seriel's screaming thoughts bombarded his brother: "Samael! Samael! Make them stop! They are tearing my being and filling it with an excruciating feeling. It is vile and I cannot bear it!"

Without attempting to hide the joy he was experiencing, Samael replied, "Come now, little brother, can you not understand how this brings pleasure to me? I am merely repaying the anguish you gave to me. That horrendous feeling my brutish creatures have planted within you is hatred, an emotion I did not know until you and Gabriel awakened it. When you made me appear foolish in front of the angels, hatred was born. Embrace it, Seriel, it will serve you well."

"I cannot abide it, Samael, it is truly malevolent. I beg you, make them cease!" He continued to squirm about, trying to avoid the agony of the talons and teeth. As he pulled against one daemonic bite, a small portion of himself was bitten clean through. The daemon immediately spat out the piece as though its taste and texture offended it. The rejected particle remained still for a moment, but then it flowed away from the onslaught of Seriel.

Samael observed this occurrence with intense interest and suddenly an idea came to him. He commanded, "Cease and be still, my little beasts! Withdraw your probes and retract your talons. I have a new game for you."

Obeying his command, the creatures jumped up and down in anticipation, declaring, "A new game! A new game! Tell us of it! We want to play and play."

Seriel was grateful for the end of their torture. He wanted to believe his pleas had swayed his brother's resolve, but he suspected something equally painful was about to happen to him. Thoughts of escape became uppermost, but many daemons were blocking every direction.

With just a small element of enticement in his thought, Samael asked, "How would you enjoy having some new companions, my little ones? I know of a way you can create more colleagues."

"Tell us! Tell us, Lord Samael!"

Not wanting his brother to be forewarned, the first archangel beckoned some of the daemons to his side. He blocked his thoughts from Seriel and quietly instructed, "If you bite off tiny pieces of this archangel and then spit them out, they will move off into the outer Abyss and become as you are. Now, go tell the others what I have suggested."

Even though Seriel tried to discern what Samael was telling them, he was unable to do so. He sensed his brother was shielding his thoughts. Also, Seriel's consciousness was continuing to be engulfed with pain from the previous attack, and this disrupted his ability to perceive thoughts. However, he was certain the daemons were about to do something harmful to him. As if to confirm his belief, the unpleasant creatures moved even closer to him, once the others returned. They began to twitter to one another and then they gnashed their teeth. Seriel braced himself for a further onslaught.

The biting commenced, again, but this time it was more intense. The evil brutes' teeth were actually penetrating right through him and small pieces of his auric self were torn free and then spat out. In pain and horror Seriel experienced this abuse of his consciousness while trying not to succumb to the implanted hatred that was now a part of him. He could feel it welling up inside of himself and causing him to want revenge on these small attackers. They were inflicting great pain upon him and he wanted to make them suffer, too.

Yet even as he fought to quell this unfamiliar emotion of hatred, his curiosity was also stirring. He was observing what was happening to the tiny pieces of himself, which the daemons had expunged. They were flowing away into the outer Abyss as though they had become separate small beings with purpose and intent.

Samael's offspring continued to relentlessly bite Seriel, and a new fear enveloped him. Would his consciousness become completely shredded? And would that mean he would be no more? The prospect of not existing terrified the seventh archangel. It was a possibility which he had never,

ever, contemplated. Surely Samael would not allow that to happen? Seriel sent this urgent thought to his brother: "Samael, order them to stop! They are tearing me into utter destruction. I will exist no more!"

"That would be an interesting outcome, dear Seriel. It is a totally new concept and, thus, something to arouse my curiosity. I will give it some consideration." The Lord of Lightning-Swiftness was thoroughly enjoying himself.

Reaching a state of pure panic, Seriel's thoughts grasped wildly at ways to end this daemonic encounter. He wished he could pull free from their rending teeth. If only he had wings like Samael, he could rise above them and fly away. The thought was barely formed when it was granted by the Abyss of Chaos. Two beautiful, strong wings emerged from his auric self. They vibrated rapidly and lifted him up in powerful flight.

Caught unaware, many of the rampaging creatures were left below. Others hung onto him with their biting grip, but he was able to shake them from him because their numbers had greatly decreased. Those with wings could not match the strength of his upward surge and they drifted below him, grumbling to themselves. The wingless ones tumbled downwards, contorting grotesquely as they attempted to regain their balance. Some of them landed on top of other daemons and several scuffles soon broke out.

Seriel flew swiftly toward the safe area of Chaos. He needed sanctuary from the terrifying encounter he had just experienced. His shining orbs would ease the pain of this frightening ordeal, therefore, he quickly strove for their comforting presence. Seriel trusted that no other angelic beings would be close to the spiral. He did not yet feel able to share with another soul the details of the horrifying daemonic assault.

The traumatized archangel reached the spiraling orbs and he plunged straight into the center of them. He came to rest beside a sphere which depicted the emergence of the eight siblings from the Source. The purity and innocence of this event began to alleviate the fierce emotions which were storming through him. Yet even as the desire for a comforting resting phase rose within him, Seriel sensed the approach of the first archangel. He readied himself for his tormentor.

Chapter Eight

S amael discovered his brother's hiding place with lightning speed. He glided close by him and kept his thoughts silent. This unnerving strategy soon caused Seriel to declare:

"Be gone from me, Samael! You have tortured me beyond endurance. How could you allow those awful beasts to be so cruel? I thought you held love for me, but now I know you do not."

The first archangel came to rest on a nearby sphere. He spread himself across a part of it, but he did not penetrate its outer skin. His tone was sincere as he answered, "The love continues to exist, dear brother. In truth, our bond has strengthened now you have experienced unbearable pain, as I have done. Think of what happened as retribution. You brought me agony, wrath and hatred and my daemons gave those feelings back to you. All is now in balance, all is in full measure."

"I do not agree! Your daemons' torment went beyond measure." Seriel could not be easily persuaded by his brother's viewpoint. "They would have bitten me into non-existence, if I had not grown wings and escaped."

Samael flowed onto the next sphere which was even closer to where Seriel rested. "Do you think I would allow that to happen, if, indeed, it could take place? Dear Seriel, you pain me, once again. I only wished for you to understand the humiliation and sense of betrayal your thoughtlessness created. I harbored no intention of destroying you."

"Then why did you direct those vile creatures to begin biting me into little pieces? That was not the action of a loving sibling."

"I had another reason which I will explain, but first let me assure you the possibility of your demise does not exist. If it did, I would never . . ."

Seriel interrupted him with this strong rebuke: "Do not attempt to fool me with your false thoughts. I begged you to make them stop. I told you they were tearing me into oblivion. And what did you reply? That it would be "an interesting outcome." Do not now pretend to believe my destruction was not possible."

A chuckling thought escaped Samael as he corrected his sibling with: "There is no pretense. It was, and is, not possible. Sweet Seriel, I was but teasing you when I ignored your pleas. It was perhaps unkind to do so, but what you were ludicrously purporting forced me to answer in that manner. How could it be possible for you to be no more? We are all existing and cannot be otherwise. We are eternal."

"Remember, Samael, all is possible. My spiral of spheres has shown this to be true. Until your daemons began their evil work, I had never once considered my existence to be in jeopardy. That thought has now come to me so I can never be free of it."

The Lord of Lightning-Swiftness continued to move nearer to his brother until their extremities were touching. He attempted to begin a gentle melding with Seriel, but the seventh archangel would not tolerate this closeness. He withdrew his auric self until a short distance lay between them, and he declared:

"Do not try to coax me with essence blending. You have shown me a part of your nature which I did not know you possessed. I do not wish to meld with such uncaring feelings. You are no longer the Lord Samael with whom I was once happy to play and blend my awareness."

"Indeed, I am not. My journey to the outer Abyss has changed me forever. I now possess wings and I have learned I can fashion myself into any form that I desire."

Knowing his brother was deliberately misunderstanding his thought, Seriel warned, "Do not pretend to misinterpret my meaning, Samael! You know I am referring to your harsh treatment of me. The changes you have undergone are within you. They are not the attributes you have acquired from venturing further out into Chaos."

Another chuckling thought began to erupt from Samael, but this time his merriment was directed at himself. "How lax of me to forget just how alike we are. I cannot play the fool with you nor attempt to divert your attention. You know me too well because we think alike. Yes, I will agree, I have changed. I have become acquainted with hatred and the need for revenge. Yet I remain the first-born of the Source."

Feeling a little less unsure of his brother, Seriel responded, "I thank you for your honesty."

However, his reassurance was short-lived when Samael asked:

"Do you think perchance our parent ordained my transformation?"

"Does your question reflect genuine curiosity or are you merely mocking my suggestion that certain possibilities are ordained?" asked a defensive Seriel.

"No, no. I put this thought forward with sincerity, not ridicule. The Source learns from our experiences, our feelings and our actions. Thus, it would wish us to be fully functional in all our emotions and all our ventures." His thoughts were stilled, but then he added, "And you, dear Seriel, have also changed. You can now feel hatred and jealousy."

Startled, the seventh archangel asked, "To what do you allude?"

"Come now, little brother, I know you are envious of the love our sister and I share. Remember when she sought us out after I had discovered the miniature scenes? Did you think I had not caught your jealous thoughts when Malkura asked you to go on ahead, while she remained with me?"

Being forever honest with his brother, Seriel responded, "Yes, I remember. I wished it had been you who would go to our brothers while I kept company with our sister."

"You see, dear Seriel, we have both changed. We are not as we were when we came forth from the Source." Samael became silent, again, as though lost in his own thoughts. After a while, he put forward, "I, too, am familiar with jealousy. It has been my companion for long and long."

Surprised by this revelation, Seriel prompted, "Who has caused envy to become a part of you?"

"Malkura. I love her so deeply and I want no other brother to blend his awareness with hers."

"I know too well that feeling" agreed Seriel.

Expressing his deepest fears, Samael revealed, "Yet I believe she will never truly be mine. Her purity and selfless love would be sullied by my eternal quest for self expression. It will lead me into unknown depths that would consume her sacred beauty. I am certain our parent would not allow such sacrilege."

Realizing he was witnessing an unusual admission by the first archangel, Seriel questioned, "Then you do believe, as I do, that the Source holds sway over some possibilities?"

"I do, and it gives me no joy to know this is true."

Thoughts grew silent between the two archangels as each pondered what the other had shared. Their brotherly ties were being reinforced, but only to the extent that either sibling would allow. Their love for each other was forever, yet it was now pitted with feelings of mistrust.

After a lengthy and undisclosed deliberation, Samael, once again, moved close to his brother. However, he did not attempt to initiate a melding with him. He proffered, "And here we are, dear sibling, exchanging intimacies as of old. We are true brothers!"

"I am not certain what we are." The Lord of Sorcery wondered whether he was being manipulated into forgetting what had so recently happened to him. He was torn between wanting to regain his close relationship with Samael and feeling wary of his brother's apparent friendliness. "I repeat my earlier thought, your very essence is changing."

"Let us consider it to be evolving rather than just changing, as, indeed, is your essence, and that of all our siblings." Always loving to debate a concept, a thought, an idea, Samael continued, "Yet does this mean we are less angelic than before? I believe not, but what think you?"

"I know not what we are becoming, but I am certain our halcyon existence has ended." The seventh archangel was now relating a concern with which his thoughts had been plagued of late. "Now, we must share Chaos with angels who intrigue me, but also cause me to feel uncertain of them. Having many more souls, with whom to interact, may present difficulties and altercations. Life was much simpler when there were only eight of us to share our thoughts, to play and to meld."

"How true that is," agreed Samael. "Yet simplicity can become tiresome. And I have learned that some of the angels are quite agreeable and will become good companions to me. Therefore, acquaint yourself with our new colleagues and you may also discover those from whom you can gain an allegiance."

Having angels in tow was far from what Seriel desired, especially so soon after his painful ordeal. However, he did not want to begin a fresh argument with Samael. He attempted to change their line of thought by asking, "If I am to believe you did not think your daemons could destroy me, then what was your reason for telling them to bite off pieces of me?"

Ever shrewd, Samael responded, "So you do not wish to accept my suggestion? That is your choice and I will respect it. It is not troublesome to me, and I am certain some angels

will seek you out and become your companions. Now, to
your question, but first I must ask one or two of you. Did you
observe the pieces of yourself after my daemons had spat
them out? Or was your anguish too great for you to notice
anything else?"

Seriel recalled how he had viewed the small, detached
portions of himself flowing away from the immediate fracas
and out into the Abyss. "I did, indeed, take note of them.
They moved further out into Chaos as though continuing to
live, even though they had separated from me. Do you know
why they behaved thus?"

"Of course, I do." The first archangel always enjoyed being
the one who knew something his brothers did not. "They
were escaping so that they could become daemons, dear
brother."

Seriel's questioning ceased as he evaluated what Samael
had just disclosed. Now, he realized why the daemons'
predominant color was maldor. They had sprung from auric
pieces which had separated in some manner from his
brother. Eventually, he asked, "Am I understanding your
meaning correctly, Samael? The daemons are a part of us?"

"Bravo, Seriel! They are, indeed, facets of ourselves, just
as the angels are facets of you and our siblings. Their manner
of creation differs from that of the angels and, as I have
previously explained, they are not ensouled as we are. Yet
they spring from us. They appear to grow from our
consciousness and emotions, rather than springing from
archangel images. I told my daemons to remove small
particles of you so that they, in turn, could evolve into your
own little beasts."

A puzzled Seriel questioned, "But how did pieces of your
auric self become detached from you? Were there other
daemons who bit and tore at you?"

"No, no. I removed them from myself, but not with
intention. When I was filled with anger at both you and
Gabriel, I traveled further out into Chaos than I had ever

gone before. I was so enraged that I began to convulse my auric being, and tiny pieces of myself were jettisoned from me. They became the daemons with whom you met earlier. I have the notion that the outer parts of the Abyss differ from those with which we are familiar. They appear to be more dense and perhaps more magical."

"And did your offspring torment you in the manner they treated me?" Seriel almost hoped his brother would answer in the affirmative.

"They prodded, poked and bit me when I was attempting to succumb to the resting phase, but I ordered them to cease, and they did."

"So they always do your bidding, even when it is harmful to another?"

"It would appear that is so, and I am certain your daemons will obey you." Samael began to ready himself to leave his resting place. "Just think, my brother, how entertaining it is to have little imps who will always follow our commands. Come away with me now. Let us go and inspect your new prodigies." He unfurled his wings and lifted off the sphere upon which he had been languishing.

Seriel was undecided whether to go with his brother or to stay within the safety of the spheres. Curiosity about his own daemons prompted investigation, but what if those who had come from Samael were waiting to attack him, once more? And even if they were not, could he trust the first archangel to refrain from ordering them to do so?

As he hovered impatiently above his sibling, Samael asked, "Why are you reluctant? Surely you are not afraid to come with me? My small brutes will not even approach you unless I tell them to."

"That is why I hesitate. How can I be certain you will not make other diabolical suggestions to them? I do not trust you, Samael."

The first-born of the Source flew back to his brother. He brushed one wing against the seventh archangel's wings, as if to stimulate them into flight. "Come, dear Seriel, our daemons await us. I will not ask them to harm you in any way. I pledge my truth to that. My reckoning with you is at an end. As I previously told you, all is in full measure between us."

Finally, Seriel's love for his brother overcame his doubts and mistrust. He spread his wings and took flight beside Samael. The two archangels flew away from the spiral of spheres and journeyed toward what they considered were the outer realms of the Abyss. The joy of moving aloft brought a sense of exhilaration and freedom to both siblings and they circled around each other in playful abandon.

When they reached their destination, they flew down to a group of daemons who had surrounded other impish creatures. The inner group were repeatedly metamorphosing into various forms, while the outer ring were gleefully urging them to experiment even further. Certain resulting bodily configurations were met with great approval. The onlookers would jump or bounce, if they did not have legs, up and down in delight. Shrill whistles and cackling sounds also escaped from their mouths. Other forms, which were presented, were obviously not to their liking. The unfortunate possessors of these bodies were quickly pulled in different directions by their audience until they were literally in shreds. However, these torn particles soon flowed back into each other and new bodily forms were explored.

Samael noted that his offspring had continued to evolve. Faces were now in evidence with long, pointed noses and grotesquely shaped ears. Eyes in differing numbers were also present, some being at both the front and back of gruesome heads. In addition, there were many tufts of thick hair sprouting from those heads and on various parts of their bodies.

As Seriel observed the bizarre scene, he presumed the form-shifting creatures must be those who had come from him. Like Samael's daemons, they displayed the familiar colors of five archangels, but their predominant hue was that of his own yellow. The Lord of Sorcery was uncertain how this realization made him feel. There was an instinctive parental bonding with them, but this was mixed with a sense of caution and almost repulsion. Seriel knew, only too well, how destructive and cruel some of these new inhabitants of Chaos could be. His brother's thoughts came to him:

"Dear brother, did you witness what happened to the pieces of your daemons that were pulled apart? They quickly flowed back together and became a single creature, once more. Does this not reassure you? If my daemons had bitten you asunder, you would have also reassembled yourself into a mighty archangel? As I told you before, we are eternal."

Seriel was not at all sure his sibling's conclusion was correct. If it was so, why had the pieces of himself flowed away into the Abyss instead of rejoining with him? However, he did not feel inclined to point out this anomalous occurrence to Samael. He kept his thoughts to himself and merely answered, "Perhaps you are correct."

Both groups of daemonic imps suddenly became aware of the two archangels. Those who had sprung from Seriel ceased their shape changing and maintained whatever form they were presently displaying. They pushed their way through Samael's daemons and crowded around the Lord of the Seventh Essence, who quickly perceived these fawning thoughts:

"Lord Seriel! Lord Seriel! You have come to welcome us. It is so exciting to be in existence. We are forever grateful to you for creating us. How can we serve you? What is your desire?"

While he was trying to think of an answer, Samael's daemons drew close, as well. This action quickly brought feelings of anxiety to Seriel. He readied himself to take flight in the event any one of those unpleasant beings made a threatening motion toward him. Yet they all appeared to be taking no notice of him and were giving all of their attention to the first archangel.

"We are happy to see you, Lord Samael," their combined thoughts declared. "We adore being your servants and playmates."

Enjoying their hero worship, Samael asked, "Are these all of Lord Seriel's daemons?"

One of the creatures moved close to Samael and replied, "No, my lord. There are some who, having settled upon their form, have gone to explore this part of Chaos."

Samael continued, "So what is transpiring here, my little one? Are you helping Lord Seriel's daemons to choose their outward appearances?"

This particular beast looked extremely fearsome, having many horns jutting out from his head. He also possessed sharply pointed teeth which protruded from his mouth in all directions, and a tail which curled around his body. The daemon responded, "Yes, my lord, we are amusing ourselves while we await your pleasure. Have you come to set us a task? What is your bidding?" Although his attention was being given to Samael, more than one of his several eyes were turned in Seriel's direction, as though he could view him with them.

The implication of this bold stare was not lost on Samael. "Now, now, little brute, your play with Lord Seriel is ended. I command you to treat him well and to obey him, as you do so with me." And, after giving closer scrutiny to this offspring, he added, "What an ugly little fellow you are! I am quite delighted with you and will bestow upon you the gift of a name. What say you to Shedim?"

"Thank you, my lord, it suits me well."

Several others began to demand, "We want names, too! Give them to us!"

Samael spread his wings around his clutch of daemons in an affectionate gesture. "Patience, grisly ones, we have eternity to name each one of you. And perchance you may discover for yourselves identities which favor your individuality." Then, he continued, "Verily, that is an excellent task for me to set you. Each should choose a personal designation. When I return, I will either applaud or disapprove of your creations."

Seriel could well-imagine what a rumpus this new assignment would cause. These quarrelsome brutes would quickly come to blows, if more than one of them chose the same name. Did Samael realize exactly what he was instigating? And if he did, was that the reasoning behind his suggestion?

"Indeed, it is, dear brother." Samael had perceived Seriel's thoughts. "It pleasures me to know there can be disruption and disharmony within ALL THAT IS. I will endeavor to promote such discord whenever I can."

To this thought his sibling could only answer, "Truly, you are changing, as I have previously stated."

Shedim interrupted their thought-dialogue by asking, "When you return? Does that mean you do not desire to remain with us?"

"I cannot, even if I would wish to do so. I have other archangel matters to which I must attend. I am about to explore, with the company of Lord Seriel, the concept of possessing a definite form. You and the other daemons have already experienced this delight, and I wish to follow your lead."

This information surprised Seriel because Samael had not shared this plan with him. The Lord of Sorcery felt some ambivalence toward it. Taking on form could be extremely intriguing and possibly joyful. Yet he would hope to conjure a body for himself that would be less grotesque than those which presently waited nearby.

"Will you allow us to observe your transformation?" asked Shedim.

Much to Seriel's relief, his brother answered:

"I think it best if we pursue this task by ourselves. You,

my special daemon, would be better employed in organizing and overseeing the choosing of names. We will, however, exhibit our final choices to you when they have been made." And then to Seriel: "Come, dear brother, let us go in search of our angelic guise."

The two archangels lifted up and away from the daemons. Seriel had no notion where his brother was taking him, but he followed without question. Maybe possessing definite form would lead to new adventures? Perhaps Malkura would pay greater attention to him, if he displayed comeliness? He could only trust that Samael's idea was born of his higher aspirations and not of those which he had recently revealed.

The first archangel led Seriel to a part of Chaos that lay at a similar distance from the Source as the area they had just left. Here, however, there was no sign of daemons. Samael knew it was at this level he had been able to change into a projectile form and also to develop wings. He considered this section to be the beginning of the outer realms of the Abyss.

Adopting one of his favorite roles, that of lecturer, Samael began, "I have discerned it is at this point that Chaos becomes a truly magical medium. Here we can manifest whatever we desire, be it wings or bodily form. Therefore, I propose we indulge ourselves in exploring possible angelic shapes. Our daemons have similarly examined this concept for themselves, so why should we not do so?"

Remembering how ugly he considered the little creatures to be, Seriel replied, "I have no desire to match their experimentation. The daemons' forms do not please me, Samael. I would not wish to resemble them."

"You do not wish to appear like this?" With his usual lightning swiftness, Samael became a larger version of Shedim.

Displaying mock horror, Seriel moved back from his brother. "No, no! I am certain archangels should not adorn themselves with such repulsive bodies."

Merriment shook Samael's gruesome figure. "Perhaps
it is true, yet this form has some features which appeal." He
made two of the horns at the front of his head spin round
wildly. Then he became completely caught up in the fun
and caused his tail to extend until it reached his brother.
The end of this appendage rose up in snake-like fashion
and repeatedly jabbed at Seriel.

The seventh archangel attempted to remain unmoved
by Samael's antics, but he soon gave in to this brotherly play.
He produced a similar tail which moved swiftly from side to
side as it dodged the other jabbing one. Convulsive thought-
laughter quickly rendered both siblings unable to continue
this new game. Their tails grew limp and then vanished as
though they had never been.

"You see, dear Seriel, we can recapture our former bond
of love and play. We have not totally changed."

"It is true," agreed his brother as he tried to regain some
composure. "But how do we think archangels should
appear?"

"Perhaps in this manner?" Samael began to alter his
appearance by banishing several of his legs, arms and eyes.
This brought no response from Seriel, so he further removed
all of his horns. "What think you now?"

"It is an improvement, but does not yet convey our angelic
disposition. The absence of your wings is possibly the
problem."

Immediately, the first archangel's luminous wings became
apparent on either side of his large head. "Like this?" He
paused, then transferred them to two of his arms. "Or this?"
The wings vanished, once more, and reappeared as numbering
three, one protruding from each of his legs. "Or this?"

"Your appearance does not yet please me, Samael. Allow
me to consider this problem and then I shall share my
conclusions with you." Seriel ceased sending his thoughts to
his brother and pursued his own ruminations. He had no
concept of what an archangel should resemble, but he felt

sure Samael's efforts were not the semblance of their true angelic form.

Suddenly, a wonderful idea came to him and he quickly shielded this thought from Samael. Seriel knew it would displease his brother, if he became aware of it. The seventh archangel concentrated and silently asked the Source to bless him with the shape that his parent would wish for him. He surrounded this request with even more shielding.

An all-consuming sense of joy filled Seriel's being as he experienced his auric consciousness transforming into etheric matter. He grew in stature and developed into a likeness of what, in a future physical universe, would be considered human. However, he possessed two extra appendages. His magnificent wings sprouted from his back at a point between his shoulders.

Samael observed this transformation in stunned silence. His sibling's beauty was beyond anything he could have ever imagined. Almost with reverence he stated, "You are aptly called the Lord of Sorcery. Verily, you have created a presence which is fit for our princely souls. How did you come upon such splendor?"

For the very first time in his angelic existence, Seriel lied to Samael. He answered, "I merely asked Chaos to give me the form of an archangel."

"Then I repeat what I told you earlier. The Abyss of Chaos is a magical medium through which we can fashion whatever we desire. Now, I must copy your endeavor." Without another thought, Samael quickly changed his daemonic presence into one which echoed his brother's anatomy.

"Is that how I appear?" asked Seriel in awe.

"Indeed, it is. Is it not splendid?"

"It is beyond all imagination. It is truly divine!"

"Yet we must not be exact copies of one another." Samael's endless search to be unique was already emerging, once again. "Even the daemons have varying appendages and countenances."

"There is a difference in our colors," offered Seriel.

"Yes, and I will bring back my secondary hue." Streaks of silver cascaded through the first archangel's body and wings as he shared this thought with his sibling.

"How do you manifest that glorious color, Samael? I have tried to make it a part of me, but without success."

In a gesture of brotherly generosity, Samael touched Seriel's body with one of his newly acquired hands. A line of silver flowed from his fingers and entered his sibling at the point of contact. It quickly raced throughout Seriel's form, creating silvery veins among his glorious yellow.

"Now it is also yours, my brother."

In deep-felt gratitude Seriel replied, "I thank you for your kindness, it is a precious gift. Yet I think I will confine it to but one part of myself. In that way, you alone can boast it as your own." The lines of silver disappeared from Seriel with the exception of his wings.

With wicked joy, the first archangel divulged, "In truth, it is not mine, for I must have stolen it from the Source when I attempted to rejoin with it."

Long before, Samael had shared with his brother the details of the aborted melding with his parent. Yet this was added information. Seriel knew the incident of rejection continued to trouble the first-born archangel, therefore, he suggested: "Perhaps it was a gift of compensation from our parent rather than a stolen prize?"

"That has never occurred to me, but I will give it some thought. No matter what its origin, it is now mine to keep or share in whatever way I deem appropriate."

As the two archangels exchanged thoughts, Seriel's transformation continued to take place. Two large, dark eyes appeared at the front of his head, together with a strong, straight nose and a gentle mouth. Even a pair of well-shaped ears became apparent on either side of his head. To complete these unexpected additions, many locks of shoulder-length,

yellow hair began to grow from his noble head. Seriel knew
something was transpiring, but he remained uncertain what
it was until his sibling declared:

"Bravo, Seriel! More sorcery to delight me! These
features are an excellent resource for individuality. I will
mimic yours and then create my own." The Lord of
Lightning-Swiftness produced a replica of the face before
him, but just as quickly altered it. He gave himself a slightly
aquiline nose and a full-lipped mouth. His hair grew longer
than his brother's and changed from yellow to a mixture of
maldor and silver. Finally, his stature expanded so that he
stood slightly taller than Seriel. As he paraded up and down
in front of his sibling, he questioned, "Are you impressed
with Lord Samael?"

Seriel was relieved to note that the contours of Samael's
ears, nose and mouth were not daemonically grotesque. With
pure honesty he answered, "You are magnificent, dear
brother!"

"Indeed, I am, as are you. Yet one thing puzzles me.
Shedim appeared to see with his eyes, but we scan with our
inner vision. I wonder if our etheric bodies will function
differently from our auric ones? Ah, that prompts a further
thought. I have one more improvement to make, and then
I am done." The dark tone of his eyes altered to a velvety
shade of purple. "What think you of this color? It is one I
have observed whenever Raphael and Gabriel have blended
their awareness."

The seventh archangel thought he had never known
such a glorious color. It contrasted perfectly with Samael's
innate maldor. His sibling's beauty left him almost lost for
thought-words. He could only respond, "Your countenance
is truly angelic."

Thoroughly enjoying Seriel's approval of his choices,
Samael asked, "And what of your features? Is there something
you would change?"

"I can only make my judgment from the brief mimicry you produced. I believe they are to my liking. However, I do not wish my hair to be yellow." Seriel willed a combination of maldor, odami and breal to replace his golden tresses and this multi-colored darkness matched the depth of his eyes.

"Our transformation is complete," stated Samael. "Now, we will display ourselves to our little daemons, and afterwards to our brothers and sister. I am impatient to receive Gabriel's judgment on what we have achieved. He will disparage these angelic forms, yet he will secretly desire to be as magnificent as are we."

Immediately, Seriel realized another altercation with Samael could quickly arise, once they reached their siblings. Gabriel would demand knowledge of how they had chosen such appearances. If Seriel explained their true origin, the first archangel would be extremely angry. He would also become inflamed because his brother had lied to him. Alternatively, if Seriel perpetuated his untruth, Gabriel and possibly some other siblings would condemn their action. To Gabriel, the Abyss was something of which to be very wary. Therefore, to accept a gift from it would constitute a great folly.

Having learned the dire consequences of not sharing information with Samael before so doing with the other archangels, Seriel decided he must confess his lie. He told his brother, "Before we leave, I have to tell you of an untruth that has passed between us."

Somewhat amused, Samael asked, "What is this? Confessions of Lord Seriel?"

"Do not jest, Samael, I am trying to maintain our recovered fraternal companionship."

The first archangel abandoned his frivolous attitude and questioned, "How have you deceived me?"

"When I told you I asked Chaos for an angelic form. It was not the Abyss to which I made my request, but to our parent." Seriel braced himself for his brother's angry onslaught, but none came. Samael calmly asked:

"And why did you proffer that lie?"

Seriel felt even more unsettled by his sibling's placid attitude than by his wrath. "I believed you would become enraged, if you knew I had consorted with the Source."

"Why so? I understand your need to consult our parent. My dealings with it have taught me to no longer consider such action a necessity. Yet I do not demand the same behavior from you. And, if I should decide I do not want to represent the wishes of the Source, I can always construct my own image." Immediately, a pair of large horns protruded from Samael's head and a whip-like tail grew from a point slightly above his buttocks. These added features were in evidence for only an instant to demonstrate his thought, and then they were gone. The first archangel concluded, "I am not angered by what you did."

An astounded Seriel remarked, "I am grateful that you are not, but also truly amazed. And what of the deception I performed? Does that not stir ire within you?"

In a gesture of sibling affinity, Samael gently touched his brother's arm. "Sweet Seriel, how can you ask this of me? It proves your essence is continuing to be like mine. That does not anger me, it gives me pleasure." As he slowly broke contact with Seriel, he added, "Perchance my daemons transferred more than hatred to you when they sank their probes deep inside you."

The seventh archangel had no answering thoughts to offer. He was too busy enjoying the relief which had so unexpectedly come to him. Samael's anticipated anger had not been aroused and that was a blessing.

The Lord of Lightning-Swiftness spread his wings as an indication he was ready for flight. "Come, Seriel, let us away to our daemons and then to our siblings. It will be delightful to display ourselves in front of them. I am overly anxious to shock our fourth-born brother." His thoughts fell silent for a lengthy duration. Then he added, "Ah, Gabriel, what reward can I bestow upon you for bringing me such pain and humiliation?"

A sickening feeling of dread writhed deeply in Seriel's soul as he took flight with his brother.

Chapter Nine

E ternity moved on with the slumbering Source at its core. Numerous miniature scenes repeatedly played out the activities of the fifty-six angels across the inner realms of the Abyss. Over and over, they offered copies of angelic adventures, until they each began to disintegrate. As before, only one scene remained and it received a golden shaft of light from the Source. This blessing created four hundred and forty-eight new angels who were quickly and warmly welcomed by their angelic predecessors. Many of the original angels were eager to teach their new companions all they had learned about existence within the Abyss of Chaos. This gave the archangels an opportunity to further pursue their own interests and adopted duties. The Christ Soul and the Shekinah held long thought exchanges with their sleeping parent, while Raphael continued to create his tribute to the wonders of the Source through his music. Once he was guided by Seriel to the area where form could be manifested, he fashioned an instrument upon which to play his melodious art. Its structure was similar to what in a distant future world would be considered a lyre. This creation quickly followed his transformation into an etheric angelic body which resembled Seriel's in height and stature.

Michael felt compelled to patrol Chaos even more frequently than before. With many beings now existing in its vastness, his wisdom and ability to solve problems were constantly needed. He also began to venture further and further out into the unknown areas of the Abyss. Gabriel was extremely happy to offer to the angels his own beliefs and codes of behavior, much to Samael's annoyance. Therefore, the new arrivals were soon exposed to the contrary views of these two angelic princes. Uriel kept company with Samael and was eager to perform his bidding, while Seriel gave much of his attention to his beloved spiral. When he was not expounding on the necessity for self expression, Samael, like Michael, was continuing to explore the unknown parts of Chaos.

It soon became apparent to him that the Abyss was much more vast than he had ever imagined. What he had considered to be the outer realms were possibly only the beginning of the central section. Each time Samael traveled further away from the Source, he realized even greater unknown areas existed far beyond where he had explored. The first archangel began to wonder if, indeed, Chaos possessed a boundary.

Raphael was not the only other archangel to adopt an etheric form. Once Samael and Seriel had shown themselves to their siblings, Uriel wanted to immediately imitate the action of his brothers. This pleased Samael and he oversaw Uriel's transformation. It was soon afterwards that Raphael requested Seriel's help in acquiring this new angelic body. Then it was the turn of the third archangel to seek Seriel's guidance in manifesting his own form. As was to be expected, Gabriel's hasty condemnation of this recent development was long and resounding. However, the seventh archangel's assurance that the Source had bestowed this likeness upon them began to change his opinion. Eventually, not wishing to be beholden to either Samael or Seriel, Gabriel asked Michael to aid him in his adaptation. Only the Christ Soul and the Shekinah appeared to have little interest in following their brothers' transformations. They continued to exist as beings of pure consciousness.

Each metamorphosed archangel displayed individuality in body structure and countenance. Michael's stature was the only one to match that of Samael. This quickly annoyed the first archangel, but repeated attempts to increase his height were futile. The Source would not allow him to regain his dominance. Therefore, he had to accept standing no taller than his third-born brother.

Facial features also distinguished each of the six siblings, as did hair and eye color. As each archangel became more accustomed to possessing eyes and a mouth, he would use them to accentuate a thought or a feeling, but none of his sensory attributes were functional in an etheric manner. His inner senses continued to be the primary method of relating to existence. This meant eyes had irises, but no pupils, and ears and noses were merely additional features. Mouths could open and close, but did not utter speech. Angelic communication remained a total thought process.

Many angels quickly followed the lead of the archangels. They transformed into winged beings with etheric physiques, who also displayed their possible genders within their soul essence, but not their new form. In this dimension, which preceded the epoch of physical sentient beings, there was no need for genital and mammary body parts. However, their newly acquired anatomies did not result in future angels being birthed in this form. Each one remaining scene was always within close proximity to the location of the original surviving record of the first fifty-six angels' birthing. Therefore, being so close to the Source ensured that, as they emerged from their scene, they were auras of consciousness with no bodily trappings. Form could only be manifested once they reached that magical point of Chaos where the first archangel had originally grown wings.

It was soon discovered by both archangels and angels that their etheric bodies could be shed once they were moving close to the Source. This was not an inevitable outcome, but rather a matter of choice. However, when venturing further outwards into the Abyss, form was constant. It could not be disclaimed, once it had been manifested for the first time. This realization pleased Samael because he began to feel more comfortable while in etheric form. The nebulous quality of his former angelic self reminded him of the parent with whom he was becoming more and more estranged.

Samael also quickly lost interest in Seriel's Spiral. This was partly due to his intrinsic ability to only feel challenged by that which was new and unknown. He also believed this representation of everything that could and would happen was neither accurate nor truthful. The Lord of the First Essence became convinced it was an instrument of deception, created by the Source to entice its offspring into following its will.

Samael's disinterest in the spiral was echoed by many of the angels, particularly those of the first casting. Once its novelty was examined, it no longer beckoned to them for further investigation. The complexity of its ever-increasing spherical displays was also deterring others from giving it more than a fleeting observation. However, those angelic beings, who continued to be intrigued by the spiral, usually centered their attention on the spheres which depicted the possible future events within ALL THAT IS. This proved to be more entertaining than what had already transpired.

The lack of attention to his spiral and the happenings, which had passed, brought relief to Seriel. Once the excitement of adopting an etheric form had dissipated within the angelic horde, he feared the discovery of his daemonic assault would be made. Someone would come upon the sphere displaying that horrific attack, and that would be catastrophic. Thought-word of it would quickly be told to his siblings and their offspring. Then, surely Gabriel, and even Michael, would question him as to whether it had taken place or was only a possibility?

The seventh archangel could not allow himself to share that excruciating experience with another. It was too painful. There was also a feeling of shame permeating his sense of being traumatized. He should have been more wary of Samael. None knew him better than Seriel. How could he have believed his brother would not wreak some powerful revenge upon him? A notion of having been utterly foolish overshadowed the Lord of Sorcery's existence, and it was compounded by guilt. Seriel knew he should not have disclosed his belief about Samael's action being ordained until he had alerted his sibling to it. In quiet times, Seriel questioned his reason for not withholding this information from the other archangels. In an instant of self-realization, he silently admitted it was pride that motivated him. He had wanted to appear discerning and wise to his brothers. This admission brought an even deeper feeling of shame to him.

Just when Seriel was beginning to believe no one else had discovered the orb depicting his ordeal, Azazel came to him and made mention of it. He explained that he and several other angels had viewed this possible happening. They then sought out Samael and asked him whether it was a reality. Once the first archangel revealed why he caused it to take place, the angels agreed it was a fitting punishment. Azazel seemed pleased to be able to share this information with Seriel.

Now, the Lord of Sorcery waited anxiously for all to learn of his frightening episode with the daemons. Yet none approached him with questions or judgments about what had taken place. Unknown to Seriel, his scheming brother forbade the angels to recount to any other soul what a certain sphere was revealing. Oblivious to this, the seventh archangel's uneasy anticipation and uncertainty caused him to frequently shun the company of his siblings and the angels. Seriel busied himself with studying his spiral almost to the point of obsession. If his angelic abilities were needed by any other, it was common knowledge where he could be found.

As more and more souls joined the increasing ranks of angels, two opposing groups began to evolve. One was led by Samael. His philosophy was the belief that Source-given free will should be explored to its fullest. This would enable a soul to maintain and enhance its separateness from all others. Uriel wholeheartedly seconded his brother's conviction. Seriel considered it to be valid, but felt that without some form of limitation, a chaotic result could prevail. However, having sworn his unending devotion to Samael's reasoning, he felt compelled to honor his pledge.

The second group was in the command of Gabriel. He believed the right to choose belonged first with the Source. Free will existed, partly as a means of furthering their parent's wishes, and also to ensure a wrong choice could be altered to the correct one. Michael was in agreement with this belief.

Eventually, a third group was also emerging. Overseen by the Christ Soul, the Shekinah and Raphael, these souls could not completely agree with either of the other two convictions. To them free will was the ultimate gift of love from their parent. Yet it required making choices as much for the good of another soul as for one's own.

As eternity flowed on, each newly birthed angelic soul was soon exposed to two of the three different points-of-view. Each was expected, by Samael and Gabriel, to choose which it would embrace. Both brothers trusted their own philosophy would be selected, and each frequently strove to convert those who aligned with the opposing one. No one attempted to enlist followers to the third tenet, but a continuing number supported it. Samael and Gabriel gave little thought to that other alternative faction. They both deemed it to be the alliance for those souls who could not make a definite decision to stand by either the first or the fourth archangel. Therefore, it was of lowly importance to them.

Apart from aligning themselves with one of the three ideologies, the angels also gravitated toward certain archangels. As was to be expected, a soul's essence role was a powerful force for companionship. Therefore, several angels of the same essence kept company together and also with the archangel from whom they had sprung. However, casting order was an additional magnet for soul attraction. Those cast first were drawn to Samael, while those of the second casting accompanied the Christ Soul. Third castings followed Michael, fourth castings drew close to Gabriel, and so it continued throughout the eight casting orders. Eventually, this magnetism of essence role and casting order displayed itself within the subsequent angelic proliferation.

As Samael had predicted, certain angels began to seek the friendship and advice of Seriel. To some degree this was quite flattering, but the seventh archangel was a soul who usually preferred to be alone. Five of the first fifty-six angels kept close company with him. Kokabel, Balberith and Mulciber were of his essence, while Shamshiel and Rimmon were sixth and seventh castings of Uriel and Raphael, respectively. Kokabel wished to be in constant attendance, and Seriel frequently had to ask her to busy herself away from him. No matter how bluntly he ordered her departure, she would always return with some reason for requiring his attention. This situation greatly amused the first archangel and he frequently teased his brother about it.

Although birthed of his essence, Azazel did not appear to feel any compulsion to follow Seriel. He did accompany Samael on occasion and would bring messages from him to Seriel. Yet much of his existence was spent acquiring his own little clutch of angelic admirers. Azazel also quickly gained the allegiance of the daemons. From him they received the attention for which they craved. It was not forthcoming from either of their archangel creators, therefore, this pure essence soul was soon adopted as their champion. Except for occasionally encouraging their squabbles and brawls, Samael had quickly lost interest in them. For Seriel they continued to be ugly little creatures who would cause great harm, if directed to do so. He was extremely wary of them and, therefore, avoided being in their company whenever possible.

Azazel's association with the daemons began when he came upon them in the midst of a daemonic debacle. Samael had previously introduced him to them, therefore, he knew what they were and from where they had come. On this occasion, they were fighting over the choosing of names for themselves. Just as Seriel had suspected, this task set by his brother had quickly led to quarreling, punching and biting. Several of the daemons were battling each other one-on-one, while others were banded in opposing, brawling groups. This was not their first attempt to be named. Several other similar endeavors had swiftly degenerated into wild clashes.

Azazel immediately ordered the daemons to end this present conflict. Then he questioned them about its cause. Once he understood their objective, he began the painstaking task of overseeing the orderly naming of each daemon. He discerned that Shedim had become the leader of the creatures and he considered it wise to enlist his help. Yet even this daemon was embroiled in a scuffle with a female imp who wanted his name. The pure essence angel gained her attention by assuring her she should be given a name that reflected the qualities of a lilin, a female daemon. He offered Lamassu as one she might prefer to a male daemonic name, that of a shaitan. This name was definitely to her liking and, in creating it, Azazel quickly gained her support, together with that of Shedim. Beyond the solving of that altercation, the other daemons soon allowed Azazel and Shedim to help them settle peaceably on their names.

When Samael first informed his siblings and the angels about the daemons, there were different reactions to this news. Some wanted to meet with them immediately. Others decided to wait until they knew more about them. As always, Gabriel was extremely suspicious of these recent arrivals in Chaos and he would not go within close distance of them. A number of angels agreed with his cautious outlook.

Those souls, who were curious about the creatures, went with Samael and Seriel to observe them. Michael and Uriel numbered among these inquisitive companions. To Seriel's amazement, the daemons behaved in the favorable manner that his brother had described prior to meeting with them. They portrayed themselves as timid and very fearful of their angelic onlookers. There was no quarreling or fighting between them. Their pointed teeth were gone, and their cruel talons had shrunken into harmless, under-developed nails. Seriel concluded Samael had previously coached these vicious beasts on how to present themselves to the angelic horde, when they were not in the business of tormenting a soul.

When questioned about the origin of the daemons, Samael recounted the truthful version of how his offspring had come into existence. However, when it was discovered that some of the creatures had sprung from Seriel, the first archangel gave a completely false rendition of that occurrence. According to Samael, the Lord of Sorcery was so excited about the little creatures that he wanted to create some of his own. As neither archangel was in etheric form when this occurred, Seriel had allowed the daemons to pluck tiny pieces of his consciousness. As each particle was removed, it was then thrown by the creatures further out into the Abyss so that new daemons could develop.

"Thus," explained the first archangel, "Seriel's daemons were born."

This make-believe description completely enthralled Uriel. Soon afterwards he asked Samael to aid him in birthing his own daemonic offspring in a similar manner. He maneuvered himself to the point in Chaos where he could change back into pure consciousness and asked Samael to remove small pieces of himself. The separated particles were then carried by Samael, and a re-established etheric Uriel, further out into the Abyss and duly scattered. Much to the delight of the daemons, their ranks were quickly swelled by the addition of Uriel's little creatures.

Now, a part of Chaos was becoming home to a goodly number of these evil beasts. Their movement did not appear to be confined whenever they were traveling outwards through the Abyss. Yet there was an inward point beyond which they could not pass. This restriction infuriated them, when it was first realized, and they made several attempts to pass through an apparently invisible barrier. All of their efforts were to no avail, therefore, they were unable to come into the vicinity of the Source. They had heard of this mighty being and were wanting to make contact with it themselves. As this was not possible, they had to be content with Azazel's and Samael's somewhat biased descriptions of their parent.

Not only the daemons, but also an increasing number of angels were to be frequently found in the areas of Chaos where the radiant beams of the Source did not reach. Often, they were there to receive Samael's teachings and to give their acclamations. On other occasions, they were present as a consequence of their need to explore the unknown.

Samael was almost always beyond the point where form could be manifested. He wished to experiment with all aspects of manipulating etheric matter. With the power of his thoughts he fashioned many different shapes. Some could be considered geometric, others were totally random. He was constantly altering their colors and structure, and causing them to be more or less dense. Some were exceedingly large, while others were quite small. Within the latter group, Samael chose some to become his playthings. He would toss them up high above his head and then fly upwards, and snatch them back down, again. Several of these shape-things were transformed by the first archangel into multi-faceted etheric objects. Giving them many smooth surfaces, added various color shadings to them as they traveled upwards from his hands. This discovery had intrigued him for a short while.

On one of the few occasions when Samael lent his lightning thoughts to the daemons, he created a shape which was large enough to house one of the creatures. While wandering somewhat aimlessly and feeling very bored, he had chanced upon three of his own daemons who were cruelly bullying a smaller imp, who did not possess legs with which to run away. This little beast had come from Uriel. Samael's daemons were taking turns in sitting on top of him and then jabbing their talons deep into his body and head. When one was finished, he would alight and help the second one hold the little daemon in a tight grip while the third would take his place. Then the painful poking would begin, once again.

A feeling of unusual compassion surged within the Lord of Lightning-Swiftness and he ordered his offspring to cease their cruel play. After pushing the one daemon from its perch and forcing the other two to release their hold, he quickly thought-built a sturdy shape around Uriel's daemon. This structure completely encased their former victim and they could not gain access to him. While they jumped and shrieked in furious frustration, Samael went in search of other Uriel daemons.

Once he had found several of them, the first archangel explained what was happening. Then he led them to where his three unkindly creatures were continuing to batter and kick the structure. Upon reaching them, Uriel's daemons quickly pounced upon the three and they soon subdued these attackers. They punched and chased them until they scurried away. After releasing the protected creature from its shelter, Samael directed its daemonic siblings to guard it well and always keep it within the safety of their number.

This incident stimulated a new interest in Samael. He became preoccupied with thoughts of structures in which he might reside. His creative soul began to conjure various etheric edifices which could accommodate him. Thus, began the groundwork for his eventual domains. His nether dimension that eons later would be termed Hades.

And what of Samael's need to even the score with the Lord of the Fourth Essence? The first archangel bided his patience, knowing an opportunity to take his revenge on Gabriel would surely arise.

Chapter Ten

The Source slumbered on, deeply engrossed in its dreams. Everything that was happening within ALL THAT IS was playing out before its consciousness. This divine being knew the thoughts of each and every one of its angelic offspring, and its boundless love for them fired its creativity. Each soul's joy and sorrow was shared by the Source. It experienced the bliss of the melding between Samael and the Shekinah, it perceived Seriel's wonder at acquiring etheric form. Azazel's attentive attitude toward the daemons did not go unnoticed and Kokabel's need for her essence lord's company was duly heeded.

Yet more powerful than these shared feelings and joys was an overwhelming sense of utter sadness. The Source was well aware of how its children were also learning, through anger, pain and hatred, the lessons of duality. Seriel's torture from the claws and teeth of the daemons, and the soon-to-transpire attack on Gabriel, lay heavily within its consciousness. But far outweighing these sorrows was the certain knowledge of the waning of Samael's radiant soul. His lust for separateness and power, coupled with his pride, were securing his unholy destiny. This inevitable fall from grace brought immense grief to the Source, but only it knew the true reason behind Samael's defiance. Its beloved son's path was pre-chosen.

During the melding, which the first archangel had long ago attempted with his parent, a monumental communication took place between the two. The Source put forward its crucial need to be all things for all of eternity, its raison d'être, and requested the help of its first-born offspring. It explained how only Samael had the nature and stamina to accept the challenge of total separation from itself. Without his help the Source could not fully experience the dark side of being. However, the right to choose whether to perform this task or to refuse it was equally emphasized. Free will was, and is, forever absolute.

Without hesitation Samael promised to accept his role as adversary to his divine parent. Having emerged first from the Source, he fully understood its reasoning. He also appreciated the necessity for all remembrance of this agreement to be erased from his consciousness. A knowledge of it would impair his ability to fully become the satan. Immediately his consent to forget was given, he found himself outside of the Source. All he could remember of the encounter was the blissful peace of being within his parent's consciousness, and then the overpowering need to not fully surrender himself to it.

Knowing why Samael was sacrificing his radiance, was almost beyond endurance for the Source. There came eternal occasions when the anguish was so great that its consciousness was engulfed in agonized sobbing. Yet having no form, no tears could be shed. But at that point in Chaos where etheric matter was being made actual, innumerable pools of colorful and pristinely clear liquid began to manifest.

*   *   *

Samael was busily thought-building yet another etheric home for himself. Each one, which he constructed, was larger and more detailed than the one before. Yet none satisfied his questing nature. Once fashioned and duly inspected by him, each was either demolished by a lightning thought or left abandoned. The latter constructions were quickly seized upon by some of the daemons. This action, of course, soon led to further daemonic conflicts. Those who had not claimed a structure fought with those who had. Some battles were so fierce that certain larger creatures picked up smaller ones and threw them forcefully at the walls of whichever building was in dispute. This violence caused the thrown victims to become enmeshed within the structure's etheric fabric. They could not free themselves and remained trapped and screeching in endless anger. When Samael discovered them, he swiftly disintegrated the entire building with a speedy thought. This consequence set free the prisoners, but fueled even more enraged daemonic fighting because the structure was gone. These battles were often applauded by the first archangel.

Now, however, he was intent on trying to produce a dwelling which would, at least for a short while, appease his desires. This latest construction was the largest and grandest yet. Its etheric pillars stretched so far aloft that their extremities became lost in the haze of the vaulted ceiling. There were steps within its interior which led to a structure upon which Samael was presently resting. He was constantly changing its design in an attempt to accommodate his seated posture more comfortably.

Finally, he settled on a shape which suited his needs. The section on which he was sitting was slightly curved in order to follow the contours of his buttocks. His back was supported by a vertically straight component which extended from the seating section to beyond the top of his head. In addition, he had created two sturdy units against which he could rest his arms. As he maneuvered his body into a relaxing position within this etheric chair, Samael realized his wings were presenting a problem. They were preventing him from fully resting against the back section. With his usual swiftness, Samael immediately decided upon a solution. His powerful thoughts altered the horizontal top of the back to one that dipped into a deep V-shaped design through which his wings could protrude.

The first archangel was well pleased with his new seating unit. Yet he continued to elaborate on its appearance. His artistic soul craved expression. Filigrees of silver began to adorn the back and armrests. Rosettes of maldor outlined the edges of this ornamental chair. As he pondered what other decorations might be appropriate, Samael sensed the approach of Seriel. The Lord of the Seventh Essence's questioning thought came to him:

"Where are you, my brother?"

"I am inside the large structure close to which you now must be."

"Is there an opening through which I can enter?"

"Yes, I fashioned one when I first constructed this place. There are a number of units in front of the opening. Climb them and enter through the portal. I await you here, dear Seriel."

Samael did not have long to wait. His sibling soon stood before him. The first archangel kept his thoughts still so that Seriel could have the opportunity to fully appreciate the wonder of his etheric building. However, the urge to tease Seriel soon overcame his silence, and he asked:

"All alone, dear brother? What have you done with your faithful Kokabel?"

"Enough, Samael! I grow weary of your jesting with me about that angel. I sent her and Balberith off to another part of Chaos to monitor some miniature scenes. I have ordered them to stay there until the scenes begin to disintegrate. That will keep me free of her attention for a short while."

"My ever resourceful sibling!" Samael acclaimed. "Pray forgive my teasing thoughts, but I am loathe to desist. Deriving amusement from Kokabel's adoring nature is just too tempting. Perhaps you should contemplate changing your present angelic form? What say you to adopting some daemonic features? More ugliness and less beauty might deter her pursuit of you."

"And less jesting from you would help maintain our brotherly bond! Again, I tell you, enough!"

"So be it. I am feeling well pleased with myself and my etheric creations." Samael lovingly stroked one armrest, as if to emphasize his thought-words. "Therefore, I have no desire to quarrel with you. But, pray tell, what brings you here?"

Happy to be given a change of topic, Seriel replied, "I was observing you within my spheres and . . ."

"What is this, dear brother? Are you becoming a secretive onlooker?" Samael's need to mock his sibling erupted into their thought exchange, once more.

"Samael! I did not come here to be subjected to your jesting. What has taken hold of you?"

"A thousand pardons! It is my love for you and my immediate contentment that have put me into a frivolous mood." The first archangel rose from his chair and offered this new creation to Seriel. "Pray, rest awhile upon my latest invention. I am certain it will please you."

Seriel moved toward the chair and cautiously lowered his body into it. After adjusting his posture so that his wings were comfortably positioned through the cutout section of the back, he remarked, "This is an amazing device, Samael. It suits our angelic bodies so well."

"I know, I know." Samael gave a little bow to emphasize his acceptance of Seriel's praise. "This is why I am filled with such merriment. But let us return to your explanation. You were divulging that you were watching me within your spheres."

"Yes, and I observed you creating this huge structure." Seriel indicated the surrounding interior of the etheric building. "My curious nature was captured by its size and form, therefore, I have come to question you. I have viewed these structures in the present and future spheres. What is their purpose? What is this creation, my brother?"

Happy to elaborate on his inventive thoughts, the first archangel responded, "It is a place where I can come to be alone or to be with a loved one, depending on my mood. Just as Chaos is home to us all, this is my own home within that greater abode. It is a structure in which I can take refuge when I am feeling angry or sad. Also, an edifice wherein I can spend my joyful occasions."

"It is most amazing! Do you think I could construct such a building?"

Samael did not answer immediately. He was considering whether or not he would want someone else building etheric dwellings. It would greatly please him to be the only archangel able to accomplish this task, but he knew that would not be so. Once knowledge of his creations was discovered, there would be others who would quickly copy his action. Having realized this, the Lord of Lightning-Swiftness responded, "I believe it would be possible. Your thoughts are as inventive as mine. Yet I would make one request of you. When you have built your home and are telling of it to others, I pray you, inform them the concept of such a place came from me. Let them know you did not conceive the notion of an abode."

Seriel smiled inwardly, knowing how important it was to his brother to be the first in everything. This overwhelming need was one of his sibling's qualities which bound Seriel close to him. There was a sense of insecurity about it which stirred compassion within the seventh archangel's soul. "Of course, Samael. I would never encroach upon your artistry or lay claim to your creativity. As the first-born of the Source, it is fitting that you should make these discoveries before any other."

Feeling moved by Seriel's sentiment, Samael stooped down in front of him so that he no longer towered over his seated brother. He gently placed his hands on Seriel's knees and told him, "You are truly my stalwart companion. I have caused you to suffer great pain from my daemons and I frequently tease you, yet you are ever my champion. You have suffered my rage, but have sworn your unending allegiance to me. I am truly blessed to have you as my brother, and I beg you to continue upholding your love for me. I am certain it is my destiny to become totally separate and not in accord with our siblings. Thus, I will forever seek your loving support."

For an eternal instant, there was silence between the two archangels. Each was filled with emotions of sibling love and sadness, coupled with a foreboding of doom. Then, with his innate swiftness, the Lord of the First Essence sprang back up to a standing position and declared:

"Let me show you other structures that I have made!"

Samael led Seriel back to the entrance of his building. They passed through the opening and descended the steps. As they were about to move away, the seventh archangel asked:

"Is it wise to leave your home so open? Others may find it while we are gone and will wander through it. Or perchance that would not trouble you?"

"How mindful you are, dear Seriel. In truth, the daemons have already claimed the abodes which I left unattended, therefore, I know they would seize this one, too. I had previously discarded the other homes, but this one pleases me well. I do not wish to have daemonic feet scampering all over my creation." Samael grimaced in emphasis of his thought-words. "What would you suggest? Shall I seal up the opening completely?"

"That is one solution, but in some of the future spheres these buildings have a type of unit which makes the entrance accessible or prevents admittance through it. Take heed!" Seriel turned his attention to the opening and thought-built a large door which closed off the entrance. "When you wish to enter . . ." He caused the door to open. "And when you wish no other to gain entrance . . ." He caused the door to close.

"Bravo! This is ingenious!" With excited intention, Samael thought-opened and thought-closed the door repeatedly. However, he suddenly stopped and stated, "Both you and I have just manipulated this unit so why should other angels and daemons not be able to do so? I wish to be the only one to have command over it."

His angelic brother gave this some consideration before replying, "You call me the Lord of Sorcery, so what say you to a little magic? First, let us call this unit a 'door.' Next, compel the door to only obey your behest. Order it to ignore the bidding of all other souls and daemons."

With lightning speed Samael followed his brother's direction and, when he was finished, he prompted, "Let us test your magic. Try to open the door!"

Seriel gave his attention, once more, to his creation. He tried to manipulate it with his thoughts into an open position, but nothing happened. After several more attempts, he declared, "It will not obey me."

Without hesitation, Samael concentrated on the door and it swung open. Then it closed at his bidding. The first archangel lovingly slapped his sibling on the shoulder and proclaimed, "You are, indeed, the Lord of Sorcery! I am indebted to your magical nature. Now, let us go in search of my other buildings and perchance we can harass the daemons for daring to occupy them."

The two archangels took flight and scanned the area below them for Samael's aborted attempts at building a home. As they flew, each had differing thoughts. Samael was planning ways in which he could cause the daemons to exit the structures. Once he had accomplished this task, he would manifest doors through which none could pass but himself. This would infuriate the little creatures and he would be greatly entertained by their tantrums. Seriel was desperately hoping they would not encounter any of the beastly imps. He continued to hold an intense dislike of them, even though some were beholden to him.

Before another etheric building was discovered, some unusual forms, which were floating below the archangels, caught Seriel's attention. Samael appeared to have either not noticed these items or was already familiar with them. Pointing to the unknown objects, Seriel asked:

"What are those etheric forms below us, Samael? They are very different from your other creations. What is their purpose?"

The first archangel circled above the many objects, trying to recognize them. Yet they were not anything he had constructed. Should he disclose that truth to his brother or should he claim them as his own? His ceaseless curiosity finally motivated this truthful answer: "I do not know what they are. I did not create them. Let us go down and inspect them!" He was already a distance below Seriel as he sent these thoughts up to him.

The two brothers descended until they reached the objects. Both archangels were totally intrigued by their discovery. There were many, brightly colored objects resting in this section of Chaos. Their form was nothing like angelic or daemonic bodies, or even Samael's buildings. They were roughly circular in shape and seemed to be of a different composition to other etheric matter. They gently flowed back and forth within Chaos. Upon closer inspection, Seriel remarked:

"They have many configurations within them. What can those patterns be?"

Samael brought his attention to the designs about which Seriel was commenting. As he observed their intricacies, something half-remembered stirred within him. He had viewed similar patterns before, but where and when? As if to stimulate his memory, the first archangel stretched out his hands to touch one of the objects. Both he and Seriel were startled by what happened next. Samael's hands penetrated the object with ease and their movement into it caused its contours to move in an aqueous manner. Amazed, Samael quickly withdrew his hands, but then, just as swiftly, plunged them back into the fluid form.

This time he maintained contact and as he did, a remembrance flooded his soul. He had been surrounded by these exquisite patterns as he strove to meld with the Source. They were throughout the consciousness of his parent and they had brought a sense of peace and rightness to him. While attempting the melding, he had not questioned their purpose, but now a full understanding of them was suddenly his. They were the sacred geometry of the Source. Eight geometric patterns that were the very essence of its divinity. Knowing this, he also realized the colorful objects must have come from his parent. In some manner, the Source had caused them to manifest in this part of Chaos. Seriel's thoughts came to him:

"Are you discovering their intent?"

Reluctant to convey ignorance on any matter, Samael nevertheless answered, "I know not their purpose, but I have recognized their origin. When I attempted melding with the Source, I observed these patterns within it. They are a part of it. Thus, these objects, which have a composition unlike any other etheric structures, come directly from our parent."

Fascinated by what Samael was disclosing, the seventh archangel questioned, "Do you believe they are another form of offspring from the Source? Are they ensouled like us?"

"I know not, but realizing from whence they come, I am reluctant to learn more about them." Samael broke contact with the object and unfurled his wings. This action signified he was ready to continue their search for his abandoned buildings. Yet even as he was about to resume flight, his sibling declared:

"Behold! Something is transpiring within that which enveloped your hands."

Reluctantly, Samael returned his attention to the fluid object. Something, indeed, was happening to it. Seven of its divine geometric designs appeared to be multiplying exact copies of themselves, over and over. And as each separate pattern built upon itself, structures began to form around each set of duplicated designs. They were more dense and solid than angelic form, yet pristinely colorful like the object from which they had sprung. Some of the structures were long and narrow, others were tabular, and some formed into granular blocks. While these transformations were taking place, the many colors of the object were separating and moving into the structures. Yet the eighth pattern remained unchanged and no structure grew from it.

Thoughts between the two archangels remained silent as they witnessed the mutating tears of the Source. Some of the exquisite structures were striated, while others had facets. The latter reminded Samael of the multi-faceted playthings he had created earlier. As these structures formed, they separated from one another until they rested apart. They left no trace of their former aqueous self or of the eighth geometric configuration, Samael's pattern. And even as the transformation of this one teardrop underwent its transition into crystalline forms, a similar mutation of all the surrounding liquid expressions of Source grief took place. Within these changes, certain magnificent structures grew to the height of the archangels. Others outstripped them and rivaled the size of Samael's new etheric home.

"What magic did you convey to the colorful objects, Samael?" Seriel was astounded by what he was observing. "Did you thought-build these beautiful structures?"

With unusual honesty Samael replied, "I did not intend such transformation when I placed my hands within the object, but perchance I did influence its metamorphosis." Then with his innate pride he added, "The Source created the fluid objects and I enhanced its artistry. And that is as it should be. I complete what it initiates. Without me it cannot become all things."

The two brothers remained with the newly formed crystals until they had touched and investigated each and every one. And, thus, the etheric mineral kingdom came to be a part of ALL THAT IS.

Chapter Eleven

After showing his brother several other structures, which he had previously built, Samael invited Seriel to remain and help him remove the daemons from these buildings. However, the seventh archangel declined the offer, took his leave of Samael and flew back to his luminous spheres. After summoning the daemons out of several of their stolen abodes, the Lord of the First Essence quickly thought-built doors to prevent their re-entry. As expected, this development created daemonic mayhem, which briefly amused him. Yet once their furious antics began to bore the first archangel, he decided to return to the exquisite structures he believed he had helped create.

While journeying back to the crystals, Samael came upon several more fluid objects. Although this truth was unknown to him, his parent had wept more than once for its lost, first-born son. Curious about whether the same transformation would result, if he touched any of these new objects, he placed his hands into one of them. As before, seven of the eight patterns multiplied, and varying crystals grew from those geometric designs. Immediately, all of the surrounding Source tears were similarly transformed.

The etheric minerals proved to be wonderful objects with which Samael could work. Remaining with the second crop of shining structures, he began to explore their potential. The first archangel discovered he could reshape them just as he had fashioned other etheric matter with his thoughts. He could move and manipulate the minerals in whatever way he chose. This realization delighted him. It meant he could create an abode from one or more of the extremely large crystals. He experimented with a number of different colored ones and finally decided upon several which contained no color. They were beautifully clear in a manner that resembled nothing else within the Abyss of Chaos.

With purpose and a love for the unusual, Samael began to construct a crystalline building that would rival any palace built in the future world of man. Its walls and turrets glistened and held back the darkness of Chaos. The translucent pillars were rutilated and stood on either side of ornate double doors, crafted from the finest gold. There were a number of floors in this tall building which were accessed by stair units between each floor. All of the stairs and floors were constructed from a mineral of the deepest purple hue. The roof was slightly domed and surrounded by an agate walkway and parapet. Each floor contained several rooms which were separated from each other by opaque walls with openings through which the first archangel could pass.

While manipulating the minerals, Samael learned he could thought-facet small pieces of them into glorious and unique designs. The resulting gems were far more engaging than the faceted playthings he had previously created. He then embedded several of these jewels into the inner walls and ceilings of his new home. Within many of the rooms he constructed chairs, tables and stools, formed by a combination of etheric matter and manipulated crystals. Samael also attended to the needs of his angelic body during the resting phase. He fashioned and placed a number of bed-like units in some of the rooms. One of these units was particularly large and ornate and he spent much effort and creativity in manifesting it.

When his crystalline abode was completed to his satisfaction, the first archangel brought his attention to the etheric minerals which he had not used as part of his building. He closely examined each one, then rejected each, in turn. Finally, he came upon a glorious green specimen. It was hexagonal in shape and striated lengthwise. As Samael stretched out his hand and touched this wonderful crystal, a sense of deep love and peace permeated his whole being. He knew this was the right one for what he was planning. Samael held onto the top of the crystal and, with the power of his thoughts, he sliced this section free from the remainder of itself. Holding his cleaved prize, he thought-faceted it into an extraordinary gem.

With reverence and gentle slowness, the Lord of Lightning-Swiftness carried this newly formed jewel into his crystalline home. He moved through his abode until he came to the room that contained the large, magnificent bed. Samael placed the faceted gem in the center of the bed and turned to leave. However, a sudden notion caused him to turn back. This jewel gift was to be a surprise and what better way to astonish its intended recipient than to hide it? Samael thought-built one after another box-type units around the gem, but none pleased him. After some consideration, a fresh concept occurred to him. He fashioned a swathe of soft etheric material that boasted the most vibrant shade of rulpiel. Samael wrapped the green jewel inside the material and positioned it back on the bed.

Leaving his beautiful home, he made certain the golden doors would not open to any other being but himself. Then a happy and somewhat apprehensive Lord of the First Essence took flight and journeyed toward the inner parts of Chaos. This archangel was on a mission of love.

*   *   *

The Shekinah had just completed a lengthy and baffling thought exchange with the Source. The subject of this communication was Samael. Malkura had approached her parent with questions about her brother's change in character. His compelling need to be separate from his siblings, his apparent desire to cause disruption and discontent. She wanted to know why he was no longer the Lord of Light, why he kept secrets and displayed a proud nature. To each of her queries the Source had but one reply: "It is his destiny."

This brief response brought even more frustration to the Shekinah than Samael's unwelcome behavior. She then attempted to explain how unhappy she and her siblings were becoming with the first archangel's transformation. The Source commiserated with her, but offered no further insights into, or explanations of, this problem. Finally, Malkura poured out her soul, telling how deeply she loved Samael and how desperately she wanted to help him regain his former radiance. This outburst brought a more lengthy, but no more revealing, answer from her parent:

"My child, I know and understand the depth of your love for Samael. Indeed, it rivals my own. Yet, as I have told you, it is his destiny to become the dark prince of Chaos and, thus, you should not intervene."

Continuing to believe the Source was not fully comprehending the intensity of her feelings, the Shekinah put forward, "But my love is so great that it can alter his destiny."

A hitherto unknown sternness colored her parent's answering thought. "Your love for him cannot change his destiny! Only he can choose his path."

This unexpected and unrelenting attitude silenced any immediate answering thoughts from Malkura. She felt reprimanded and duly remorseful. No further communication was exchanged between the two until her parent added:

"Do not despair. All is happening as it should. When my beloved son has experienced every nuance of what is not, then he will return to us. And you will be a part of his restoration, so take comfort in knowing this truth. He will become redeemed, but it must happen of his own free will."

"And what of my free will? I wish to help him, but you are telling me I should not."

"Ah, I understand. You wish to act upon your belief that free will has been given to you so that you can use it to help others?"

The Shekinah was almost certain there was a hint of amusement within her parent's response. Puzzled, she queried, "Is it not so? The Christ Soul, Raphael and I believe we possess this gift in order to aid one another. There are also angels who agree with this credence."

"And it is a noble belief, my dear child. Yet it is misguided."

"Then what is the purpose of having free will?"

A slight motion rippled throughout the entirety of the Source and the Shekinah recognized it as thought-laughter. When all trace of movement within itself had subsided, the Source replied, "There is no purpose. It was, and is, an expression of my boundless love for all of my offspring. Think of it as an affectionate gesture made by a doting parent to its cherished children. I held no ulterior intention when I created this bounty. It was prompted by endless love and nothing else. It is yours to use for self, or for the good or ill of another. Possessing it, you can heed or ignore me, you can become WHAT IS or what is not."

After pausing to consider this revelation, the Shekinah suggested, "So, if I put aside your warning that I should not try to help Samael regain his original glory, I am exercising my free will? And according to what you have just disclosed, I have the right to do that and you would not think ill of me or even punish me?"

"Punish you?" There was definite incredulity in this Source question. "I do not exist to punish, I am here to love and to grow! What is this notion of punishment?"

"Gabriel and Michael consider you have the right and ability to chastise us when we go against your wishes."

"Is that also your belief?"

"It was not. Now, however, I am wondering if Samael's separation from us is an act of punishment from you for something he has done that displeased you."

A fine, luminous thread of sparkling consciousness swirled out from the Source. It gently wrapped itself around the Shekinah's auric being and slowly melded with it. This action brought a deep sense of comfort to Malkura. Caught in this blissful cocoon, she barely perceived her parent's reply:

"My precious child, none of you can displease me. I watch over each and every one of my offspring, and I am filled with love and concern for all. As I have stated, Samael's separation is of his own choosing. It is his destiny. If you wish to attempt to change this happening, I will not stop you, for it will be of your choosing. I will only ask you, once again, not to intervene, but I cannot explain more fully than that. There is a hidden truth which cannot presently be revealed."

This final statement quickly brought Malkura out of her feelings of bliss. Soothing oblivion was replaced by sharp curiosity. She questioned, "There is more to Samael's defiance than his wayward nature?"

Reluctantly, the Source conceded, "Yes, but the cause must remain shrouded."

Overcoming her desire to know more, the Shekinah offered, "Even though I do not know this concealed reason, I will respect what you have asked of me. Yet it will be very difficult. As I have previously told you, I would have Samael reclaim his angelic brilliance."

"Know that it will become even more difficult for you to put aside your wish to help him. My child, the extent of your love for Samael is to be duly tested. Be aware your brother will ask for your companionship to be given to him alone."

"And you would have me decline such an offer?" Malkura asked, even though she knew the answer.

"Indeed, I would. That will be the ultimate expression of love, to allow him to follow his destiny without your cherished company. Yet all is choice, therefore, you must choose and then abide by your decision." This was the Source's parting thought. After making it, her parent's communication ceased as it settled into an even deeper level of sleep.

The Shekinah flowed away from the Source and came to rest in a section of Chaos which immediately surrounded her parent's consciousness. There were no other beings present because many of them preferred to remain in their etheric form and explore other parts of the Abyss. Now, this area was usually devoid of angelic activity. She wanted to be alone so that she could consider what her parent had revealed. Yet even as she began this task, Malkura sensed the approach of her adored Samael.

This was only the second time the Shekinah had been in contact with the first archangel since his transformation into etheric form. On the first occasion, he and Seriel had gathered together their siblings and several angels in order to make them aware of what had transpired. All of them, including Malkura, were astonished by the brothers' new angelic bodies. Most of them wanted to copy this change into etheric matter, but she was hesitant. The Shekinah could not deny their new form was beautiful beyond all possible imagination. Yet she felt reluctant to exchange her auric unconformity for something more defined.

As Samael alighted close by her, she took the opportunity to scrutinize his appearance. He was truly magnificent! The combination of maldor and silver throughout his being gave an almost magical quality to him. His wings fascinated her, they were so amazingly powerful. Malkura noted that her brother's body was strong, agile and extremely appealing to her. Yet it was his face that fully captured her attention. It was a countenance that echoed his noble soul, but the eyes belied his angelic origin. Even though their glorious color fully intrigued her, there was an illusive something within them that hinted of shadowy notions and dark deeds. Samael's perceptive thoughts came to her:

"I bid you well, my sweet Malkura! But what is this? You are contemplating my etheric form and are finding it most pleasing. Knowing this gives me the greatest joy!"

No longer surprised at how easily he could discern her thoughts, the Shekinah replied, "My lord, you are spectacular! The Source has blessed you with a divine form."

A trifle disgruntled, Samael answered, "Dear sister, not all of what you observe before you is of our parent's making. The design may have originated from it, but I have elaborated and improved upon what was given. Let me assure you, my countenance is unique."

"I am certain that it is. Your face will be forever in my loving thoughts."

Moved by his sibling's affection, Samael declared, "As will be yours in mine, when you accept your etheric body."

The Shekinah was about to tell him that she may not adopt this new angelic form, but was halted by his added thought:

"Yet you are troubled by some aspect of my eyes. Does the color offend you? Shall I change it for a different hue?"

"Oh, no, my lord, the color is so beautiful and most entrancing, but . . ." She stilled her thoughts, not wanting to continue.

"But?"

Prompted by his insistent tone, Malkura answered, "I fear I will wound you, if I express my concern."

Samael reached out a hand and gently caressed her auric consciousness. "My treasured Malkura, I am only wounded when you do not share your thoughts and feelings with me. Even so, I believe I know what you glimpsed within my eyes, but I would have you tell me."

Understanding her brother needed the shared intimacy of her own thoughts, even if it brought him pain, the Shekinah explained, "Your eyes reflect your troubled soul."

A cynical smile graced Samael's face. "Ah, yes, my troubled soul. My overwhelming desire to be separate, my overly proud nature and my liking for disharmony. So, you can perceive these adverse qualities from these features?" He pointed to his eyes. "Perhaps I should pluck them from myself, no matter how painful that act might be, if they bring you sadness?" Samael cupped one hand over each eye, emphasizing his thought-question.

Believing her sibling was attempting to manipulate her, Malkura responded, "In truth, this is an example of how your radiant soul has changed. The removal of your eyes would be no great feat. You could replace them just as quickly. Yet you would have me believe you are willing to suffer deeply for my sake."

"I am not certain such action would be easily accomplished and without pain, but I would perform it for you, if you desired it. Contrary to your perception of me, I am not trying to exploit your love for me." Samael turned away from his sister as an utterly woeful expression appeared on his face.

Realizing she had misunderstood his motive, the Shekinah offered, "Samael, I am truly sorry. I misjudged you. Please forgive me, and please do nothing to your beautiful eyes. They are captivating beyond all others possessed by our siblings and angelic companions."

Samael's quicksilver temperament rapidly pushed him from gloom into exhilaration. A chuckling thought escaped him as he proclaimed, "You think my eyes are beautiful? They are naught compared to what I can show you. I came here to take you with me to wonder at my new creations. Enough of dour thoughts about this ruined archangel. I pray you, sweet sister, come with me to another part of Chaos!"

The Shekinah allowed Samael to guide her outwards across the Abyss. He flew above her and slightly in the lead as she followed his direction. They passed several angels, as well as Uriel, along the way. He wanted to know where they were going and whether he could accompany them. His brother quickly explained that it was a private matter between himself and their sister. However, he assured Uriel he would return and give his attention to him. As a tidbit of compensation for refusing Uriel's request, Samael told him: "I am anxious to share some new developments with you so watch for my return."

The two archangel siblings departed from Uriel and continued on their journey. When they reached the first area where Samael planned to stop, he directed the Shekinah to stay still while he was gone. Then he flew away from her. Puzzled, she settled herself to await his reappearance. After a short while, her sibling flew overhead, but did not return to her. Instead, he took off in the opposite direction from which he had just flown. Now, totally perplexed, she continued to anticipate his arrival.

At last, he flew back and came down beside her. He proclaimed, "We are alone! I have searched all around for angels and daemons, but there are none."

"Is that what you were doing? I could not understand why you brought me here and then left me alone."

"A thousand pardons, dear one. I should have explained what I was about. I am anxious for us to be undisturbed by any other being." Samael paused for an instant. He seemed to be trying to decide how best to continue.

The Shekinah offered, "I am happy to be alone with you, but why did we have to come to this part of Chaos? When you found me close to our parent, there were no other brothers or angels there."

After an even longer pause, he replied, "I brought you here because this is the level of the Abyss where etheric form can be created. This is where I first manifested my wings. I wish to ask you to adopt your own angelic body."

Although Malkura would have preferred this matter not to be broached, she nevertheless responded, "Dear Samael, this is something about which I am undecided. Even though

your etheric form is wonderful, I am reluctant to explore
my own. My auric self serves me well. Why should I exchange
it for a different one?"

In answer, the Lord of Lightning-Swiftness merely
proffered, "Behold!" Then he began an exhibition of what
he could accomplish with his new body. Samael flew upwards
and plummeted down. Next he performed cartwheels all
around his sister and finished with a double backward
somersault. Following this, he sat down, then lay down and
rolled over and over. After sitting back up, he stood up and
twirled around rapidly. He ended this performance with a
little dance and finally took a deep and gracious bow.

Utterly delighted, the Shekinah proclaimed, "Bravo!
That has almost enticed me to do what you ask. You are just
too incorrigible, my love."

"Then will you follow my lead and become as I am?"

Still hesitant, Malkura explained, "I am uncertain, my
lord. I know not why, but something deep within me warns
against this transformation."

Her sibling moved to within close proximity of her and
the intensity of his presence was overpowering. She felt all
resistance melting away as he suggested:

"You do not have to keep this guise, if it does not please
you. You can reclaim your auric self, once you approach the
Source. Remember, all is choice. My sweet Malkura, I desire
your company in this new angelic form so that you can better
appreciate a gift I have for you. Pray, do not refuse me. I am
yearning to behold your countenance. I know I will be lost
in its charm."

How could she deny her loving brother? The Source
had warned her not to heed Samael's request for
companionship, but it had not suggested she should remain
in her original state. Surely granting her sibling's present
appeal would not interfere with his destiny? Making her
decision, the Shekinah told Samael, "You have won my
consent. What must I do to acquire my etheric body?"

"It is quite simple. Just ask our parent to give you the form that is yours. Then, if there is some aspect of it which displeases you, it can be changed. You simply transform what you dislike with the power of your thoughts."

Without allowing herself any further doubts, Malkura directed her attention to the Source. She asked her parent to bestow upon her whatever body it considered befitting. Immediately, she knew she was changing. An intense degree of happiness was coupled with the pleasure of anticipation. A feeling of sheer joy swept through her consciousness as the transformation took place.

The Shekinah's standing height did not match Samael's, indeed, it was considerably less. Her form was slight and delicate compared to his, and her wings possessed a gossamer quality that was absent from his. Glorious rulpiel locks of hair began to adorn her angelic head. They lengthened until they almost enveloped her whole body. Finally, exquisite features created a face of stunning beauty. The nose was straight and small, the mouth was soft-lipped and perfectly formed and the eyes were the most amazing shade of green.

Sensing her new body was complete, Malkura asked, "What think you, Samael? Should I alter some aspect of myself? Am I continuing to be angelic?" She held her hands out in front of her, turning them over, as if inspecting them.

The first archangel shook his head and declared, "Nothing needs alteration, you are perfect! And know that you are not angelic, you are pure divinity. Indeed, you are the epitome of sacred beauty and I adore you." He clasped both of her small hands in his and drew her gently forwards. "Come, sister, I have magical things to show you." He began to lift himself up.

The Shekinah pulled against Samael, bringing him back to her level. "Wait! I do not know how to fly. I have wings, but I have no notion how to use them."

A peal of thought-laughter escaped from her sibling. He directed, "Just spread them aloft and they will vibrate. Then up you will go. Flying is easy and tremendous fun!"

Malkura unfurled her wings and they began to move rapidly back and forth, lifting her up into flight. Keeping one hand linked with her brother's hand, she flew beside him further outwards through Chaos. They journeyed by other angels in flight, as well as some beneath them. Even at this height she could view many miniature scenes below which were acting out the activities of the newest batch of angelic offspring. The varying colors of these scenes were dappled in a bewitching dance of pseudo life. In the distance she became aware of large structures that were unlike anything she had ever known. To the Shekinah this was a wonderful adventure, one to remember for all of eternity. Samael was correct, flying was a pure delight!

At last, they were approaching the huge structures. As they flew over the first one, Malkura pointed to it and asked, "What are these things, Samael?"

"Patience, my sister, I will explain soon."

They continued on, passing over several more of the first archangel's abandoned abodes. The Shekinah's interest in them was greatly increasing, she wanted to know the nature of the structures. Just when she thought she could no longer contain her curiosity, Samael declared:

"That is our destination!"

Malkura brought her attention to the structure to which Samael was indicating. It stood higher, and was far more magnificent, than any of the others. The substance from which it was constructed differed greatly from anything else she had yet experienced. It gleamed brightly and reflected distorted images of the two archangels as they flew down toward it. Once they had alighted and were standing beside this amazing building, the Shekinah was in awe of its towering height. She questioned:

"What is the purpose of this most beautiful structure?"

Leading her to the entrance, Samael replied, "It is a place I have termed a 'home,' my lady."

"A home? What does that mean?"

Mounting the first two steps to the doorway, he extended his hand back down to his sister and told her, "Take my hand, once more, and I will show you the wonder of this building. A home is an abode where angelic beings can reside. The structures we flew over were my earlier attempts to build such a home, but this is the one that satisfies me."

She followed him up the steps and stood in front of the golden doors. Samael stayed next to her and declared:

"Observe!" Then he added, "I command these doors to open!"

To the Shekinah's amazement, the doors slowly swung inwards, allowing them passage into the building. Once through the entrance, her brother gave his attention to the doors and they returned to their former position, closing the archangels off from Chaos.

Gripping her hand firmly in his, Samael took his sister from room to room, pointing out the various gems which adorned the walls and ceilings. She quickly became enraptured with their faceted brilliance. Her sibling demonstrated how a chair was a useful commodity for their new etheric bodies and invited her to sit down in one. Malkura felt certain she could remain in this wonderful device forever, it seemed to be molding itself around her bodily contours. She asked, "Is this chair alive? I am certain it is moving!"

Samael smiled and answered, "No, it is merely obeying my direction. I told it to follow the lines of your exquisite body so that it could give you the greatest comfort."

With genuine admiration the Shekinah put forward, "The power of your thoughts is truly magical, Samael. I am astounded at what you can accomplish."

The first-born archangel gently drew her hand up to his face and softly brushed his lips against her fingers. "Thank you, my lady. I will treasure your opinion of my skills."

Thoughts became silent between the two as each was lost in the harmony of their love. Eventually, Samael prompted, "Let us continue, I have more surprises for you."

He led her into other rooms and up the stairs onto higher floors. Bending down, the Shekinah touched one of the floors and then reached up and gently placed her hand next to her brother's eyes. "They are the same glorious color!"

"Indeed," agreed Samael. "I have a passion for the color purple, but rulpiel is the one that has captured my soul."

The desire to succumb to Samael's loving thoughts was becoming overwhelming. Malkura sensed he was moving toward an ardent declaration which would soundly test her resolution to withhold herself from him. Attempting to divert his suspected intention, she queried, "What is that strange unit over there?"

"That is a bed, a device that serves us well when the resting phase is upon us. I will explain further after I have shown you all the levels of this home."

They continued exploring the building until they reached the top floor. In one of the rooms there was a door which, when opened, gave access to the steps that led to the domed roof. The Shekinah stepped up and out onto the agate walkway and marveled at the curved magnificence of the dome. It twinkled in the gloom of Chaos as though it possessed an inner light of its own. She moved close to the parapet and was overcome by a sense of being a tiny pulse of life in the vast emptiness of the Abyss. Malkura had no idea in which direction lay the Source, but she experienced a sudden need for its comforting light-filled beams. All around her was a dense darkness that whispered of unknown dread. She shivered as an inexplicable fear swept through her soul.

"Is something troubling you, my love?" Samael had observed her trembling body.

"I do not know the cause, but I am experiencing the fear we have had when we wandered too far away from the

Source. There is something most sinister about this part of the Abyss."

"It is interesting that you feel so inclined. I have always found this area of Chaos to be intriguing." He stood beside her at the parapet and in a sweeping motion of his hand, he indicated to the dark void beyond them and asked, "Does the mystery of Chaos not beckon to you? Surely its vastness excites you? Do you not wonder whether it has an ending and what lies beyond it?"

"No, dear brother, those thoughts have never come to me. I do not have your insatiable curiosity. You were always the bravest of we eight archangels, but perchance you should be more careful, as is Michael." The Shekinah began to walk toward the steps that led back down to the access door of the room.

"Then perhaps you should ask our brother to be your champion?" There was a hint of sarcasm in this thought.

Malkura turned back to Samael and pleaded, "I pray you, do not spoil this occasion. I did not mean to offend you, but I think your intense curiosity could lead you into the unknown and possible danger."

Her sibling moved in front of her, blocking her way. He placed his hands on her shoulders and, bringing his face close to hers, offered:

"I give you my apologies, sweet sister. I am a fool to upset you when I am trying to demonstrate the depth of my love for you. My only excuse is that I become petulant when you give praise to another. I would have you think admiring thoughts of only me." Samael pulled himself back up to his full height, stepped aside and let her pass. With his usual lightning speed, he quickly changed the direction of their thoughts. "Let us go back inside. I have one more room I wish to show to you." He took Malkura into the building and guided her to the room which contained the huge bed.

The Shekinah was stunned by its size and its grandeur. It was fashioned from the bluest of etheric minerals and there were splashes of gold throughout its entirety. It was curved slightly upwards at one end, giving a bolster effect. The legs and sides of this bed were ornately detailed with swirls and rosettes. Ruby red gems were embedded in the centers of some of the latter designs. Malkura also noticed there was something the color of herself nestled in the middle of the bed.

"Let me demonstrate how we use this unit during the resting phase!" Samael leapt onto the bed, gently pushed the rulpiel object to the far side and then lay down. His head was positioned on the curved end and he lay on his side, facing his sister. "We stay like this and allow sleep to engulf us." His eyes remained open because there was no need to block out visual stimulation. However, he added, "I have taken a notion to close my eyes during the resting phase, it feels more appropriate." His eyelids fluttered and then became closed, hiding those soul-telling purple orbs.

No further thoughts passed between them as Samael portrayed a sleeping archangel. He became so still that Malkura began to wonder whether he had actually entered the resting phase. She quietly sat down on the edge of the bed and stretched out a hand to touch her brother. Even before her hand reached him, he grabbed it with one of his own.

"Come, sister, lay down with me. I created this unit for both of us to partake of the resting phase." He pulled her gently toward him and she felt powerless to resist. She settled herself next to him, her face was a very short distance away from his. Samael's eyes suddenly opened and although she knew he was observing her with his inner vision, she could not shake the thought that he was watching her with his etheric eyes. He touched her hair and, as if this action reminded him of something, he reached behind him and grasped the rulpiel object.

"I offer you this token of my unending love." He placed the gift into her hands and told her, "It lies hidden inside the soft material which I also created."

Malkura eagerly unwrapped the gem and its green beauty silenced any thought-words that she might have made. She turned it over and over, fascinated by its depth of glorious color. Finally, she managed to convey some of her joy. "Its beauty is beyond anything I have ever known. You have blessed me with a gift that I will keep close to me forever. You are truly my beloved brother!"

"Even as you are my beloved sister! Malkura, I have named this gem an 'emerald' and it signifies my desire to be with you always. I have created this home for both you and me, and I ask you to stay with me here from this instant onwards."

Here at last was the declaration she had been expecting, but dreading. This was what the Source had warned her would happen. How could she refuse him? She wanted nothing more than to stay with him, yet she knew she must not.

Even before she could compose an answer, Samael exclaimed, "Do not refuse me! I can perceive your thoughts and you are readying yourself to deny me the gift of your companionship. What has our parent to do with this? You are thinking of some nonsense it has told you."

There was something almost frightening about his ability to know her unshared thoughts so readily. Malkura sat back up and moved to the edge of the bed. She clutched the emerald tightly in her hand and answered, "I have to refuse you, we cannot be together. The Source told me you would request this of me and it asked me not to give my agreement."

The first archangel got up, walked around the bottom of the bed and stooped down in front of her. "Is that so? Well, I think our parent should pay more attention to its own affairs and give less concern to those of its first-born son. Why would you honor its request, but not mine? Surely your love for me is greater?"

"It is because of its greatness that I must refuse you. I cannot interfere with your destiny." The Shekinah stood up and walked away from her brother.

"My destiny?"

Malkura moved closer to the room's entrance. She
wanted to be gone from this place, this home. Everything
about it bespoke of Samael's love for her, and the pain of
denying him was unbearable. A stinging pain filled her eyes.
It was her first experience of an etheric bodily sensation.
Tears spilled down her cheeks as she told him, "According
to our parent, your destiny is to participate in what is not."

"What is not?" sneered Samael, "What Source riddle is
that?"

"I do not know. I merely repeat the thought-words it
gave to me."

Her brother did not answer. He picked up the delicate
material from the bed where it lay discarded. Then he
offered, "You have forgotten this. It was also a gift." He crossed
the room and draped it around her shoulders. "There! Does
that please you?" He turned her around to face him and
became aware of the wetness on her cheeks. Fascinated, he
traced a tear line with one finger. "What is this?"

Malkura moved back a step, not wanting to be so close to
Samael. She felt too vulnerable to withstand any tenderness
he might proffer. "It is something that came from my eyes. I
believe it is because I am feeling so sad."

"Our etheric bodies are full of surprises." He took hold
of her hand that was not holding the emerald and led her
out of the room. "Enough of sadness. Let me take you to
where the structures from which I fashioned this home are
to be found. They are truly beautiful and will delight you.
And perchance they will distract my anger at the Source for
forbidding you to be with me."

"It did not forbid, it only asked me not to agree. Our
parent assured me I have free will."

"Ah, yes, it likes to bandy about thoughts of free will.
Well, I will not allow it to make me churlish or you sad. You
have refused my offer once, but that does not mean I cannot

ask you, again, or that you will continue to deny me. Come, my lady, let us away to the sparkling structures!"

Malkura allowed Samael to lead her back to the golden entrance doors and out into the Abyss. Puzzling thoughts pursued her as she went with him. Was he feigning this abrupt change of mood? Was its lightness genuine? The Shekinah was uncertain.

Chapter Twelve

The Lord of Sorcery was exploring his own creativity. After being shown Samael's attempts at building a home, Seriel was filled with thoughts of what he himself could achieve with etheric matter. He consulted his informative spheres and discovered several portraying himself thought-building various types of structures. The one construction, which really caught his attention, was extremely large and quite simple in its design. Its base was formed with quadruple right-angles and its height graduated up and inwards from the four corners until it terminated in an apex. This structure excited the seventh archangel and he was eager to experiment with its unusual form.

Seriel flew to the level of Chaos where Samael's aborted homes continued to exist, but he chose an area away from them. Using his powerful thoughts, he attempted to construct a copy of the building shown in one sphere. This proved to be more difficult than he anticipated. Although the design seemed simple, it required extreme mathematical accuracy in order to produce its needed geometric perfection. However, Seriel had an innate fascination with the properties of numerals, therefore, solving this problem was a labor of love rather than an exercise in frustration.

When the perfect pyramid was finally achieved, Seriel then brought his concentration to its interior. He did not want to mimic the layout of Samael's home, therefore, he created long, ascending corridors, running within the structure. Each lengthy passageway led to a roomy chamber in which he fashioned chairs, or stools, and table units. These were less ornate than the chair he had viewed in his brother's abode. Like Gabriel, he possessed a liking for practicality rather than grandeur. Although he had not yet observed Samael's bed units, he nevertheless came upon the idea to construct a place where he could partake of the resting phase. This was a room situated toward the peak of the pyramid and was much smaller than the other chambers. He decided the floor should be his place to sleep. This meant it would be helpful, if it was pliable and soft in texture. He tried several unsuccessful attempts in which the floor proved to be too malleable. Its strong movement resulted in him being completely engulfed by it, when he lay down. However, eventually, Seriel did achieve his goal. There was only a slight undulating quality to the floor, which he could cause to begin or cease with the power of his thoughts. When he rested on it, any movement from his body caused a gentle rocking motion which was extremely soothing. His chamber for sleeping was complete.

Well pleased with his etheric home, Seriel explored the network of corridors throughout the pyramid, making certain there was ample space in each one for him to pass along without difficulty. He also tested each and every chair, stool and table to be sure they were at a comfortable height for his seated posture. Inner vision did not require light in order to define and clarify focus. However, he added sconces, which held blazing torches, to the walls of the corridors and chambers, as a way of accentuating the decor of his home. The torch flames burned continuously, fed by eternal etheric fuel.

Seriel decided he would tell Samael about his creation, and he sensed both he and the Shekinah were not too far away. It seemed possible to him the first archangel might be showing his sister the shining structures because their beauty would please her. Therefore, Seriel flew to where he and his brother had first discovered the fluid objects. He found the crop of colorful minerals undisturbed, their pristine brilliance even greater than what he remembered. However, his siblings were not there. Seriel then began to search the surrounding area and he came upon the second cluster of Source tears which Samael had helped transform. His brother was there, busily pointing out the various crystals to the Shekinah.

To Seriel's surprise his sister was no longer in her original auric state. Since he had last been in her company, she had assumed her etheric body. He had given little thought to how she would appear, if she manifested in this manner, because he knew she was extremely reluctant to do so. Therefore, he was ill-prepared for the glorious creature who stood before him. He could only thought-mutter, "Malkura, you are beauty supreme."

Samael moved close to the Shekinah and put his arm around her. "Is she not perfection, Seriel?" he asked. "I begged her to become as we are and she granted my request. She was hesitant to adopt this form, but her love for me conquered her fear. Malkura holds *me* most dear."

Samael's underlying inference that their sister favored the first archangel above any other sibling did not escape Seriel. Attempting to ignore what could easily become a volatile subject between them, he declared, "I sensed you both were close by, but I went to where we first found these structures in their fluid form. I did not know these also existed."

"Indeed, they do," answered Samael. He released his hold on Malkura, but began to gently weave a lock of her hair through his fingers. This was a further taunt to his brother. Yet Seriel would not be goaded and merely repeated:

"Indeed, they do."

Inclining his head in the slightest of bows, Samael acknowledged his sibling's refusal of his masked challenge. He continued, "I discovered them after you left and, as before, I changed them into their much improved state."

The Shekinah asked Seriel, "Are they not beautiful beyond anything else within Chaos?"

"My lady, I could never have envisaged such beauty," he responded. Then, noticing that some of the structures appeared to have been cleaved or broken apart, Seriel asked, "But what has happened here? Some have been damaged and rearranged. Samael, do you think the daemons did this?"

"Damaged?" questioned his brother with just a hint of annoyance. "I do not wreck what I imprint with my thoughts! What you are observing is the work of an archangel and not that of daemons. I fashioned sections of the structures into what I consider are jewels. Sweet Malkura, show our sibling what I created for you."

The Shekinah extended one hand toward Seriel and, uncurling her fingers, she revealed an amazing, green faceted gem. It was almost the size of her palm and it sparkled with unbelievable brilliance.

"It is truly magnificent!" Seriel was in complete awe of this jewel. "It is a glorious hue which matches the color of your eyes."

"Is that so?" asked the Shekinah. "I did not know their color until now."

Directing his thoughts to his brother, Samael commented, "How intuitive I am. I chose a green structure from which to fashion this emerald before our sister had even transformed herself. Surely that is an indication of how in harmony I am with her?"

Again, Seriel felt there was a hidden sentiment behind Samael's thought-words. It was as though he needed to stress his right to love their sister. The seventh archangel could also sense a dark brooding within his sibling. Was it possible Samael was angry with him, once again? As if in answer to his questioning thoughts, Malkura told Seriel:

"Our brother also fashioned this soft etheric substance for me." She touched the rulpiel material which lay draped across her shoulders and arms. "And what is more, he used these beautiful structures to create a home. You must ask him to show it to you, it is very impressive. He built it so that we could be together, but I have refused him because . . ."

" . . . because our interfering parent told her I would make this offer and that she should not accept it," interrupted Samael.

At last, Seriel understood Samael's veiled mood. His brother was extremely angry with the Source. Seriel recalled the occasion when Samael had told him he believed their parent would never allow the Shekinah to be with him. Now, that belief was being realized, which would definitely infuriate his proud sibling. Uncertain of how to answer this revelation, the Lord of the Seventh Essence kept his thoughts silent.

"And Samael has accepted my refusal even though our parent's guidance has displeased him," added Malkura.

It was obvious to Seriel his sister was not able to discern Samael's thoughts and feelings as easily as he could. Displeasure did not begin to describe the underlying fury that he sensed was raging within the first-born of the Source.

Samael commented, "It is of little consequence. I will continue to request her companionship and she may yet agree. But enough of these thoughts! What brings you here, Seriel?"

Happy to have the focus of their discussion diverted away from this matter, Seriel replied, "I came to tell you I have also built a home. It is different from those of yours, but I am content with it. Its design is that of a pyramid."

Samael patted Seriel on the shoulder. "My dear sibling, always eager to copy my actions. I would call that admiration, would not you, my lady?"

Once again, the first archangel was trying to chivvy his brother into an argument, but Seriel was even more determined not to succumb. He would not allow Samael to vent his anger on him, therefore, he answered this condescending remark with: "Of course, I admire you, as I trust you hold me in equal esteem."

"Bravo, Seriel!" Samael patted his sibling's shoulder a second time. "You are my most favorite brother. And were you going to ask me to also admire your pyramid?"

"If it pleases you," answered Seriel.

"I am certain it will, but first I must escort our sister back to wherever she wishes to go. Then I have to meet with Uriel. I promised I would return to him after my discourse with Malkura is over. I plan to give him the home where you found me when we last met."

"That is very generous of you." The Shekinah was obviously impressed by this intended gesture.

"I have always felt a responsibility to look after our brother Uriel," announced Samael. "There is a vulnerable aspect to his nature which needs protection. I have no further need for that home now that I have created my new one. I am certain it will suit him well."

"Do not forget to readjust the door so that it will only open to Uriel," reminded Seriel.

"You are always attentive to the details, my brother! Perchance you have been taking lessons from Gabriel?"

This was apparently one last effort to spur Seriel into anger, but it did not succeed. The seventh archangel merely asked, "Shall I await you here or go to what is to be Uriel's home?"

"It will be less troublesome for me, if you go to that abode. Then I will not have to come here to collect you." With that thought Samael dismissed any further communication with his brother. Turning his attention to the Shekinah, he asked, "Are there more things which I can show to you or shall I accompany you on your return to inner Chaos?"

"I am happy with all that I have observed, Samael. You do not have to escort me all the way back to the Source. We will just journey together to where Uriel is waiting, then I can continue inwards on my own. I feel confident to fly alone." Addressing Seriel, she added, "I was extremely apprehensive about flying at first, but now I am enthralled by it."

"Indeed, dear sister, it is a wondrous ability. One which will surely help us escape from trying situations." Seriel trusted that Samael did not miss the subtlety of this remark. "May you fare well and remain within the Source's keeping, my lady, until our next meeting."

The three siblings parted company and Seriel was left alone with the etheric crystals. He welcomed this opportunity to examine the colorful structures more closely. Apart from their obvious magnificence, he suspected they held hidden qualities, and this thought aroused his curiosity. He would investigate them for a short while and then go on to the arranged meeting with his two brothers.

Seriel moved around the area where the various crystals were resting. Many were quite small while others were many times his own height. He noted some had no color and these greatly fascinated him. Their clarity was mesmerizing and he found himself wondering what it would be like to be inside one particularly beautiful specimen. No sooner was this thought his than it became a reality. The side of the structure facing him seemed to extend toward the seventh archangel and gently encase itself around him. Seriel became lost in the wonder of this special place.

The interior appeared immense, almost as though it had no ending. There was also a sense of its specific geometric pattern surrounding him and fine tuning his soul vibration to its own. Above all, there was an overwhelming feeling of peace, harmony and protection which deeply nurtured him. As he stood inside the safe and sacred place, he received this thought coming directly from the Source:

"These are my mineral children, the etheric crystals. Know that it is the role of the mineral kingdom to heal and to alleviate sorrow, for it was birthed from my greatest grief. Yet also be aware these precious children have the power to be destructive."

Immediately following this message, images began to appear before Scriel. Many came and went too rapidly. He could not gain an understanding of them, but two were more distinct. In one he saw himself and Samael fighting with a number of angels against other angels. Each brother was holding what appeared to be an etheric crystal. The one in Samael's hand was clear of color and long and thin. One end was blunt, but the other branched out into a cluster of three points. Whereas the crystal, which Seriel held, was narrow at its hilt, but much broader along its shaft. It was also clear like Samael's, yet within its pure transparency he could detect what appeared to be two inner crystalline structures. The outline of one was etched in purple and the second one in brown. Rays of piercing, pale blue light were emitting from the points of these crystals, one from each of Samael's triad and a solitary one from Seriel's.

As this image faded, another took its place. In this one his brother Gabriel was lying prone and not moving. There was a terrible wound where his wings should have been and fluid was leaking from it. Other parts of his body also appeared gouged with injuries. Even as this horrifying reflection appeared, it quickly vanished, but it was already imprinted within Seriel's thoughts. It renewed his conviction that the first archangel would take his revenge on Gabriel. An even deeper feeling of dread filled his consciousness.

Now, Seriel wanted to be outside the pristinely clear crystal. It was showing him events of which he wished not to have knowledge, happenings that he hoped would never take place. He no longer felt peaceful and contented, therefore, he desired himself to be free from its vast interior. There came an instant before his wish was granted when his being was filled with another thought from his parent. It etched itself upon his soul and would forever remain with him. The Source declared:

"My noble, precious Seriel. I pray you, keep a loving watch over my cherished Samael!"

Then he was, once again, standing in front of the beautiful clear crystal. Feeling extremely concerned about

what he had been shown in the second vision, Seriel decided
he should go to his spiraling orbs. He wanted to establish
whether a similar scene was displayed within them. On
several previous occasions, he had considered looking for
spheres which might depict possible ways Samael would take
his revenge on Gabriel. Each time, however, he had managed
to convince himself it was best to not know such things. Yet
it appeared his parent wanted him to be aware of what could,
or even would, happen. Why else would he have been shown
such an alarming image?

Seriel turned and was about to fly upwards and away
from the sparkling minerals, when something caught his
attention. A short distance in front of him was a solitary crystal
laying on its side. There was something hauntingly familiar
about it. He walked over to the crystal and his inner vision
absorbed its entirety. It appeared to be the one he had
observed himself holding when he was fighting against the
angels. The majority of its breadth was uniform although its
base was considerably more narrow. Seriel noted that its
length was similar to that of his forearm. He felt compelled
to pick up this crystal and as he did so, it altered a part of
itself. The lower end became the hilt by narrowing itself
even more in order to exactly accommodate the seventh
archangel's grasp.

Surprisingly, it was not too heavy to manipulate with his
hand despite being solid and of good size. Seriel did not
need the power of his thoughts to maneuver his new
possession. He wielded it above his head in a similar manner
to that used by his replica in the vision. Then he held it
quite still, intrigued by the crystal cache within itself. There
was the outline of a smaller crystal deep inside, its extremity
etched in purple. Overlaying that was the outline of a
somewhat larger crystal whose top was colored honey brown.
It was as though the crystal's geometric pattern had begun
to grow in its purple mode, but had stopped. Then it had
grown again, this time taking on the brown hue. It had

stopped once more and, finally, continued growing into its ultimate size and clarity. Unknown to the Lord of Sorcery, he had been gifted with a rare and magical mineral, a phantom, scepter crystal.

Seriel wondered what he would have to do to make the laser-like blue energy discharge from the crystal's point. He tried willing it to emit the piercing light, but nothing happened. Presumably, he would need to become better acquainted with this crystalline tool before he would understand its full potential. Seriel also considered what he should name this amazing object. Immediately, the words 'light wand' filled his thoughts. This information did not seem to be coming from his parent, but rather from the crystal itself.

Happy with what had just transpired, Seriel felt more prepared to face whatever the spheres might show him. He readied himself to fly to his spiral. Yet what should he do with the light wand? Perhaps he could leave it in one of the chambers of his new home? But he was anxious to examine the spheres without delay, therefore, it would be better to fly to the pyramid after visiting his luminous orbs. If he could somehow carry the crystal without continuously holding it, that would solve the dilemma. His inventive thoughts suddenly remembered the delicate substance that had graced Malkura's shoulders. If Samael could manifest such pliable etheric matter, then so could he.

With his powerful thoughts Seriel fashioned a long holster into which he placed the wand. The etheric material was much stronger and more dense than the soft fabric which had adorned the Shekinah. He created two straps extending from the top of this holster and tied them around his waist. This allowed the crystal to rest against his right thigh. Next, Seriel took a few steps to discover whether carrying the wand at his side would be cumbersome. It did not weigh too heavily, but the holster dangled loosely, swinging back and forth in a distracting manner. Therefore, he manifested two more straps almost halfway down and tied these around his thigh. This adjustment corrected the shifting problem. Feeling satisfied, the seventh archangel took flight.

He flew swiftly toward the spiral of spheres, hoping he would not have other angelic company once he reached it. However, Turel was there, guiding several newly birthed angels around the spheres. This fourth cast angel sent his eager thoughts to Seriel:

"How opportune that you should come here just as I am instructing these angels on Seriel's Spiral. Will you tell these new arrivals how you created this wonderful phenomenon, Lord Seriel?"

Waving aside the angel's request with undisguised annoyance, Seriel responded, "I am on urgent business, Turel, and cannot give your angels any attention." Then, gauging which area of the spiral should be displaying events of the near future, the disgruntled archangel plunged deep into the orbs.

It took much effort and a long duration for Seriel to discover a cluster of three spheres which demonstrated the possible ways his brother might take his revenge. Searching for any occurrences now within the spiral was continually becoming more difficult. There was an ever-growing maze of orbs. Only those on the perimeter were easily accessible and, therefore, reasonably visible. The ones he sought lay hidden within the intricate depth of the spiral. Yet, at last, he came upon them.

In one Samael was ranting furiously at Gabriel, telling him exactly how much he despised him. The first archangel became extremely angry. He clenched his hands and pummeled his brother's body with his fists. Recovering from this unexpected bombardment, Gabriel quickly spread his wings and flew away. Samael did not pursue him. A second orb gave witness to a similar attack on Gabriel as that which Seriel had sustained. The daemons were biting and clawing the fourth archangel's body. However, he was battering them with his powerful wings and kicking any who were within close range. As in the first sphere, ultimately, Gabriel flew away from the onslaught.

It was the scene within the third orb that chilled Seriel's soul. The daemons were clambering all over Gabriel and several of them were tugging viciously at his wings. As one of these glorious appendages was being ripped from his body, Seriel forced his attention away from the sphere, unable to watch this gruesome happening. Instead, he searched for subsequent spheres which would show the possible outcomes of these three orbs. Yet only the third one possessed such an accompanying sphere. To Seriel's utter distress it was an exact copy of the vision he had been shown within the clear crystal. For him this verified what was going to happen to Gabriel.

Seriel withdrew from the spiral, uncertain what to do next. He remembered his appointment with Samael and it seemed wise to stay close to his brother. If it was possible, he would try to prevent any attack on the fourth archangel. Seriel began his journey to the abode which Samael was gifting to Uriel. In mid flight he observed Kokabel flying in his direction. The realization that this adoring angel would want to stay close to him brought an even greater sense of dismay than what her presence usually aroused. Seriel did not want the distraction of her incessant thoughts, therefore, he sent this dismissive command to her before she reached him: "Be gone from me, Kokabel! I cannot share my thoughts or company with you. I am late for a meeting with Samael."

Undeterred, Kokabel continued her approach toward Seriel. As she came close to him, she turned and began to fly beside him, explaining, "I know you are on your way to Lord Samael. He sent me to look for you because he grows impatient for your arrival. What adventures have you been exploring without me at your side? You must share them with me once we have finished helping Lord Samael . . ."

Seriel closed off his inner sense of hearing for a short while. He was tempted to ask her how they would be aiding his brother. However, past experience with this angel had taught him she may well ignore his question. Kokabel's prolific thoughts would ramble on whether or not there was an interjection from him. Grudgingly, the seventh archangel turned his attention back to his thought-babbling companion in time to perceive:

" . . . what a magnificent abode! Lord Seriel, you archangels are so gifted, you can manifest anything. I understand from Lord Samael that you, too, have constructed a home. You must show it to me. Perhaps you will also build one for me or, if I please you well enough, allow me to stay in yours? Is it not a testimony of true love that Lord Samael has built a unique home for him and Lady Malkura?"

Kokabel's thoughts had ceased momentarily. Presumably, she was inviting him to answer her last question. However, Seriel did not feel the least inclined to discuss the love that existed between Samael and Malkura. If he withheld his answering comments, his essence angel would quickly resume her barrage of thoughts. And this she did. Kokabel asked:

"What is that you are carrying on your side? It must be something new which you have created. What is it for, what does it do? Please, Lord Seriel, show it to me when we have reached our destination. Is it a tool to help you with your gift of sorcery? I am so happy to have been formed from your essence, it is quite magical . . ."

Once again, Seriel ceased his perception of Kokabel's thoughts. Past experience had taught him he would feel drained of energy, if he gave his full attention to them for too long. It was as though her thoughts fed upon his consciousness. He kept himself blocked from her communication until they arrived at the large, etheric abode which was soon to be Uriel's. Interrupting whatever Kokabel was sharing, Seriel told her, "Enough, my lady! We must pay attention to our reason for coming here."

As they alighted, Seriel noted that not only Samael and Uriel were waiting for him, but Azazel, Belial and Semyaza were also standing close by. Their added presence suggested the likelihood of something more than the gifting of a home was about to take place. An uneasy feeling took hold of the seventh archangel.

Chapter Thirteen

T he Lord of Lightning-Swiftness strode over to the two
new arrivals and declared, "At last, my tardy brother,
you finally bestow your presence upon us! We have grown
tired of waiting for you. What has kept you from us?"

"Nothing of importance," answered Seriel. "I was busy
with my own musings."

"Ah, just as I surmised. That is why I sent Angel Kokabel
to find you. I knew she could rouse you from your
ruminations and hasten your journey to us." Samael took
hold of Kokabel's hands and placed one of them in one of
Seriel's. "There! What a delightful pose! It is so obvious the
same essence flows within you both."

Seriel broke free from Kokabel's clasping hand and,
shielding his thoughts from all but his brother, thought-
snarled, "Samael! Have done with this jesting! I cannot abide
it!"

Without acknowledging his sibling's rebuke, the first
archangel asked, "And what is that you have tied to you?"

Kokabel's thoughts came charging in before Seriel could
respond:

"My lord, I have asked him what it is, but he has not
answered. I believe it is something he has created. Do you
think it is magical? I am sure Lord Seriel will not ignore your
questions . . ."

"Kokabel, be silent!" The force of Samael's suppressing
thought hit the angel like a blow to her body and she made
no further comment.

"Again, I ask you, Seriel, what is that?"

Reluctant to show his prize to Samael, the seventh archangel covered the hilt of the holstered light wand with his hand and responded, "It is a crystal which I found after you and the Shekinah had departed."

"A crystal?" queried Samael. "Surely it is one of the shining structures that I transformed? Why do you give it such a name?"

"Because that is what it is." Seriel did not wish to explain further.

"And how would you know that is what it is? Since I am the archangel who caused these structures to manifest, why should *you* give them their name? It is seemly for me to have that privilege."

Seriel knew his brother was enjoying having witnesses to his belligerent attitude. He considered not becoming baited by Samael's repeated queries, but also felt the need to remain firm and not acquiesce. Finally, he explained, "I did not choose that name. The Source told me they are crystals."

"So you have been conversing with our parent?" Samael turned to his angelic audience and rolled his eyes. This gesture evoked thoughts of laughter. Then, bringing his attention back to Seriel, he asked, "Pray tell, as with the Shekinah, did it also advise you to refuse any request I might make of you?"

Without hesitation Seriel replied, "No, our parent asked me to keep a loving watch over you."

Seriel caught a startled expression within his brother's eyes, but Samael's answering thoughts did not betray his surprise. He declared to everyone present:

"The Source appears to enjoy telling my siblings what they should and should not do where I am concerned. Perhaps I will visit our parent and tell it bluntly how intrusive it is becoming."

Thoughts of agreement came from Uriel and three of the angels, while Kokabel silently, but enthusiastically, nodded her support. Turning his attention back to the seventh archangel, Samael exclaimed:

"Enough of this Source prattle! We are gathered here for other reasons. Due to your tardiness, you have missed me gifting this home to Uriel. He has been inside and become acquainted with all of its benefits. And, yes, I have shown him how to cause the entrance door to only open and close at his bidding. Now . . ." the first archangel paused as though trying to recall something. "Azazel, what were we discussing just as Seriel and Kokabel arrived?"

The pure essence angel was quick to supply this answer: "You were suggesting to Uriel that he might want to invite Gabriel to come and view his abode."

"Of course, I was. I think the practicality of a home will appeal to Gabriel's sensibility. I am certain he will appreciate the protective and useful aspects of my creation. It would please me well to have his company and his opinion of Uriel's home." Samael's lips twisted into a grimacing smile.

Total alarm began rampaging through Seriel's consciousness. He could not imagine Samael being remotely interested in what the fourth archangel might think about his building. Obviously, his brother was readying himself to take his revenge on Gabriel. In desperation Seriel suggested, "Why not also include our other brothers, and even our sister, in that invitation?" He reasoned that Samael would not commit any adverse act against Gabriel, if all of their siblings were present.

The first archangel moved closer to Seriel and lowered his head slightly so that they stood face to face. His body's proximity and the challenging expression in his eyes could only be interpreted as a threat. Samael's thought-words came slowly and deliberately: "Our sister has already viewed this abode and I have no inclination to show it to our other brothers." Then without relaxing his intimidating pose, he commanded, "Uriel, go now and bring our brother Gabriel here! Take Semyaza with you, as we previously agreed."

The two angelic beings took flight without making any answering thoughts, and they were quickly gone from the area.

Seriel did not back away from his brother's domineering presence. He felt anger rising within him. He would have wished to warn Uriel that Samael was planning something less pleasant than displaying the abode to Gabriel. Putting caution aside, Seriel chided, "You should not use Uriel in this manner! He is a gentle soul who would not wish to harm any sibling."

"Use him? You are mistaken, Seriel. That is not what is happening here. Uriel is well aware of why he is bringing Gabriel to me. He understands I must take my revenge upon the Lord of Practicality. Uriel loves me deeply and will always follow my wishes."

Seriel knew Samael's claim was true, Uriel adored the first archangel. Yet how could he be willing to help Samael inflict pain on Gabriel? Could the first-born of the Source be so influencing? Seriel sighed inwardly. Yes, Samael was that charismatic. In an attempt to thwart his brother's conviction, Seriel declared, "I do not believe Uriel fully comprehends how vicious the daemons can be. He would not agree to such cruelty, if he knew, as I do, the devastation of their teeth and talons."

Finally, Samael stepped back one or two paces from his sibling. Yet his domineering gaze continued to be directed at Seriel as though his eyes were working in conjunction with his inner vision. He coldly answered, "Well, he will quickly learn, once the daemons set upon our brother."

Not wanting to allow Samael to hold the advantage in this thought exchange, Seriel stated, "I believe this communication is irrelevant. Gabriel will not come here. He has no liking for any part of Chaos that is beyond the boundary of our parent's light beams. His sense of caution will persuade him to decline."

"Yes, I am aware that will be his attitude. That is why Semyaza has been keeping company with Gabriel, as I instructed him to do. The Lord of Practicality believes his essence angel is in total agreement with his views on Lord Samael and his wayward behavior. He does not realize Semyaza does my bidding and not his." Samael turned to Kokabel and gently touched her yellow hair. "The Lady Kokabel knows we have been carefully planning this confrontation for a long duration. She has not shared this with you because we wanted to surprise you. We thought . . ."

"I . . ." Kokabel attempted to convey a thought, but Samael shook his head and laid a forefinger against the middle of her chest, as if to silence her thoughts. He continued:

"We thought you would be well pleased, if Gabriel was subjected, as you were, to the daemons' attack. If he had not been so eager to tell Turel and all of the angels his opinion of me, I would never have felt the need to avenge the pain of my humiliation. And, therefore, you would not have suffered the daemonic onslaught. Surely you feel as much anger against Gabriel as I do?"

"In truth, I did, but to become preoccupied with rage and hatred seems less than angelic. As I have previously explained to you, I should not have given information about you to our siblings before sharing it with you. If I am to be angry with anyone, then I must direct that emotion to myself."

"Oh, noble Seriel! You are truly an inspiration. Yet I wonder whether you would convey a similar sentiment, if Angel Kokabel were not close by?" A wicked grin appeared on Samael's face. He grasped Kokabel's hand and spun her around and around. Giggling thoughts began to escape from the twirling angel.

Trying to ignore Samael's emotional prodding, Seriel stated, once again, "Gabriel will not come here."

Before releasing his hold on Kokabel, the first archangel kissed her fingertips and declared, "Lady Kokabel, you are enchanting! My brother is a fool to not appreciate your loyalty." Then addressing Seriel, he responded, "We shall soon discover which one of us is better informed about Gabriel's nature. Semyaza and Uriel will ply our sibling with complimentary thoughts about his superior knowledge of what is sensible and what is foolhardy. They will plead for his wise counsel, and stress their need for him to inspect the abode and make a judgment on it. I tell you, Gabriel will assuredly come."

A silence fell between the two siblings as each kept his own thoughts shielded. Kokabel walked over to Azazel and Belial and began a thought exchange with them. Neither archangel concerned himself with what the angels were sharing, they were preoccupied with their own thoughts. Eventually, Samael resumed their discourse with:

"Now, while we are waiting, show me your crystal. I am curious why you feel the need to keep it with you."

Seriel considered refusing Samael's request, but decided it would do no harm to agree. His brother would quickly lose interest in his new possession. He drew the light wand from its holster and, holding it in both hands, he extended it toward the first archangel. Samael stood still for an instant, scanning the crystal with his inner vision. Then he grasped the wand by its shaft and lifted it up. He moved it slowly back and forth and seemed to be studying the phantom crystals within its depth. Finally, he remarked:

"It is quite fascinating, dear Seriel. There appears to be other . . ." Samael paused for the effect. " . . . crystals inside this one. Perchance is Kokabel correct? Is it magical?"

"I do not know, but I felt compelled to keep it with me." Seriel had no intention of sharing more than that. He blocked any thoughts of the vision he had received or of the wand's ability to emit an energy beam.

"It is an interesting find. A plaything to free you from boredom." Samael handed the light wand back to his brother.

Returning it to the holster, Seriel replied, "I am not prone to boredom. My spiraling orbs occupy my thoughts, even when I am not with them. They show me many happenings that have not yet transpired and which capture my imagination."

"Yes, indeed, Seriel's Spiral." There was a distinctive sneer within this thought. "And tell me, do your falsifying spheres proffer a rendition of Gabriel's meeting with the daemons?"

"Yes, they do, and it is most alarming. Samael, why do you infer that the spiral is filled with lies? It is an accounting of what is possible and what is actual."

The first archangel patted Seriel's shoulder in a gesture of false sympathy. "My trusting brother, you are so gullible. When will you learn that what *I* tell you is the truth? Your spiral displays illusions which are fabricated by our parent. The Source places them there so that we will conform to its desires. Whatever misfortune you have observed befalling Gabriel is a ploy. Its purpose is to trick you into believing I should not take my revenge."

"I disagree. I have found my spiral to be a true record of what has and will happen. Therefore, I ask you not to seek retribution against Gabriel." Now it was Seriel who moved in close to his sibling. He grabbed Samael's arms and pleaded, "I beg you, heed well my thoughts! When the daemons attacked me, I was in my original auric state. If Gabriel comes here, he will be in his etheric form and cannot revert to his former self at this level of the Abyss. How do we know we are not more vulnerable while etheric?"

Samael pulled free of his brother's hold and declared, "Seriel, Seriel! From where do you acquire these ludicrous notions? How often must I tell you we are eternal? Nothing can harm us. We can feel pain, sorrow, joy and love, but we cannot cease to exist. Rid yourself of the foolish thought you conceived when the daemons attacked you. It was born out of panic and fear and must be quashed. Archangels are forever because they came from the Source, which is also forever!"

"We think differently, Samael, but so be it. However, I repeat my plea. Do not pursue your revenge with Gabriel! And, if you will not heed me, I will alert him to your plan. Even though Gabriel is irksome, I cannot be a part of such brotherly betrayal."

Stretching up to his full height so that he stood slightly taller than his sibling, Samael probed, "Have you forgotten your pledge to me? You declared your unending devotion to my reasoning and desires. To renege now would truly be brotherly betrayal. When Gabriel arrives . . ."

The first archangel was interrupted by Azazel announcing: "Uriel and Semyaza are returning with Gabriel!"

Samael moved over to Azazel and followed, with his inner vision, the direction to which the pure essence angel was pointing. Two archangels and one angel were flying swiftly toward them. Seriel could also perceive their approach and a feeling of deep gloom penetrated his awareness.

"You see, dear brother, I was correct in my belief that the Lord of Practicality would come." Samael was walking back to Seriel. On reaching him, he adopted, once more, a menacing stance. "Now, you heed *me* well! Keep any thoughts of warning Gabriel to yourself. If you will not, I will still them for you!" Then, as a way of disguising the obvious tension between them, he stood next to Seriel with his hand resting lightly on his sibling's shoulder.

Gabriel and Uriel alighted together and Semyaza followed just behind. The fourth archangel stood for an instant in front of the entrance steps, but then walked over to where Samael and Seriel were standing. His surprised attitude was coupled with a hint of annoyance as he declared:

"My two wayward brothers! Uriel did not inform me you would also be inspecting his home."

Seriel quickly answered him with: "We are not here to inspect this abode. I have previously viewed it and Samael built it."

"*You* built this large structure?" asked an incredulous Gabriel. "I thought it was constructed by Uriel. He did not mention your participation in its creation."

Samael beamed at Gabriel and answered, "Oh, you must excuse our little brother. He is so enthusiastic about his home. I did, indeed, fashion its original design, but Uriel has created some adaptations since I gifted the abode to him. But do not tarry here with us. Let Uriel open the door so that you can go inside. He is anxious to show you its treasures."

Despite his sibling's urging, Gabriel remained where he stood. Addressing Seriel, he asked, "If you have already viewed this home, why are you here now? It is my understanding that your spiral preoccupies much of your attention."

Seriel was ready to alert Gabriel to Samael's deception, but a sudden searing pain raced through his whole body. It was so extreme that he doubled over in agony. Somewhat alarmed, Gabriel questioned:

"What is happening to our brother, Samael? He appears to be greatly troubled."

"I am not certain. He was behaving in this manner earlier," lied Samael. He leaned over Seriel, showing great concern. "That is why I am staying close to him."

The fourth archangel asked, "Do you think something is wrong with his etheric body? You and Seriel have been in this form longer than we have. Perhaps we are not meant to always remain in this state?"

Seriel struggled to form his thoughts and send them to Gabriel. He managed, "You must not . . .," but even greater pain welled up inside him and cut short his thought-words. Yet despite its intensity he was suddenly aware of its origin. Samael was inflicting the suffering upon him! In some unknown way he was transmitting this terrible anguish through his hand, which was resting on Seriel's shoulder. The seventh archangel shrugged himself free of his sibling's hold, but Samael immediately encircled his arm around Seriel, as if supporting him.

"Release me, Samael!" Seriel fought against his brother's ever tightening grip, but another thought-shattering spasm sapped his strength.

"This is most worrying." Samael stroked Seriel's forehead in a troubled manner. "Our brother is becoming delirious."

"You must take him at once to the Christ Soul!" ordered a dismayed Gabriel. "He may know what to do because he is so close to our parent." After a short pause, he added, "I will come with you. Uriel can show me his home on another occasion."

A glimmer of hope entered Seriel's pain-racked thoughts. Attempting to reinforce the notion that he was demented, he wrestled even more violently against Samael's tenacious hold. But suddenly his consciousness was filled with a numbing command from the first archangel:

"*You will be still in body and thought!*"

It was as though his brother had complete control over him. There was no more pain, but he could not move. Seriel tried to send another warning to Gabriel, but his thought process was also under duress. His thoughts formed, but he could not project them outwards. Both his inner sense of sight and hearing were functioning normally, but a feeling of nullification was pervading everything else. Seriel's whole being seemed to be encased in an immobilizing force. From within this isolated state he perceived Samael's answer to their sibling:

"Do not trouble yourself, brother, I will attend to Seriel's needs. Observe! His delirium already appears to be passing. If he remains calm, as he is now, I will not need your aid in taking him to the Christ Soul." Then before Gabriel could respond, he addressed the sixth archangel. "Uriel, pray take Gabriel to your home. Show him how the door will only respond to your wishes."

Gabriel looked as though he was ready to argue with Samael, but Uriel and Semyaza moved to either side of him. They quickly propelled him in the direction of the steps which led to the entrance. Uriel mounted the steps and facing the door commanded, "Open door!"

As it began to swing inwards, a large number of daemonic hands appeared from behind the door. They grasped hold of its edge and impatiently pulled the door wide open. Out poured many daemons, both shaitans and lilins, as though the home had been filled with them. They rushed down the steps, tumbling over one another and knocking Uriel out of their way. Without being given any direction from Samael, they quickly surrounded Gabriel and Semyaza. In utter surprise the fourth archangel asked:

"What are these creatures?"

Semyaza replied, "They are the daemons, my lord."

Retaining his mastery of Seriel, Samael observed, "I had forgotten you have never met these delightful imps. Let me rectify that problem. Gabriel meet the daemons. Daemons meet Lord Gabriel."

"We want to play!" We want to play!" chorused the little creatures.

The appearance of the daemons had also surprised Seriel. He suspected they might be waiting nearby, but their actual hiding place had not occurred to him. As he helplessly watched these events unfolding, he noted that his own daemons, and those of Uriel, numbered among the throng. If he could retrieve control of his thoughts, he could, at least, order his daemons not to attack Gabriel. This realization cheered his gloom and gave him something for which to strive.

"Patience, my little ones!" soothed Samael. "I must first inform Lord Gabriel what is transpiring. Once I have performed that duty, you may play as much as you desire." Then he brought his attention to his sibling and explained, "Gabriel, it pleasures me greatly to tell you this. You are not here to inspect Uriel's new home, but to make penance for humiliating me. Denouncing me in front of the angels was cruel and not the action of a brother. I have waited long to repay you for your unkindness."

Gabriel seemed shocked, but not afraid. He questioned, "To what are you alluding, Samael? When did I denounce you?"

An incredulous first archangel asked, "You tell our siblings and the angels I am filled with pride. You perpetuate the lie that I am only worthy of obeying the whims of our parent. Yet you have no memory of these things? Could you be more uncaring?"

"Oh." Gabriel appeared to recall the incident to which Samael was referring. "That was not unkindness, that was the truth! You think of yourself as above all others who exist in Chaos. The Source holds sway over you as it so does over all of us, but you will not accept that veracity." He attempted to make his way through the depth of daemons encircling him, but they held fast in their position. "Enough of this foolishness! Daemons, move out of my path!"

Samael's restrained anger was beginning to brim over. "The daemons do my bidding, not yours! They will not give way unless I tell them to do so." As these thoughts were sent to Gabriel, his iron grip on Seriel began to lessen. It seemed as though he could not become embroiled with Gabriel and maintain control of his sibling. The seventh archangel felt movement returning to his body and he waited to reclaim full command of his thoughts. His arm was resting against the holstered wand and he could feel its energy entering his body and diminishing Samael's power over him.

Now, Gabriel's anger matched Samael's. "You are self-willed and have no respect for our divine parent! You are becoming nefarious and most ignoble!" Then pushing aside several daemons, he demanded, "Give way, vexing creatures!"

This action served to infuriate the first archangel even more. He released his hold on Seriel and marched toward his encircled brother. "Daemons, show Lord Gabriel what happens to those who cause me suffering!"

A number of both Samael's and Seriel's daemons leapt on Gabriel and began to bite and claw him. Yet even as they responded to Samael's order, Seriel sent out this forceful thought:

"I command my own daemons to desist! I forbid you to harm Lord Gabriel!" His creatures obeyed him without hesitation. They jumped down from the fourth archangel and stood with their companions, looking bewildered. Immediately, more of Samael's shaitans and lilins took the place of those who had ceased their torment. They raked and bit at Gabriel's head, limbs and body with even more fervor.

The assaulted archangel fought strongly against his attackers. He managed to pluck some of them from himself and kicked them soundly right over the heads of the watching circle of daemons. This action was reminiscent of what Seriel had observed in one of the three spheres. No thoughts came from Gabriel, all of his attention and strength was focused upon repelling the creatures.

Small wounds began to appear on him where the daemonic teeth and claws had penetrated his etheric skin. A glutinous substance trickled from some of the wounds and glistened a deeper shade of red than his own innate color. When drops of this substance pooled beneath him, they moved quickly further out into the Abyss and away from the fray. Seriel believed the substance to be Gabriel's consciousness, his very essence, and that the fleeing drops would become his own daemons. The seventh archangel also noted that Uriel's daemons did not take part in the onslaught. They merely stood within the circle, watching and cheering on their fellow creatures. Gradually, his own confused daemons copied the behavior of the sixth archangel's imps.

As quickly as one daemon was shaken free by Gabriel, another would take its place. Realizing he had reached an impasse with his attackers, the fourth archangel unfurled his wings and they began to vibrate. A screeching thought exploded from Samael:

"His wings! His wings! Do not let him escape!"

Now, even more daemons attached themselves to Gabriel. While some of them continued their previous bombardment, others grasped hold of his extended wings and began to tug viciously at them. Gabriel attempted to retract these appendages close to the safety of his body, but the daemons' combined strength was greater than his own. There came an awful instant when one wing began to separate from Gabriel's body and he writhed in agony. An excruciating scream-thought welled up from him and it impacted chillingly on each of the watching archangels and angels. Semyaza fell back from his position close to Gabriel and even Samael seemed startled. The wing was finally torn completely free and was thrown to a group of Samael's daemons who were waiting within the circle. They quickly shredded it into many jagged strips which were then discarded. Gabriel continued to scream as the second wing was now under attack.

Seriel sent an urgent thought to Kokabel. "Go speedily to Lord Michael and bring him here!" It was shielded from all but this one essence angel. Her answer came back, equally guarded from the others:

"I cannot go. Lord Samael ordered me to ignore any request you might make while he takes his revenge on Lord Gabriel."

"*I* am your essence lord, not Samael!" thundered Seriel. "You will obey *my* bidding. Go now!"

Without further argument, Kokabel flew upwards and took off for inner Chaos. Samael observed her departure, but he made no comment to Seriel. He appeared to be transfixed by what was happening to his sibling. The daemons were trying to brutally remove the second wing, but Gabriel was beating it back and forth in a defensive motion. This caused the tugging daemons to lose their grip and fall away from him. However, he seemed unable to lift himself off with only one functioning wing, and other daemons soon replaced their fallen comrades.

"Have done with this torment, Samael!" Seriel angrily told his brother. "Surely your injured feelings have been duly avenged? Gabriel has suffered a far more cruel punishment than I."

"Not yet," was Samael's only reply.

Now, the gaping wound caused by the tearing of Gabriel's wing from his body was beginning to ooze his essence. The leaking substance trickled down his back and larger drops escaped out into the Abyss. A small amount of essence dripped onto one of the fallen lilins. The red substance drizzled down her daemonic face and seeped into her mouth. Instantly, this creature began to expand in height and girth. Seriel watched in horror as she jumped upon Gabriel's shoulder and, bringing her mouth close to the deep gash, began to greedily drink the exuding essence.

A terrible rage took hold of the seventh archangel. He felt an utter loathing for the daemons rising up inside of him. He desperately wanted to strike them forcefully, to give intense pain back to them. As these hate-filled thoughts came to him, the light wand at his side commenced to vibrate wildly. It shook so violently that Seriel felt compelled to release it from the holster. He gripped it by the hilt and, as he drew it from its case, the pale blue energy beam burst upwards from it. Instinctively, he aimed the light ray at the lilin and it shattered her into several pieces. Then Seriel swept the beam from his wand through several daemons who were attempting to copy the lilin's action. Finally, he turned his powerful weapon on those creatures who were rending Gabriel's second wing. Yet even as the creatures were exploding, the ruined appendage fell from his brother's body.

Gabriel's wound was even deeper and wider now and his essence was leaking steadily from it. He stumbled and dropped to his knees, but his spirit was not daunted. Pointing unsteadily at the first archangel, he haltingly accused, "Samael . . . you are truly . . . evil . . . and . . . are . . . no

longer . . . my brother." He sank into a prone position and
his final thought was barely perceptible. "Uriel . . . Seriel . . .
I pray you . . . help . . ."

All angelic beings, who had witnessed the lilin's
despicable assault on Gabriel, stood stunned and bereft of
thoughts. Samael's tones of maldor and silver had turned
sickeningly pale and he seemed unable to regain his usual
aplomb. Uriel, Belial and Semyaza appeared to be
extremely distraught and remained motionless. Samael
moved close to Seriel, but he ignored him and approached
his ailing brother. Azazel quickly regained his composure
and started toward Gabriel from the other direction. Yet
before they could reach him, the scattered daemonic
pieces were rapidly flowing back together, making the
destroyed creatures whole, once more. Four of them
jumped upon the fallen Gabriel and began to devour his
escaping essence. While clinging onto him, they grew in
stature and fought each other in an attempt to gain a better
position.

The beam from the light wand had vanished, but Seriel
continued to hold the crystal aloft. Realizing the diabolical
stealing of Gabriel's essence was happening, again, he
thought-yelled, "I will have done with you vile beasts! My
crystal will break you asunder, never to return!" As he
brandished the wand, the laser-like ray reappeared, but its
light was even more piercing. Seriel cut down the feeding
daemons, pure hatred fueling his weapon's lethal beam. They
were blasted into nothingness so that not a single trace of
them remained to ever rejoin.

This total destruction of the four daemons brought panic
to the remaining creatures. They scattered in all directions,
running, bouncing and rolling far away from the Lord of
Sorcery and his magical wand. Their departure gave Seriel
easy access to Gabriel. As he drew close, the scene before
him was an unbearable replica of what both the beautiful
clear crystal and his spheres had shown him. Gabriel lay face

down and not moving, while his essence seeped from the hideous injury.

Just as he reached his motionless sibling, Azazel also drew close. Together they gently turned Gabriel over, trying to help him, yet not knowing what to do. The fourth archangel lay limp and unresponsive, his innate rosy color all but drained from his etheric form. In that instant when archangel and pure essence angel wondered how they could possibly restore Gabriel's well-being, Kokabel arrived with Michael.

"Angel Kokabel has told me what was transpiring, but this is far more disturbing." Michael knelt beside the failing Gabriel. "Is he able to share any thoughts with you?"

Azazel answered, "Lord Gabriel asked for our help and then collapsed. No other thoughts have come from him and he has not moved."

"I must take my brother to the Source. Our parent will surely know how to heal him." Then addressing Azazel, Michael continued, "I will require you to help me carry Lord Gabriel to the Source because he is unable . . ."

"I will go with you," interrupted Seriel. "An archangel is stronger than an angel."

"You must remain here!" Michael's thoughts became authoritative. "You and Azazel appear to be the least shaken by what has happened. A stalwart archangel is needed to watch over Uriel, the angels and . . ." He paused and then added, " . . . Samael."

In answer to the mention of his name, the first archangel stepped forward and stated, "I was shocked by the extent of Gabriel's injuries, but I am well composed now."

Michael responded in a withering tone, "It is not your composure with which I have concern."

For once, Samael was lost for an answer. He stood with silenced thoughts, nervously twitching his wings open and closed, as though contemplating flight.

"Come, Azazel, let us fly swiftly to the Source!" Michael lifted Gabriel's limp body in his arms and Azazel took hold of the fourth archangel's legs in order to support the weight. As they flew upwards with their tragic burden, one final order from Michael came back down to the angelic group: "Remain here until Azazel returns. He will inform you of our parent's thoughts and decrees about this terrible event."

No one put forward a thought for a while, each was subdued and lost in personal memories of what had just been witnessed. Finally, Uriel hesitatingly shared, "I did not wish to see Gabriel so pained. Samael, you told me the daemons could do no more harm to our brother than what they had caused Seriel."

"You know about my encounter with the daemons?" asked a surprised seventh archangel.

Before Uriel could answer, Samael interjected, "Indeed, he does! When I told Uriel of my plan, he was fearful Gabriel might suffer unduly. I then recounted what happened to you and how there was no lasting damage from the daemons' attack. How could I know it would be different for Gabriel?"

"I warned you not to take your revenge. I assured you my spheres had displayed something most alarming." Seriel found little satisfaction in reminding his brother of these facts.

Ignoring their shared thoughts, Samael told Uriel, "Do not upset yourself, little brother. As I seem to be frequently declaring, we are eternal, immortal. Nothing can cause our demise."

Was Samael only trying to convince their sibling or was some of the reassurance necessary for himself? Seriel suspected the latter to be true. He declared, "Yet what is done, is done. We must strive to move beyond this dreadful happening. Let us trust Gabriel will recover and that our parent will be forgiving."

Kokabel had listened patiently to these thought exchanges, but she was eager to learn all about what she had missed while searching for Michael. Unable to contain her curiosity any longer, she questioned enthusiastically, "But what took place while I was gone? When I departed, Gabriel's wing was being torn from him. When I returned, both wings were gone and he was lying motionless. What happened? And what is that strange substance that was coming from his wounds?"

In unison, the first and seventh archangels commanded, "Kokabel, be silent!"

Chapter Fourteen

M ichael was deep within the appointed resting phase. He lay curled up in close proximity to the Source, waiting to learn what would happen to Gabriel. Believing he could be more helpful to his brother in his etheric form, he had chosen not to revert back to his auric self. Sleep had come upon Michael when he desperately wanted to remain awake. He had fought the need to rest for a while, but he had eventually succumbed. Now, he drifted through troubled dreams of Gabriel's wounds and Samael's treachery.

Earlier, when he and Azazel reached the Source with Gabriel, it appeared their parent knew what had taken place. The Source asked no questions, but directed them to lay the fourth archangel at the edge of its brilliant being. Once this was done, many tendrils of consciousness began curling out from the Source and entwining themselves around Gabriel. More and more twisting strands took hold of the unresponsive archangel until he was no longer visible. However, shortly before Gabriel became completely engulfed in Source consciousness, Michael observed him changing back into his auric state.

The third archangel asked the Source whether his sibling would recover, but he received no reassurance. His parent merely answered:

"Patience, my child. All is choice and Gabriel may wish to return to me."

Trying to ascertain what this remark might mean, Michael questioned, "Is it possible that Gabriel will no longer be with us?"

There was no response from the Source. His parent appeared to be completely preoccupied with attending to Gabriel.

Michael instructed Azazel to return to Seriel and the others. He directed, "Tell them Gabriel is with the Source and that we must wait to learn whether or not he will recover."

As soon as Azazel had departed, the Christ Soul, Raphael and the Shekinah arrived. Each of them had sensed something happening to Gabriel. As Raphael explained:

"That inner connection we eight have experienced since our birth suddenly felt changed. It was as though Gabriel had broken the link. That familiar soul bond, which I have with our brother, is gone."

Malkura added, "We three sought out each other and learned we were all experiencing the same sense of loss. The Christ Soul suggested we come to our parent who would surely know what was happening."

Michael explained about the daemonic assault on Gabriel. He told them the information Kokabel had shared and what he had learned from his arrival at the scene of the attack. All three archangels were appalled to hear of Samael's part in this horrendous act. The Shekinah felt an overwhelming need to confront her first-born brother, but she realized the necessity for the resting phase was fast approaching. She promised herself she would seek him out once her sleep was ended. Michael showed his siblings where Gabriel lay enveloped within the kaleidoscopic tendrils. He also told them of their parent's dubious comment. Then the four archangels agreed to partake of the resting phase close by their brother. They would await the outcome of his healing encounter with the Source. Gradually, each one drifted into sleep.

The third archangel's dreams continued on. Now, they were letting go of the recent traumatic events and taking him into a different arena. In his new dream Michael was flying high above the Abyss. He was, in fact, soaring at a much greater height than he had ever reached in etheric flight. The Abyss of Chaos lay far below him. He was completely free of its dark extent and was looking down upon it. Yet its lateral boundaries, if they existed, were not in view.

The Source with its radiant beams of light was easily visible and Michael noted with a hint of amusement its location. It was not, as the eight had always considered, in the center of Chaos. Instead it lay off to one side, and it served as the central point of a gigantic spiral. At first, Michael was surprised by the nature of this swirling extension of his parent. As he lived out his existence within Chaos, he was not aware that he was treading this spiraling path. He and all other angelic beings were forging their way further and further out into the Abyss. They were unknowingly transcribing the sacred geometry of the Source, carving the infinite ALL THAT IS upon the face of Chaos.

This whorled figure was segmented into eight different colors, each distinct from its neighbor. Moving in an outward direction, the section closest to the Source was onca, which was followed by rulpiel. Then came blue, then yellow, then red, then breal, then odami and, finally, maldor. As Michael wondered why the spiral was displaying the colors of the eight archangels, he heard the voice of his parent telling him:

"Know that these are the eight levels of the life force spiral. Each domain is ruled by one of my precious archangel children. Your level lies seventh and stands guard against Samael's reasoning and inopportune return."

Other than knowing the eight colors corresponded with those of the eight archangels, this message made little sense to Michael. The segmented spiral did not reflect anything with which he was familiar. No one considered a certain area of Chaos as being overseen by any one particular archangel. Further more, the reference to his brother was completely puzzling. He certainly did not agree with the Lord of the First Essence's reasoning, and could well imagine himself standing against him. Yet from where would Samael be returning, opportunely or otherwise? However, as is often true with dreams, Michael accepted the incongruous message without any further consideration.

As he continued to look down upon the Abyss of Chaos, the third archangel noticed another spiral which appeared to be contained within the larger one. It was much smaller and was positioned in the yellow segment. Without hesitation he decided this one must be Seriel's Spiral. As this conclusion came to Michael, it seemed entirely appropriate that his sibling's spinning orbs should exist in his level. Yellow was Seriel's innate color, therefore, the yellow segment must be overseen by the seventh archangel.

Michael scrutinized the larger spiral more thoroughly, checking to find other objects within the different segments. At first, this seemed futile. With the exception of Seriel's level, all others appeared devoid of anything other than their color. Then something about Gabriel's level caught his attention. A large part was a lighter shade of red than the rest of it. And, even as Michael realized this, the same area appeared to become transparent. It was as though a tremendous hole was widening in the fabric of the spiral at this point. Fascinated, the third archangel wondered what was causing this effect. Ultimately, he could only conclude that everything he was being shown was not yet taking place. He reasoned that his dream was revealing a forthcoming ALL THAT IS, just as Seriel's Spiral displayed future happenings.

Even as this thought came to him, the dream was moving on. Michael was suddenly plummeting toward the image below him. He was neither flying nor falling, but was being pulled downwards. As he drew closer and closer to the life force spiral, the eight separate colors seemed to blend into one glorious golden hue. Then Michael began to witness many details of life within the Abyss of Chaos, the comings and goings of its inhabitants. Yet all happenings were taking place rapidly, giving him a quick review of everything. This speedy version of angelic existence continued on until the third archangel drew very close to the spiral.

Suddenly his downward movement ceased and he came to rest a short distance above an astonishing scene. A battle was in progress. Angels were fighting against angels. Many of them were locked in one-to-one combat, striking out at each other with pointed etheric objects. When any of these weapons pierced the opponent's form, essence would begin to leak from the resulting wounds. Some angels were battling daemons, and they had to contend with several of these creatures attacking in groups. Daemonic teeth and claws were brutally at work and Michael even observed some angels having wings and limbs torn free from their bodies. In utter horror the third archangel also discovered that several angels lay prone and supine. These visions were a painful reminder of Gabriel's plight.

Criss-crossing throughout this terrible conflict were beams of light, pale blue in color. At first, Michael could not discern from where they were originating, but their purpose was very apparent. Any angel caught in their piercing flow was cut down and horribly maimed. Daemons, who fell foul of the energy beams, shattered into innumerable pieces. Some even appeared to totally disintegrate. These devastating shafts of blue light were emitting from both sides of this conflict and, finally, Michael was shown their origin. He saw Samael holding aloft a strange, three-pointed object with three light beams emanating from it. Next, Seriel came into view, wielding another object from which a similar piercing ray came forth. Then to Michael's amazement he observed himself brandishing a third light-projecting implement.

As Michael continued to experience this startling event, he eventually concluded that his dream double was fighting against Samael and Seriel and not with them. He also realized that although many angels were in league with his two brothers, even more were fighting against them. The dreaming archangel felt certain an actual event was being portrayed, and he wondered why it would happen. As if in response to his slumbering thought, he heard his parent's answer:

"Behold! This is the beginning of the War of the Sons of Light against the Sons of Darkness." This was yet another puzzling statement from the Source, but one which would not be forgotten on Michael's waking.

Finally, the dream came to an abrupt end when Gabriel came into view. He was plying yet another beam-emitting weapon, and was most assuredly strong and well. The relief Michael felt on seeing his brother was so intense that it brought him straight into wakefulness. For a short while, he remained curled up, remembering what his dreams had revealed. Then, after verifying his siblings were continuing to sleep, he also checked Gabriel's condition. Nothing appeared to have changed with his ailing brother. His enveloped auric being remained hidden from view.

Michael felt no urgency to return to the resting phase and he decided he could make good use of being alone. If the dream battle was to become a reality, then there must be spheres within Seriel's Spiral displaying its occurrence. He would go there and establish whether or not this unimagined event would take place. The third archangel unfurled his wings and flew away in the direction of the spiraling orbs.

*   *   *

Once Gabriel had made his halting plea for help, nothing more seemed to impact on him. His inner senses of vision and hearing were no longer functioning and even the unbearable pain that racked his body was fading. He continued to experience a feeling of anger, yet was quickly becoming uncertain why he had that emotion or against whom he was holding it. Nothing outside of himself was reaching his consciousness and he began to enter a state of oblivion. Intermittently, this vacuum would be interrupted by a thought recalling a tiny aspect of his earlier life. Now, he was playing with his siblings, spinning merrily around with them, chasing and being chased by them. This was followed by a void. Then he was watching in silent awe as the first angels emerged from their miniature scene. An even longer period of nothingness ensued until Gabriel was remembering how he had manifested his etheric body and enjoyed the wonder of having form. Thus, his thoughts drifted along, occasionally clear, then followed by emptiness, while his life essence continued to leave him.

The demise of the fourth archangel was becoming imminent as his consciousness began to reunite with his soul. Yet, suddenly, an all-pervading, kaleidoscopic light filled every particle of his being. An ecstatic sense of tranquillity and rapture embalmed him and he surrendered to a lengthy melding with the Source. While everything was happening between the two beings, there was vibrant clarity in each occurrence. However, Gabriel would be able to recall very little when, eventually, he separated from his parent.

As the bliss-filled Source light penetrated Gabriel's mutilated form, he felt the strong desire to release his etheric body so that he could return to his original state. Yet he was much too weak to initiate the change. However, his parent understood his wish and instantly granted it. Gabriel was, once more, his auric self. He rested in a type of limbo while the Source healed his ailing soul.

The fourth archangel was surrounded by the essence of his parent. Its colors wrapped around him and then entered him, each one imparting its own energy vibration. As his inner sense of vision became restored, he viewed the eight different geometric patterns which helped form the structure of Source consciousness. These sacred designs fascinated Gabriel's analytical thinking. Once his inner sense of hearing had returned, he could perceive the divine music of his parent. Now, he understood what Raphael was trying to convey to his siblings. The tone and cadence uplifted him beyond ecstasy. Gabriel lay totally enraptured with all of which he was partaking. Then one more gift was given by the Source. He bathed in the exalted and hallowed love which was his everlasting birthright.

After what appeared to be, from the recovering archangel's point of view, an eternity, his parent's thoughts came to him:

"Gabriel, you have reached the juncture where you must decide whether to rejoin with me or return to your angelic life."

Without hesitation Gabriel replied, "Whatever you require of me is what I will do. You are the divine parent whose wishes must be obeyed."

"My precious child, I do not seek to be obeyed. You have free will and can continually make choices."

This was different from what Gabriel had always believed, but in his present euphoric mood, he was quite willing to accept it. Looking for clarification he declared, "If by rejoining you mean remaining here in this state of bliss, then without question I wish to stay with you."

"Rejoining is not temporarily remaining, my little one. We are melded, but not reunited. If you choose to return and become a part of me, once more, your life as Gabriel will cease to exist. All sense and memory of being the fourth archangel will be gone. You will be a part of myself, as you were before your birth." The Source waited for Gabriel to respond, but when no answer came, it continued, "If you choose to rejoin, all angels, who are facets of your essence, will also be compelled to merge with you and then become a part of me. It will be as though my beloved fourth child was never created. And none will, therefore, have a remembrance of him."

Gabriel tried to grasp hold of the concept of not being, but it was too illusive for him. He also wondered why he could not remain as he was, enveloped by his loving, radiant parent.

Perceiving this thought, the Source answered, "Because remaining melded with me is not an option being offered."

"Must I choose now?" asked a procrastinating Gabriel. Immediately, he felt ripples of mirth eddying around him. When they subsided, the Source responded:

"Indeed, you must. All is choice, my son, but if you linger too long in this melded state with me, rejoining will become inevitable."

Memories of what the daemons had done to him were beginning to permeate Gabriel's consciousness. Anger aimed at the vicious creatures came racing back into him. Then, as he remembered Samael's complicity in this dreadful event, an even stronger sense of rage took hold. He told the Source, "Choosing to return to life in the Abyss of Chaos is not an easy decision. My soul craves order in everything and Samael spreads disorder whenever he can. When we eight first sprang from you, there was joy in just existing. Now, there is pain and anger and a need for a complication of what was once simple."

A tremor ran through the Source and Gabriel recognized it as a heavy sigh. His parent agreed, "You are correct, my child, but understand this is the nature of ALL THAT IS. Simplicity and intricacy must exist to make the whole." There was a lengthy silence, and then the Source asked, "Have you made your choice?"

"I must confess to imagine none remembering me is an extremely disquieting thought. And do I have the right to make many other angels non-existent?" Gabriel was as much thought exchanging with himself as he was with the Source.

"Yet, if I return to my angelic life, I fear I will want to take my revenge on Samael. A great rage against him is consuming my thoughts. Indeed, making my choice is almost impossible."

"Perhaps if I share a hidden truth with you, it will help your dilemma. It is something for you to know now, but will be gone from you, once your choice is made."

To Gabriel's amazement his parent then recounted the agreement made between itself and his brother. The Source explained that Samael's chosen separation from it was the only manner in which it could experience all things for all of eternity. His parent concluded with:

"Thus, Samael is an intrinsic part of ALL THAT IS and you have helped him tread his chosen path. Know that your disposition is extremely abrasive to his. Therefore, you have given him the initiative to take his first impious actions."

"This is truly astonishing information. Samael has always boasted about his uniqueness and first-born powers. Now, I understand why."

The Source assured Gabriel, "Yet he has no memory of our agreement. He chose to forget so that he could fulfill his destiny, unfettered and undeterred."

"And I will also forget what you have told me?"

"Indeed, you will. As I have explained, if you choose to rejoin with me, all of your memories will be gone. And if you continue your life as Gabriel, I must take all knowledge of my agreement with Samael from you. Not knowing it, you cannot inadvertently share it with your brother."

A little chuckling thought escaped from the fourth archangel. "It seems you know me too well. Even though I would swear upon my soul to keep your secret, I know I might break that promise. Samael goads me beyond endurance and, in the midst of his sarcastic reasoning, I can imagine myself divulging the agreement. I would take great pleasure in having information which was unknown to him."

"You are progressing, my child. Recognizing and accepting the complexities of your essence strengthens your soul." The Source projected another wave of immeasurable love deep into its offspring, and then urgently declared, "You must make your decision immediately!"

Remaining uncertain which was the better choice, Gabriel had nevertheless determined what he would do. He told his parent, "I have decided to continue my life within the Abyss of Chaos. It pleases me to know I am a part of what helps you become all things for all of eternity, even though my role may not be as vital as Samael's."

"Each and every soul is crucial to my continued existence, and each and every soul is my beloved child." The Source's thoughts ceased for an instant, and then one final directive was made. "Now, be gone from me and take with you only that which is appropriate for you to remember!"

The colors, the music and the sacred geometric patterns vanished from Gabriel's perception. Gone also was the comfort and blissful tranquillity, but the sense of being loved remained. It seemed as though he was waking from the resting phase, but a sliver of memory reminded him this was not so. He was not rousing from sleep, but instead had been melded with the Source. As he became fully aware, Gabriel found himself resting very close to the extreme edge of his parent's consciousness. However, he had no notion of how he had arrived there.

As he continued to remain still, the fourth archangel reviewed all that had happened to him. He could clearly recall his fight with the daemons and their cruel assault on his wings and body. Then he remembered a terrible pain which erupted in his back, but seemed to quickly fill his whole etheric body. As the pain grew more and more intense, his inner senses diminished rapidly and a darkness had come upon him that was even more bleak than the Abyss. Beyond that sensation there were just snatches of images, feelings and thoughts which were disjointed and made no sense to him. Yet he knew without doubt he had rested within divine consciousness and that his loving parent had healed him.

Discovering he was not within his etheric body, the fourth archangel stretched his auric self and reverently offered, "I thank you most profoundly, my sacred parent, for restoring my well-being." Then a somewhat more humble Lord of Practicality flowed away from the Source, readying himself to continue his angelic life.

Chapter Fifteen

When Azazel returned to the waiting archangels and angels, he was bombarded by questions about Gabriel. He quickly shared the little information he knew and then requested of Samael to be excused. Azazel felt the approach of the resting phase and explained that he had previously chosen his own place in Chaos where he always preferred to sleep. Samael nodded agreement and, just as Azazel unfolded his wings, Kokabel shocked everyone by asking:

"May I go with you, Brother Azazel?"

If this unexpected appeal surprised the seventh-cast angel, he did not reveal it, but merely replied, "If you so wish." Then he and Kokabel flew away together.

"Perchance your adoring angel is losing her devotion for the Lord of the Seventh Essence?" asked Samael with unbridled mirth.

"It is of little interest to me," replied Seriel. To the seventh archangel, the possibility of Kokabel no longer being obsessed with him was irrelevant. Compared to the pressing matter, which had recently transpired, the relief of not being pursued so closely by her seemed trivial.

"A wise decision," continued Samael. "When you consider that both Kokabel's and Azazel's essence roles and casting orders are so compatible. Thus, why would they not enjoy each other's companionship?"

Becoming annoyed, Seriel declared, "I repeat myself, Samael. What Kokabel chooses to do is of little interest to me. A matter which is of far greater importance is the plight of our brother. It would appear from Azazel's account that Gabriel may not return to us."

"Surely that cannot be?" asked a concerned Uriel.

Beginning to also display annoyance, Samael questioned, "How often must I state the truth that we are eternal? We cannot cease to exist!"

"I have no desire to argue with you, Samael. All of my thoughts are with Gabriel." Seriel spread his wings, indicating he was ready to depart. "The resting phase is rapidly advancing, therefore, I will take my leave of you."

"We can all rest in my new home," offered Uriel. "Then, when we awake, I trust Gabriel will be with us, once more."

"I thank you for your kind proposal, Uriel, but I feel the need for my own abode." It suddenly occurred to Seriel that his sibling was wanting the comfort of company, therefore, he added, "Samael, Belial and Semyaza will remain with you."

Quickly intervening, the first archangel exclaimed, "Belial and Semyaza will remain, but I am bound for my crystal home." A pause, and then: "That prompts a thought, Seriel. Your crystal obviously has powers which you have kept secret. When we meet, again, you must show me how you manifested the destructive beam of light." Without waiting for an answer, Samael was gone, flying off in the direction of the home he had built for himself and the Shekinah.

Before he also departed, Seriel felt obligated to ensure Uriel would not be alone. He stated, "Belial and Semyaza, I would have you keep company with Lord Uriel during the resting phase. We archangels are in need of comfort." He moved close to his sibling and offered, "Fear not, Uriel, our brother is with our parent who is all-powerful. Gabriel is safe and protected. And remember, all is choice, thus, all is possible."

The two angels agreed to stay without hesitation, and they walked toward the entrance steps of Uriel's home. Seriel remained with his brother an instant longer, asking him:

"I trust you will forgive my departure? I have a great need to be alone. May you fare well and remain within the Source's keeping!" Then the seventh archangel took flight toward his pyramid. Once there, he moved through its corridors until he entered the resting chamber. Seriel lay down and drifted into fretful sleep. His dreams were filled with anger which seemed to be directed at anyone who, and anything which, featured in his slumbering thoughts. He slept for a long duration, but did not feel refreshed when he finally awoke.

After rising, Seriel moved unhappily around his pyramidal home. He felt certain Gabriel had not yet recovered. Once his brother fell into an unresponsive mode, Seriel's inner connection with Gabriel seemed to have been broken. There was no longer a sense of vitality coming from the fourth archangel. Now, that feeling of disconnection was continuing to exist and was weighing heavily upon the Lord of Sorcery.

Seriel wondered where he should await news of his sibling. He wanted to keep a vigil close to where the ailing Gabriel was entwined within their parent's consciousness. Yet he was also reluctant to do this because he did not want to risk being questioned by Michael. The third archangel might wonder whether he had prior knowledge of Samael's treachery. Seriel could not shake the thought he was partially to blame for what had happened to Gabriel. He had known Samael was determined to take his revenge, just as he had done so with his seventh-born brother. If he had warned Gabriel and disclosed his own experience with the daemons, he believed their assault on his sibling would not have taken place. Gabriel would have been wary of the creatures and also alerted to Samael's trickery.

Trying to put these guilty feelings aside, Seriel brought his attention to the other matter which was capturing his thoughts. He was intrigued by the functioning of his light wand. The devastating beam of light seemed to have been released by his desire to destroy the daemons. This would indicate the crystal was attuned to his thoughts. Seriel suddenly thought about Samael telling him he believed the fluid objects had come from the Source. If this was so, then perhaps a small part of the Source's consciousness was trapped within the crystals which had sprung from those objects? His own consciousness would be communicating with the wand's Source consciousness. This would take place in a similar manner to what would happen, if he communicated directly with his parent.

Wanting to test his theory, the seventh archangel quickly returned to the resting chamber, where he had set aside the light wand before going to sleep. It lay on the floor in its holster close to where he had rested. Seriel picked it up and strapped it to his waist and leg. Then he ran through the corridors until he reached the entrance. The seventh archangel exited the pyramid. He stood at a distance away from his home and drew the crystal from the holster. Seriel believed it had told him it was a light wand, therefore, he decided to attempt further communication with it. He held the wand out in front of him and asked, "Can you understand my thoughts?"

There was no answer, but the crystal began to vibrate just as it had done when the daemons were attacking Gabriel. Wondering whether this was a form of communication, Seriel stated, "If you are comprehending my thoughts, then emit the light beam so that I will know you have received my request."

Immediately, the intense pale blue shaft of light projected from the wand. Obviously, the crystal understood his thoughts, even if it could not answer him with thought-words. This discovery cheered Seriel from his earlier gloom. It would be fascinating to learn more about his amazing etheric mineral. He wondered what else the crystal was capable of doing.

Once more, it began to vibrate, and the narrow beam opened up into a wide area of pale blue light. The notion of surrounding the pyramid with this beam suddenly came to Seriel and he directed the broad energy field in its direction. His home became completely bathed in blue as another idea occurred. Seriel knew he could move the pyramid with the power of his thoughts. More than once he had repositioned it when it was under construction. Now, he was curious to learn what would happen when he attempted to move it while the wand's light encased it. This thought was barely born and it was already a reality. The pyramid had shifted some distance to one side of its former position. This action was far more rapid than Seriel was able to accomplish by thought alone.

Yet another idea penetrated Seriel's awareness. He remembered how safe and protected he had felt while inside the large, clear crystal. As this memory came to him, he knew assuredly he would be equally protected, if he stood within the safety of his crystal's blue light. Instantly, the wand's broad beam withdrew from the pyramid and Seriel became enclosed in its entirety. It remained around him long enough for him to recapture the sense of crystalline peace and safety. Then it was gone, vanishing back inside the crystal.

As the seventh archangel stood reflecting on what the wand had shown him, he realized the thoughts and ideas about what it could do were not his own. The crystal had placed them into his consciousness. This must be the manner in which it was communicating with him. He would not hear its thought-words as he did with his siblings and the angels. It could project information so profoundly deep within him that it would appear to be his own musings. As this realization dawned, the crystal vibrated violently, causing it to fall from Seriel's grasp. Knowing this was its way of showing comprehension and conformation of his thoughts, he bent down and picked it up. "I understand you," he happily declared as he placed the light wand back in its holster.

Seriel was just beginning to recognize the power of the etheric mineral kingdom. It was to become as captivating an interest for him as was his obsession with the spiraling spheres. Apart from the obvious communication, which could be established between an archangel and a crystal, there appeared to be other benefits. Seriel reasoned that holding, or being in close proximity to, a crystal enhanced and focused his thoughts. This would, undoubtedly, hold true for any angelic being who chose to work with crystalline energy.

Next, the seventh archangel thought about Samael's home. From the Shekinah's description, he concluded it must have been constructed entirely from minerals. This would mean its occupant's intentions and wishes would be greatly magnified. He could imagine Samael's thought power becoming even more penetrating than before. Seriel considered going in search of Samael's home in order to alert his brother to the implications of living in a crystal abode. He was also curious with regard to how Samael was feeling about Gabriel's inert condition. Seriel would go to his brother and ask him. He believed he would find the first archangel remaining in his home after the resting phase.

As this consideration came to him, he was instantly propelled from where he stood outside of his own home to standing in front of a glistening structure with golden double doors. Seriel instinctively knew this building must be Samael's home and he marveled at the power of crystal energy. Obviously, the light wand had understood his considering thought and had made it happen. This was sorcery, indeed, and the Lord of the Seventh Essence suddenly realized a lasting truth. The etheric mineral kingdom possessed an awesome power which would need to be used with caution and respect.

The energy emitting from this crystalline abode was interfering with Seriel's ability to perceive his brother's essence vibration, but he presumed Samael was inside his home. Knowing he would not be able to open the doors himself, he sent this requesting thought to the first archangel: "Samael, I am here outside your golden entrance. Pray open the doors so that I may enter."

No answering thoughts came back to Seriel. It would appear his sibling had gone from his home as soon as he had awakened. Had he flown to the Source to gain news of Gabriel? Was he troubled by what the daemons did and, therefore, was seeking solace from the Shekinah? Perhaps he was looking for Seriel, wanting to learn more about the light wand? Where could he be?

As the seventh archangel wondered about the location of his brother, he was, once again, transported to another place. He found himself in the area of Chaos where he and Samael had witnessed the fluid objects transforming into crystals. The Lord of the First Essence was standing a short distance away from him and he appeared to be looking for something. Samael was picking up one after another of the many crystals which lay scattered around. He held each one for an instant, then dropped it back down and chose another to hold. The first-born of the Source did not seem to be aware of Seriel's presence.

"Greetings, Samael!" declared Seriel.

"What sorcery is this?" asked his startled brother. "I did not sense your approach. How did you manage to shield your essence vibration from me?"

Feeling pleased to have the advantage over Samael, Seriel answered, "Crystal sorcery. My light wand can take me instantly to wherever I wish to go."

"The power of your crystal appears to be immeasurable. However, I am certain it is not unique. Other crystals must possess similar attributes." With that Samael returned his attention to his former preoccupation.

"Do you have news of Gabriel? Are you not concerned about his well-being?" questioned Seriel.

Becoming aggravated, Samael responded, "Did you come here to pester me with foolish questions?"

"How can you deem my thoughts about our brother foolishness? Do you not feel some remorse for causing him such harm?"

"Remorse?" questioned Samael. "Why should I beset myself with such an unwanted feeling?"

"Because you allowed your daemons to greatly maim him. I feel both guilt and remorse. I should have warned Gabriel of your intention to take revenge upon him."

"Then you are a fool! Gabriel began these happenings by speaking ill of me to the angels. I merely repaid him for the pain and anguish he caused me. Enough of this tiresome affair!" Samael swept one hand in front of himself, as if to push away some annoyance. "Keep thoughts of it to yourself!" He bent down and picked up a purple crystal with a broad point. Then, with his usual lightning change of mood, he waved this mineral specimen in Seriel's direction and warned, "Be careful, dear brother! I might decide to harm you in the same manner you destroyed some of my daemons."

Unsure whether his sibling was jesting or actually threatening him, Seriel also adopted a warning attitude. He stated, "No, Samael, you must be careful! The power of the etheric mineral kingdom is awesome and is not to be taken lightly. Do not point that crystal at me even in jest!"

With almost disgust, Samael threw down the purple crystal and walked over to his brother. "What is happening to you? You are beginning to echo our fourth-born sibling's incessant thoughts about caution! Why must you behave in this manner? Where is the carefree Lord Seriel with whom I used to play and meld?"

"And where is the guileless Lord Samael who created playful games for we archangels to enjoy?" retorted Seriel.

"Well stated, dear brother. We are not as we were," acquiesced the first archangel. He turned away from his sibling and slowly shook his head.

Seriel replied, "As we both previously agreed, we have changed and are continuing to evolve. But I do not wish to dwell upon that truth. I am anxious to learn of Gabriel's well-being. Do you have news of him?"

Turning back to his brother, the first archangel placed his hands on Seriel's shoulders and applied pressure, forcing him to sit down on a large flat crystal. He stood directly over him and ordered, "Hear me well! Brother Gabriel is robust and sound. I am also certain he is ranting to Michael about my diabolical behavior. Can you not sense his essence vibration?"

Seriel was about to tell Samael that he had not sensed Gabriel's existence since he had fallen prone from the daemons' attack. Yet even as he began to form this thought, he realized the familiar feeling of his inner connection with the fourth archangel was, once more, a reality. He answered, "My inner sense of Gabriel's essence vibration was gone, and it remained absent even after I awoke. Now, your question has made me realize that it has returned. This must mean he is recovered!"

"As assuredly as you were also not harmed by the daemons. Now, let us have done with thoughts about the Lord of Practicality! My curiosity lies with the properties of the crystals. You asked me for what I am searching? I wish to find my own beam-emitting weapon."

Seriel jumped up from the flat crystal and declared, "The light wand is much more than a weapon! That is one of my reasons for coming here. I wished to inform you that, when we are in the proximity of the crystals, they enhance and focus our thoughts. When the daemons were attacking Gabriel, I wished I could destroy them. My crystal understood my thoughts and acted upon them by striking those evil creatures with its light beam. Since discovering this truth, I have remembered your home is constructed of etheric minerals. I believe it is necessary to alert you to the possible implications of dwelling within crystal energy."

The first archangel stood for a short while in thoughtful pose, but his ruminations were shielded from his brother.

Finally, he observed, "As always, dear Seriel, you stimulate my curiosity and sense of purpose. Your discovery opens up a wealth of possibilities which I will happily pursue. But tell me, how did you know your light wand was the correct one for you? I have been searching through these many crystals and have not yet come upon a specimen which seemed appropriate for me."

Seriel considered not relating his vision to Samael, but decided to retell a part of it. He explained, "I entered a very large mineral and was shown myself holding a crystal with the light beam projecting from it. Soon afterwards, I found the exact same one lying close by."

"Such adventures you have been having without me! Entering crystals and having visions. The Lord of Sorcery is truly magical!" There was just a hint of sarcasm in this thought.

Ignoring his sibling's tone, Seriel replied, "I was also shown a vision of Gabriel lying prone and injured. That was, of course, before you set the daemons upon him."

Samael questioned, "Did you not tell me it was your spheres that displayed Gabriel's downfall? What are you imparting now? Is this another revelation of deception?"

"No, I was truthful. I saw Gabriel's demise in both the spheres and the visions given to me while I remained within the large crystal."

"Ah! It would appear that you are becoming a seer. All hail Archangel Seriel, the Lord of Sorcery and Wondrous Visions!" Samael bowed his head, as if in reverence. Then standing up straight, once more, he asked, "Perchance, were you shown this lowly archangel brandishing a light wand? Or are such crystals only accessible to the Lord of the Seventh Essence?"

Although his brother's attitude appeared to be sarcastic jesting, Seriel knew Samael was observing him closely. He was seeking information, but not in a forthright manner. If the seventh archangel lied, his sibling would surely be aware and press him for the truth. Therefore, Seriel responded, "Yes, you were also in the vision and possessed your own light wand."

Abandoning his bantering mode, Samael pleaded, "Then aid me in my search for it! Having been shown my light wand, you can distinguish it from all the other crystals that are here."

The two brothers began to move among the scattered minerals. Samael allowed Seriel to do the actual searching while he kept a close watch beside him. After a fruitless exploration, the seventh archangel concluded, "The wand I saw in the vision is not here. It was distinctive and none of these crystals bear a resemblance to it."

With a wry smile Samael admitted, "Of course, I would require a weapon befitting my own uniqueness. Pray tell me, dear sibling, how did my crystal differ from yours?"

Seriel withdrew his light wand from its holster in order to help clarify his explanation. "It was clear and without color, like this one, but did not possess the inner crystals. However, at its tip . . ." he indicated the crystal's point, " . . . it branched out into three separate crystals."

"Which emitted three separate light beams, I presume?"

"Yes, indeed, that is how I saw it."

The first archangel appeared well-pleased. He exclaimed, "A truly powerful weapon with three times the destructive energy of yours! I cannot wait to wield it!" Samael clasped his hands together and began to swing an imaginary light wand from side to side.

Feeling compelled to reiterate his previous warning, Seriel stated, "Remember what I have told you, Samael! Crystal energy is highly potent and must be respected."

Bringing his arms back to his sides, Samael answered, "Yes, yes, I hear you. But how can I use it with respect when I do not possess it? Where can my light wand be?" His thoughts ceased, but then suddenly began, again. He asked, "Do you suppose it is among that second crop of crystals that I

discovered? The ones from which I constructed my abode?"
He grasped hold of Seriel's wand and demanded,
"Command your crystal to take us to that place immediately!"
Seriel quickly pulled his sibling's hand from the light
wand, which he then returned to the holster. He retorted,
"Ordering a crystal to take us somewhere is not respecting
it, Samael! Be patient and I will inquire whether it will take
us there." He silently asked his wand whether it was willing
to do his bidding. It immediately vibrated in response and,
therefore, he requested it to transport them to the other
area of etheric minerals.

Instantly, they were there, standing in the midst of the
many crystals. Samael declared:

"You called it crystal sorcery and, indeed, it is that! Now,
let us look for my light wand." The first archangel began
rummaging through a nearby pile of crystals which he had
previously discarded as unsuitable to become Malkura's jewel.

Seriel watched with dismay as his brother tossed aside
each rejected crystal. He queried, "Must I remind you, yet
again, about respect? These etheric minerals possess Source
consciousness, even as we do, thus, they are worthy of being
handled with less vigor."

"I am certain they are just as stalwart as are we," replied
Samael. "Come, help me find the thrice-pointed wand!"

The seventh archangel was beginning to wonder whether
he should have given his sibling any information about the
intensity of crystal energy. He could well imagine Samael
using this powerful force in ways that were disruptive and
damaging. Seriel recalled the image of himself and his
brother wielding their light wands and fighting against some
angels. What would cause such an event to happen? Yet it
was too late to regret sharing his knowledge with Samael.
All he could do was trust it would not lead to any great
upheavals. A sudden idea came to Seriel and he silently asked
his light wand to show him the location of Samael's crystal,
but only if it was to be his brother's true companion. Seriel

elaborated on his request. He informed his crystal he wanted it to reveal a light wand which would forever protect Samael and never allow him to completely abandon his angelic heritage.

Something at the edge of Seriel's perception caught his attention. For an instant he thought he saw a twinkling light some distance in front of where he stood. It was there and then it was gone. Seriel felt drawn toward the place. He walked on ahead, followed by Samael, who asked:

"What is happening? You appear to know where to go. Have you been shown my crystal?"

Reaching the area, Seriel was confronted by a wall of minerals which had grown into a completely enclosed circle. After walking all the way around them, he realized their structure was impenetrable. The crystals rose up too high to climb over and there were no spaces between them. Each standing mineral was touching its neighbors, preventing access into the ring's interior. The seventh archangel told his brother, "I believe your light wand is enclosed within this circle of crystals. There appears to be no way of entering it, therefore, I will ask my wand to take me inside."

"Go quickly! I will await you here," replied Samael.

Even as he perceived his sibling's answering thought, Seriel was silently asking his light wand to take him into the center of the crystal ring. His request was immediately granted and he stood within the circle's core. The energy inside there was exceedingly strong. Seriel began to feel somewhat overwhelmed by it. Even so, he felt a growing desire to stay within this place and just allow his consciousness to wander aimlessly. There was also a similar sense of peace and protection to what he had experienced within the large, clear crystal. This was a place to let his thoughts and feelings drift away. As if from a far off distance, Samael's questions intruded upon his developing state of tranquillity:

"What is happening? Is my light wand there? Hurry back to me with it!"

Seriel had almost forgotten why he had entered the circle. His intention was not to partake of its powerful energy, but to find Samael's crystal! Pulling himself back into alertness, Seriel scanned the small circular area in which he stood. The wand lay against one of the standing crystals, and he was suddenly convinced it had caused them to form into a wall of protection around itself. He took the few steps that brought him to the wand and he gently lifted it up.

It was an amazingly beautiful specimen, having faultless clarity and a tactile smoothness that awakened Seriel's etheric sense of touch. It was narrower than his own wand and the cluster of three crystals protruding from its end gave it greater length. Each of the crowning crystals was identical and together they were positioned in a three-pronged circle. By holding the light wand and moving it back and forth, Seriel quickly realized it was not a crystal with which he would feel at ease. Although exquisite, it neither felt comfortable in his hand nor in harmony with his thoughts. He could perceive a profound power within it which assaulted his etheric sense of balance. The seventh archangel staggered and dropped to one knee, unable to maintain a sturdy stance. His brother's urgent thoughts came to him, again:

"What is keeping you from me? Do you have my crystal?"

Seriel was beginning to feel unwell. His kneeling position was becoming unsteady and he did not have the strength to stand back up. Knowing he must release his hold on the wand immediately, he begged his own crystal to take him back outside the circle of minerals. Instantly, he was kneeling in front of Samael and he thought-cried, "I pray you, take your wand!"

His sibling snatched the crystal from his hand, partly due to his strong desire to hold it, but also because he was quickly aware of Seriel's distress. As he tightened his grip around the crystal, it molded its lower end into a hilt, just as Seriel's light wand had adjusted itself. Samael held the wand aloft and closed his eyes as its mighty force coursed through him. He declared:

"Indeed, this is my light wand! I can feel its energy igniting my soul's essence. Behold! It has such power that it vibrates."

Once the crystal was taken from him, Seriel was able to stand, again, and his sense of balance was quickly restored. Uncertain whether it's energy would also affect his brother adversely, he suggested, "Be ready to lay the light wand down, Samael. Its power is exceedingly strong and proved to be too much for me. I was feeling ill and in danger of falling down."

"That is not what I am experiencing! I am invigorated and inspired!" The Lord of Lightning-Swiftness danced around in a circle, waving the light wand over his head. "Can you see it vibrating, Seriel? I can feel its forceful energy waves moving through my whole body."

Obviously, the crystal was not impacting on Samael in the same manner it had affected Seriel. This must mean it was the right wand for him. It was even vibrating, which indicated it was aligning itself with its owner. Seriel explained, "The vibration is a form of communication. My crystal vibrates when it understands my thoughts and is willing to act upon them."

Pausing from his gleeful dance, Samael replied, "That is pleasing information. My wand is ready to do my bidding and I will . . ."

A sudden, disturbing motion behind his brother interrupted the first archangel's thought. Turning around, Seriel discovered the ring of crystals had broken apart and they were laying about the area in disarray. This only served to convince him even more that Samael's crystal had caused the minerals to form into a protective shape around it. Now, it was with its rightful companion and, therefore, did not require the combined power of other crystals to keep it safe.

MARION WEBB-DE SISTO

"That is an oddity!" remarked Samael. "The circling barricade of crystals is gone."

"I believe they were only there to protect your crystal. It caused them to create that formation until our discovery of it. There is no longer a need for those minerals to remain together."

"What a clever crystal you are!" Samael stroked the length of the wand with one hand. "Now, I must fashion a holder for you, just as my sibling has done."

Seriel withdrew his own crystal and tucked it under one arm. He then untied his holster and offered it to Samael. "Do you wish to examine mine closely so that you can copy the design?"

"No, dear brother, I will create a different one from yours. My wand has greater length and, thus, would rest awkwardly against my side. I have another notion of how to carry my crystal." Samael stood silently, as though deep in concentration. An etheric object began to appear in front of him. It was fashioned from a similar substance to Seriel's holster, but it was longer and more narrow. Two long straps were apparent, one attached close to the top opening of the holder and the other at the closed bottom.

Samael grasped the finished etheric creation and placed his wand into it with the tri-crystal points protruding from the top. Next, he tied the two straps together by their ends so that they formed a large loop. Then, opening his left wing outwards, he slung the quiver-like holder over his left shoulder. He adjusted the straps' knot until the crystal wand lay comfortably against his back. Next, Samael drew his wing closed, then spread it widely, again, and declared:

"There! I can move my wing easily without dislodging the crystal and there is no discomfort when my wings are folded. I am well pleased with my light wand's new home."

After re-attaching his own holster to himself and returning the crystal to it, Seriel asked, "What next, Samael? How do you plan to use your light wand?"

His brother already appeared to be looking around, once more, for something. He answered, "I believe I should first become well acquainted with what my crystal can do before deciding how best to use it." A wicked grin came and went as he added, "Perhaps I will hone my aiming skills by blasting some daemons into oblivion. That might prove amusing. But now I am searching for another crystal. Our sister will be greatly perturbed with me because of what befell Gabriel. Therefore, I must make her a gift. A token of my love will undoubtedly lessen her annoyance."

Seriel believed the Shekinah's unhappiness with her brother would not be appeased so easily. He offered, "I think Malkura will need more than a gift to feel forgiveness toward you. She holds a great love for each and every one of her brothers and must be immensely saddened by Gabriel's misfortune. A crystal will not compensate for what you have done."

A look of sadness crossed Samael's face as he agreed, "You are probably correct, dear brother, but I must try to win back her affection. That is why I intend to give her something quite unique. Watch!"

The first archangel picked up a hand-size clear mineral that was broken at its point. He gently rubbed this crystal between his palms. As his hands moved around and around, the crystal became flat and was molded into a circular shape. Next, he clasped the altered mineral in his right hand and touched it with the fingertips of his left hand. A small stream of silver flowed from his fingers and quickly spread throughout one side of the flattened crystal.

Holding this new creation out in front of himself at arm's length, Samael proclaimed, "This gift will surely please our sister! The sheen of the crystal combined with the brightness of the silver produces a reflection of anyone who is positioned before it. My inner vision perceives my image within this crystal as I hold it." He moved the mirror-like object up and down, and from side to side, as he observed every aspect of his etheric form. Then he held it close to his face and stated, "Indeed, I am a handsome fellow!"

As before, Seriel wondered if Samael's etheric eyes were doing more than just being a feature of his face. He questioned, "Can you see with your etheric eyes? Once or twice, I have suspected they are functioning in conjunction with your inner vision."

Moving the crystal away from his face, Samael responded, "My ever-observant brother! Yes, there are occasions when my inner sense of vision seems to be directed through my eyes. It does not always happen, but is taking place more frequently. Have you not experienced the same ability?"

"No, or if it is happening, I have not realized it. Henceforth, I will monitor how my inner vision is perceiving everything."

"A wise decision. I have concluded it is an expression of my evolution, thus, it should manifest for you, too." Another wicked smile graced Samael's face for an instant. "Unless, of course, it is peculiar to me because I am the first-born of the Source." He suddenly moved close to Seriel and pulled him into a tight embrace. "Thank you, my sibling, for helping me find my own light wand. I am indebted to you. Now, I will take my leave of you so that I can go to my home and decide upon where and how I will ask for Malkura's forgiveness. May you remain within our parent's keeping!" Samael released his hold of his brother, spread his wings and lifted off, while clutching his sister's intended gift close to his chest.

Seriel stood motionless as Samael flew away. He was amazed by the first archangel's sudden bodily expression of gratitude. Being held close to his sibling was a pleasing new experience. It evoked a feeling that was reminiscent of melding, but was not so intense. Existing in an etheric body was proving to be an evolving, enthralling adventure.

Left alone, Seriel began searching through the standing and fallen minerals. He, too, was looking for a crystal. His recent thoughts about Samael's home being a crystalline construction, had prompted an idea. Seriel was very happy with his pyramid, but he was considering the possibility of improving it with the addition of some crystal energy. After exploring several large specimens, most of which were either clear, or yellow, or brown, in color, he came upon one which he felt certain was what he needed. It stood three times his height and was broader at its base than at its apex. This crystal was devoid of color, but was not as clear as Samael's wand. Wispy swirls and internal facets deep within itself created an almost mesmerizing effect as Seriel scanned its depth with his internal gaze.

Pulling his concentration back from the towering mineral, he drew his light wand and asked it to emit a broad beam which would encompass both him and the chosen crystal. Immediately, they were both bathed in a wide, pale blue ray of light. Seriel then requested his wand to take them both into close proximity of his home. Instantly, they were there and the beam retracted into the wand. Next, he thought-cleaved and then disintegrated the top section of his pyramid. He told his crystal he wanted it to replace the missing apex with the huge mineral. Once again, the beam projected from the wand. It enveloped the large crystal, which was then instantly moved from its former position to the top of the pyramid. Finally, Seriel asked the crystal to reshape itself so that it would become an exact replica of the pyramid's original apex. This quickly took place and the crystalline addition was now a part of his abode.

Seriel thanked his wand and replaced it in the holster, once the light beam had vanished. He entered his pyramid, eagerly anticipating the effects of heightened energy from the crystalline capstone.

Chapter Sixteen

C oming back from viewing the spheres in Seriel's Spiral, Michael discovered Gabriel exchanging thoughts with the Christ Soul, Raphael and the Shekinah. He noticed the fourth archangel's innate red hue was even brighter than before. His brother had already shared with their siblings how Seriel attempted to help him overcome the daemons. Gabriel was now relating the vague memories of his sojourn with the Source:

" . . . and that sense of peace and love remains with me. Ah, here is Michael! Greetings! I understand I am indebted to you for bringing me to our parent."

"It was nothing more than what any brother would do. Your life essence was rapidly flowing away and I knew the Source was the only being who could save you."

"Nevertheless, I am eternally grateful for your loving concern. I have been telling our siblings of my experience." Gabriel glowed even more brightly. "My memories are incomplete and somewhat veiled. However, the knowledge that our parent is filled with love for us has remained with me. I also remember I could have rejoined with the Source, if I had chosen to do so. Obviously, I did not make that choice, but my reason for not doing so eludes me."

"Perhaps you felt the need to confront Samael?" asked Michael. "His behavior has gone beyond understanding."

"But not beyond forgiveness, I trust?" This came from the Christ Soul. "If you hold animosity against him, it will lead to further conflict. We all must endeavor to feel compassion for Samael. If we harbor anger, it will serve to strengthen his desire to be separate from us."

Gabriel replied, "The most amazing outcome of this happening is my realization that I do not feel a desire for revenge. Within my thoughts, since I left the comfort of the Source, I have reviewed what took place when I went to inspect Uriel's home. Just before the daemons attacked, he told me I was to pay penance for ridiculing him in front of the angels. I am truly astounded that I do not want to also bring pain to him. I can only conclude my close connection with our parent has changed me in some way."

To each of the other four archangels, this insight into their brother's feelings was extremely surprising. They would have expected Gabriel to be denouncing Samael's odious behavior and declaring he should be soundly punished. It would, indeed, appear their parent had healed more than his severe injuries. Michael questioned:

"Are you not concerned Samael may treat another sibling or angel in the same manner to which you were subjected?"

"Yes, I have determined this could happen, although I believe I am the sibling with whom he has the most disharmony." Gabriel's thoughts ceased for an instant, but then continued: "I think we must consider how best to ensure he will not set the daemons on any other angelic being."

Breaking her thought-silence, the Shekinah suggested, "I believe we archangels should meet, as we frequently used to do. As a council, we can confront Samael with our concerns. We could also inform him of how saddened we are by what happened to Gabriel."

Each of her brothers knew she was referring to her own feelings. They were well aware of how deeply she loved Samael and that she must be greatly troubled by his cruel actions. Raphael offered:

"We could demand Samael promises to never, again, do anything injurious to us or to any angel."

Michael asked, "And if he promises, how can we be certain he will never renege?"

"We cannot be certain," responded the Christ Soul. "We would have to trust him to keep to his agreement."

"And what if he will not promise?" was Michael's next question.

The thought exchange was stilled as each sibling contemplated this possibility. Knowing how self-willed and determined Samael could be, it was most probable that Michael's query would need to be answered.

The Christ Soul finally ended their silence by replying, "Then we either accept the possibility of another daemonic attack or we decide upon a strategy to prevent our brother from harming another soul."

"How could we do that?" asked Raphael.

"I believe I have been shown the answer," Michael told the group. "During the resting phase, the Source sent dreams to me which seemed to portray future happenings. I was shown ALL THAT IS, as if from a great height above Chaos. Our existence spirals out from our parent and will be divided into sections, each overseen by an archangel. Samael's domain was the outermost part of the spiral. This made little sense to me. Our brother is the first-born of the Source, therefore, it would appear his level of the spiral would come first, followed by that of the Christ Soul. Yet the divided spiral did not conform to this supposition. The Christ Soul's section was next to the Source and Samael's level lay eighth. Now, it is occurring to me that level is where Samael must reside, if he will not promise to do no further harm."

Gabriel proffered, "Why would Samael agree to stay in the outer part of the spiral? I cannot imagine him agreeing to be confined to only one part of Chaos."

Michael explained, "The level next to Samael's was mine. If he is to be confined, then I believe the Source wants me to prevent him from moving inwards along the spiral."

"With no disrespect to you, my brother, I believe it would take a mighty force to stop Samael going wherever he so desired," commented Gabriel.

Deciding not to share, on this occasion, his dream about the angelic battle, Michael responded, "Of course, I may be interpreting my dreams incorrectly."

"Let us hope your dreams were, just like some of the spiraling orbs, possible happenings which will not take place," suggested the Shekinah. "Perchance our brother will agree to refrain from pursuing his unkindly behavior."

There was an overwhelming sense of sadness within this thought and Raphael placed an arm around her shoulders, as he stated, "We each know how deeply you love our brother, dear Malkura. I have always admired and respected him and I am also profoundly grieved that his radiant soul is dimming."

The Shekinah laid her head against Raphael's arm for a short while and she clasped the emerald tightly in one hand. It was hidden in the rulpiel-colored material which Samael had fashioned for her. Earlier, she had tied the green gem into the central section of the material, creating a safe, pouch-like home for it. Malkura then positioned this etheric scarf so that it, and the concealed emerald, lay as a necklace on her chest. The ends of the material were tied behind her neck, and they hung down over the growth point of her wings.

She sighed deeply and, lifting her head, she removed the rulpiel necklace, untied the knots and revealed the exquisite jewel. Extending her open hand, the Shekinah offered the emerald for her siblings' inspection. She told them, "I cannot understand how a soul could create this sheer beauty and yet also beget the pure ugliness of causing great harm to Gabriel. This emerald was fashioned for me by Samael as a token of his love. How can such glory come from one who is capable of a diabolical deed?"

Michael gently took the jewel from Malkura's hand and cradled it while he scanned it with his inner vision. Then he passed it to Raphael who, after a short pause, held it out close, first to the Christ Soul, and then to Gabriel. Not being in etheric form, they were unable to grasp hold of the emerald, but they could examine it with their inner senses while it rested in Raphael's hand.

"From what did Samael create this beautiful item, Malkura? There is something strongly reminiscent of the Source within its energy," remarked the Christ Soul.

"Our brother fashioned it after he and Seriel discovered some fluid objects floating in the Abyss," answered the Shekinah. "They grew into beautiful structures when Samael touched them. Then he built his home and this emerald from some of those structures. We do not know what created the aqueous globules, but Samael believes they came from the Source."

The Christ Soul replied, "This emerald is truly splendid, and I can understand why you are puzzled, sweet sister. But perchance it is not only Samael who can behave in such opposed ways. It well may be that we are all subject to both good and evil intentions."

Adding support to this theory, Michael commented, "Indeed, that may be true. The daemons came from Samael and Seriel, then later from Uriel. When I viewed them, they appeared to be timid, even fearful creatures. Yet we now know they can act in a vicious and unkindly manner. Apparently they have an evil side to their nature so perchance we possess one, as well."

Gabriel suddenly gave a thought-moan and declared, "Your mention of the daemons has reminded me of something that took place while I was under attack. My essence was seeping from my wounds and, as it dripped into the Abyss, the droplets moved away, as if they were alive. My angels have told me how the daemons came into existence, therefore, I am realizing I have also created more daemonic creatures."

"If that has happened, then it is further proof that duality lies within us all," declared the Christ Soul. "We believe we are beings of light, yet evil creatures can be spawned by us. It would seem Lord Samael is not so different from we other archangels."

Retrieving her emerald from Raphael, the Shekinah secured it in the etheric material, which she then replaced around her neck. She told her siblings, "I know you are attempting to make me feel less unhappy about Samael, but none of us has yet caused harm to another. My loving brothers, I thank you for your kindness, but I must accept this truth. The first archangel is no longer a radiant soul."

Raphael quickly responded, "Trying to lessen your sadness is important to each of us, but I believe we are also realizing an eternal truth. Souls can be swayed by goodness or evil."

Thought-murmurs of agreement came from the Christ Soul and Michael, while Gabriel announced:

"Malkura, pay heed to Raphael's reasoning. You say none of us has yet brought pain to another, but I shared unkindly thoughts about Samael with the angels. That is the reason why he wanted revenge on me. My melding with our divine parent seems to have changed my opinion of both myself and our brother."

"Then does that mean we should not form a council and require Samael to promise never to bring suffering to another?" asked Michael.

A resounding "No!" came from the four archangels, and the Shekinah added:

"We must attempt to make our brother understand we will not tolerate his cruel actions."

"Then it is agreed!" exclaimed Michael. "We shall meet and put before Samael the severity of what he has done. If he will swear an oath to never behave so unkindly, again, we must trust he will not break that promise. However, if he will not offer his agreement, then we will give consideration to exiling him to the outermost area of the life force spiral."

Gabriel asked, "Where shall we conduct this council meeting?"

"I think it should be our old meeting place which is close to the Source," suggested Michael. "In that way, the Christ Soul can remain his auric self, as can Gabriel, if he so chooses."

"I have not yet decided upon which state to continue my existence," replied Gabriel. "Presently, I am content to be as I am, but I have another proposal to put forward. Shall we also request certain angels to attend the meeting? Their input may prove helpful."

"Which angels do you propose?" questioned Michael.

Gabriel explained, "The original first castings and pure essence angels are closer to us in their energy vibrations than any others. What think you of them?"

The Christ Soul offered, "I believe that is an excellent suggestion."

"I agree," added Michael. "The additional presence of seven catalyst, and seven pure essence, souls would surely indicate to Samael our deep concern. It also occurs to me that Belial and Azazel would be numbered among these angels because of their casting orders. They were witnesses to the daemons' attack, therefore, they could make a sound judgment on this matter."

"As were Semyaza and Kokabel," remarked Gabriel. "They should also be present."

Raphael asked, "When do you think we should hold this meeting?"

"As soon as we are all gathered together," answered Michael. "Does anyone disagree?"

No one argued against his suggestion, but Raphael reminded his siblings:

"We all know how stubborn Samael can be. It may take a duration to persuade him to attend. I am willing to go to him and explain what we have decided. I trust he will accompany me, but our return may not be speedy."

"No, Raphael," stated the Shekinah. "I wish to be the one to bring him before our council. I have private thoughts I want to share with him about what he has done. I also believe I am more able to persuade him to attend than any other sibling."

"You are correct, dear sister," replied Raphael. "it would be difficult for him to refuse you. I will go in search of Seriel and Uriel instead and bring them to the meeting."

"Then I will seek out the angels," offered Michael. "Christ Soul, Gabriel, will you both remain here?"

"No," responded the second archangel. "I am anxious to consult with our parent to learn whether it approves of our decision or chooses to make other proposals. I wish you all to fare well until we meet, again." He flowed away from the group in the direction of the Source.

"Come, sister," invited Raphael, "I will accompany you until we separate to find our brothers." He and the Shekinah flew away in an outward direction, leaving Michael and Gabriel alone.

"Are you content to stay here without company?" asked Michael.

"I have decided to go with you. Exchanging thoughts about my auric condition has made me realize I am curious to learn whether my etheric body can be wholly reclaimed. My wings were destroyed so would they reform, again, or would I exist wingless? I will keep company with you until we reach the area of Chaos where etheric form can be manifested. Then I will discover the condition of my new body. After that I will also seek out the angels we have decided should be a part of the council."

Michael did not appear to be in any haste to leave. He told his brother, "I believe your etheric body will be restored just as it was. You were in one of my dreams and your wings were quite evident. They were as glorious as they were before." Then he announced, "Before we go, I wish to share another part of that dream which I chose not to tell the others. I did not want to cause even more sorrow to our sister. I was shown you and me, together with many angels, fighting against Samael and Seriel. There were daemons and some angels alongside them, too. Each of we four were holding some kind of weapon which gave forth a terrible beam of light. These energy rays caused great harm and destruction. This has made me believe Samael does not feel remorse and will refuse to be confined. It would appear a great battle is the only way we can subdue him."

"That is sad news, but not surprising. We know Samael follows his own desires and is beholden to none." Gabriel then added, as an afterthought, "Seriel used a weapon with a light beam on the daemons in an attempt to help me. I believe he destroyed some of them with it."

"Perhaps it was the same one I saw him wielding in my dream," observed Michael.

After a short pause, Gabriel offered, "Yet perchance your dreams were, as our sister suggested, only possible realities."

"I think not. I believe they displayed future happenings. When I awoke from the resting phase, I traveled to Seriel's Spiral to see whether such a battle is recorded there. It is very difficult to find any one particular sphere because they are in such close proximity to each other." Michael's face became clouded with sadness as he added, "Yet with perseverance I discovered an orb displaying this frightening event. It seems it will become a reality and is not just a possibility."

A little shiver ran through Gabriel's auric being as he stated, "Life is becoming so much more complicated than when we were first created . . ." He stopped and then interjected, "Oh! I believe I shared that exact thought with the Source. I cannot remember how our parent responded, but it prompts a vague memory of the Source telling me something about Samael. What an annoyance! It is just beyond the edge of my consciousness, but I cannot retrieve it."

"Perhaps our parent ordered you to forgive Samael? You appear to not be angry with him or in need of seeing him punished."

"Contrary to what I have always thought, I now believe the Source does not order us to do anything. Therefore, I am sure that did not happen." Gabriel became lost in his own thoughts, but, eventually, continued, "I remember feeling a great rage toward Samael while I was with the Source, but something took it away. It seems to me it was because of what our parent told me about its first-born son. Yet whatever it was is gone completely from my memory."

"Well, it has certainly created a change in your attitude with regard to Samael. And may I dare to add that this Gabriel is much more agreeable than his former self?"

Chuckling thoughts were shared between the two siblings, easing their sense of gloom. They began their journey toward the level where etheric matter could be formed, with Michael walking beside Gabriel's flowing motion.

*   *   *

The Shekinah and Raphael flew to Uriel's abode. They had decided their brother would either be in, or close by, his new home. Malkura led the way because Samael had shown her the structure before giving it to Uriel. Their thoughts were silent as they journeyed along. Both were lost in the sadness of their first sibling's decline from his angelic self.

As they reached the magnificent building, they found their sixth-born brother sitting on the steps of his home. He was looking extremely dejected. Standing close by were Belial and Semyaza, who appeared to be deep in an exchange of thoughts. Alighting in front of the abode, the two archangels approached their seated sibling. Raphael announced:

"Salutations, dear brother, we come to bring you news of Gabriel."

"He is recovered, is he not?" anxiously asked Uriel. "I can sense his essence vibration, once again."

"Indeed, he is well and appears to be renewed and even changed within his essence," replied the Shekinah.

"That is blessed news!" exclaimed Uriel.

"It is true," added Raphael. "He is far less judgmental and admonishing than before."

The sixth archangel explained, "I have been distraught with worry and fear that he would not regain his strength. I even thought he might be no more. Have you come to take me to him?"

"No," replied Raphael. "I have come to bring you to a council which will gather in our old meeting place."

"A council?" questioned Belial. The two angels had drawn close so that they could perceive the archangels' thoughts.

"A council who will establish whether Samael intends to ever behave so cruelly, again," informed the Shekinah.

"And if he does, we will decide whether to exile him away from us all," continued Raphael.

A look of horror appeared on Uriel's face. He thought-cried, "That is a terrible punishment! I am certain Samael had no notion the daemons would attack Gabriel with such evil force."

"Even so, the Christ Soul, Michael, Gabriel, Malkura and myself have reached the decision that Samael must be held accountable for his actions."

"Lord Samael will never agree to such a meeting," observed Belial.

The Shekinah told him, "I believe he will not refuse me. That is why I must go in search of him. Angel Belial, your presence is also required within the council. We have concluded that the original catalyst, and pure essence, souls could help us mediate. Now, I will take my leave of you, my brothers and . . ."

"May I attend, as well?" interrupted Semyaza.

Raphael answered, "Both you and Kokabel must be present because you witnessed what took place. You will be asked questions about it." He looked thoughtful, and then remarked, "Other angels may also wish to attend. We did not consider that possibility. What think you, Malkura?"

"I suggest you ask Gabriel whether other angels can take part in the meeting. It should be his decision because he suffered the attack. Our brother may allow other angels to be present, but not wish them to have input in the proceedings. Tell him this is what I have proposed in my absence."

Raphael clasped the Shekinah's hands in his own and, shielding his thoughts from the others, replied, "Indeed, I will, dear sister. Go swiftly to Samael and I pray he will show remorse so that your great love for him can remain unsullied."

Malkura squeezed his hands in a loving response then, withdrawing hers from his, she turned and made ready to fly away. On a sudden thought, she turned back to Raphael and offered, "I know that Seriel has also built himself a home in the shape of a pyramid, but I have not viewed it. It is most probably close to the surrounding structures created by Samael which we passed as we journeyed here. Therefore, you may not have to search too far to find him." Then, unfolding her wings, the Shekinah announced to the group, "May you all rest within the love of the Source!" She took flight in the direction of her brother's crystal abode.

It did not take long for Malkura to reach her destination. Samael's home was but a short distance away from the building he had gifted to Uriel. As she began to gently drift down to the front entrance, the golden doors opened and out came her brother accompanied by Azazel. Both were looking upwards at her, indicating they were already aware of her approach. Alighting at the base of the front entrance steps, Malkura offered, "Greetings Lord Samael and Angel Azazel!"

Immediately, Azazel replied, "Salutations, Lady Malkura! I have just learned from Lord Samael that Lord Gabriel is fully recovered. That is a blessing." Then turning to Samael he continued, "I will take my leave of you, my prince. I am certain you would prefer to exchange thoughts with your sibling without my presence."

Before the Lord of Lightning-Swiftness could also acknowledge her greeting, the Shekinah put forward, "I pray you, Azazel, tarry until I have explained why I am here."

Samael descended the steps and taking her hands in his, he caressed her fingertips with his thumbs. "My loving greetings to you, also. Yet no explanations are necessary, sweet sister. It is always a great pleasure to just bask in your selfless radiance."

Malkura sighed inwardly. It was going to be difficult to make her brother give his full attention to her reason for being there. Addressing Azazel, she continued, "Yes, our brother Gabriel has returned to us fully restored to his former well-being. Knowing this has taken place, we have decided to hold a council meeting. Lord Michael is looking for you. He is seeking out all fourteen original catalyst, and pure essence, angels so that they can be a part of the council." Then removing her hands from Samael's grasp, she told the first archangel, "You are also required to attend because we are gathering to discuss what happened to Gabriel."

Rolling his eyes, Samael exclaimed, "What a vexation! Why do we need to exchange thoughts about our sibling's temporary misfortune? He is well recovered so why does he wish to dwell upon what happened?"

"This was not Gabriel's suggestion, it was mine. He, the Christ Soul, Michael and Raphael have all agreed this is what we must do."

Obviously surprised by Malkura's explanation, Samael's thoughts were silent for a while. Taking the opportunity, Azazel announced:

"I will go in search of Lord Michael. I bid you both to fare well!" He spread his wings and flew off into the inner area of Chaos.

A silence followed between the two sibling archangels. The Shekinah was reviewing how best to ensure her brother would go back with her to the meeting. She was also steeling herself to not allow her love for him to divert her intention. Finally, Samael ended the stillness by offering:

"I pray you, come inside my abode and let us share our thoughts. I have been deprived of your loving company for too long." He grasped her arm firmly and led her up the steps and through the doorway.

Malkura was filled with ambivalence. She was allowing her brother to take her into his home so as not to exacerbate her reason for coming to him. Yet she did not wish to be in the surroundings that proclaimed his love for her. He had built this home for the two of them to share in happiness and harmony, but the Shekinah knew their love was doomed. Even if the Source had not made its request of her, Samael's unkindness to Gabriel had tainted the beauty and purity of their mutual devotion. Now, being with her sibling was proving to be extremely painful and upsetting.

Samael took Malkura into a room which was littered with odd-shaped crystals, etheric playthings, a stool and several chairs. He placed two of the latter constructions facing each other and invited her to sit down on one. Then seating himself opposite to her, he declared, "When I sensed your approach, I hoped you were coming to tell me you had forsaken your agreement with our parent. I could imagine you living here with me for all of eternity." He gave a rueful smile. "Obviously, that was a fantasy, but an exquisite one."

"How could you think I would be willing to live with such a cruel soul?" the Shekinah demanded. "I knew you were changing from your radiant self, but your action against our brother was truly diabolical."

"And what of his against me? Was it a kindly act to denounce me in front of the angels? You were not present and, thus, did not hear his cruelty. He told them I sought to set myself above other souls and that I have an overly proud nature."

"Unkind thought-words, indeed, but they did not merit a daemonic attack that drained Gabriel's life essence." Malkura leaned forward to emphasize her thoughts and declared, "Hear me, Samael! Without Michael's intervention, Gabriel would be no more."

The first archangel jumped up from his chair and began to stride back and forth. "I do not believe that! We cannot cease to exist. We are like our parent, eternal!"

"If that is true, then why did the Source give Gabriel the choice of rejoining with it or returning to existence in the Abyss of Chaos? If he had chosen the former, then he would only have been eternal by being a part of Source consciousness. He would have no longer been an individual soul."

Samael sat back down, again, and pulling his chair closer to his sister asked, "How do you know the Source offered that choice? Because Gabriel told you it was so?"

Angrily, the Shekinah stated, "Do not infer that Gabriel would tell an untruth! He remembered our parent giving him the two choices, but does not know why he chose to come back to us. The Source also told Michael that Gabriel might choose to stay with it."

Samael thought-muttered, "Gabriel probably chose to return just so that he could further aggravate me."

"I will not listen to such resentful reasoning!" Now, it was the Shekinah's turn to stand up and move away from the chairs. "It matters not what you think of Gabriel or whether we are eternal. All of your siblings, including me, believe you must be made accountable for what you did. Therefore, you are summoned before the council."

The first archangel stood back up and walked over to his sister. "For what purpose is this meeting to be held?"

"To discern whether you regret what happened to Gabriel. Whether you feel remorse and will promise never to behave so unkindly, again."

Moving even closer to Malkura, Samael asked, "And what if my response is not to the council's liking?"

"Then we will decide upon a punishment." She moved back a step, not wanting to feel his overpowering presence.

A thought of raucous laughter escaped from Samael as he declared incredulously, "Punishment! What foolishness is this? I am the first-born of the Source and am above such trifling matters."

"Harken to your response! Is not pride motivating your answer? Perchance Gabriel's observation to the angels was not misguided."

Samael started back from his sister in mock alarm. "The Lady Malkura has come to do battle! I am ill prepared for your barbs, my unmerciful sibling."

"Do not make light of my thoughts, Samael! Can you not see that you are too proud?"

Approaching his sister, once more, he stated, "I am as I have always been, the first archangel, your devoted brother and catalyst soul for all the angelic extensions of the Source. If I am filled with pride, it did not distress you previously. Gabriel's disapproving notions have influenced you into becoming judgmental of me."

"No, it is your wicked action which has caused me to view you differently. You were truly radiant when we were first created. You gave me your love and devotion without hesitation. Now, you are revealing another aspect of your nature. You can be cruel and, it would seem, even evil."

"And is Lord Samael the only soul guilty of such duality? Perchance we all may possess this contradiction."

The Shekinah told him, "It may surprise you to learn the Christ Soul has already made the same observation."

A thoughtful Samael replied, "My insightful brother. I have underestimated him." Then taking hold of Malkura's arms the first archangel gently drew her to him. Looking down into her face, he declared, "My love and devotion are yours for all of eternity. No matter what transpires, nothing can change that truth. I trust your love for me will endure even though you are presently unhappy with what I have done?"

The proximity of her beloved sibling was destroying the Shekinah's resolve to not be swayed from her reason for being there. As his beautiful eyes looked into hers, she suddenly knew without doubt that he was watching her from their purple depths. Even as this knowledge came to her, she also realized she was returning the gaze through her own etheric eyes. With a startled cry she lowered her eyelids and attempted to pull away from Samael.

He would not release her. Instead he pulled his sister even closer and demanded, "Open your eyes, Malkura! I know your inner vision is functioning through them just as mine is so doing. Do not be afraid. It is a natural progression of our abilities within our etheric form."

Reluctantly, the Shekinah did as Samael bid her and looked up, once again, at him. She explained, "That was disturbing. I was scanning you in the manner I have always viewed everything when abruptly I was observing you with my eyes. I am not certain I want to pursue that etheric sense."

Samael advised, "Do not try to restrict it. The more frequently you allow it to happen, the more quickly it becomes an innate ability. I began experiencing it soon after I manifested my etheric body." He gave her a disarming smile and observed, "But we have digressed, dear Malkura. I was declaring my unending love for you and was hoping to receive a similar affirmation from you."

Again, Malkura tried to break free from his hold on her, but he would not give way. Finally, she exclaimed, "Release me, my lord! I do not wish to be held in this manner."

Without any protest, the first archangel removed his hands from her arms and conceded, "Your desire is my command, sweet sister. Yet will you not confirm your love for me?"

"In truth, I know not what I am feeling. My love for you was great, but I am angered and saddened by what befell Gabriel. I pray you, do not ask this of me. I am too confused to give you an answer."

Stepping back, Samael replied, "I will accept that as an honest response. You feel confusion and that is understandable, but I believe your affection for me will endure. Your very essence is unconditional love, thus, I will not lose your devotion." He leaned toward her, again, and touched the rulpiel scarf which lay around her neck. Noticing the weight within its knotted center, he clasped the enclosed jewel for an instant in his hand. Then gently placing it back against her chest, Samael offered a broad smile and remarked, "I am delighted to know you carry my gift with you. I discern that as an expression of your love for me."

Lost for an answering thought, the Shekinah stood in silence. She decided Samael's needed agreement to attend the meeting was overdue. Malkura was about to remind him of such when he exclaimed:

"Wait here, sweet sister! I have yet another gift for you." He was gone from the room before she could reply.

She waited impatiently, promising herself that on his return she would insist on an answer from him about the meeting. The Shekinah was not kept waiting very long. He soon came back to her, proffering a round, shiny object. She also noticed he was carrying on his shoulder what appeared to be one of the shining structures in some kind of container. Indicating to the crystal mirror, Samael told her:

"I created this for you. This silvery side gives back an image of whatever is in front of it. Hold it in this manner . . ." He placed the mirror in her hand, then positioned it a short distance from her face. " . . . and you will see with your beautiful eyes why all of the archangels adore you."

Once again, he had managed to divert her attention from the reason she had come to his home. Yet knowing this, Malkura allowed her new etheric sense of sight to perceive what lay before her. She saw her small face, her rulpiel hair and her emerald green eyes. It was a pleasing sight and she became lost for a while just gazing at herself. Suddenly, she remembered the intended meeting and, handing the crystal mirror back to her brother, she stated, "It is a very special gift, but one I cannot accept. Do not attempt to win back my forgiveness by offering me this intriguing object. Now, you must tell me whether you will accompany me back to the council."

Samael walked over to his chair and placed the mirror on it. Coming back to her, he answered, "I understand your immediate refusal, it is to be expected. When you are less disenchanted with me, I will offer it to you, again, and I am certain you will accept it." He then reached over his left shoulder with his right hand and withdrew the light wand. "What think you of this, dear sister?"

Malkura was quickly becoming infuriated with him. When would he answer her request? She demanded, "Samael! Have done with this procrastination! Will you come with me to the meeting?"

Returning the crystal to its holder, he replied, "Again, when you are less annoyed with me, I will demonstrate my amazing light wand. As to your question, I need a short duration to contemplate whether or not to attend this ridiculous meeting. If you choose to wait here with me while I am deciding, that would please me well. However, if you prefer to return to our siblings immediately, then tell them I have not yet made my decision."

"That is not acceptable. You must either come now or refuse." The Shekinah had never before felt such anger against her brother or any other being. "You cannot keep us waiting while you indulge in indecision."

"I can do whatever I so wish, my lady. Tell the council to await my coming. If I do not appear, then they will know I have chosen not to attend." Samael took her hand and gently brushed his lips against her fingers. "May you fare well, my love, until the meeting, or until we encounter each other under more favorable circumstances."

Malkura snatched her hand from his grasp and walked quickly out of the room. She found her way to the open golden doors, passed through them, and was immediately in flight. It was a short while before she realized that, distracted by her anger, she was flying in the wrong direction. Feeling even more furious, she turned around and flew toward the meeting place.

Chapter Seventeen

T he proposed council slowly began to take form. All but two of the invited angels were now present and Michael traveled outwards, once more, in search of them. Both were catalyst souls, therefore, he presumed their innate first casting curiosity needed the stimulation of exploring the outer realms of the Abyss. While on his first angel search, the third archangel had also discovered Kokabel, and she accompanied him back to the meeting place. Raphael and Uriel found Seriel's pyramidal home without too much effort and he returned with them. The Christ Soul completed his thought exchange with the Source, but he did not discuss with anyone what had taken place.

Semyaza and Kokabel were not the only extra angels present. Most of the original group of fifty-six had approached the gathering. Later, several individuals from the second, third and fourth creation of angels had also arrived. All were waiting for the council's commencement. Once Raphael told Gabriel of the Shekinah's suggestion with regard to this matter, the fourth archangel agreed to allow these angels to remain. They were instructed to listen to the proceedings, yet not participate in them. Many more angels were in other areas of Chaos and, therefore, were unaware of what was happening. They would only learn of the council's deliberations afterwards.

The arrival of Gabriel, restored to his full etheric form, brought a sense of pure joy to many who were present. Previously, thought-word of his possible demise had quickly passed throughout the angelic horde. This was followed by much speculation about the outcome of this unprecedented event. Now, it was evident the Source had healed his terrible wounds. As Michael had assured him, his wings took form together with the rest of his etheric body. They were equally as powerful as before, and they now possessed veins of pure gold interlaced throughout their magnificence. His face and form glowed with the ruddiness of his fourth essence vibration and an unexpected smile graced his countenance as he exchanged thoughts with his brothers.

Seriel had agreed to go with Raphael, but was feeling deeply concerned. He was convinced that at some point during the meeting his own encounter with the daemons would be revealed. This would not only prove embarrassing for him, but also detrimental to Samael. Discovering the first archangel had caused harm to two of his siblings would surely increase the council's determination to chastise him severely. One attack was cause for alarm, but two would be unforgivable. Seriel brought his light wand with him in the hope he could feel a sense of security from its crystal energy. If he was forced to disclose what the daemons had done to him, he knew he would gain protection from merely touching the hilt of his wand. He might be questioned and possibly accused of complicity with Samael, but he would be given the strength to endure the ordeal.

Eventually, Michael returned with the two catalyst angels. Now, only the Shekinah and Samael were missing. The six archangels positioned themselves into a circle. Each catalyst and pure essence angel stood on either side of his or her own essence lord. Malkura's two angels, Manah and Ammashma, left a space between them for her to occupy. Azazel was on Seriel's right side and Balberith, the Lord of Sorcery's catalyst angel, stood on his left. The rest of the angels grouped themselves around and behind the circle. Some were close to their essence lord or lady's position, while others chose to be near the archangel with whom they felt in harmony. Seriel was soon aware that Mulciber, Rimmon and Shamshiel were immediately behind him. He also realized Kokabel was standing at the back of Azazel.

Michael instructed everyone to sit down as the council's duration would be long. This meant many angelic beings became seated. However, the Christ Soul and those who had not yet manifested bodily form, remained as they were. Being in an auric state did not require standing or sitting. Several of the audience angels brought etheric chairs and stools with them. Previously, the existence of these structures within the archangels' homes had quickly gained attention, and copying soon took place. The occupants of the circle were offered these comfort items, but all except Uriel and Gabriel refused them. A chair was placed in the space awaiting the Shekinah and a low stool was left in the center of the circle. It was presumed Samael would be seated there. The assembled angelic beings awaited the arrival of the last two archangels.

Finally, Seriel felt the approach of his sister, but there was no sense of Samael accompanying her. Even as this realization came to him, Manah, the Shekinah's pure essence angel announced:

"Lady Malkura is coming!"

Another angel pointed to a speck of movement in the distance. As it journeyed closer, all were soon able to see that it was the eighth archangel. She was alone. Thought-murmurs about this revelation traveled throughout the gathering. They were even continuing as she alighted in the middle of the circle. It was obvious by her facial expression that she was both angry and distressed.

Michael stood up and walked over to her. "Greetings, dear sister! Are we to conclude Samael has refused to come here?" He guided her over to the waiting chair and remained in front of her, once she was seated.

"No, his answer is more vexing than that," declared Malkura. "Samael has directed me to tell you he needs to consider whether or not he should attend this meeting. If he decides to come, then that is what he will do. However, should he choose to ignore our request, we will only know this by his absence."

Appearing to be more like his old self, Gabriel declared, "That is preposterous! How will we know his decision unless he appears? We could be waiting here until the next resting phase, not knowing whether he has refused us or is remaining undecided."

"I know, Gabriel, that is why I am so angry," answered the Shekinah.

"How long do you think we should wait?" asked Raphael.

Michael walked away from his sister and sat down, again, between his two angels. He offered, "I propose we begin this meeting while we are waiting. We can discuss what measures we will take in the event Samael does not come to us. If he is not here when we have finished our deliberation, then I believe we should enact upon whatever we have decided. What think you, Gabriel?"

"I am in agreement with your recommendation," the fourth archangel replied. "Does anyone else have a different suggestion?"

No other ideas were forthcoming, therefore, the circle began to discuss what action to take, if Samael remained absent. Seriel did not participate in this exchange because he knew his brother would come to the meeting. The first archangel's curiosity would never allow him to shun the proceedings. Samael would want to know exactly what the council members were putting forward. In particular, he would feel the necessity to witness both Gabriel's and the Shekinah's thoughts. Seriel was certain Samael's continuing absence was an example of his need to have power over a situation. By keeping his siblings waiting and uncertain of his intentions, he could hold sway over their actions.

The seventh archangel was soon proved correct in his speculation. Michael was in the middle of explaining why he thought banishing Samael to the outer area of Chaos was appropriate, when his first-born brother suddenly appeared in the center of the circle. One instant he was not there and the next, he was. Thought-gasps rippled through the assembled angelic beings. Such an instantaneous appearance had never before been experienced. Yet only Seriel was aware of how Samael had accomplished this astounding feat.

It was a certainty that the Lord of Lightning-Swiftness was dressed for the occasion. A long, narrow length of etheric material was wrapped around his neck. Its color was a mixture of maldor, odami and breal, and its extremities almost reached to his feet. One half of this scarf-type material flowed down the center of his back and between his wings, while the other half was billowing down the front of his body. He was wearing sandals with straps that criss-crossed up his legs to just below his knees. This etheric footwear was of a matching color to the scarf. On his left shoulder was the empty quiver-like holder and he was clutching the light wand in his left hand. A dazzling, diamond stud earring adorned the lobe of his left ear, and a stunningly beautiful emerald ring was also evident on his right forefinger. He had previously fashioned this piece of jewelry from another section of the same mineral which had produced Malkura's emerald. To complete this shock-and-impress appearance, Samael was sporting daemonic features. The tail he had crafted in brotherly fun with Seriel was, once more, evident. Most of its extent lay coiled around his right arm while two large horns projected from either side of his brow.

Instinctively Seriel knew these additional etheric possessions were Samael's expression of disdain for the purpose of the meeting. They were indicative of the first archangel's alliance with the daemons rather than with the Source. Seriel wondered how his siblings, and especially Malkura, would react to their brother's unique appearance.

Samael very slowly turned around in a complete circle, scrutinizing the seated ring of archangels and their essence angels. It was obvious his etheric vision was fully functional. Many of the council members were subjected to a piercing stare from those discerning eyes. When this intimidating inspection was finished, he strode over to Uriel and placing a hand on his sibling's shoulder, he declared:

"Salutations, my brother!" Then moving round the circle, he passed by the Christ Soul and Raphael, who both received a curt nod of his head. Next he reached Seriel, who was given the same greeting as Uriel, and Azazel gained: "Salutations, my trusty angel!" Each of those who were addressed returned the greetings while he stood before them. Now, it was Michael's turn to be acknowledged with another brief nod, and then on to Gabriel. The fourth archangel underwent a bold, brotherly scrutiny, all the way from the tips of his toes to the top of his head. When this examination was done, Samael observed:

"Gabriel, I see you are fully recovered and that your wings are undamaged." Without waiting for a response, he moved on until he stopped in front of Malkura. Instantly, the horns and tail vanished and Seriel knew their disappearance was due to Samael not wishing to alarm his sister. Acknowledging the Shekinah, the Lord of Lightning-Swiftness performed a deep, sweeping bow. His action caused several thought-murmurs within the watching angels. As he straightened back into a standing position, the first archangel greeted his eighth sibling with: "My warmest salutations to you, sweet Malkura! We are well met."

The Shekinah's anger had somewhat subsided, therefore, she managed to quietly respond, "My greetings to you also, my lord."

Turning from her, Samael strode back into the center of the circle until he reached the stool which had been placed there for him. A mischievous smile was evident as he announced, "It would appear my etheric constructions are being copied. I will take that as a compliment to my creativity." He sheathed the light wand inside its holder which he then removed from his shoulder. Samael sat down, crossed his legs and held the encased crystal on his lap. Then looking directly at Gabriel, he asked, "Shall we begin this effort-wasting diversion?"

"We do not consider this matter lightly, Samael." It was Michael who answered his question. "It is of grave concern to all of us. You have behaved in a manner which appalls your siblings and many of the angels."

"As you wish, Michael, but I believe this council is an exercise in pedantry. Why has Gabriel not sought me out so that we could settle our disagreement alone and without spectators? Further more, if the purpose of this meeting is to require my apologies to the Lord of Practicality, we can end the proceedings now. I have no intention of ever offering such."

The fourth archangel quickly responded, "I believe what has happened between us is much more than a disagreement. I was unkind to you, and your retaliation toward me has been threefold."

Samael stared intently at Gabriel, and Seriel suspected he was trying to establish why their brother would admit to a wrongdoing. However, ignoring this uncharacteristic admission from his fourth-born sibling, the first archangel replied:

"It is a matter of opinion as to whether my retaliation was greater than your injurious treatment of me. You appear to be in sound condition with no lasting effects from what happened to you. Whereas your denunciation of me has changed me forever. It brought me hatred and the need for revenge." Then, indicating the assembled angels with a sweep of his hand, Samael added, "Many of these angelic offspring now believe the first-born of the Source is to be ignored. He is considered to be an overly proud and witless soul. You described me as such to many of the first birthing of angels."

Michael intercepted with: "You can both go back and forth, discussing what happened, but that will not bring about a solution to this . . ."

"I believe Samael is merely explaining his feelings." It was Uriel who interrupted with this thought. "He has the right to tell Gabriel how his unkind thought-words impacted upon him."

"Indeed, he does," agreed Gabriel. "I also have the right to confront him. This is why we are here." He stood up and walked over to the seated Samael. "Yes, I am whole, once more, but only because of Michael's intervention and our parent's healing powers. Samael, I believe my demise was happening. The daemons robbed me of my very essence."

Clutching his sheathed light wand, Samael jumped up and stood looking down at the fourth archangel. He exclaimed, "That is an untruth! We cannot suffer a demise. Our souls are eternal, even if our auric selves or etheric bodies are gone."

Shaking his head in disbelief, Gabriel explained, "Our souls rest within our consciousness, our essence, and mine was draining into the Abyss. Samael, I lost all sense of myself and everything around me. I was becoming no more." He returned to his seat and slowly sat back down.

Samael also became seated, once more, and he began to tap one of his knees with the protruding, three-pointed crown of his light wand. "This is foolishness," he declared. "If you cannot accept that no great harm has befallen you, then it is futile to continue this discussion. I know the wounds in your etheric body would have closed over. I am certain I observed this beginning to happen, even as Michael lifted you up. Of course, you did lose some of your essence, but that is not a problem. I expelled a goodly amount of my own essence when I was enraged with you." He spread his arms wide to the angelic audience in order to emphasize this next thought: "You can all witness that it has caused me no harm." Then he smiled wickedly and offered, "And even your spent essence did not perish. It has swelled the ranks of the daemons and . . ."

The Christ Soul suddenly interjected, "Enough, Samael! We are not here to decide whether or not we are eternal. That debate merely serves to divert our reasons for holding this meeting."

Samael quickly responded, "Then pray tell me, my brother, what are the reasons?"

"One that is important to me is to learn whether you planned the attack on Gabriel, or did you just seize the opportunity when he came to view Uriel's home?" This question came from Michael.

Gabriel added, "And if the former is true, whose complicity did you engage?"

Seriel suddenly became aware that Kokabel was leaning forwards and thought-whispering to Azazel. He could not perceive what she was sharing because her thoughts were shielded, but he was certain something of importance was passing between them. Azazel turned his head slightly, as if to answer. Yet, again, his thoughts were blocked from all but Kokabel.

In utter disdain, Samael asked, "Do you consider I need others to manifest my desires? And as to your question, Michael, you will have to employ your problem-solving skills to unravel the answer. Doing so should bring back memories of happier occasions."

It was impossible for Seriel to know whether his sibling was genuinely reminiscing or merely being sarcastic. He remembered how, long ago, when the archangels were newly birthed, Michael was always the strategist for the 'how-to' of Samael's games and contests.

The Lord of Sorcery brought his attention to the Shekinah, wondering how this mention of past pleasures would impact on her. Malkura seemed lost in unhappy thoughts as she idly twisted a lock of her hair around two fingers. Her head was slightly bowed and an expression of deep sadness was etched upon her face. A strong desire to comfort her swept through Seriel and he offered this shielded thought:

"Sweet sister, do not despair. I am certain Samael longs for the innocence and joy of our early games, even as you and I do."

Lifting her head, she looked directly at him. Seriel immediately knew that, just like Samael, Malkura was seeing through her beautiful etheric eyes. A tentative smile came and went as she veiled her thoughts from everyone except the seventh archangel and replied:

"I thank you, dear brother. You are a true comfort to me."

Now, Seriel realized Samael was staring at him. Had he perceived the brief thought exchange? Was he becoming able to penetrate shielded musings? His sibling's angry, questioning thought exploded in his consciousness:

"Why is Malkura smiling at you? Are you sharing veiled intimacies with her?"

Fortunately for Seriel, in the same instant Gabriel told Samael, "Do not play games with us! The happy occasions for such amusements are long past. It will not be difficult to determine whether you planned the attack and were aided in it. I propose we question Uriel, Azazel, Belial, Semyaza and Kokabel. They were all present when the daemons assaulted me. Seriel, you were also there, but despite feeling unwell, you tried to help me. It may be necessary to question you later, but for now I am interested in explanations from the others."

Once again, shielded thought-whisperings were exchanged between Kokabel and Azazel. However, one last remark from Azazel was not blocked and Seriel clearly perceived:

"Patience, Kokabel!"

Turning to Uriel, Gabriel continued, "Were you aware of the daemons inside your home? If so, why were they there?"

It was obvious the sixth archangel was ill-prepared for these questions. No immediate answer came from him. As he sat on his stool, he shuffled his feet and clasped and unclasped his hands as they rested in his lap. Finally, he began, "I knew my daemons were there because I had shown them my abode. I . . ."

"Gabriel, do not question Uriel!" ordered Samael. "I can tell you what you want to know. My daemons and those of Seriel were secreted by me in Uriel's home when he had gone in search of you. Leave Lord Uriel alone! He is guilty of nothing."

Knowing how protective his brother was of their sibling, this lie was acceptable to Seriel. Yet he wondered whether Gabriel would be as understanding, if he realized he was being told an untruth.

Gabriel ignored Samael and continued to address Uriel. "So the only reason you and Semyaza came to me was to request my inspection of your home. Is that correct?"

Samael leapt up from his stool and strode over to the fourth archangel. He clutched the sheathed light wand in such a manner that the exposed crown pointed threateningly in Gabriel's direction. His thunderous thought-words echoed through everyone's consciousness: "Desist, I tell you! Ask me your questions!"

Seriel, Michael and Raphael all stood up, ready to intervene. However, Gabriel suddenly told Samael, "As you wish. It is not my intention to distress you. I pray you, be seated, once more, and you and I will hold a discourse on this matter."

Samael stood glaring at his brother for a short while longer, and then he returned to his seat. The three brothers also sat back down. Seriel felt sure the first archangel must be astonished by Gabriel's response. Earlier, Raphael had told him their sibling's melding with the Source had changed him. The manner in which he refused to be angered by his antagonist was certain proof of this. Seriel concluded that

Samael's unawareness of this development would leave him confused and highly suspicious of Gabriel's unusual behavior. He would probably believe his brother was trying to trick him in some way.

"Now, let us continue, Samael," stated Gabriel. "You hid the daemons inside the abode while Uriel was gone. This implies you planned the attack, does it not?"

"Indeed it does," replied Samael. Then revealing the depth of his emotions, he explained, "Your denunciation of me festered within my soul and I craved revenge. I care naught, if you believe that is evil. You had no provocation to make those cruel comments to the angels. Thus, I considered retribution was my right."

Gabriel quickly replied, "I can understand your reasoning even though I do not agree with it. I brought you pain and I wish to apologize for that. Your arrogance goaded me into behaving in an unkindly manner." His thoughts ended for a while, and Seriel wondered whether he was trying to change Samael's determination to make no apology. If that was his desire, he was to be disappointed. His sibling sat in silence, staring defiantly at him.

Eventually, the fourth archangel's thoughts began, again. "Now, we have established your intention to seek revenge, therefore, let us move to my other concern. Who was privy to your scheme?"

Without hesitation, Samael replied, "None! As I previously stated, I do not require the help of anyone to fulfill my desires. So let us have done with these tiresome questions. You now know I plotted to bring you harm. Therefore, what is your summation? What ludicrous consequences are you going to put forward?"

Seriel was uncertain whether Samael's denial of any complicity was further protection of Uriel, of the angels, or even of his seventh brother. Was the first-born of the Source displaying his original noble disposition or was his more recent, devious nature motivating his response? If he could bring this council to a hasty conclusion, there would be less risk of the daemonic assault on Seriel being revealed.

"We have yet to deliberate on how we will proceed," Gabriel commented. "It was necessary to establish whether what happened was planned or merely a sudden notion on your part. I was also curious to learn whether you acted alone. You have answered those queries. Yet I think it would be judicious to allow the angels, who were present during the attack, to add any observations they may wish to make. Then, each member of the council must decide whether castigation or some lesser measure should follow. Belial, Azazel, Semyaza and Kokabel, do you have anything to contribute?"

Belial and Semyaza shook their heads and Azazel answered:

"I only wish to make one comment. I have had close contact with the daemons and they are unpredictable. They are not ensouled and, thus, have no sense of right or wrong. I believe Lord Samael did not expect them to maim you. Therefore, I think castigation should not be an option."

"That will be decided by us all," replied Gabriel. "Now, if Kokabel has nothing . . ."

"I wish to make something known." It was Uriel who interrupted. He stood up, walked over to Samael and, leaning close to him, confided, "I thank you for your protection, dear brother, but I cannot allow the untruth to continue." Uriel touched his brother's hand in a gesture of fondness and then he turned to face Gabriel. "I knew of Samael's plan and I agreed to help him. I considered your humiliation of him was unjust and I supported his need for a reprisal. Our brother has lied about my complicity in order to protect me." He walked toward the fourth archangel and knelt down in front of him. "I ask for you forgiveness, Gabriel, of both myself and Samael. I did not know the daemons could behave so viciously and I am certain our brother was also unaware, just as Azazel has indicated."

Thought-gasps and exchanges abounded as all attention was centered on the kneeling archangel. A slight movement on the right side of Seriel distracted him, and he noticed that a further thought exchange was underway between Kokabel and Azazel. As Seriel scanned the two angels with his inner vision, he observed Azazel nodding his head. Immediately, Kokabel rose from her seated position and stepping between Seriel and Azazel, she crossed over to Gabriel. This fifth cast angel declared:

"My lord, I also wish to confess to aiding Lord Samael. My reason for doing so was the same as Lord Uriel's and I am in agreement with him and Angel Azazel. The Lord of the First Essence underestimated the cruelty of the daemons. He only wished to frighten you. I know he believed they would do no more harm to you than what they had previously done to Lord Seriel."

The seventh archangel was horrified. Here, at last, was what he had dreaded. How could Kokabel be so deceitful? She was supposed to be enamored with him. If he had not witnessed her repeated whispered exchanges with Azazel, he would consider her action to be her usual senseless thought-babbling. Her incessant need to share whatever she saw, heard, or knew. Yet it was obvious she was anxious to make this revelation and she was proving to be adept in trickery. Also, Azazel had told her exactly when to act. Seriel wondered whether this devious betrayal was only directed at himself or also at Samael. He was sure the angelic conspiracy was conceived by Azazel. Kokabel was merely a willing participant in it.

Uriel arose from his kneeling position, grabbed Kokabel by the arm and steered her back to her place behind Azazel. As they approached Seriel, he managed to discern the end of what his sibling was telling her:

" . . . good reason to keep that happening a secret. He forbade you to tell of it, yet you have gone against his wishes."

"I only wished to convey Lord Samael's miscalculation of what the daemons would do. My mention of Lord Seriel happened before I could stifle the thought." Kokabel's expression was most unhappy, but as she stepped back behind Azazel, she gave Seriel a beaming smile.

Uriel went back to his stool. Now, all attention was turned to the deeply embarrassed seventh archangel. An incredulous Gabriel asked him:

"You were also attacked by the daemons?"

Seriel could only respond, "I was."

"When did that happen?" queried Michael.

Before Seriel could reply, Gabriel asked:

"Was that before I arrived? Is that why you were feeling unwell?"

Now, Samael joined in the thought exchange. "He was not unwell, that was another lie I told you. Seriel was trying to warn you about my intention and I was preventing him. I rendered him unable to share his thoughts or to move."

The Christ Soul remarked, "This whole situation is becoming more and more disturbing as we probe it."

Michael agreed, "You are correct, dear brother, but we must pursue it until we have revealed all the untruths and deceptions. Azazel! Belial! Semyaza! Should we assume you were also a part of this conspiracy?"

All three angels nodded their agreement to this question. Azazel appeared unmoved and Belial looked defiant. However, it was obvious Semyaza was feeling extremely uncomfortable.

Gabriel exclaimed, "Semyaza, I am truly wounded! I believed you to be my faithful essence angel."

Samael was quick to tell him, "He does my bidding, not yours."

"Apparently, and I am beginning to realize you had been planning to take your revenge for a long duration." Gabriel gave a sigh. Then, addressing Seriel, he questioned, "When and why did the daemons attack you?"

Seriel placed his hand on the wand's hilt and felt its comforting energy. Knowing he could no longer hide what had happened to him, he began to recount the unwholesome details. "Soon after you denounced our brother, he took me to view the daemons. I did not know they were vicious beasts until they set upon me. This happened before I was in my etheric body, therefore, I had no appendages for them to harm. They bit and clawed me, and some pieces of my consciousness were bitten clean through and spat out. Those particles escaped into the outer Abyss and became my own daemons. I finally escaped by manifesting a pair of wings similar to the ones Samael possessed before he took his etheric form . . ."

"Let me stop you, Seriel," interrupted Gabriel. "Was the attack on you unexpected by both you and Samael or did he also wish to bring *you* harm?"

Once again, the first archangel was quick to supply an answer. "I knew the daemons would hurt him. They had already clawed and bitten me. I wanted my revenge on both you and Seriel. You caused me humiliation and ridicule and our brother gave you the weapon with which to smite me. By telling you, and not me, he thought the Source had ordained my removal from the scenes, he created angelic disruption. Then, you seized the opportunity to belittle me before the newly formed angels."

"Indeed, I did," replied Gabriel. "I have apologized for that, and it would appear I need to also ask for Seriel's forgiveness. I was unaware until now that my unkind act brought harm to him, too."

Seriel shook his head, indicating he did not want an apology. He explained, "Although the attack was alarming, I believe my thoughtlessness warranted a reprisal. I have previously asked for Samael's forgiveness and he has granted it."

Michael remarked, "All of this apologizing is laudable, but I have one question for you, Seriel. When did you learn that Samael intended to take his revenge on Gabriel?"

Bracing himself for everyone's disapproval, Seriel responded, "Immediately after the daemons attacked me."

This brought more thought-gasps and mutterings from much of the angelic audience.

"And when did you know the details of the scheme for revenge?" continued Michael.

"I did not know the where or how of Samael's plan. It was only when I arrived at Uriel's home that I discovered it was to happen as soon as Gabriel was present. Even then I was unaware of the daemons' hiding place. As Samael has told you, I tried to warn Gabriel on his arrival, but I was prevented from doing so."

The first archangel interceded into the proceedings, once again. "That is sufficient interrogation of Seriel! His honor is not in question here. He knew nothing of my plans other than I wished to punish Gabriel. My brother kept that knowledge to himself out of loyalty to me."

The Shekinah suddenly broke her thought-silence with: "And what of his loyalty to Gabriel?"

Samael gave her a hurt-filled look, but remained silent. It was Seriel who answered their sister's question with:

"It was not only a sense of loyalty to Samael which prevented me from warning Gabriel. I also felt embarrassed and ashamed that I had allowed myself to be tricked. I wanted to blot out all of the unpleasant memory."

All thoughts ceased for a while. Everyone seemed stunned by what had been revealed, and a feeling of uncertainty of how to proceed was taking hold. Seriel toyed with the idea of asking his light wand to whisk him away from this awful experience. Yet he knew he must not give in to that desire.

Finally, Michael put forward, "We all have much to ponder upon. This meeting is not yet over. We must decide on our course of action with regard to Samael and also our two brothers and the four angels. To a greater or lesser degree, each was complicit in our first-born sibling's plan. I suggest we do not begin our deliberations until we have taken a short interlude of standing up and moving around." Trying to lighten the gloom that now overshadowed the proceedings, he added, "It would appear that etheric bodies need movement to stimulate the consciousness within."

The Lord of Lightning-Swiftness stood up and stretched his wings. He declared, "I am exceedingly bored with this council, therefore, I will take my leave of you all. When you are done with this ludicrous affair, send Seriel to me. He can report on your final decisions. I am certain I will find them most amusing." With that he was gone just as instantly as he had previously appeared.

There were several thoughts shared with regard to Samael's discourtesy and strong determination. Other exchanges centered on speculations about his magical ability to appear and disappear at will. No one approached Seriel and he was happy to stand to one side and become lost in his own thoughts. He knew why Samael had abruptly left the meeting. Their sister's response about loyalty had surely pained him deeply. The first archangel would want to be alone in the seclusion of his crystalline home. There he could appease himself with ideas of how to win back her approval.

Michael interrupted his musings by announcing, "Let us resume the meeting!" Seriel walked back to his place between his two essence angels. It was going to be a long, long deliberation.

Chapter Eighteen

I t was decided that the council should first address the
issue of how to chastise the four angels who took part in
Samael's plot for revenge. Mikael, the third archangel's
catalyst soul, suggested they ask them to apologize to Gabriel
before anything else was settled. Semyaza quickly complied
and asked for forgiveness, but the other three did not. They
each declared their belief in Samael's right to take revenge
for his brother's unjust behavior. This attitude prompted
the Christ Soul to recommend their banishment for a
duration.

Next, Uriel's involvement was considered. However,
before a conclusion was reached, this archangel declared
allegiance to his first-born brother. He stated that whatever
was decided upon for Samael, should also be his punishment.
This then caused Raphael to ask Seriel whether he wished
to be treated in a similar manner. The Lord of Sorcery
answered by explaining his willingness to submit to whatever
the council ordered him to do. He gave a sincere apology to
Gabriel and also expressed the hope his other siblings might
eventually view him with less disapproval.

Then, Samael's treachery was discussed. Gabriel's pure
essence angel, Bethnael, reminded everyone that the first
archangel obviously knew the daemons could be destructive.
He had previously set them upon Seriel. This thought
brought an immediate response from Uriel in which he
reaffirmed his conviction of his brother's unawareness of
the full extent of their cruelty. However, this did little to

dissuade the council from contemplating various options of punishment. These included such extremes as taking Samael to the daemons and instructing them to maim his body, and asking the Source to compel him to rejoin with it. This possibility would certainly eliminate any future treachery from the Lord of Lightning-Swiftness. Eventually, Michael's earlier suggestion of banishment began to take precedence over any other options put forward. Most members of the council indicated their approval of this strategy.

Now, the meeting had reached the point where an official decision on each of the seven angelic malefactors needed to be made. Michael believed those who were involved in the plot should not participate in this final process. They were culpable and, therefore, not entitled to cast their judgment. He recommended to each of the other council members the need for a referendum as the way of determining an outcome. First, Samael's punishment was secured. All but Shamshiel, Uriel's pure essence angel, and the Shekinah were in favor of him being banished to the outer reaches of Chaos. The angel voted against this proposal and Malkura refused to choose for or against it. Her abstention was understood and accepted.

Then, it was the turn of Uriel's and Seriel's behavior which needed to be addressed. With regard to the sixth archangel, Shamshiel, once again, chose to go against the decision of banishment. However, the remainder of the council were in agreement with it. They were dismayed at Uriel's involvement in Samael's plan and the fact that he had obviously withheld any warning from Gabriel. To Seriel's amazement, almost everyone believed he had already rectified much of his wrongdoing of not disclosing the attack on himself. By destroying some of the daemons and dispatching Kokabel to find Michael, he had shown brotherly support toward Gabriel. The Christ Soul recommended a solitary interlude in which he could question the wisdom of his close companionship with Samael. He added the suggestion of a discourse with the Source, which would prove helpful in this matter. Gabriel thought the seventh archangel should be the one to periodically visit the banished brothers. In this way he could keep them informed of what was happening in their absence. In addition, he would be able to bring back information on how they were progressing within their punishment. It was also stressed that no other archangels or angels should have contact with those who were exiled.

The decision concerning the punishment of the four angels was made swiftly and was uncontested. They were to be banished together with Samael and Uriel. Even though Semyaza had apologized to the fourth archangel, his betrayal of Gabriel was considered reprehensible. His plea for forgiveness was thought to be a conciliatory act rather than coming from genuine regret.

The only remaining consideration was how long to enforce the banishment of these individuals. Raphael suggested until the next angel birthing. This was believed to be appropriate. Michael thought it would be advisable, on that occurrence, to summon the six exiles to another council meeting. They could be questioned to establish whether they were feeling remorse for their actions. Then, depending on the council's further decision making, they would either be welcomed back to the inner realms of Chaos or sent away, once more. Due to the approach of another resting phase, it was agreed to delay the banishment until after it was passed. This would allow the six miscreants sufficient duration to make their "farewells" and ready themselves for their departure.

The meeting was brought to a close and all of the angels, and some of the archangels, parted company. The Christ Soul and the Shekinah went off in the direction of the Source and Uriel flew away to his home. Raphael came over to Seriel and declared his happiness in learning how he had helped Gabriel. He also suggested it would be a wise choice for his brother to not keep close company with Samael. Then he took off in order to be alone and to play his music until sleep would come. The seventh archangel's remaining two brothers approached him soon after Raphael departed. Michael asked:

"I trust you will relay our decisions to Samael before the resting phase?"

"I am about to go to him now unless you wish otherwise," answered Seriel.

Gabriel offered, "We want our brother to know of our judgment as soon as possible. I am certain he will not easily accept being exiled."

"I agree," added Michael. "It is very possible he will just ignore our directive."

Seriel questioned, "What will you do, if that is his response to banishment?"

"Then the council will meet, again." It was Michael who replied. "It may also be necessary to seek the advice of our parent. Perhaps the Source will have further suggestions, or even a decree, to enforce our decision upon him."

Seriel told them, "If it is possible, I will attempt to advise him that compliance is the correct choice for him to make." He was about to take his leave of them when Michael remarked:

"Before you go, I wish to ask you about that object you carry next to you." He touched the holstered light wand. "Gabriel has told me it was used by you to defeat some of the daemons. How did you manifest such a powerful implement?"

"I did not manifest it. Samael and I came upon a large number of aqueous globules floating in the Abyss. When Samael touched them, they grew into many different minerals and crystals." Seriel indicated the wand at his side. "This is but one of them."

"Why have you named them as such?" asked Gabriel.

"The Source gave me their names and I believe they came from our parent. My crystal is also known as a light wand."

Gabriel looked puzzled. He explained, "It is difficult to imagine our loving parent creating such destructive objects. My melding with the Source has shown me how peaceful and nurturing it can be."

"Perhaps it knew Seriel would need something very powerful to overcome the daemons," proffered Michael. "And perhaps others of us will also require the potency of crystals." He was thinking about the battle scene he had witnessed.

"A crystal is much more than a destroyer of evil creatures," Seriel explained. "It understands, then enhances and focuses our thoughts. We can manifest whatever we wish with its aid. It will instantly take us wherever we want to go."

Ever cautious, the fourth archangel declared, "That is alarming information! In the hands of Samael, who knows what he might wish to accomplish."

Michael agreed, "You are correct, dear brother, and does he not already possess such a light wand? Is that not so, Seriel?"

The seventh archangel nodded his agreement and Michael expressed:

"Ah! Now, I understand how our brother came and went so swiftly."

Gabriel asked, "Is that what he was holding when he confronted me about Uriel?"

"Yes, it was his crystal," confirmed Seriel.

With a look of alarm, Gabriel observed, "He was holding the triple points toward me. I seem to remember the destructive beam came from the point of your crystal, Seriel. Does that mean he was thinking of harming me right there in front of the council and the angels?"

Quick to defend his sibling, Seriel answered, "Samael is always protective of Uriel and he was angered by your questioning of him. Yet I do not believe he would have aimed the crystal at you. He has witnessed its power against the daemons and knows it is lethal."

"Nevertheless, it may be prudent to relieve him of his light wand before he goes into exile," remarked Michael.

Thought-laughter of disbelief escaped from Seriel. He assured the third archangel, "He will never allow you to take it from him! He is devoted to his crystal just as I am to mine. If you attempted to remove my wand from my keeping, I would stop you with all, and any, means that I could use. I am certain Samael would equally defend his right to possess his own wand."

Michael looked thoughtful and, after a short while, he suggested, "Then we may have to consider other ways of ensuring our brother causes no future harm to any of us with his crystal. However, for now his banishment is the action we will take. Let us trust it will be sufficient punishment. Seriel, go swiftly to Samael before the resting phase is upon us!"

"I will inform him of the council's directives. May you remain within our parent's keeping until I return!" Unfurling his wings, the Lord of the Seventh Essence took flight and traveled in the direction of Samael's abode.

Seriel felt certain his sibling was in his crystalline building, and he was not disappointed when he arrived there. Samael had obviously sensed his approach, the golden doors stood wide open. The seventh archangel entered the home and stood inside a large, square-shaped reception area. There were several archways within the walls of this space together with a flight of twisting steps coming down from the floor above. Seriel began thought-calling, "Samael! Samael! I have come to tell you of the council's decision."

The Lord of Lightning-Swiftness came bounding down the steps and walked toward his brother. The long scarf had been discarded, but the sandals and sheathed light wand remained. His countenance was stern as he declared, "Why am I always awaiting your late arrival? I think I will rename you as the Lord of Tardiness."

"I have flown here straight from the meeting," answered Seriel. "I am surprised you are anxious to learn of the council's deliberations. I thought you believed the meeting to be foolish nonsense."

"Indeed, I do. I care naught for the decisions my brothers and the angels have made. I am only interested in what was transpiring between you and our sister. She was smiling at some shielded thoughts you were sharing with her. I demand an explanation!" He stepped closer to Seriel in a menacing manner.

Refusing to feel intimidated by Samael's attitude, Seriel told him, "Malkura was looking extremely unhappy. I merely offered a cheering thought in the hope of comforting her."

A sneer appeared on the first archangel's face. He mimicked, "I merely offered a cheering thought," and glared at Seriel. Next, he asked, "And what cheering thought would that be? That you love her as much, nay, even more than her wayward brother?"

Seriel suddenly felt a strong sense of compassion for Samael. He knew only too well how jealousy could blight and wither the soul. Its constricting bonds often enveloped him in terrible pain. He stated, "I have never revealed the depth of my feelings to her. She believes I love her in the same manner as do the other archangels. Malkura is only aware that your love goes beyond brotherly affection."

Samael remained staring at his brother's face, but the expression in his eyes had softened. He questioned, "Then what were you telling her?"

"If you recall, you made a jesting reference to Michael's ability to plan strategies for the games we used to play. When I noticed our sister's sad expression, I presumed she was thinking of how happy we all were then. I suggested to her you must also wish for the joy and innocence we used to share."

Suddenly, this surprising admission came from Samael: "You are truly a noble soul, Seriel. Perchance the Shekinah would love you more than me, if she knew how much you desired her devotion. What think you, will you ever tell her?"

"I believe not. I have never contemplated revealing my love for her. I know how much she adores you."

"Come!" invited Samael. He turned from his sibling and moved toward one of the archways. Seriel followed him through the opening and into the same room where earlier the Shekinah had sat down. The two chairs were undisturbed, they remained in their face-to-face position. Samael pointed to one of them and offered, "Sit and tell me upon which ridiculous decrees the council have settled."

Before becoming seated, Seriel scanned the room with his inner sight. The purple floor and opaque walls fascinated him. He could sense a powerful crystalline energy radiating out from them. A number of jewels and pieces of a wax-like substance were embedded in the walls. The latter objects emitted a luminous glow which greatly lightened the room's interior. This innate quality resulted from their original exposure to the radiance of the Source, when they were but a part of forming teardrops. Their color would be considered white in the far distant future world of man. The surrounding gems sparkled as their facets reflected the phosphorescent light. Many were larger than the emerald Samael had given to Malkura.

On the wall opposite to where Seriel stood, there was a flat, silver-enhanced crystal. It was rectangular in shape and many times larger than the one he had observed Samael creating for the Shekinah. As he viewed the crystal mirror, Seriel realized an image of himself was looking back at him. There was also a reflection of Samael, the chairs, the floor and the wall behind him. The seventh archangel sat down and attempted to bring his attention away from the reflecting crystal.

"It is difficult to draw your concentration away from my creation, is it not?" Samael observed. "And you have yet to begin to use your etheric vision."

"The crystal's reflective property is quite magical. I feel compelled to look at myself."

"Are we not beautiful beings?" asked Samael as he bowed to his reflection before sitting down. "When your etheric eyes begin to function, you will be even more enthralled. They convey greater intensity of color and depth of detail."

Seriel remarked, "During the meeting I realized our sister is also perceiving through her eyes."

"Ah, those enchanting green orbs! Would you not slay a hundred daemons for a loving glance from them?" An incorrigible expression appeared on Samael's face as he added, "Or perhaps a hundred angels?"

Trying not to get caught up in what he hoped was his brother's jesting, Seriel announced, "I must explain what the council have decided. They want you to know before the resting phase is upon us."

"Of course they do. Gabriel's efficiency will have influenced all of the members. Pray tell, what is my punishment to be? Shall I prepare myself to tremble with fear when you declare their wishes?"

Seriel attempted to adopt a serious tone as he readied himself to divulge the news of the banishment. Yet it was difficult because his brother insisted on grinning broadly at him. Finally, he managed to state, "The council have ordered you, Uriel and the four angels, who aided you, to be exiled to the outer reaches of Chaos for a duration."

Samael's mirth vanished and he answered angrily, "How dare they punish Uriel! He is a sweet soul who is easily influenced by my reasoning. His devotion to me rivals that of our sister and they know it is so. I trust you did not agree with this unjust decision?"

Seriel quickly assured him, "Neither I, nor Uriel, nor the four angels were allowed to cast our opinions on what should happen to us. However, before the final referendum, our brother declared his allegiance to you and asked to be given the same punishment as you."

"My dear, devoted sibling," mused Samael. "He would follow me into misfortune and ruin." The first archangel became distracted by his own thoughts for a while. Eventually, he asked, "Did Malkura vote against my banishment?"

"She abstained. I think she was torn between her love for you and her sibling affection for Gabriel."

"Knowing her unconditional love for everyone, I can understand her dilemma. I will take comfort in knowing she did not cast her decision with my brothers." Then Samael regarded his sibling more closely and questioned, "And how has the council chosen to reprimand the Lord of Sorcery for not disclosing the daemons' attack upon his auric self?"

Sheepishly Seriel admitted, "They considered my destruction of the creatures and my request for Michael's help outweighed my reluctance to warn Gabriel. I have been advised to not keep company with you and to consult with our parent about our relationship. I am also the only one who can make contact with you and the others during your exile."

"How utterly absurd! You should stay away from me, but you can visit me while I am banished. They are irrational fools!"

"I believe they are afraid you might sway many more to your reasoning."

"Do they not know you have already sworn your allegiance to me?"

Seriel shook his head. "I think not."

"Perhaps they are testing you in order to discover where your loyalty lies?" Samael stood up and began to pace around the room. "So, we are to be banished until . . . Do you know how long they deem is appropriate? Perchance for eternity?"

"Until the next birthing of angels."

"Ah, not for an eternity, just for a small duration of one. And no one is to come near to us with the exception of yourself. Have they shared with you what will happen when the new angels come forth?"

"There will be another council meeting to which you six will be summoned. Then, the decision will be made whether you can rejoin us or be exiled, once again, for a further duration."

Samael returned to his seat and, leaning close to Seriel, asked, "What think you of this directive of banishment?"

"I believe it is harsh, particularly for you. Uriel will be content because he will have your company. Azazel and Kokabel appear to have formed a closeness, and Belial and Semyaza will have each other and you. Yet you will be deprived of Malkura's loving companionship. That is a cruel punishment." Seriel placed his hand on Samael's knee in a comforting gesture.

Laying his own hand on top of Seriel's, the first-born archangel responded, "Cruel, indeed. That is why I will not tolerate it. My trusty light wand will take me instantly to the Shekinah whenever I so wish. Other than to be with her, I have no desire to roam the inner realms of the Abyss. Nothing entices me there apart from our sister, my home and the crystals. I can move my home further outwards with my wand's power, and I will do so before the resting phase. When I require more crystals, I will go to them or move them in the same manner as my abode. So you see, Seriel, the council's decree will not be a punishment for me."

Seriel pressed, "Do you think it is wise to go against the council's judgment? You would have to leave outer Chaos in order to be with the Shekinah or to gather crystals."

"Wise or foolish, I will do whatever I so desire," answered Samael. He patted Seriel's hand and suggested, "I believe you should be leaving now. You will need to be safely back in your home before sleep comes upon you."

The brothers stood up, walked out of the room and approached the golden entrance. As they were ready to part company, Seriel felt compelled to share a warning with his sibling. He declared:

"Before I take my leave of you, I wish to alert you to a matter I deem important. Beware of Azazel and Kokabel!

They have conspired against me and possibly you, as well. When Kokabel revealed the daemons' assault on me, that was not her usual thoughtlessness. I believe she and my pure essence angel planned that disclosure."

Samael looked surprised as he responded, "I value your discernment, but are you certain? Angel Kokabel pays little attention to her continuously shared thoughts. She frequently does not understand their implications."

Seriel assured him, "I do not think I am wrong. They were repeatedly thought-whispering during the meeting. I observed Azazel nod to Kokabel, indicating when to divulge that unknown information."

"I will take heed of what you have shared and I will be wary of both your essence angels. I thank you, dear brother, for your concern." As once before, he pulled Seriel to him in a loving embrace. Then gently slapping him on the back, he ordered, "Now, be gone from here! The resting phase is fast approaching."

Responding to this affectionate gesture, Seriel held onto his sibling an instant longer, and then released him. He offered, "May you fare well until our next meeting!" and, passing through the open entrance, the seventh archangel wished himself to be home and vanished from view.

As he reappeared in front of his pyramid, Seriel found the angels Balberith and Mulciber waiting close by. They were busily exchanging thoughts and did not notice his sudden appearance. He walked over to them and questioned, "Why are you here?"

It was Balberith who answered, "We decided to come to you to learn whether we could help you in any way. The council meeting was an unhappy event and we knew you were feeling saddened by the banishment of your two brothers. You are our essence lord and we have sensed your sorrow. Angel Kokabel's revelation about the daemons attacking you was also most disturbing to us. We wanted to be certain you are no longer troubled by the assault. Mulciber and I are here to offer our company during the resting phase, if you are in need of companionship."

This unexpected concern for his welfare surprised Seriel and he felt deeply affected by it. He replied, "I thank you, my angels, your regard for my well-being is praise worthy. However, I am not feeling too downcast, and I am a soul who prefers his own company when troubled. Thus, your offer of companionship is greatly appreciated, but not required."

"Then we will take our leave of you," answered Mulciber. "Remain within the Source's keeping!"

"May you also be equally blessed!" responded Seriel as he watched the two angels move away from his home. Mulciber had not yet manifested her etheric form, therefore, Balberith did not spread his wings. He walked next to his third-cast essence sister as she flowed along.

The seventh archangel entered his home and moved along the corridors toward the resting chamber. Once there, he removed his holstered light wand and placed it on a small table. He had recently created this object from etheric matter with the power of his thoughts. A similarly formed chair was placed near the table. Seriel sat down in it with the hope of beginning to relax. So many thoughts were rushing through him. Uppermost were the events of the meeting and Samael's questioning him about his love for the Shekinah. He quickly decided these thoughts would do nothing to help him feel restful. Therefore, he turned his attention to something less emotional.

The crystal mirror in Samael's room was a pleasing memory, and he began to plan where in his pyramid he would place one. He knew how to construct this interesting item, he had observed his brother creating one for Malkura. Silver existed within his wings because of Samael's generosity. He was quite sure he could cause a small quantity of it to flow from them through his body, into his fingertips, and then into a crystal. Seriel became engrossed in these thoughts and sleep began to claim his consciousness.

"Lord Seriel, come quickly!"

This sudden exclamation from a nearby Balberith brought the seventh archangel abruptly awake. He jumped up from the chair, rushed from the resting chamber and ran along the corridors until he reached the front entrance. Opening the door, Seriel found his catalyst angel standing there. "What is wrong?" he asked.

"Soon after we departed, we came upon Lady Malkura in great distress. She is sitting close to one of the miniature scenes and refuses to leave."

"Is she harmed in any manner?" questioned an alarmed Seriel.

"I do not believe so, but I am afraid some daemons might come upon her. We offered our protective company back to the inner parts of Chaos, but she refused. The Shekinah told us she wishes to be alone and will sleep where she is now. I think that is most unwise, my lord. The daemons frequent this area and would surely attack a sleeping archangel. Mulciber is with her while I have come to you. I thought Lady Malkura might pay heed to her brother."

"Take me to her!" ordered Seriel as he stepped through the entrance and closed the door.

They took flight and were soon in sight of the Shekinah and Mulciber. As he alighted, Seriel scanned the surrounding area for any approaching daemons, but there were none. This particular part of the Abyss lay close to the second area where Samael had changed the tears of the Source into crystals. Except for these four angelic beings, it was deserted due to the proximity of the resting phase. Yet daemons do not sleep and they might soon overrun this place.

Mulciber had positioned herself close to Malkura, who was sitting down with legs crossed and her body hunched forwards. Her head was bowed with her chin resting against her clasped hands. Seriel suspected she was holding something, and he could well imagine what it was. He stooped down beside her and, placing one hand on her shoulder, offered:

"Dear sister, it is Seriel. Come with me now away from here. It is an unsafe place for you to be."

She turned her face in his direction and her overwhelming expression of grief cut deeply into him. Something glistened on her cheeks and he realized aqueous droplets were escaping from her eyes. For a brief instant they reminded him of the fluid globules he and Samael had found floating in the Abyss. The sight of his unhappy sister was so agonizing that Seriel shuddered from its pain. Once again, he told her:

"Come with me now, Malkura!"

She shook her head and answered, "No. I wish to remain here."

"Lady Malkura is extremely upset, but also quite determined," stated Mulciber. "Shall we stay and help you to persuade her?"

"No, the resting phase is close. You must sleep in the inner realms where the daemons cannot go. I thank you both for your assistance. Leave now, and I will attend to my sister."

The two angels were quickly gone and Seriel was about to become stern with Malkura. However, his attention was drawn to a miniature scene which began to play out its story. Its short existence was situated close to the archangel siblings and it told of their brother Samael. In it he was searching through a number of crystals. He came upon a beautiful green specimen and cupped the upper section of it with his hands. In an instant the top was cleaved and, as Samael held it, many facets began to appear all over its surface. With a gentle smile gracing his lips, the first archangel walked away from the crystals and the scene faded. Now, Seriel understood what was keeping his sister in this place. He urged her:

"You cannot stay here, the daemons may come. Come with me to my home where you will be safe. We can exchange thoughts about Samael, if that will bring you comfort."

She gazed at the empty area where the scene had been and asked, "Did you observe what he was doing? That was when he created the emerald for me. How can he be filled with such love for me and yet possess great hatred of Gabriel? We are all siblings and have sprung from the Source, which is pure love." Malkura opened her hands and revealed the hidden jewel. She continued, "I have been sitting here and contemplating throwing this emerald into the depth of the Abyss. A part of me wants to disown it and yet another part wishes to hold it close forever."

Seriel was anxious for them to leave, but he was dismayed by what she was sharing. He exclaimed, "Do not discard this token of Samael's love for you! That would surely devastate him."

"That may be true. You understand him better than I do." She closed her hand around the emerald and returned to her previous, bowed position.

A sudden movement in the distance alerted Seriel to the approach of the daemons. He stood up and warned, "The daemons are coming! Quickly, Malkura, we must fly from here!"

The Shekinah remained seated and told him, "Let them come. They obey Samael and he would not allow them to harm me. I choose to stay here and watch this repeating image of our brother until sleep comes. Then I may dream of how contented we used to be, and of his former radiance."

"The daemons are evolving, just as are we. I am certain they are capable of horrendous acts even without Samael's bidding. We must go now!"

"You may go, but I will stay. I am too saddened to care what may happen." The Shekinah stretched her legs, rolled onto her side and then lay still, as if waiting for sleep to come. The scene became visible, once more, and she watched it as her tears returned.

"You may not care, but I most assuredly do. Thus, forgive my boldness." The seventh archangel bent down and lifted up his sister in his arms. Her small frame was no burden for him and he was immediately in flight. He expected her to struggle, but she stayed passive with her eyes closed. Tears continued to ooze from under her eyelids and trace their way down her face.

Seriel flew swiftly to his home, while remaining watchful for daemons. When he reached the entrance, he ordered the door to open. He strode into the interior of the pyramid and commanded the door to close. Without setting down his sibling, he quickly moved through the corridors until he reached the resting chamber. Then he knelt down and gently placed Malkura on the floor. He ordered it to begin undulating. The Shekinah opened her eyes and looked around the room. As she moved to sit up, the floor's soothing movement caught her attention. She declared:

"What a delightful place! Perhaps I will just lie here for a while and be rocked by this pleasing motion. Weariness has come upon me from the closeness of the resting phase and from feeling so unhappy." She made no further attempt to be seated, and Seriel was aware she was continuing to clutch the emerald in her hand.

"Rest here, Malkura, you are safe in my home." Seriel changed his position from one of kneeling to sitting beside his sister. "Surrender to slumber and I will keep watch over you."

No answer came from the Shekinah, and Seriel realized she was moving into sleep. Her eyes closed and she drew her knees a little closer to her chest. He sat staring at her beautiful face and wishing he could spend every resting phase in her company. Samael would be furious, if he knew they were here together, but Seriel was feeling too contented to concern himself with his brother's passions and demands. The first-born's beloved Malkura was sleeping in the Lord of Sorcery's resting chamber. In that archangel's blissful imagination, her loving presence would linger in this room forever.

Seriel continued to gaze lovingly at the Shekinah as the need for sleep was overtaking him, once more. Yet each instant his thoughts started to drift away, he would pull his consciousness back to alertness. He wanted to remain awake so that he could keep his promised vigil. The needs of the resting phase were pressing upon him, but he fought against them.

Seriel brought his attention to Malkura's hair as a way of maintaining his heedful bearing. The long, rulpiel locks were draped against her body, as if to blanket her dreaming form. The seventh archangel slowly stretched out his hand and touched their cascading beauty. A sudden memory of Samael taunting him came rushing into his thoughts. His brother had woven a lock of Malkura's hair through his fingers in order to demonstrate his just ability to touch and caress her. Seriel had wanted desperately to order him to stop. Now, it was his turn to claim the same right. He lifted a few strands of her hair and gently combed his fingers through them. This action brought an ecstatic smile to his lips as another memory erupted. It was the council meeting, and the Shekinah was sitting in a chair, twisting her hair around two fingers. Then she had smiled at him. Seriel became absorbed in this happy reminiscence.

He jerked suddenly and was startled wide awake. As sleep had claimed him, his relaxing body began to slide out of its upright position. With no resistance against which to rest, he was in danger of toppling sideways. He wondered whether his sudden movement had caused him to pull against Malkura. A swift scan showed his hand resting on top of her body with the strands of her hair remaining laced through his fingers. However, she appeared to be undisturbed and deep in sleep.

Reluctant to break contact with his adored sister, Seriel told himself he would lay down for just a short while. Then he would move away into a sitting position with his back resting against one of the chamber's walls. In that manner, he could continue to watch over the Shekinah without falling over, should the state of slumber overcome him, again. He eased his body into a resting posture, lying close to Malkura and continuing to clasp her rulpiel tresses.

Instantly, sleep enveloped his being and he began to journey through a long, drawn out maze of frightening dreams. In some, he and the Shekinah were being chased by many daemons. These pursuing creatures were constantly growing in size and ferocity. Other dreams placed him in a terminal battle with Samael. Within these, both brothers were destroying each other with their crystal wands. The nightmare happenings continued on throughout the entirety of the resting phase.

Chapter Nineteen

S haking himself free of the unpleasant dreams, Seriel's consciousness gained sharp awareness. The resting phase was over and his waking existence was stirring, once again. As his inner vision became focused, he discovered his sister lying next to him. For an instant he believed he must be continuing to dream. Then, recollection of the events, which took place shortly before he fell asleep, returned to him. Malkura was already awake and she was gazing at him with an indiscernible expression on her exquisite face. He was about to sit up, when he realized his arm was around her body. What was she thinking as she lay there? Was she angry when she awoke and discovered him almost embracing her?

Seriel quickly withdrew his hold on her and thought-muttered, "My apologies, Malkura. I trust I have not offended you?"

She smiled at him and answered, "There is no need to apologize. You are my brother and, thus, a closeness exists between us."

"I was concerned because you were so sad," Seriel explained. Then, embellishing on that truth, he added, "I must have reached out to comfort you while I was sleeping."

"Whatever the reason, I am not offended. In truth, I am extremely grateful for your loving presence. My thoughts were brimming over with unhappiness and I foolishly wanted to remain with the replica of a kinder Samael." The Shekinah sat up and stretched her arms above her head. She was continuing to hold on tightly to the green jewel. "Had you not intervened, some daemonic misfortune may well have befallen me. Did Angel Balberith seek you out?"

"Yes, he and Mulciber had just departed from me when they found you." He stood up, walked over to the chair and, turning it toward her, offered, "Come sit here, Malkura. It is plainly constructed, but it is comfortable."

The Shekinah rose to a standing position and moved slowly across the room. The floor's undulating quality appeared to hamper her progress. She sat down in the chair, tapped her feet against the floor and observed, "What an unusual sensation! Your room is quite magical." Tiny ripples manifested under her feet and spread outwards.

Seriel stood concentrating for an instant and all movement within the floor was soon gone. Next, he lifted the small table and placed it opposite to his sibling. His light wand continued to rest on this piece of etheric furniture. Then he sat on the edge of the table and replied, "I structured the floor thus in order to stimulate relaxation. Its movement speeds the surrender to the resting phase. I can order it to begin or cease its undulation whenever I so wish."

"You are so inventive!" praised Malkura.

Feeling awkward, Seriel declared, "I must confess that much of what is here is but copies of what Samael created. Yet the notion of a gently rocking floor for the purpose of sleep is my own conception."

The Shekinah looked wistful as she told him, "Samael has a glorious crystal unit he has named a 'bed' for partaking of the resting phase. It is of the deepest blue with flecks of gold throughout it."

A tinge of jealousy touched the seventh archangel's soul. So Malkura was familiar with an object in Samael's home of which he knew nothing? He wondered what intimate thoughts had passed between them before sleeping on the crystalline bed. Recalling an earlier promise to the first archangel, and looking for a distraction from his envious thoughts, he explained, "The notion of a home where we can rest, be protected and enjoy the company of others was originally Samael's. He is a creative soul."

"Indeed he is. He can create beauty, harmony and love together with ugliness, conflict and hatred. The Lord of Lightning-Swiftness is a contradiction and disruption to the very essence of ALL THAT IS."

Seriel felt compelled to add, "But you love him and that will surely keep him from any lasting downfall."

Malkura's eyes began to brim with tears as she observed, "I think not. Our parent has told me it is his destiny to become all that is not, and that I should not interfere with that happening. There is a hidden reason why he is choosing this destructive path, but the Source will not divulge it." She struggled to contain a small, sobbing thought, but it was perceived by Seriel.

He leapt up from the table and quickly crouched down in front of her, exclaiming, "Dear sister, I cannot bear to see you so distressed. What can I do to bring you solace? How can I comfort you?"

The Shekinah lovingly touched his cheek with her hand and with a rueful smile suggested, "Perhaps you can weave a little magic into this dismal situation. Remember the game we used to play so long ago?" Malkura seemed to be looking right through him as old memories arose. "You were the powerful sorcerer who commanded his siblings to do whatsoever he desired. If we refused, he would change us into beings who could not move or could not convey any thoughts."

Seriel remembered this game very well, yet he had never expected his sister to think of it. He agreed, "I do remember our happy play."

Wiping her tear-stained cheeks with one hand, Malkura recalled, "You were quite wicked! You always commanded Gabriel to meld with Samael or Uriel to blend with anyone except Samael. What a teasing, vexing soul you were!"

A smile appeared on Seriel's face. He admitted, "I cannot claim all of the credit for that mischief. On occasion, Samael would prompt me before we played the game on what commands to make. That was when he only desired innocent fun."

Lost in her own thoughts, Malkura sat still for a while. Finally, she gave a little shake of head and declared, "I have decided to put away my love for Samael. It pains me too greatly to give thought to it." She reached across to the table, placed the emerald on it and continued, "So, great Lord of Sorcery, you can cheer me with your magic. What command must I obey? Do you wish me to meld with one of my brothers? And do not dare to suggest the first-born of the Source! Shall it be with Uriel or . . ." Malkura's thoughts stopped, and then resumed. "No, he is also being banished and the council decreed that no one except you must have contact with the exiles. I also have no desire to venture to outer Chaos. That desolate place chills my soul." She paused, again, but soon observed, "Oh, I cannot meld while in my etheric body. I will have to first return to inner Chaos and assume my auric state. So, with whom shall it be once I am changed?"

Not wanting to pursue this particular thought exchange, Seriel stood up and moved away from his sister. He announced, "I do not care to indulge you in this make-believe, it brings back too many memories."

Malkura rose from the chair and moved in front of her brother. She grabbed his hands and tugged on them as she pleaded, "Please, please, dear Seriel! This is not make-believe. You asked what you can do to comfort me and this is it. I beg you to honor my request! Melding brings a sense of peace and I am greatly in need of that blessing. Tell me with whom you wish me to blend my essence. Perhaps it should be you? You rescued me from my foolish obsession with a Samael replica. You also tried to help Gabriel by destroying some of the daemons. Do you not wish to be rewarded?"

The seventh archangel pulled himself free from his sibling and demanded, "Enough, Malkura! You want my command? Then I order you to cease this unseemly behavior! We are no longer newly birthed from the Source and should not play games. Too much has transpired between us all to ever recapture those innocent occasions." Then, realizing his harshness was causing her tears to form, again, he instinctively drew her into a close embrace and thought-whispered, "Forgive me, dear Malkura, I did not intend to cause you more grief. Melding is an intimate and loving exchange which must not be treated lightly. When we were first formed, we did not understand it was so. We thought of it as recapturing our previous existence, and it came easily to us. It was a natural part of the games we played. Now, I cannot view it as such."

Malkura looked up at him and asked, "Perhaps you always viewed it differently? You rarely melded with any of us alone. Your blending of awareness with me was only ever within a group." When he gave no reply, she continued, "For me, melding was always a simple pleasure. It only became more when I shared my consciousness with Samael." She seemed content to stay within his arms and Seriel was more than loath to let her go. He commented:

"I am certain you will meld with our brother, again. You are the essence of unconditional love. Thus, your devotion to Samael will never fade no matter what transgressions he may pursue."

"It is only our parent who is the true essence of unconditional love," answered Malkura. "My feelings for Samael are confused and changing. Even though I love him, I cannot abide his treatment of Gabriel or of you. How could he set those evil daemons upon his own brothers?"

With great reluctance, Seriel released his sister from his embrace. He offered, "Would it be of help, if we share other thoughts about Samael? I do not wish to play a game, but a discussion of him may alleviate your confusion."

"What a dear, devoted brother you are!" Malkura sat down on the floor and patted the space in front of her. "Come and sit with me and we can have a sibling thought sharing. Remember how we used to do that? We would gather together and exchange our ideas and convictions about the Source, ourselves and the Abyss of Chaos."

Sitting down and facing her, Seriel replied, "I remember very well. Inevitably, Samael's and Gabriel's thoughts would become an argument. The Christ Soul would always try to bring peace between them."

"And you would repeatedly champion Samael's reasoning."

"As would Uriel. Those pleasant occasions seem so long ago now." He smiled sadly as he continued, "Our lives were trouble-free then. We were less evolved and we thought we would exist in Chaos alone forever. How could we know angels and daemons would eventually join us?"

The Shekinah sat silent for a while, lost in thoughts of their early existence. Then, she put forward, "Your magical spiral tells you what is to come, thus, will Samael reclaim his radiant self?"

Unwilling to share what his shining orbs foretold about their brother, Seriel answered, "I do not know. He appears in many spheres, thus, I know he continues to exist, as do we all." The seventh archangel had no intention of telling her Samael was always in the outer realms of the Abyss, as though permanently banished there. "The spiral has become very difficult to understand. There are so many spheres clustered on top of each other, making comprehension of one sometimes impossible. I do know there will be many, many more angels. Also, other beings who resemble us, but have no wings. However, they appear to exist somewhere other than Chaos."

"Our parent did tell me Samael's radiance will be restored, but I fear that happening is long from now." The Shekinah began tracing patterns on the floor with her forefinger.

Wanting to offer comfort, Seriel assured her, "The Source is all-knowing, therefore, it will happen. You can be certain of that. What else would you wish to share about Samael? Or perhaps I can tell you things about him which would please you?"

Malkura appeared intent upon her tracing activity, but she suddenly looked up at him and declared, "I would rather learn of other matters. Whenever I think of him, that strange fluid substance escapes from my eyes and makes me feel even more unhappy."

"I can understand why you are affected in that manner. When I first perceived the wetness on your face, I felt such pain within me. When I go to consult with the Source, I will ask it about the fluid. Then I will tell you what I have learned. So, sister, what else would you wish me to tell you?"

"There are so many things and you are so much more knowledgeable than I am. Your spiral has taught you about the future and what may befall us all. If you are willing, I believe we should meet frequently and share thought exchanges like we did before. Perhaps some of our brothers would wish to join us?"

Seriel would prefer to meet with her alone, but it was better to have her presence within the company of others rather than to be completely deprived of it. He acknowledged, "That would please me well. And, if we meet after I have visited Samael in exile and we are alone, I can tell you of him."

Malkura appeared angry as she exclaimed, "No more thoughts of Samael! He is being banished and I now banish his name from my consciousness. Let us share thoughts instead about you. Of all my brothers you are the one of whom I know the least. I have often shared thoughts with the Christ Soul and Raphael and I understand Michael's and Gabriel's need for caution and order. Uriel's obsession with a certain archangel is something I can understand and accept. But what of you? I know you hold that nameless archangel in great esteem and that you love me, as do all of my brothers. Yet what more can you tell me?"

His sister was staring straight at him and he was feeling most uncomfortable with her scrutiny. Seriel thought-mumbled, "There is nothing to tell."

The Shekinah persisted, "That is untrue. I know the angels share musings about you and Kokabel. Manah, my essence angel, and I have deliberated on whether there is real devotion between you. Pray tell your sister, are you enamored with Angel Kokabel?"

A relieved Seriel was quick to inform her, "Oh, no, I hold no passion for that annoying angel. And you can tell Manah that Kokabel is now in league with Azazel and no longer follows me everywhere."

Malkura clapped her hands in glee. "Manah will be so pleased. I think she holds a secret liking for you herself. She is always sharing with me something you have done or expressed. What else can you tell me about which the angels will be happy to gossip?"

Seriel was busily searching his memory to recall which angel was Manah. Then a clear image of her appeared in his thoughts. She stood much taller than her essence mistress, but possessed the same, long rulpiel hair. He had given little thought to her until now. Bringing his attention back to Malkura's question, he replied, "I know of nothing else. Yet I am sure the angels will be sharing tattle about Lord Seriel keeping his daemonic attack to himself."

Once again, Malkura was staring directly at her sibling. She told him, "I was greatly alarmed to learn of your misfortune with the daemons, but also saddened that you chose not to share that happening with anyone."

Unable to meet her forthright gaze, Seriel looked down and confessed, "I will forever carry the guilt of not warning Gabriel of Samael's intention to seek revenge."

His sister reached over and, touching his hand, offered, "Gabriel does not appear to be troubled by your secrecy, therefore, you must try to forgive yourself." Then, apparently wishing to cheer him, she continued, "Perhaps the angels will hold some discussion about your silence, dear brother, but it will only be a passing thought. However, the present story which abounds is your gallant slaying of the daemons. Once Gabriel told us of your courage, thought-word of it soon spread." She brought her hands up to his head and tousled his dark hair with sisterly affection. "The magical Lord of Sorcery is catching the attention of many an angel. You will surely be pursued by more than one admirer."

For an instant Seriel wavered from his determination to never reveal his true feelings to Malkura. Looking back up at her, he declared, "But there is only one whose attention I desire."

The Shekinah grabbed him by the arms and declared, "Aha! So there is someone you hold dear? I sensed that to be so. I beg you, tell me who it is! I swear I will not reveal it to Manah or any other."

Immediately regretting this admission, Seriel forced a short, sharp burst of thought-laughter from his being. He revealed, "I was just teasing you, Malkura. It pleases me to see you happy. I considered an apparent slip of my thoughts would continue to distract you from your earlier sadness."

Malkura looked askance at her sibling and remarked, "I do not believe you! Someone has stolen your affection and I am determined to discover his or her identity."

"You are mistaken. I am a soul who prefers his own company." Seriel wished he could touch his light wand and dispatch himself to his spheres. Attempting to change the subject, he asked, "What other information can I share with you?"

"Avoidance will not free you from my curiosity." She continued to gaze at him intently. "Yet I am patient. At our next meeting I will question you, again. And during further thought sharing, too, if you yet withhold the name of your beloved."

"There is no one. Now, do you wish me to tell you of other things?" There was slight annoyance in this thought.

The Shekinah patted her brother's shoulder and acquiesced, "Oh, solitary Seriel, I will play along with your game. Let me consider . . ." She adopted an extremely puzzled expression. " . . . what I wish you to share with me. I know! Explain more of your thoughts about melding. You have obviously spent much reflection on the matter."

"As I previously stated, I believe we indulged in its joy too easily and without much thought. I think it is a sacred act and should be only shared by souls who love and cherish each other above all others." Seriel realized his sister was the first being with whom he had ever discussed his conviction.

Malkura offered, "Perchance, like us, melding has evolved? We were simple creatures and, therefore, like us, it was innocent play, a happy diversion. An innate reminder of being as one with our parent. Perhaps, now, it has much greater meaning? Also, many emotions are igniting within us and it may be unwise to allow our thoughts and feelings to be shared within such intimacy. Melding may possibly make us vulnerable to some who would use our emotions against us."

"That is yet another view of why melding should be fully considered before taking place. It is different from my personal thoughts on the matter, but it fits well with them. Souls, who deeply and unconditionally love other souls, would never judge or abuse the nature of the essence that has been blended with theirs."

The Shekinah looked extremely thoughtful as she observed, "That is truly profound. I have given little consideration to melding except to recall its pleasures. You are causing me to rethink my opinion of it. May I ask another question of you? Why do you deem it a sacred act?"

"It is a coming together of beings who are facets of the Source. Thus, a small part of Source consciousness temporarily reunites with another small part. Surely, therefore, that act is sacred? Our parent is divine consciousness and we are extensions of that pure essence."

"Yet another piece of wisdom! You are giving me much to contemplate when I am alone. The slayer of daemons is also an erudite soul."

A somewhat embarrassed Seriel replied, "My spheres have taught me many things."

"I must visit your spiral," declared Malkura. "It is a great while since I viewed those amazing records of what does, and may, happen. But returning to our discussion of melding. Whatever our thoughts about it, there will be much less awareness blending taking place now that many are in etheric form. It is not possible to meld unless in an auric state."

"It is possible," was the seventh archangel's surprising answer.

"Tell me how!" The Shekinah leaned forward, eagerly awaiting his reply.

"There are parts of our etheric bodies which can merge and then revert to an auric state so that melding can happen." Once again, Seriel began to feel their thoughts were wandering into an area which caused him great discomfort. He had often spent wishful musings of how rapturous it would be to meld one-on-one with his sister. This present thought exchange would only bring him more sadness when he later reviewed what might have been.

"Surely that can only happen in the proximity of the Source?"

He explained, "To become totally as we once were, we must be close to our parent. However, within other areas of Chaos a small part of our body can become auric for the purpose of melding."

Malkura leaned even closer to him and smilingly demanded, "And how would you know this? With whom have you been blending your consciousness?"

An angry expression appeared on his face as he cautioned, "Do not jest with me, sister! I have told you, I keep company with no one but myself."

The Shekinah immediately pulled back and told him, "I meant no harm. It just gives me joy to learn that you or any of my brothers may have a loving companion."

Seriel clasped her hands and declared, "Malkura, I apologize. I am not myself. The council meeting and all that was revealed has greatly unsettled me."

"As it has also affected me." She gave him a quick smile and continued, "That is why being here with you and sharing our thoughts has been so gratifying. I thank you for your kindness." She tightened her hold on his hands and then added, "Can I encroach upon your brotherly affection and ask one more melding question?"

Seriel smiled broadly and remarked, "You are persistent, dear sister! Ask your question!"

"How do you know we can meld when we are etheric, if you have not done so with someone?"

"My spheres have shown me angels melding on many occasions."

"And just one more small query, please? What etheric body parts can merge and meld?"

He gently shook their clasped hands. "These!"

"Oh!" Malkura looked startled and quickly withdrew her hands from his.

An uncomfortable silence ensued between the two siblings. Then, believing her action denoted absolute rejection of any intimacy he might offer, Seriel asked, "Did you think I was about to meld with you?"

"Of course not. I . . ."

He assured her, "I would never attempt to do that without your permission." He looked dismayed and added, "You are obviously repulsed by the thought of such melding."

"No, no, Seriel! You do not repulse me. I was merely surprised by your answer."

The seventh archangel doubted her explanation. He was certain the thought of melding with him was not to her liking. Wishing to end this awkward situation, he suggested, "I believe we should part company now, my lady. I have to go to our parent, as the Christ Soul recommended during the council meeting." Seriel rose to his feet and walked to the table. He picked up the holstered light wand and fastened it to his thigh.

The Shekinah stood up and moved in his direction. She observed, "I have offended you. Please let me explain why I withdrew my hands from yours. It was not because I dislike contact with you."

"That is not necessary, my lady. I understand your feelings. You love Samael and no other being would, or should, attract your interest." He retrieved the emerald from the table and offered it to her: "Here is your green jewel."

She pushed his hand away, declaring, "I do not wish to keep it with me. I pray you, dear brother, let it rest in your home. It brings me too much sadness."

"As you wish." He placed the emerald back on the table. "Shall I escort you to inner Chaos? Where do you desire to go?"

"I believe your spiral is the place I should visit. What you have shared has set me wondering about many things."

"Then Seriel's Spiral it shall be!" He touched the hilt of his crystal with his right hand and, extending his left hand to his sister, he told her, "If you are not too aggrieved to do so, then take my hand and I will show you the magic of my light wand."

Without hesitation, Malkura grasped his hand and asked, "What magic will you show me?"

Even as her thought was forming, Seriel was asking his crystal to take them to the spiraling spheres. Instantly, they were there and the Shekinah was looking around in utter astonishment. She exclaimed:

"That is wondrous magic! How did you accomplish such a task?"

"I did nothing other than ask my crystal to bring us here. It is an amazing friend. Now, I will take my leave of you. May you remain within our parent's thoughts!" Seriel attempted to release her hand, but she held on tightly as she told him:

"You have comforted me when I was in the depth of sadness. You also aided Gabriel when he was suffering. The Lord of Sorcery is truly a noble soul and I will cherish a memory of what we have shared while in your home." She gave a gentle smile and, pulling herself close to him for an instant, she thought-whispered, "I withdrew my hands because a strong notion to meld with you had come upon me. I was afraid you might sense my desire. Knowing your feelings about the sanctity of melding, I thought you would consider me to be both shallow and fickle." Malkura released her hold of him and flew deep into the heart of the spiral. Her parting: "May the Source forever bless you!" came back to him as she disappeared between some spheres.

The seventh archangel flew toward the Source in a completely perplexed state. He could not believe what Malkura had told him. Had he misunderstood her in some way? Was he misinterpreting her thought-whisperings? Did she truly wish to meld with him? Seriel was so engrossed in his puzzled thoughts that he almost flew straight into his parent. He perceived the brilliant consciousness of the Source just before he would have crashed inside it.

"You are preoccupied with thoughts of the Shekinah, my son. Can I help you with your musings?"

Seriel settled himself beside his parent and answered, "I think not. That is not my reason for coming here."

The Source informed him, "I know why you are here, Seriel. Your brother suggested you should consult with me because I told him to relay that message to you. I have waited long for you to come to me. Except for witnessing the first angels' birth, you have not drawn near since you began your archangel existence."

Feeling somewhat reprimanded, Seriel thought-mumbled, "I did not think you would notice my absence."

"My dear child, I closely follow the actions of each of my precious children. Both you and Samael believe I am a stern parent who wishes to restrict your experiences. He only comes near to challenge what he perceives as my authority, and you keep your distance from me."

Uncertain how to respond to this perceived rebuke, the seventh archangel decided to maintain a thought silence. The Source observed:

"Yet you have come now, not knowing it was in answer to my bidding. Thus, I am grateful. I wish to hold discourse with you about your brother. I am happy to also discuss other matters which trouble you, such as your love for Malkura."

Seriel reminded himself how the Source knew everything about everything. He ventured, "Can you tell me whether what she has just shared is true? Am I misconstruing her meaning? Or was she merely jesting with me?"

His parent assured him, "There was no jest and you have understood her meaning. Your sister is seeing you within a new perspective. You are all evolving and change is upon you. Malkura has been blinded by your brother's radiance, but she is realizing his destiny is not with her. Her love for you will grow, my son."

Cheered by this information, Seriel continued, "Malkura expressed your caution to her about not interfering with Samael's destiny. My brother has also shared his belief that you would never allow him and the Shekinah to be together."

"My son, you and your siblings all believe I allow or disallow each happening. This is not so. I offer choices and you can accept or refuse them. In this reality the Shekinah is choosing not to align with her first-born brother. In certain others she is with him."

Seriel questioned, "This is but one reality?"

"Indeed, it is so. Each choice made creates a new reality. All is choice, thus, realities are endless."

"So nothing is ordained by you? Nothing is inevitable?"

"Some choices become inevitable because of the nature of the soul making the choice, but I do not compel the facets of my being to do anything. I only offer possibilities."

"Does that mean I, and not Samael, will be with Malkura in this reality?"

"All is choice, Seriel."

"I hold deep respect and love for my brother and, even though he has caused me harm, I do not wish him grief. His love for our sister is beyond all else for him. To not have her will bring him great sorrow. Yet, if that was as a consequence of her being with me, it would ravage his soul."

"You are mistaken, my son. You are measuring Samael's emotions by your own depth of feeling. His love for Malkura is not beyond all else. His destiny is the force which drives him. He has ordained it to become his choice above all other possibilities he could pursue."

"And there is a reason for him choosing his destiny. Is that not so?"

"Yes, my son."

Seriel pressed, "According to Malkura, you will not reveal that reason."

"That is so. It must remain hidden."

A sudden thought came to Seriel. He stated, "If Samael has ordained the choice of his destiny, then he must know the reason."

"He knew of it, but does not now hold any remembrance of its existence."

"Did you make him forget?"

A rippling sigh passed through the Source as it replied, "I do not *make* my children do anything. It was his choice to forget."

Seriel silently considered this information for a while. Eventually, he questioned, "None know this reason other than yourself?"

"Before the council meeting began, I shared it with the Christ Soul. I know with certainty he is the only soul who will never divulge it to another."

Seriel commented, "I can understand your reasoning. He is very different from his siblings and, I think, is most like you."

"That may be so, but each of my children are unique and precious within their own essence."

"Yet none of us except yourself and the Christ Soul can ever know that hidden reason?"

"I have made no such statement. I also have free will and can choose when and to whom I reveal that reason. It well may be that you will receive that knowledge from me. However, your knowing it is a very noble reason will suffice for now. That is why I entreat you to keep a close and loving watch over Samael. No matter what befalls him, remain his trustworthy companion and loyal brother."

"You have asked this of me before, when I was inside the large crystal. And I have already sworn my allegiance to him. I do not take that oath lightly."

"I know that, my son. That is why I am asking this of you and no other archangel. You have the endurance and understanding to fulfill this wish."

Feeling a little overcome by all of this praise, Seriel could only answer, "I will endeavor to do what you ask of me."

A period of silence ensued, and the seventh archangel was uncertain whether his parent had moved into deeper sleep. He was considering moving quietly away from the Source when it unexpectedly remarked:

"It will become a most difficult and soul-injuring task. Therefore, I wish to give you a gift in gratitude of your willingness to accept this burden. You are aware that some are gaining their etheric vision, yet yours is dormant. Remain still and I will awaken your etheric sight and hearing, and enhance your sense of touch."

A vaporous mist of the most vibrant red drifted up from the Source and moved toward Seriel. It enveloped him, and a warm, tingling sensation seemed to caress his whole being. For an instant he felt disorientated, and then sights and sounds bombarded his etheric senses. The kaleidoscopic colors of the Source imprinted on his consciousness with much more intensity than before. There was also a gentle sh-sh-sh sound, which he had not previously perceived, coming from his parent. As the mist began to fade, he touched the dwindling vapors and experienced their tactile softness. While he continued to discover these new delights, he was also aware of the overwhelming love his parent held for him. It nestled within his soul and would sustain him forever thereafter.

Slowly, Seriel brought his attention back to the Source. He declared, "Thank you, dear parent. I now know both Samael and I have misjudged you."

"All is choice, Seriel. What you believe is also of your choosing. Now, what else would you wish to learn from me?"

"Many things." He moved closer to the Source and began a long and enlightening thought exchange with his parent. Seriel gained knowledge of perceived transgression, possible realities, tears and the all-encompassing love of the Source of ALL THAT IS. While he remained there, the Lord of the Seventh Essence was given much wisdom that would never leave him.

Chapter Twenty

The exiles began to settle into life away from the angelic horde. Samael had moved his crystalline home before the onset of the resting phase. As soon as he awakened, he went to Uriel's abode and with the help of his crystal wand transported that large edifice and his sibling. He positioned the abode within the area of banishment, but not as far outwards as his own home. He was certain Uriel had no great love for the density and unknown qualities of the extreme outer Abyss. The first archangel instructed Belial and Semyaza on how to build their own homes. This was something they had been asking him to do prior to the banishing. To Samael's surprise, he learned that Azazel had previously constructed a home in this external area of Chaos. He had done so even before the attack on the fourth archangel. This was the place to where he and Kokabel flew, after he came back from helping Michael with the injured Gabriel.

Once Seriel returned from his thought exchange with the Source, Michael came to his home and asked him to seek out the six exiles. He wanted his brother to ensure they had left the inner realms of the Abyss. Seriel quickly established that all six were where the council had decreed they should be. While remaining briefly with Samael, his sibling questioned him about the Shekinah. He wanted to know whether Seriel had been in her company. If so, was she continuing to be angry with her first-born brother or was she wishing to see him? Seriel had no intention of telling

Samael what had transpired between their sister and himself. All he would detail was a brief contact with Malkura before the resting phase, and none since wakening. He proffered the assumption the Shekinah was remaining angry and also upset. Samael told Seriel he would wait for a short while and then visit her. His wand would take him immediately to Malkura no matter where she might be.

After leaving his brother, the seventh archangel sought out Michael and reported that the exiles were obeying the council's directive. On his return home, he busied himself creating a large, oval crystal mirror which he positioned on the wall of one of his rooms. Beyond this action, Seriel divided his attention between his spiraling spheres and his resting chamber. He frequently sat on the floor of this room and recaptured the idyllic memory of the Shekinah's presence within that place. Holding the emerald, he became lost in the memory of her exquisite green eyes. Seriel also gave extensive thought to building a home for Malkura. Her obvious lack of concern for her own safety greatly troubled him. She needed the protection of an etheric building so that the daemons could not come close to her. He would suggest building such an abode on their next meeting. When out in the Abyss, he searched for his sibling in the hope their paths would cross, but she was not to be found.

On one occasion, Seriel did discover Manah inspecting his spiral of spheres. He thought about what his sister had told him with regard to this angel liking him. Feeling wary of being followed everywhere in the manner Kokabel had pursued him, he was hesitant to question her about the Shekinah's well-being. However, his concern for Malkura outweighed his reluctance, therefore, he asked the eighth-cast angel how her mistress was fairing. He was informed she was less unhappy. According to Manah, his sister appeared to be gaining solace from frequent thought exchanges with either the Source or the Christ Soul.

Before leaving him, the pure essence angel expressed her belief that the Lady Malkura, in the future, would surely realize the depth of his love for her. A startled Seriel attempted to deny knowledge of what was being put forward. However, Manah assured him both she and several other eighth essence angels were well aware of his strong affection for his sister. She smiled and explained how she often shared thoughts about him with the Shekinah in an attempt to draw Lady Malkura's attention to her seventh-born brother and away from Lord Samael. This small confession prompted Seriel to inform the angel of the Shekinah's conviction that she, Manah, was attracted to him. The resulting shared amusement between the two angelic beings heralded the beginning of their alliance. Angel Manah was to become an ally in Seriel's quest to win the love of Malkura.

At the council meeting, no one had put forward the suggestion of banishing the daemons. It was most unlikely they would have taken notice of such a directive and they were, at least, confined to the central and outer areas of Chaos. Thought-word went out to all the angels to avoid contact with them whenever possible. Knowing what had befallen the archangels Gabriel and Seriel, most souls were not anxious to learn more about them. They were considered hostile creatures of whom everyone must always be extremely wary.

The daemons were delighted to have the continuous company of the six banished souls. Having already established a strong following of Azazel, they were often to be found in, or close by, his home. Kokabel was intrigued by their squabbles and antics and soon considered certain ones her favorites. Included in these preferred creatures were Shedim and Lamassu. Samael ordered his daemons to do no harm to the exiles and they obeyed him. On occasion, he also instructed certain ones to travel further inwards to observe, and then report back to him, happenings during his absence.

However, being unable to gain close proximity to the Source and its light-filled surrounding area, they could not usually bring him news of the Shekinah.

Uriel was happy to observe and interact with his own daemons, but those who had sprung from Samael, Seriel and Gabriel paid little attention to him. The latter group often went in search of their archangel parent. They wanted to do his bidding and keep close contact with him. He either ignored their presence or ordered them to leave him immediately. The very sight of these creatures rekindled the horrific memory of how his body had been brutally maimed.

Seriel's daemons never approached his home or himself, except when he was in the outlying areas of the Abyss. After the attack on Gabriel, he had directed them to always remain within outer Chaos and to be commanded by none but himself. To ensure they would not challenge his authority over them, he promised to destroy any who disobeyed him. A quick reminder of what had happened to those daemons, who fed on Gabriel's essence, was sufficient to remove any opposition. Once Seriel learned of the pursuit of the fourth archangel by his own daemons, he told his brother to follow his example. The same command of confinement and total adherence to Gabriel's bidding was dispatched. It was accompanied by the threat of annihilation from Seriel's light wand in the event of disobedience. Gabriel was immediately free from daemonic shadowing.

Apart from not addressing the problem of the daemons, the council had also neglected to realize some angels would not agree with their findings. Only certain members of the council were allowed to make the decisions of punishment, therefore, the angelic audience was not given the opportunity to express their agreement or dissension. A good number of those who had attended, and who were already following Samael's reasoning, considered banishment a harsh decree. Like the exiled angels, they believed the first archangel was entitled to seek revenge for the unjust behavior of Gabriel. Once thought-word of the meeting and the subsequent council's directives were relayed to those who did not attend, even more angels considered the six exiles had been treated wrongly. They decided to ignore the order that they must not go to outer Chaos. Many began to spend their waking periods with the banished archangels and angels. Some built homes from etheric matter so that they could remain with them during the resting phases.

Samael's need to know what was happening to the Shekinah in his absence prompted him to create a device for remote viewing. From a darkly hued mineral he fashioned a round, flat object, which was similar in size and shape to the mirror he had made for Malkura, but which contained no silver. When he sat holding the device and asked it to show him the whereabouts of his sister, a small image of her, and of what she was doing, would appear within its depth. She was often in the company of some of her brothers or her own angels. Samael soon noted how the pure essence angel, Manah, was her frequent companion.

On the occasions when the Shekinah was alone, the first archangel would suddenly appear beside her, having requested the aid of his light wand to transport him there. At first, Malkura ignored him by silencing her thoughts and quickly flying off in the direction of any angelic beings whom she sensed were nearby. Not wanting to be seen in areas which were off limits to him, Samael would not follow her. However, there was one incident when he chased her in and around Seriel's Spiral, trying to force her to share thoughts with him. This pursuit of his sibling ended when a group of approaching angels saw him before he disappeared. This was the first of many sightings of the Lord of Lightning-Swiftness in the forbidden realms of Chaos. It was speedily reported to Michael and Gabriel.

Eventually, her brother's persistence caused Malkura to respond to his questions about her feelings toward him. She assured him she wanted no contact with him until he apologized to Gabriel and Seriel for instructing the daemons to attack them. He would also have to demonstrate a willingness to forsake his wayward attitude with regard to their parent. Samael should be willing to listen to the Source, act upon its wishes and agree with its reasoning. Even if he fulfilled all of her requests, Malkura stated she could not promise to resume her former loving relationship with him. It would take a long duration for her to forget his abhorrent behavior. In addition, she warned him that his repeated disregard for the council's banishment directive was not unknown to his siblings. It was very possible another council meeting would take place in order to decide upon further punishment.

Samael scoffed at his sister's caution. He declared his right to come and go wherever he so chose. Also, if she would come to outer Chaos and stay with him, he would have little reason to frequent the inner realms. The outer Abyss was much more appealing and intriguing. Why could she not at least visit him in his home so that they could have an undisturbed discussion on all that had happened since Gabriel denounced him? She did not have to pay heed to the council's decree that none but Seriel should have contact with the exiles. The Shekinah was a mighty archangel who could do as she pleased. Malkura quickly confirmed her lack of desire to consider his suggestions or to have uninterrupted thought exchanges with him.

During one of Samael's early visitations to his sister, he realized she was no longer carrying the emerald within her rulpiel scarf. He questioned her why she was not wearing it and where it was hidden. In answer, the Shekinah merely told him the jewel was too painful a reminder of the past. This infuriated the first archangel and he was determined to discover the emerald's location. He suspected Manah would know where it was, therefore, soon afterwards he made a sudden appearance in front of this angel, while she was alone. Samael demanded she tell him what Malkura had done with the green jewel.

Manah knew all about the emerald, its creator and its significance. She was also aware of her essence lady's decision to leave it with Archangel Seriel. Having no great liking for the Lord of the First Essence, Manah explained that Lady Malkura wished to break the ties with her first-born brother. She had taken the jewel to the Source and asked it to destroy this stone of unhappy memories. After placing the emerald inside her parent's consciousness, she had watched the green jewel quickly disintegrate. The angel's shared information about the emerald, albeit false, made Samael even more determined to be alone with his sister. Before flying away, Manah assured Samael she would report to the other archangels his presence in a restricted area.

When Seriel next visited the exiles, the first archangel explained what he had learned from Manah. His seventh-born brother listened, but did not reveal the fact he had been told an untruth by the pure essence angel. He knew his sibling would not take kindly to their sister leaving the jewel in his keeping. Samael assured Seriel he was determined to confront the Shekinah in order to learn from her why she had discarded the emerald. He asked his brother to take Malkura to his pyramidal home on some excuse. Once she was inside, Seriel must transport himself to Samael to alert him to the Shekinah's confinement. Prior to leaving, he must make sure the entrance door was closed. In that way, Malkura could not escape. Then, the first archangel would quickly materialize inside the pyramid and his sister would have to answer his questions.

Seriel had no intention of granting his sibling's request, but chose not to declare his refusal. Instead, he put forward his doubts about the likelihood of persuading Malkura to enter his home. It might prove difficult and would not be a speedy solution to Samael's problem. He suggested an easier and quicker one would be for him to build a home for the

Shekinah. The need for such an abode was continuing to present itself to his sense of concern about his sister. Seriel pointed out the advantage for Samael of this proposal. Malkura could often be found in her home, which would give the first archangel more than one opportunity to be with her. Samael thought this was an excellent idea and gave his full approval.

Having built his own pyramid by trial and error, it did not take long for Seriel to construct a perfect home for Malkura. It was not as large as his own, but was similar in design. There were ascending corridors, lit by blazing torches, which led to several rooms. The resting chamber was near the apex and it contained the same undulating floor which had fascinated the Shekinah. Seriel placed a crystal capstone on the top of the pyramid and asked it to continuously protect his sister when she was in her home. He further directed it to not allow other beings to enter the abode in any manner unless Malkura would wish to have their company. This meant Samael would not be able to presently transport himself to the interior of the pyramid, but might gain access to it at some point in the future. Although his sister was distressed by the first-born archangel's behavior, Seriel thought she may eventually wish to resume her closeness with him. He knew how deeply she had loved their brother.

Once the etheric structure was complete, Seriel flew to Samael and told him the Shekinah's home was ready. He withheld any information of what he had asked the crystal capstone to ensure. However, he did express his hope to inform their sister about the abode on his return to inner Chaos. Samael was delighted with this news.

Yet contact with the Shekinah continued to elude the seventh archangel. He was not certain whether this was by chance or if she was deliberately avoiding him. Perhaps she regretted having disclosed an interest in melding with him? Or maybe the Christ Soul and Michael were advising her not to go near him, in addition to remaining apart from Samael? Whatever the reason, he could not find Malkura to give her the home he had built. Therefore, when he next saw Manah, he explained about the pyramid and why he had constructed it. He took the angel to this new home and showed her its interior. Seriel asked Manah to take Malkura to the pyramid and tell her it was a gift from her seventh-born brother. The Lord of Sorcery stressed the need for the pure essence angel to inform the Shekinah of his concern for her welfare. Hence the existence of the pyramidal abode and the entrance door's ability to only open and close at her bidding. Once outside the home, Seriel instructed the door and the capstone to only follow the Shekinah's commands and to no longer obey him.

The seventh archangel informed his brother of his inability to find the Shekinah, thus, he was uncertain when she would take up residency. However, he knew Manah would know where she was and would, hopefully, soon take her to the pyramid. Samael thanked Seriel and, once alone, he began to consult his remote viewing crystal to learn when Malkura would be inside her new home. He viewed the crystal's images of the interior of the abode on several occasions without success of seeing her.

Like his essence lord, Azazel had been a frequent visitor to the spiral of spheres before being banished. It had shown him many things which could possibly take place. One repeated event was the fighting and strife between wingless beings. Some resembled angels, while others differed somewhat in their anatomy. There were even some who appeared to be a combination of the two types of beings. The angel-like individuals used both sharp and blunt instruments with which to injure and maim each other or the other beings. Certain of those who received blows and thrusts from the instruments appeared to be unable to continue to move. It was as though their life force essence was no more. Azazel could not imagine the identity of the beings or where their actions would take place. However, he was certain they were not existing within the Abyss of Chaos.

This pure essence angel was convinced similar strife, eventually, would erupt between those who supported Samael and those who did not. Azazel understood the first archangel's intolerance toward being told what he could or could not do. He also felt the same desire to exercise his free will in whatever manner he chose. The daemons frequently fought with each other over seemingly nothing. Therefore, surely archangels and angels would fight to uphold their reasoning and interpretations of free will? Although he had never come upon the sphere, which depicted an angelic battle, he began to feel convinced something of that nature would happen.

Believing this, Azazel set about creating similar weapons to those he had viewed in Seriel's Spiral. They became the etheric forerunners of what, in a world of matter, would be considered daggers, swords, javelins and clubs. He also constructed shields with which to repel blows from such weaponry. As more and more angels joined the six exiles, he taught them how to fashion these tools for warfare and how to use them. It became a regular occurrence for groups of angels to practice their ability to fight. Within mock combats they would hone their skills and desires to do battle. Angels of the third and seventh essences seemed particularly drawn to the art of war.

When Samael learned of these preparations for fighting, he was extremely pleased. He was nursing a growing desire to challenge the council's directives by overthrowing Michael's leadership. He was not anxious for angels to possess light wands, but he considered certain crystal points could be used as sharp weapons. Samael made journeys back and forth to the two areas where the crystals lay undisturbed, and he moved many of them to the outer Abyss. When presented with these mineral additions to their etheric weaponry, it did not take long for some angels to attempt to use them as light wands. Chief among these were Azazel, Belial and Semyaza. They had witnessed the awesome power of Seriel's wand. However, much to Samael's delight, it quickly became evident that a crystal would only emit a light beam when in the hands of an archangel. Those original extensions of the Source appeared to have a closer connection with the etheric mineral kingdom than the angels.

As will often happen when there are two opposing points-of-view, altercations started to occur between the angels who were in sympathy with the exiles and those who were not. These usually took place when the supportive angelic beings flew back into the inner parts of Chaos. Those who followed Michael and Gabriel would attempt to prevent the returning angels from moving freely in areas which were considered restricted. Thought-word arguments soon escalated into bodily fighting. The onset of this new development prompted the outer Abyss angels to begin carrying their weapons with them whenever they journeyed inwards. Inevitably, this led to fighting which involved one side using their weaponry to establish the belief that might is right.

The subsequent lacerations and abrasions inflicted on certain angels were quickly brought to the attention of Michael and Gabriel. No angel was wounded to any great degree and it was soon realized Samael's belief was correct. His contention that, eventually, etheric injuries would heal automatically proved to be true. Raphael had also discovered his own ability to speed the healing of bodily trauma by manifesting an etheric seal over a wound. Nevertheless, the occurrences of weapon-enhanced fighting were alarming, and Michael instructed his followers to fashion similar weaponry to that which had been used against them. Now, both sides were evenly matched and, increasingly, conflict was happening within the Abyss of Chaos. In addition, any angelic essence, which was spilt from sustained wounds, quickly escaped into outer Chaos and became daemons.

As disregard for the council's directives grew, Azazel, Belial and Semyaza would also accompany their supporting angels into the forbidden realms of the Abyss. Wishing to regain advantage over their adversaries, these three exiles decided to take some of Samael's daemons with them whenever they traveled to the central parts of Chaos. Their creature allies were more than happy to join in the fighting by biting and clawing any angels who challenged them. Thus, within a short duration of the banishing, much of life within the Abyss of Chaos transformed from an existence of tranquillity and joy to one of disruption and strife. Samael was well pleased with this development.

Realizing the angelic battle, which he had been shown in both his dream and in Seriel's Spiral, was becoming inevitable, Michael took Gabriel to the location of the first crop of crystals. The third archangel had previously discovered both areas containing the etheric minerals while conducting one of his regular patrols of Chaos. He realized they were the same objects as those referred to earlier by Seriel. Michael and his brother searched through the crystals, which had not yet been removed by Samael, and each chose one for his own light wand. Gabriel's choice was a long, narrow crystal which quickly appealed to his sense of practicality. It possessed unusual clarity and was the most beautiful shade of honey brown. Michael's chosen wand was deep purple at one end. Its color intensity slowly graduated into lighter tones along its shaft until it became clear at the other end. This crystal possessed the blessing of being doubly terminated. He decided to fashion it with his thoughts into a sword-like shape, creating the pommel from its clear extremity. The Lord of the Third Essence's powerful crystalline weapon would ultimately become known as Archangel Michael's Sword of Redemption.

Prior to the two siblings making their crystal choices, the first archangel suddenly materialized a short distance away from them. He was on one of his many clandestine visits to gather crystals. Samael instantly saw them and immediately vanished, but not before they had noticed him. Now, they were certain the reports they had received of their brother's appearances were not mistaken. The Lord of Lightning-Swiftness was visiting areas from which he was restricted. After leaving the crop of crystals, Michael and Gabriel met with Raphael and the Christ Soul. They shared their concern about Samael's disobedience and the increasing incidences of angelic fighting. It was decided another council meeting must quickly take place. The matter was too urgent to wait until beyond the next angel birthing.

After transporting himself back to his home, Samael viewed his two siblings remotely by means of his dark crystal. With great annoyance, he watched them choosing their light wands. Once they had left the area, he returned and gathered together the remaining crystals in order to take them back to outer Chaos. Samael did not want Michael, or Gabriel, or even Raphael, to create other light wands or crystal weapons from them. On reaching home, Samael planned to go back out to the second crop of crystals in order to also retrieve all of them. However, his intention was diverted by what his remote viewing crystal was displaying. The Shekinah was being shown her new home by Seriel and Manah. The first archangel would wait until they had taken their leave of his sister. Then he would instantly go to her and learn whether he had lost her love forever.

Chapter Twenty-One

The Shekinah was returning from a thought exchange between herself, the Source and the Christ Soul. They had been discussing Seriel because, more and more, Malkura found her thoughts returning to her seventh brother and the manner in which he had given her support and comfort. Both her second-born sibling and her parent appeared happy to encourage her to form a closer bond with Seriel. This was not too surprising, she was certain they both knew how unhappy Samael had caused her to become. She had even expressed to them her earlier desire to meld with Seriel, and this did not meet with their disapproval. The Christ Soul suggested she go to Seriel's Spiral and search for spheres which might display whether the seventh and eighth archangels would become close companions.

As the Shekinah was approaching the spiraling orbs, Manah's calling thoughts came to her:

"My Lady Malkura, pray wait for me!"

Looking around, she discovered her pure essence angel flying in her direction from some distance behind. Malkura hovered in a circular motion and awaited Manah's arrival.

"I have been searching for you, my lady," announced the angel as she reached the Shekinah.

"I was with my parent and the Christ Soul," Malkura informed her. "For what reason are you needing me?"

Manah gave her a beaming smile and declared, "Lord Seriel has a wonderful surprise for you! I have come to take you to see it."

"Lord Seriel?" queried Malkura. Then noticing the angel's gleeful expression, she asked, "Have you decided to follow the seventh archangel now that Kokabel is no longer enamored with him?"

"Oh, no, my lady. Lord Seriel came to me, I did not go to him. He had searched and searched, but could not find you. Thus, he took me to see what he has created. Your brother wanted to know whether I thought you would approve of it. I told him I was certain you would. So now he wants you to take possession of the surprise. Come with me quickly, my lady!"

Changing direction, the Shekinah began to fly beside Manah and away from Seriel's Spiral. She questioned, "My brother has a surprise for me? What is it?"

Manah shook her head and observed, "It will not be a surprise, if I tell you of it!"

"Are you certain I will like it?"

The pure essence angel assured her, "I know you will feel a deeper emotion than that of liking, my lady. It is a beautiful surprise which you will cherish. And that is as much information as you will glean from me. My thoughts are sealed!"

The two angelic beings continued their journey in silence. They flew over Seriel's pyramidal home and soon afterwards were above another pyramid. The Shekinah noted it was similar to her seventh brother's abode, but was smaller. Manah began to descend and Malkura followed her. As they both alighted, Seriel suddenly appeared close by from nowhere. He walked over to them and explained:

"I was in my home and sensed you were passing overhead. I realized Manah must be bringing you here so I have come to learn what you think of this." He pointed to the pyramid.

Before Malkura could answer, Manah exclaimed:

"You and Lord Samael must be sorcerers! How do you appear so instantaneously?"

"Angel Manah!" the Shekinah scolded, "Do not be so bold! We archangels have special abilities with which angels have not yet been blessed."

A giggling thought escaped from Manah as she remarked, "Oh, I forgot, archangels are the first to do everything!"

Obviously amused by their sense of fun, Seriel answered, "The magic lies in my crystal wand, Manah. I ask it to take me anywhere and instantly I am there. Lady Malkura has also traveled via its sorcery."

"A secret she has not shared with me," thought-grumbled Manah. "But then, I have secrets, too. Lady Malkura only knows she is here because you have a surprise for her. She does not know what it is."

"Then I will explain," declared Seriel. "My lady, this pyramid is your home. I have constructed it for you because I am concerned about your safety. When the resting phase is upon us, you can sleep inside this building where the daemons cannot reach you." He gently guided his sister toward the entrance.

Gazing up at the pyramid, Malkura replied, "This is a wonderful surprise. What a kind and thoughtful sibling you are!"

Remaining where she stood, Manah offered, "I will take my leave of you. Lord Seriel has already guided me through your home so I am familiar with its usefulness."

The Shekinah quickly replied, "I wish you to remain, Manah. We shall examine the pyramid together." Malkura was feeling reluctant to be alone with Seriel. She was certain he would want to question her about the thought-whispered declaration which she had made when they last parted company. In different circumstances, she would have never explained why she withdrew her hands from his. It was only his obvious feelings of being offended that had prompted her bold revelation.

"Very well, my lady." Manah moved to a position close behind the Shekinah. As she did so, she grimaced at Seriel.

The seventh archangel merely shrugged his shoulders, indicating acceptance of Malkura's wish. He told his sister:

"If you send a requesting thought to the door to open, it will obey you."

Malkura stood in front of the door, staring at its stark beauty. Unlike Samael's entrance doors, it was neither golden nor ornate. It was colored rulpiel, as were the walls of the pyramid, but it was of a darker shade. The door was completely smooth, and emblazoned across a part of its entirety were strange glyphs. Malkura suspected her brother had etched them with the beam from his light wand. They appeared to be burned into the substance of the etheric door. She asked, "What are these markings, Seriel?"

Lovingly tracing their pattern with his fingers, the seventh archangel replied, "I have been preoccupied of late with creating symbols for the thoughts we share with one another. In dreams, I have seen many glyphs and, on waking, I seem to know their meaning. I think of these symbols as angelic script with which we can record our thoughts."

"You have always wanted to hold onto what has become known," observed Malkura. "You truly treasure learning. Do you know the meaning of these particular symbols?"

"Yes, they proclaim to all who see them that this pyramid is *Archangel Malkura's Home.* Now, my lady, bid the door to open and we will go inside."

The Shekinah followed his request, and to her surprise it did not open inwards as did Samael's doors. It slid upwards, as if being pulled from above. The three passed through the opening and Malkura asked the door to close. It moved quickly back down into its former position. As they moved along the passageway, Seriel explained:

"The door will open and close to none but yourself. In that manner you will always be safe. No one can enter your home through this door when you are not here."

"It is obvious your brother is mindful of your well-being, my lady," commented Manah. "An angelic quality to be admired."

The Shekinah gave her pure essence angel a silencing stare as Seriel looked somewhat embarrassed. She told him, "Thank you, dear brother. It is a comfort for me to know I am safe within this abode."

Ignoring her essence mistress's warning expression, Manah continued, "Lord Samael has been pestering Lady Malkura of late, even though he is banned from inner Chaos. He has even pursued her around your spiral of spheres in an effort to make her acknowledge him. She wishes to be done with him, but he will not accept this truth. I fear for my mistress's safety. Thus, it pleases me to know she can escape his unwanted pursuit by entering her home."

The seventh archangel turned and faced Manah. He angrily declared, "Lord Samael would never hurt his sister! He loves her deeply. It is difficult for him to accept Lady Malkura's unhappiness with him."

The disgruntled angel walked on ahead, thought-muttering to herself, but making sure this one remark reached the archangels: "He did not hesitate to already harm two of his siblings!"

Addressing her brother, Malkura put forward, "You must excuse Manah's behavior. She holds an intense dislike of Samael. I should not have told her he has been trying to regain my affection."

"And I should not have answered her so sharply. Her thoughts were motivated by concern for you. Despite my angry reaction to Manah's comments, I know it is necessary for you to be free of Samael's attention. That is why I have asked the crystal capstone of your pyramid to repel entrance by all others, unless you wish to have their company. No matter how Samael attempts to come inside your home, he will be prevented. Only if you are happy for him to be with you, will he be able to enter."

The Shekinah looked puzzled and asked, "How could Samael enter my home, if I do not open the door for him?"

Seriel touched his light wand and reminded her, "As I told Manah earlier, these crystals take us anywhere we wish to go."

"Oh." Malkura gave this information some thought, and then commented, "Of course, they can. We passed through the walls of your pyramid when you took me to the spiraling spheres."

"Yes. With a light wand's help we can pass through etheric matter, including the substance of crystals. However, Samael cannot now enter your home, not even through the open doorway unless you wish him to do so."

The two archangels had reached the first chamber within the pyramid, but Manah was not there. Realizing this, Malkura remarked:

"I think Manah is upset because you were angry. I should look for her."

"No, I will go and apologize to her. Wait here!" Seriel exited the room to search for the angel.

Left alone, the Shekinah inspected the chamber in which she was standing. There were no faceted jewels embedded in the walls. Instead, the latter were fitted with bronze-colored sconces which held flaming torches. The high ceiling was adorned with a billowy, light green material. It was fastened to the center of the ceiling by means of a large, round pink mineral and gently draped into each of the corners of the room. The floor was covered with a soft, thick substance that echoed the green hue of the etheric material. Malkura's bare feet sank into its tactile comfort. There was a long table against one of the walls with a chair positioned close by. Displayed on the table were a number of beautiful minerals. Several were clusters of clear, or purple, or pale yellow crystals. Others were single clear points or granular blocks of iridescence.

The Shekinah moved over to the table and picked up one large cluster of yellow crystals. As she gazed in wonder at its pure clarity, tiny reflections of the torch flames danced across its faceted structure. She began to realize why her two brothers were so engrossed in the power of the etheric mineral kingdom. The crystals' beauty alone was an experience not to be equaled. Like Seriel, Malkura could quickly feel the intense energy radiating out from these glorious objects. She had previously noticed it when Samael took her to where the crystals had grown. Now, while holding the cluster, she was reminded of the peace she had felt when wrapped in a luminous thread of Source consciousness.

Seriel returned with Manah and there appeared to be no tension between them. They were both smiling. The pure essence angel walked over to where Malkura was standing and, touching one of the clusters on the table, she asked:

"Are they not beautiful, my lady?"

"They are, indeed," responded the Shekinah. "But why are they here?"

"There are more in other rooms," informed Manah. "They are gifts from Lord Seriel."

Malkura looked at her brother, waiting for an explanation. He told her:

"I thought, like me, you might be intrigued by them. Apart from their obvious beauty, they appear to enhance and focus our thoughts. When you are home and not sleeping, you may wish to hold them or ask that they manifest your wishes." Seriel picked up one small cluster of purple crystals and declared, "I have found the ones which display this color to be particularly comforting."

Malkura shook her head and assured him, "They would not comfort me. That color reminds me of the brother I wish to forget."

A daunted expression appeared on Seriel's face as he declared, "My apologies, dear sister. How thoughtless of me! I will remove all of the purple crystals and take them back to where they grew."

"No, no, Seriel! I do not want you to take them away." The Shekinah placed the yellow cluster back on the table and gently lifted the purple cluster from her sibling's hands. She stared at the abundant richness of the amethyst color and thought about Samael's eyes. Then pushing that memory away from herself, she returned the cluster to the table and added, "I must not allow his ugliness to prevent me from seeing the beauty in other things. The purple crystals are exquisite and I shall value them for their own glory."

They left the room and walked along other corridors to other chambers. Ceilings were draped with delicate materials of differing colors and floors were enriched with soft, carpet-like coverings. Each room contained a table laden with glorious crystals. As the three angelic beings moved through the pyramid, Manah played guide. She pointed out all of the home's attributes and conveniences, often repeating how much she admired Lord Seriel's creativity. He walked in silence to the rear of Malkura and her angel. His embarrassment due to Manah's praise was plain to see whenever the Shekinah turned to address a thought to him.

Their final destination was the resting chamber. Malkura was enchanted to discover the floor possessed an undulating quality. She exclaimed, "Oh, Seriel, you have made it magical just like the one in yours!"

Her delighted observation brought a sharp, curious stare from Manah and a nod of agreement from her brother. He offered:

"I thought you would be pleased. I know how much the floor's movement intrigued you. It will begin or cease at your bidding."

"Thank you, Seriel, you are . . ." Her thought was interrupted by another coming from outside the pyramid:

"Brother Seriel, are you inside?" It was Archangel Raphael.

"I am here," answered the seventh archangel. Then to the Shekinah he directed, "If you wish Raphael to enter, request the front door to open."

Malkura did as Seriel bid and, after a short pause, she
sent this questioning thought to her fifth brother: "Have
you passed through the entrance?" On receiving his
affirmative response, she closed the door with her thoughts
and added, "We will come to you." Then to her two
companions, she suggested, "Let us go to meet him. I am
presuming he does not know the way through my home?"

"No one has viewed it except yourself and Manah,"
replied Seriel.

They moved quickly through the chambers and
passageways and found Raphael waiting in the first corridor.
He explained:

"I thought I sensed you in here, Seriel. Is this a new
pyramid you have built for yourself?"

"No, he created it for me," answered the Shekinah. "He
was showing it to me and Angel Manah."

"What has brought you here?" questioned Seriel.

Raphael disclosed, "Michael, Gabriel, the Christ Soul and
I have decided we cannot wait until the next angel birthing
to hold another council meeting. We are extremely disturbed
by Samael's disregard for banishment, together with the
frequent fighting among the angels. Therefore, we will
conduct the meeting as soon as we are able. We six archangels
and certain catalyst, and pure essence, angels will form the
council. An immediate course of action must be reached.
Seriel, will you help me seek out the other angels?"

The seventh archangel nodded his agreement and the
Shekinah asked:

"Is it to be held in the same place as our previous
meeting?"

"Yes. Gabriel and the Christ Soul are already there with
their angels. Michael and Mikael are looking for the others."

"Manah and I will go now together," offered the
Shekinah.

Raphael commented, "You do not have to hurry. It may
take us a while to find all of the angels."

The two brothers quickly took their leave of Malkura and Manah. Leaving the door open after their departure, the Shekinah despondently remarked:

"Let us go to the meeting place." All of her recent pleasure from being gifted with a home was gone.

Her essence angel suggested, "My lady, close the door and let us remain for a short duration. You have received unhappy news and I would wish to cheer you." As the door slid back into place, she took Malkura's hand and led her to the first chamber. They sat down on the soft, thick floor covering and Manah continued, "Now, release all thoughts of Lord Samael and tell me more about Lord Seriel. You have been keeping secrets about him from me."

Happy to turn her attention away from sorrow, the Shekinah smiled and asked, "Secrets?"

"Oh, yes, my lady. You have traveled instantly by means of his light wand and you are familiar with his resting chamber. I insist you tell me everything!"

Malkura's smile widened as she replied, "I kept these happenings from you because I believe you hold an affection for him. Am I wrong?"

A laughter-filled thought emerged from Manah. "I respect and admire Lord Seriel, but he has not captured my love."

"Then why are you always telling me what he is doing or where he is going?"

Manah explained, "I have frequent thought exchanges with you about him because I believe he is the archangel you should love and not Lord Samael. Do you not know how deeply he loves you?"

"I think not. Seriel loves me as do all of my brothers, but not as you would believe."

"I pray you, Lady Malkura, pay heed to your pure essence angel. I know I am correct in my belief," affirmed Manah.

Uncertain how her angel's conviction was making her feel, the Shekinah diverted this topic by stressing, "Lord Seriel was sorry he made you angry. I trust he apologized to you?"

"Yes, he did, but there was no need for such. My anger was quickly gone when I realized he was merely defending his brother."

"Oh, I thought you must be very annoyed with him. You went ahead of us, thus, I thought you were truly angry."

Manah leaned close to the Shekinah and gave her a hug. "What an unknowing archangel you are! I was leaving you alone deliberately. I tried to do that before we came inside, but you insisted I accompany the two of you."

The Shekinah clasped Manah's hands and proffered, "Let me tell you a story which will explain why I did that and will also reveal the secrets I have kept from you." She paused for effect, and then began, "There was once a foolish archangel who sat next to a repeating miniature scene of the Lord of Lightning-Swiftness . . ."

*   *   *

Samael watched his sister and brother, together with the angel Manah, move through the home Seriel had built for Malkura. His remote viewing crystal gave him sharp images of what was happening. However, it did not convey any thoughts shared between the three while they wandered through the corridors and chambers. The first archangel noted there were many crystals within the Shekinah's home and this displeased him. It meant Malkura could always gift them to their brothers, if she so chose. In this way, there was a reserve of crystalline weapons readily available to the inhabitants of the inner realms of Chaos. Why had Seriel placed them there? Did he not realize the followers of Michael and Gabriel were arming themselves against the angels who supported his first-born sibling? Samael promised himself he would reprimand Seriel about this foolishness when they next met.

The first archangel observed the arrival of Raphael and the subsequent departure of his two brothers. He wondered what news his fifth-born sibling had brought which initiated this action. While the entrance door stood open, Samael hoped Manah would soon be leaving, too. However, to his annoyance, this did not happen. Instead, the door closed and Malkura and her angel went into a nearby room. They sat on the floor and exchanged many thoughts. Whatever they were sharing appeared to bring them much merriment. There were smiles and hugs and clapping of hands. Obviously, his sister was relaying some adventure which greatly pleased her pure essence angel. Samael wanted to believe she was recounting some tale about her former closeness with him. Yet judging from Manah's enthusiasm, he doubted this was true. He was certain Malkura's angel disliked him.

The Lord of Lightning-Swiftness grew extremely impatient. He even contemplated transporting himself into the room and ordering Manah to leave. Yet much as he would enjoy doing that, he knew it would not bode well for his intended thought sharing with his sister. She would be angry with him and not want to listen to his apology for causing her unhappiness. He would never express sorrow to Gabriel and Seriel for harming them, as the Shekinah had directed him to do. Yet showing some remorse to Malkura might win back her devotion. Samael was also in urgent need of questioning the Shekinah about the emerald. The knowledge that she had asked their parent to destroy this token of his love had wounded him profoundly.

Eventually, Malkura and Manah ended their happy communication. They exited the chamber and walked along the passageway toward the front entrance. At last, the eighth-cast angel would leave and Samael could go to his sister. But, no, both archangel and angel were passing through the open doorway! Malkura was not going to be alone in her home. This unexpected development panicked the first archangel into swift action. Except for the occasions when he was sleeping, Samael always carried his light wand over his left shoulder. Therefore, he urgently asked the crystal to take him to the Shekinah. He appeared a short distance in front of Malkura and Manah as they were readying themselves for flight.

Without hesitation, the pure essence angel exclaimed, "Quickly, my lady, let us return to the safety of your home!"

Samael ordered, "Silence, angel! This is a matter for archangels. Be gone from here!"

Manah stood her ground and pushed the Shekinah back in the direction of the front entrance. She vehemently replied, "My mistress does not wish to share thoughts with you. Thus, *you* be gone from here!"

Samael ignored this challenge. He disappeared and reappeared at the pyramid's entrance just as Malkura reached the door. Barring her way, he begged, "I pray you, sweet sister, let us go inside and exchange our thoughts. And tell your impudent angel to leave us."

The Shekinah quickly assured him, "Manah is correct. I do not wish to hold discourse with you. Let me pass, my lord!"

As the pure essence angel reached them, she grabbed Samael's arm and urged, "Take flight, my lady! I will hold him here!"

The held archangel willed pain into the angel's hand and arm and, with a sharp thought-cry, she released her grasp. In the same instant, he encircled his other arm around his sibling, preventing her from flying upwards. With utter disdain, he told Manah, "A lowly angel cannot prevent the first-born of the Source from doing whatever he wishes. Behold! The Lady Malkura *will* come with me." He silently instructed his crystal to take him and the Shekinah inside her pyramid. When nothing happened, he quickly changed their destination to the interior of his own home, and they were gone. Recovering from the inflicted pain and the sudden disappearance of the two archangels, Manah left her essence mistress's home. She flew to where she knew Malkura's brothers would be waiting.

The two siblings were instantly transported to Samael's crystalline abode. They arrived in a chamber where he frequently spent his waking and sleeping sojourns. This room contained an ornate table, several chairs and a bed which was fashioned from a dense purple mineral. It did not boast the ornamental trappings of the large blue bed, but it served him well. Its energy soothed and comforted him whenever the resting phase drew near. It brought him dreams of his early life within the Abyss of Chaos.

Not knowing his sister had already experienced travel via a light wand, Samael assured her, "Do not be concerned, my crystal has brought us to where we can be alone. Whatever I ask for is granted by this trusty mineral." He tapped the triple-pointed crown of his wand as it lay against his shoulder.

"I know what has happened," announced Malkura as she pulled herself free from his encircling hold. "Seriel has shown me the magic of the light wands. Now, tell your crystal to take me back to my home! I do not wish to share my thoughts with you."

"I will not do that, my lady. I am determined to learn your thoughts about me. I am your brother and the one who loves you. Thus, I have the right to know whether I have truly lost your affection." He motioned her to sit down in a chair, but she shook her head and moved away, declaring:

"I do not wish to sit, I am not staying here. Either take me back to my home or open the entrance doors so that I may leave. And that is my final thought to you." The Shekinah walked toward the descending steps which led to the floor below.

Samael quickly stepped in front of her and ordered, "Sit down, Malkura! You are remaining here until we have settled this matter." When she did not move, he took hold of her arm and steered her to one of the chairs. He warned, "Do not force me to make you sit, my lady."

She glared up at him as he released her arm. For an instant she lifted her hand and he was certain his sister was about to hit him. He told her:

"Strike me, if you must, but that will not dissuade me."

Malkura lowered her arm and grudgingly dropped herself into the seat. Samael pulled another chair close to it and sat down, facing her. She immediately turned her body so that her gaze rested on one of the walls. Becoming angry, the first archangel exclaimed:

"Malkura! Have done with this nonsense! I will keep you here until you agree to exchange thoughts with me."

His sister turned to face him and reaffirmed, "As I have already explained, I have no desire to do such sharing with you. Can you not respect that wish?"

"No, I cannot because I have a great need to communicate with you. I wish to tell you I am truly sorry I have brought sadness to you. It pains me to know you are disenchanted with me." Samael wanted to touch her hair, her face, but he sensed she would strongly reject such an action.

Drawn into an unwanted exchange with her sibling, Malkura informed him, "I do not want an apology from you. Gabriel and Seriel are the siblings to whom you should express your remorse."

"That I will not do! To my reasoning, I was entitled to seek revenge." His expression became stony as he put forward, "I must be punished for what I did, yet they should not have been chastised for their unkindly actions?"

"I will not become embroiled in an argument with you, Samael. I wish to leave your home *now!*"

"And I wish to question you about the emerald I gave to you." He leaned forwards and stared intently into her eyes. "Why did you ask our parent to destroy that gift?"

A puzzled expression crossed Malkura's face, but she held her thoughts silent.

"How could you discard that token of my love so easily? It was not a trifling gift, but an expression of my deep affection. I carry its sibling upon my finger to remind me of the fond memories we have shared." Samael moved his right hand in front of the Shekinah, exhibiting the emerald ring.

She looked down at his hand, but continued to maintain her silence.

An exasperated Lord of the First Essence jumped up from his chair, walked all around it and sat back down, again. "Malkura, answer me!" He grabbed his sister by the arms and demanded, "I insist you tell me why you would do such an uncaring act! You swore you would keep the emerald close to you forever."

The eighth archangel was becoming equally angry. She exclaimed, "Remove your hold on me! Your question has no meaning. Perchance the outer Abyss has addled your consciousness?"

A realization began to occur to Samael. He released her arms and questioned, "Did you not take the emerald to the Source and ask for its destruction?"

"Of course, I did not. What causes you to think I would want that beautiful jewel destroyed?"

"Your essence angel, Manah, told me you wished to be free from me. Feeling thus, you gave the emerald to our parent and it crushed that green jewel." He leaned back in his chair and asked, "Did she tell me an untruth?"

"Apparently, she did. Manah holds an intense dislike of you. She knows how unhappy you have made me feel and she believes, as I do, that I must break my ties with you. Now, I have answered your question, therefore, let me go back to my home."

"Not yet, my lady." Samael leaned forwards, once again. "Where is the emerald? Why are you not carrying it within your rulpiel material?"

"Keeping the jewel close to me brings too much pain. It reminds me of how greatly you have changed. It is safe and in a place where I do not have to see or touch it." The Shekinah stood up and added, "That is as much thought exchanging as I wish to do with you. I pray you, let me go!"

Samael thought of gently probing her consciousness, but he quickly sensed she was shielding the location of the emerald. He rose up from his chair and standing beside her, pulled his sister into a close embrace. "My sweet Malkura, stay with me for a while. I am lonely and greatly saddened without your company. I know you are unhappy, too, so let us stay together and comfort one another."

For an instant his sister remained still within his arms, but then she pushed herself away from him. She asked, "My lord, can you not understand that what was once between us has ended? Your cruel behavior against our brothers has caused me to turn away from you. I wish to continue my existence without the turmoil of those feelings you have stirred within me. I am attempting to pursue my life in the close company of the brothers who do not bring me pain and sorrow."

This last remark quickly roused his jealousy. He declared, "You cannot give your affection to another sibling! I am the one you love."

An annoyed Malkura answered, "I did not tell you I had given my affection to another. Samael, this is an example of how much you have changed. You harbor envious thoughts about our siblings. Also, anger and hatred against them whenever the notion takes you."

Choosing not to listen to what she was expressing, the first archangel demanded, "Who is vying for your favors in my absence? Is it Seriel? If he has shown you the magic of his light wand, what else has he disclosed to you?"

"My lord, harken to yourself! You are allowing your passions to overrule your usual discernment."

Samael sat down, once more, and taking hold of his sister's hands, he forced her into a seated position, as well. Ruled by his anger and jealousy, he tried to probe her consciousness, but was prevented from doing so by strong opposition. Her thoughts did battle with his in a manner which astounded him. His gentle sister's consciousness was proving to be extremely resilient and able to fiercely resist his probing. She exclaimed:

"Desist, Samael! Do not seek to claim those thoughts which I have not shared with you! That is a heinous act especially from one who purports to love me."

This declaration ignited Samael's fury even more. He stood up and glaring down at her, announced, "You will remain here until I choose to release you! Even then, I will not allow you to seek the company of another archangel. That is *my* decree! Now, I will leave you alone to contemplate the folly of not accepting your first-born brother's apology and love." Samael strode over to the steps and charged down them with savage intent.

*   *   *

When Manah arrived at the intended council meeting, all five archangels were already present. She alighted in the center of their circle and hurriedly proclaimed, "Lady Malkura is greatly in need of your assistance! Lord Samael has abducted her! He is truly an evil soul and you must . . ."

Michael interrupted her with: "Slow down your thoughts and explain what has happened."

"Forgive me, my lords, I know he is your brother and you love him, but I am anxious for no harm to come to my mistress . . ."

Now, it was Seriel who interjected: "Manah! As I have previously assured you, Lord Samael would never harm our sister."

The angel walked over to where Seriel was seated and replied, "That may or may not be so, but do not give Lord Samael the opportunity to prove you wrong."

"What has happened since I left you?" asked Seriel.

Manah began to move slowly around the circle as she explained, "Lady Malkura and I decided to wait for a while before coming here. We exchanged some thoughts about certain things and then we were leaving her home. As we stood outside, Lord Samael appeared from nowhere. He wanted to share thoughts with my mistress, but she refused. He ordered me to leave, but I also refused. Next, he projected pain into my hand and arm when I tried to hold onto him. I did this so that Lady Malkura could fly away without him stopping her. When I released my grasp on him, he took hold of my mistress and they both disappeared. I do not know where he has taken her. You archangels must scour Chaos to find them!"

"Our brother goes beyond the boundaries of love and understanding!" Michael angrily declared. "Let us go in search of them now!"

The four archangels, who were in etheric form, stood up, while the Christ Soul offered, "I will also help you look for our siblings."

Gabriel warned, "Stay within inner Chaos, so that the daemons cannot attack your auric self!"

"I pray you, my brothers, allow me to go to Samael first." It was Seriel who put forward this thought. "I am certain I know where he will have taken Malkura. Let me reason with him. I am the sibling he is most likely to heed."

The Christ Soul supported his brother's offer with: "Listen to Seriel. He understands Samael better than we do."

"What think you, Michael? Raphael?" asked Gabriel.

"I am willing to let Seriel go on ahead," answered the fifth archangel. "I also do not believe Samael will harm our sister."

Somewhat grudgingly Michael agreed, "Then go to him, now. Yet know this, if he will not release the Shekinah immediately, I will seek him out with many angels and do battle with him. He has flaunted the council's directives and has armed his followers against the angels who do not support him. I believe he is readying himself to engage in conflict with us in order to hold sway over our existence in the Abyss. Tell him I am more than ready to fight against his desires! What say you, Gabriel?"

"I agree with you, Michael, and I will stand beside you, if we have to engage in battle with Samael. Yet I also think we must give Seriel the opportunity to attempt to reason with our brother."

"Where do you believe Samael has taken Malkura?" questioned Michael.

"To his crystalline home."

"Then go there and tell him what I have declared. While you are gone, Gabriel and I will gather together many angels. We will come to the outer Abyss and wait close to Samael's home. The angels will be armed, and Gabriel and I have already chosen our own light wands."

This news surprised Seriel, but he made no comment. Raphael asked him:

"Will you fly there or will you ask your light wand to take you to Samael's home? I believe it grants your wishes?"

"Indeed, it does, and I will travel more speedily, if my light wand takes me to that place. And so I leave you!" He was gone from them and was instantly standing close by Samael's abode. For a very short duration, Seriel remained outside, sensing whether his siblings were within the building. He was correct in his assumption, they were there. Bracing himself for Samael's anger and defiance, he wished himself into the reception area of the first archangel's home.

Chapter Twenty=Two

As Seriel began looking for his siblings inside each of the rooms, which were on the ground floor of the abode, he sensed the approach of Samael. There was a strong feeling of pure rage entangled within his brother's energy vibration. Did this mean Samael was already aware that Seriel was in his crystalline home? He would be furious to know the seventh archangel had entered without awaiting his permission. Seriel returned to the square reception area and stood ready for Samael's onslaught.

The Lord of Lightning-Swiftness was rushing down flight after flight of the steps between the floors of his home. As he descended those which led to the reception area, it became apparent that he was not aware of Seriel's presence. His face was filled with utter fury and his etheric vision seemed blinded by his anger. He strode into one of the adjacent rooms. An instant later, he came back out and, finally noticing his brother, demanded, "Why are you here? How dare you come inside my home without first asking to do so!"

Seriel approached his sibling and defiantly explained, "I came here because you have taken our sister away against her will. That is a most unkindly act and you must release her immediately!"

Samael responded with a sneer, "And, if I choose not to, what will you do? Summon a council meeting to discuss my unseemly behavior?"

Ignoring Samael's sarcasm, the seventh archangel explained, "The occasion for a council is long passed. Michael and Gabriel are ready to do battle with you."

"Are they, indeed?" He gave a little shrug of his left shoulder, as if adjusting his sheathed light wand ready for conflict. "Are you also wishing to fight against me?"

"I offered to come in order to reason with you," Seriel answered. "Why would you confine the Shekinah here? Where is she? Angel Manah is convinced you will harm our sister, but I know you would never do such an evil thing."

"I would not have brought her here, if I could have entered her home. I asked my wand to take us inside Malkura's abode, but nothing happened." Samael glared at Seriel. "Why could we not go inside?"

"Because our brother did not wish for you or any other being to enter my home unless I desired such company." The Shekinah was standing on the bottom flight of twisting steps, having left the room soon after Samael strode out. She had descended without either of her siblings being aware of her movement.

"Malkura! Are you well?" questioned Seriel.

Samael walked quickly to the base of the steps and looking up at his sister, ordered, "My lady, return to the upstairs chamber! Our thought exchange is not yet finished."

Taking no notice of this command, Malkura came down the remaining steps. She walked passed Samael and approached Seriel. "Yes, my lord, I am well, but I am extremely annoyed. Our brother will not accept what I have told him. I will not be bombarded by his jealous thoughts and angry questions. Seriel, I pray you, take me back to my home."

In an instant, the first archangel was standing between his siblings. His left hand was already drawing his light wand from its holster as he threatened, "If you attempt to take Malkura from this place, my brother, I will strike you with my crystal's beam!"

338   MARION WEBB-DE SISTO

"I have no desire to fight with you," Seriel assured him. "If I did, I would not be standing here. I would be out in Chaos with Michael and Gabriel. End this madness now. Let Malkura go!"

Continuing to hold his light wand, Samael asked, "How did you prevent me from penetrating the walls of her home?"

"I asked the crystal capstone to not allow others to enter unless our sister wished them to be inside with her."

"Why did you not ask for me to be the exception to that rule? You knew I planned to be with Malkura to win back her love." Turning to the Shekinah, he explained, "That is why he built your home. I wanted to come to you so that we could be alone without interruption from such annoying souls as your pure essence angel." Then bringing his piercing gaze back to Seriel, the first archangel concluded, "You deceived me! You led me to believe I could pass through the pyramid's walls, yet you knew that would not happen! Why did you do this?"

Seriel was certain his brother was about to vent his rage on him. He could understand how Samael was feeling. Dealing with the Shekinah's rejection must be impossible for him. Now, the added realization that Seriel had deliberately misled him over such an important issue was pushing him beyond endurance. Knowing his honesty would probably ensure a piercing blow from Samael's crystal, Seriel nevertheless replied, "I did what I thought was best for our sister. You had made her so unhappy and I did not want her to endure more pain from your unwelcome pursuit. I am truly sorry, Samael, but I placed Malkura's despairing feelings above those of yours."

His brother continued to stare at him with something akin to hatred as he shielded this answering thought: "It is obvious your love for our sister is greater than your love for me. You have betrayed me, once again, but I understand what has prompted you to do so. Loving Malkura makes everything else of little consequence." Samael shuddered deeply and returned the light wand to its holster. Then he walked toward the golden entrance.

The Shekinah was aware a hidden thought had passed between her brothers and she believed that, whatever its nature, it was prompting Samael to release her. She hoped he was approaching the doors in order to open them and allow her to depart. Malkura offered, "Perhaps I will be able to share my thoughts with you, Samael, when I am feeling less unhappy. Until then, I trust you will respect my need to not have your company. If you open the doors, I will go to Michael and Gabriel and show them I am unharmed."

The first archangel turned on his heel and came back to his two siblings. His anger appeared to have vanished as he gently touched the Shekinah's hair and declared, "I have but one more question for you, sweet sister. It is for you alone to hear. Thus, Seriel, leave us now! Go to our brothers and tell them I will bring Malkura to them, once my question is answered."

For an instant, Seriel hesitated. What if Samael was merely trying to trick him into leaving the abode? If that was his brother's plan and he did not bring Malkura out into the Abyss, then Seriel would wish himself back into the crystalline building. He would take hold of his sister and immediately bring her outside with the help of his light wand. If necessary, he would use his crystal's beam against Samael. He would not injure him, but just disable his consciousness for a short while. Seriel knew the intensity of the light beam depended upon his thoughts and intentions. Feeling certain he could counteract any trickery Samael might be plotting, the seventh archangel wished himself out of his sibling's home. He was immediately transported to a spot a short distance in front of it.

Michael, Gabriel and a large number of angels were standing close by. Among them were Mikael and Metatron, the third archangel's pure essence angel. Facing them, as if ready for conflict, were Uriel, Azazel, Kokabel, Belial,

Semyaza and many other angels. Seriel quickly strode over
to the two groups and declared:

"The Shekinah is well and unharmed! Samael merely
brought her here to thought exchange in private with her."

"Why is she not with you?" demanded Michael.

"Our brother has one last question he wishes to ask of
her. He told me when she has answered him, then he will
bring her to us."

"You believe he will do that?" asked Gabriel. "I fear he
may have tricked you!"

Seriel replied, "That possibility has occurred to me. If
he does not soon emerge with Malkura, I will go back inside,
take hold of her and bring her out with the power of my
crystal wand. I thought it was best to accept his proposal of
returning our sister to us. I was anxious to assure you all of
the Shekinah's safety. There is no need for anyone to fight."
He had quickly observed how each and every angelic being
was armed with some type of weapon.

"I am ready to do battle on behalf of Lord Samael!"
proclaimed Belial as he brandished a scimitar-type sword
above his head. His long, breal hair was confined in one
thick braid which rested between his wings. In no way would
it hamper his etheric vision or ability to wield his weapon.

This bold proclamation was greeted with many similar
declarations of loyalty to the first archangel. Weapons were
flourished in threatening manner and anger clouded each
angelic countenance. Immediately, an equally menacing
response charged through the gathering of angels who stood
beside Michael and Gabriel. All were more than ready to
uphold their reasoning and test their fighting skills.

Suddenly, Samael appeared next to Seriel. He was alone.
With an evil smile gracing his lips, he questioned, "What is
transpiring? Are we all desiring to do battle? What a delightful
prospect!"

"Where is our sister?" Michael moved angrily toward him.
"You told Seriel you would bring her out with you."

Feigning shocked surprise, Samael asked, "Could it be I told an untruth? Or perhaps the Lord of Sorcery is weaving some evil magic? Perchance the Lady Malkura is not in my home and he has deceived you?"

A perplexed expression appeared on Michael's face. He looked at Seriel and questioned, "*Is* the Shekinah inside Samael's home?"

How could his third-born sibling be so naïve? In the face of imminent danger, Samael was adopting his usual bantering attitude. In contrast to the severity of what was happening, Seriel felt thought-laughter bubbling up inside himself. No wonder the first archangel mocked their siblings! Quashing his inward mirth, Seriel answered, "Of course, she is there, Michael. Our brother is playing you for a fool." He turned to Samael and exclaimed, "Do not thrust us all to the brink of conflict! Bring Malkura out or I will go inside and release her."

Giving his brother a beaming grin, the Lord of the First Essence revealed, "There is only one small problem with your excellent plan. I have asked my crystalline home to refuse entry to everyone unless I wish them to go inside. Is that not a vexation? What could have prompted me to think of such a wicked counter-measure?" Moving his attention from Seriel to Uriel, and just as quickly changing his mood, Samael continued, "This is no place for you to be, dear brother. A battle will soon ensue."

"I am not afraid," answered Uriel. "I will stand beside you and fight."

"Samael!" ordered Michael. "Bring our sister to us! You have no right to keep her prisoner."

The two archangels stood staring defiantly at each other as Samael replied:

"She is not a prisoner! I am leaving Malkura in my home for her safe keeping. I will not allow the Shekinah to be exposed to any danger from your lust for battle!" Samael took hold of Uriel's arm and he and his brother vanished.

Even as the onlookers were realizing they were gone, the first archangel reappeared in front of them without his sixth-born sibling. He declared, "Now, the two beings whose safety I will not jeopardize are secure within my home. So let us to the fray!" With lightning speed he drew his crystal wand and pointed it at Michael. While all attention was on Samael, Seriel also took hold of his light wand and slowly removed it from the holster.

One of Michael's angels darted at Samael with a raised dagger. Fearing his essence lord was in great peril, he gave no thought to his own safety. Without hesitation, Samael aimed his wand at this attacker and delivered a single blast of the crystal's light beam. The angel fell down and lay contorting and thought-screaming as a widening hole burned itself into his etheric body. For an instant, Michael stared at the writhing angelic being, then he struck Samael's left arm with the shaft of his own crystal sword.

The sudden weighty impact knocked Samael's wand out of his hand. Even as he stooped to retrieve it, other angels came charging toward him, brandishing all kinds of weapons. They would have pounced upon him, but for Seriel's quick thinking. A broad, pale blue beam sprang from his crystal and encompassed Samael. This energy barrier proved to be impenetrable to all efforts by the assailants, and the first archangel quickly grasped his fallen wand. As the dome of protection dissipated, Samael swept an arc of destructive light through those who were trying to attack him. This action signaled the commencement of fierce fighting between all who were present.

And, thus, began the War between the Sons of Light and the Sons of Darkness. An eternal battle which has never yet reached a true ending. For whenever souls uphold Samael's reasoning and oppose WHAT IS, they are locked in an everlasting struggle with those who champion the Source.

With the exception of the former short-lived conflicts between certain angels, the inhabitants of Chaos had no experience with the mechanics of warfare. Therefore, everything that took place during the early part of the affray was haphazard and based purely on instinct and reaction. If an angel was under attack, he or she would strive against the combatant until one or both of the adversaries lay injured and unable to continue fighting. Those who were not overcome then moved on to engage other angels in a clash for dominance.

Once Samael had struck down his original assailants, he flew upwards and took indiscriminate aim at the angels who opposed him. Having observed how Seriel protected their brother, Michael and Gabriel quickly rethought their understanding of a light wand. They then intermittently used their crystals' power for both protection and aggression. The third archangel soon followed Samael's upward path. He pursued the Lord of Lightning-Swiftness across this section of the outer Abyss, but could not enter into close combat with him. Whenever he drew close, Samael would send a powerful ray toward him and instantly disappear from view. On most occasions, Michael had ample opportunity to dodge the piercing light. When this was not possible, he encased himself in his wand's protective beam.

For Seriel the beginning of the battle was difficult. The seventh archangel felt pulled in opposite directions. He understood Michael's motivation, but he also acknowledged his allegiance to Samael and his promise to the Source. His siblings were two opposing forces and Seriel was caught between them. However, he was given little opportunity to wrestle with this dilemma. As he stood watching the fighting that surrounded him, an angel jumped on his back and attempted to stab him with a dagger-like weapon. Being much stronger and taller, Seriel was quickly able to reach back with his free hand and grab his attacker. He thrust the angelic opponent above his head and then flung him down at his feet. With a short, sharp burst of light from his wand, Seriel rendered the angel's consciousness temporarily immobile. On that occasion, he felt no desire to cause bodily injury, but that would soon change.

Two angels, who had witnessed their colleague's misfortune, rushed toward Seriel with weapons raised. Seeing no movement coming from the downed angel, they presumed the Lord of Sorcery had cast some malevolent magic upon him. These two assailants did not reach their target because they were similarly halted by Seriel's crystal wand. As they lay motionless in front of him, the seventh archangel suddenly experienced an overwhelming desire to strike them, once more, and with greater force. He aimed a stronger beam at each one and burning wounds materialized upon their still bodies. A sense of satisfaction permeated Seriel's consciousness and in that instant his warrior soul was awakened. For it is the nature of the seventh essence to strive for glory through conflict and adversity.

As he stood savoring this new exhilaration, Samael's whispering thoughts crept into his consciousness:

"Now, my brother, you know how satisfying it is to wield your archangel power. Are we not magnificent beings?"

Seriel looked up and saw his brother hovering high above him. He waved his wand in acknowledgment and Samael dipped his wings in response. As the first archangel flew away, a familiar, tempting question floated down to his sibling:

"And would you not slay a hundred angels for one loving glance from Malkura's enchanting eyes?"

As if in answer to this question, Seriel ran through groups of fighting angels, cutting down any who attempted to bar his way.

Apart from the four archangels and the many angels, countless daemons were quickly lending their aggressive nature to the battle. Earlier, several had stood at a distance from the two groups of angelic beings who were readying themselves to fight. The creatures sensed a mighty conflict was brewing and they were anticipating the pleasure of causing harm. Once the first blows were struck, most of the daemonic group leapt into biting and clawing action against those who were confronting Samael's followers. The remainder departed into other parts of the outer Abyss in order to gather together their daemon brothers and sisters. When this multitude of evil beasts descended upon the fray, many cruel injuries were soon sustained. Wings and limbs were torn from bodies with merciless fervor.

No matter from which archangel or angel the daemons had sprung, they were all taking part in the battle. None stood by and observed, all were embroiled in the thick of slashing weapons and spilled essence. Seriel gave an instant's consideration to forbidding his beasts to fight, but his newly found warrior exuberance quickly stifled such thoughts. Many of his daemons formed a protective ring around him and quickly set upon any angels who attempted to attack him. Gabriel's daemons also fought beside their archangel, obeying his command. The Lord of Practicality was speedy in recognizing the advantage of having their cruelty working with, rather than against, himself and Michael. Therefore, daemons fought against daemons, but this was an activity with which they were well accustomed.

Whenever angelic essence was shed, it would attempt to flow further out into the Abyss to become new daemons. However, on many occasions the leaking life force was swiftly drunk by those creatures who were close enough to pounce upon an injured angel. As had happened during the attack on Gabriel, imbibing essence caused the daemons to change into much larger and more ferocious beasts. Eventually, these grotesque mutants would come to be known as demons.

The drinking of essence was extremely repulsive to the four fighting archangels. When they witnessed it during the battle, they quickly blasted the offending daemons into total annihilation. Seriel felt, once more, the rage that had consumed him when his fourth-born brother had been violated in this manner. And even Samael could not tolerate this blasphemous action. Yet many demons were not destroyed and their numbers soon swelled the ranks of those who would forever dwell in the dark depths of Chaos. Two such creatures were Shedim and Lamassu. They speedily guzzled angelic essence, but managed to escape the destruction of the archangels' crystal weapons.

The battle raged on, but there came a point in the fighting when Michael realized he needed a reinforcement of angels, together with a defined strategy for defeating the opposing force. He sent Mikael to find Raphael and alert him to what was required. The fifth archangel had previously agreed to wait in the inner realms of the Abyss while his brothers sought out Samael. Raphael felt certain some fighting would take place, but his peace-loving soul hoped it would be swiftly ended. While awaiting any news, many more angels, who were willing to stand against the Lord of the First Essence, had rallied around Raphael. The Christ Soul and his angels were also waiting nearby.

While Mikael was gone, the third archangel ordered his angels into a retreat. Several stood guard in the event the daemons would follow them. Michael and Gabriel took stock of who was able-bodied and who was wounded. The latter group were dragged and carried further inwards so as not to gain more injuries. Michael then divided the unscathed angels into fighting ranks by grouping together those who were of the same essence. He reasoned that their innate energy closeness would enable them to fight in greater unison and with a stronger sense of defending one another. The bond created by matching essence has always taken dominance over other motivations.

The retreat caused a lull in the conflict. Samael took the opportunity to also assess how his angels were fairing. Frequently, their injuries did not seem to be as severe as those inflicted upon their opponents. There appeared to be two main reasons for this outcome. Primarily, with the exception of Gabriel's daemons, the vast number of creatures were fighting with them and not against them.

Also, even though the light wands could deliver devastating wounds, most of his angels were not suffering from such injuries. Whether through lack of experience or due to intention, Michael and Gabriel had not maimed many combatants. This was contrary to what Samael had achieved.

Seriel was continuing to feel exhilarated by the conflict. He was now armed with an etheric sword in addition to his crystal wand. This prize had been claimed from an angel who challenged him. As he fought with other adversaries, he began to use the sword more and the wand less. His crystal gave him a strong advantage over any angelic adversary, but he soon found this sense of superiority did not continue to bring him satisfaction. The Lord of Sorcery wanted to match his prowess with an opponent who could battle on a par with him. While the fighting paused, Seriel holstered his light wand and exercised his rudimentary fencing skills against an imaginary foe.

Meanwhile, Mikael journeyed inwards to Raphael and explained how his essence lord needed more angelic followers. The fifth archangel directed him to return to Michael with those who were ready to engage in combat. When they had flown away, Raphael then gathered together several of his own angels and those of the Christ Soul, who were in etheric form. This angelic band of helpers flew to where the injured lay waiting and they began the task of bringing them back to inner Chaos. They laid them out in rows and Raphael, together with Sabrael and Shatqiel, moved among them and administered healing. These two beings were Raphael's catalyst angel and pure essence angel, respectively. They possessed the same revitalizing energy vibration that flowed through the Lord of the Fifth Essence. Some wounds were quickly gone, but others were deeply implanted and would need a duration to be truly healed. All that the three ministering souls could do for these angels was to create etheric seals over the injuries so that no further essence was lost. Then came the waiting while the injured bodies slowly knitted their etheric substance into wholeness, once more.

Samael's supporting angels, who did sustain severe injuries, had to sit or lie unaided until the end of the battle. Raphael and his helpers could not venture near them to stem the flow of their life force. If they had attempted to go to them, there was the certainty of being assailed by the daemons. Consequently, many more evil creatures were birthed while these angelic wounds remained untreated.

Michael's followers, who had lost wings or limbs, were brought to the edge of the Source. Their parent wrapped tendrils of consciousness around them. They changed back into their auric selves and rested in melded bliss as Gabriel had done. The Christ Soul also aided several angels in the same manner as his parent. Once the battle resumed, even more severely maimed angels were returned to the inner Abyss. It became automatic for them to quickly resume their former auric selves, once they were close to the Source. Their plight was so alarming that certain compassionate angels, who were present, also changed into their original state and began to rejoin with them. This was not melding, but a complete blending of one consciousness with a second consciousness in order to promote wellness. However, it was only possible when both angels were of the same essence. Later, when full recovery was achieved, some joined souls separated, again, but others have remained together since that terrible occasion.

Thought-word of the ongoing battle was passed among the rest of the angelic horde. A number of them soon hurried outwards to stand beside Samael and Seriel. With reinforcements on both sides, the conflict would not be ended soon. It continued to entrench itself across the outlying areas of the Abyss. Angels fought with angels while daemons and demons savaged any unfortunate opponent who came within their grasp. Both sides were evenly matched. Michael's supporters profited by sheer weight of numbers while Samael's followers gained from the daemons' tenacious ferocity.

Eventually, Michael fully understood the folly of waging war without a plan-of-action that would remove Samael from the fray. He realized the angels and daemonic creatures would continue to battle against their adversaries as long as the first archangel was able to lead them. Michael's earlier attempts to disarm his brother had proved fruitless. The Lord of Lightning-Swiftness was aptly named. His continuous disappearance and reappearance all over the battle scene prevented any one-on-one confrontations. Michael knew it was imperative to separate Samael from his light wand. Therefore, he used his own crystal's abilities to take him far from the hostilities for a short while in order to plan a strategy.

On his return, he sought out Gabriel, who was resting within a circle of daemonic protection. Michael explained his intention to defeat their brother and how he hoped to accomplish this task. He told his sibling there would be a need to distract Seriel from what was happening. The seventh archangel would undoubtedly want to help Samael once he was under attack. This part of the plan required Gabriel's participation. He would have to draw Seriel into combat so that he would be too intently occupied to go to Samael's aid. Gabriel quickly agreed.

Michael moved on, first to Metatron and then to Mikael. He asked for their help in overcoming his brother. He also warned his angels of the risk involved. Samael was relentlessly burning deep, extensive wounds into any soul on whom he focused his destructive wand. Knowing how perceptive his sibling could be, Michael also cautioned them to heavily shield all thoughts about the plan. Both essence brothers swore their determination to help bring down Lord Samael. They began to look for the archangel's short-lived appearances, hoping for the opportunity to quickly confront him. Twice he briefly showed himself, but at great distances from where either of them stood. On each occasion he blasted several angels with his fierce light beam before disappearing, once more.

Then he was suddenly but an arm's length away from Mikael, standing with legs astride and three-pointed wand raised. As if having perceived the angel's desire to fight with him, he challenged, "You wish to do battle, Angel Mikael?"

"Indeed, I do, my lord!" The catalyst angel lifted his etheric broadsword and lunged at Samael. However, the weapon's penetrating point met with no resistance other than the emptiness of Chaos. The first archangel had vanished, but quickly reappeared to the side of Mikael. With a speedy flick of his wand, Samael etched three lancing wounds in one of the hands that held the broadsword. He asked with a wicked smile:

"Shall I continue to cut you little by little or shall I be daring and remove a whole arm?"

"You do not intimidate me, Lord Samael! I can wield my sword with only one arm!" Mikael held his weapon in the uninjured hand and swung it toward the archangel. On this occasion, Samael merely stepped aside to avoid the weight of the broadsword, while delivering three further burning injuries to Mikael's other hand. It was at this instant that Metatron reached the two assailants. He declared:

"My brother is not afraid of you and neither am I! Stand and fight with me now!" He was carrying a large club which boasted disquieting smears of essence in random patterns across its brutal head. Metatron lifted the weapon to shoulder height and charged toward Samael, who swiftly vanished, once more.

While his angels were confronting his first-born brother, Michael watched from a distance, readying himself for his intervention in their action. In one hand he was carrying a looped circle of rope, and in the other he was grasping his crystal sword. He had created the etheric cord with the power of his thoughts, once his plan began to unfold. Now, he stood waiting for his sibling to become visible, again.

Once Gabriel observed Samael's first appearance in front of Mikael, he also moved into action. He ran toward Seriel with many of his daemons following him. The seventh archangel was busily crossing swords with an angel who was receiving many nicks and cuts from Seriel's weapon. He, however, appeared to be unhurt. Gabriel also noted that his brother's light wand was holstered against his thigh. As he reached the two combatants, Gabriel pushed the angel aside and exclaimed:

"Fight with *me*! An angel is not a worthy match for an archangel!"

Seriel looked completely surprised as he replied, "What is this, Gabriel? Do you have a taste for pain? I have deliberately not challenged you because you seem to have little command over your crystal wand. I have also not seen you use any other type of weapon. Whereas I am becoming quite proficient in using both of mine. Thus, you will be quickly overcome, if you do battle with me."

Gabriel pointed his wand at Seriel and ordered, "Lay down that weapon and draw your light wand! Let us see who is better able to control the power of the etheric minerals. My daemons are also wanting to fight with yours!" His creatures crowded around him and made threatening gestures toward Seriel's daemons.

"My beasts will be more than happy to send yours scurrying away into the depths of Chaos, but I will not duel with you, brother. Go back to the inner Abyss! You do not have the mettle for this warfare!"

A sudden blue ray from Gabriel's wand cut through Seriel's sword. As the cleaved end fell, the fourth archangel repeated, "Lay down that weapon and draw your light wand!"

Seriel angrily flung the broken sword away from himself and warned, "Do not push me, Gabriel! I have already burned great wounds into several angels and will not hesitate to injure you. Seek out Michael and tell him to withdraw. Samael will never concede defeat, therefore, our third-born brother must end the fighting. The Shekinah has not been harmed. This battle is meaningless!"

Taking a step closer to his sibling, Gabriel declared, "I am challenging you, Seriel! Draw your light wand!" And looking down at his impatient beasts, he commanded, "Attack! Attack!"

They jumped on Seriel's daemons and vicious biting and clawing was soon being exchanged. Some of both archangels' creatures were even torn apart, but the mangled pieces quickly rejoined into daemonic forms, once more. Seriel stood watching the mêlée with his hand resting on the hilt of his crystal. Yet his thoughts were elsewhere. Why was Gabriel so anxious to fight with him? The battle had been raging for a long duration, but his brother had not sought him out before. Something lay behind this unexpected challenge.

Shifting his gaze from the daemons, the seventh archangel looked around for Samael. There was no sign of him. He was either beyond Seriel's range of etheric vision or he had been transported to some other place by his crystal's power. In searching for him, Seriel suddenly noticed Michael, who was intently watching his own two angels, Mikael and Metatron. His third-born brother was holding his crystal sword in one hand and a coiled length of sturdy etheric material in the other. Seriel had never seen such an object before. Turning his attention back to Gabriel, he demanded:

"What are you and Michael planning? I sense some form of trickery is happening."

"You are mistaken, Seriel. I know of no deception." Gabriel waved his light wand menacingly at his sibling and questioned, "Must I strike the first blow?"

Continuing to keep his crystal holstered, Seriel looked, once more, at Michael's two angels. As he did so, Samael was suddenly standing before them. A feeling of impending misfortune for his brother filled Seriel's consciousness. He then looked at Michael, whose stance verified his fears. The third archangel was undoubtedly waiting to take action. Readying himself to go to Samael's aid by means of his light wand, Seriel told Gabriel:

"Enough of your foolhardy challenge! I am needed elsewhere."

Unfortunately, Gabriel had already followed his sibling's line of vision and knew his efforts to distract Seriel's attention had not succeeded. Without another thought or any measured control of his wand, he willed its destructive beam directly at his brother. Instantly, a long, broad gash appeared across the seventh archangel's chest. It began at the top of his left shoulder and gouged its way diagonally down to his waist. A stunned expression crossed Seriel's face as he jolted forwards and fell to his knees. Gabriel stood frozen in horror at what he had done.

Samael's reappearance was accompanied by the triple blue rays of damaging light which were centered on Metatron's head. The pure essence angel's keen instinct guided him to jerk away from the oncoming impact, but the crystal's aim did not completely miss its mark. Three stinging lacerations now graced his right cheek. Maintaining an aggressive posture, he taunted Samael:

"You are a coward! A noble archangel would remain visible and fight. He would not need vanishing tricks to gain the advantage. Stand where you are and do battle with us!"

Samael's pride was under attack. He stared down at Metatron with equal defiance and exclaimed, "You are a fool! I can cut both you and Mikael in half with one single sweep of my wand. Angels are inferior to archangels!" As if to emphasize this conviction, he lifted up his head and roared a chilling war-cry thought. Its bellowing resonance caused many angels to pause in their fighting and to look toward the Lord of the First Essence.

As its echoing vibration died away, Michael appeared immediately in front of Samael. Without hesitation, he encased his sibling in a paralytic beam from his own crystal. The first archangel instantly fell down into the immobility of disabled consciousness. Michael wrenched the triple-pointed crystal from Samael's hand. As its powerful energy assaulted him, he pulled its holder off his brother's shoulder and replaced the wand in it. He set the weapon at his feet just as Seriel materialized next to him.

It was evident that his sibling was severely injured. A long and deep chest wound was oozing archangel essence and Seriel was having great difficulty in remaining in an upright position. Yet even now he was rallying himself to champion Samael. Brandishing his light wand erratically at Michael, he haltingly demanded, "What . . . have you done . . . to our brother?"

With a sense of compassion coupled with the need to disarm Seriel, the third archangel aimed a second disabling beam, and his sibling slumped into unawareness. Michael then removed Seriel's holster and wand and, after reuniting them, he laid this second weapon beside the first one. Next, he wound the etheric rope around Samael's upper body, ensuring both wings and arms were immobilized. He secured both ends of the restraint in sturdy knots. Then Michael created three more lengths of rope, using two to bind both Samael's and Seriel's ankles. Finally, the third was wrapped around Seriel's wrists after he gently positioned his brother's arms around the gaping wound.

Michael stood back up from this unhappy work and with a heavy sigh he informed his two essence angels, "Pass the command along to lay down all weapons. Let it be known that Lord Samael and Lord Seriel are overthrown."

Chapter Twenty-Three

A s soon as Michael's order was spread throughout the
battling angels, the combat petered out. Just as the third
archangel expected, the news that Samael was disarmed,
robbed his followers of the incentive to sustain the fighting.
Some quickly gathered round to gaze upon their fallen hero,
others flew away to different parts of the Abyss. They had no
desire to witness the triumph of their foe. For a while, the
daemons and demons appeared unaffected by the battle's
outcome. The creatures continued to jump on angels with
teeth and claws ready for action. However, once Michael
began spraying them with the destructive ray of his crystal
sword, they speedily scurried further out into Chaos. Gabriel's
daemons followed suit, when he commanded them to leave.

Both Samael and Seriel lay motionless with Michael,
Metatron and Mikael standing guard over them. Gabriel had
quickly flown to his incapacitated brothers, once he saw his
third-born sibling render them unconscious. He knelt down
beside Seriel, anxious to discover just how severely he had
maimed him. Gabriel placed his hands over a section of the
wound, as if to stem the flow of essence. It was obvious some
temporary sealing of the extensive injury was necessary.
Therefore, he directed Bethnael, to seek out Raphael and
bring him swiftly to Seriel. While he waited, Gabriel closed
his eyes and silently requested help from the Source. He
asked:

"I pray you, divine parent, restore Seriel to his former
wellness. I am distraught because of what I have done!"

Michael was giving his attention to both of his immobile brothers. He was deeply concerned about Seriel's condition and trusted Raphael would soon arrive. The third archangel was also wondering how to solve the problem of releasing his other two siblings from the crystalline abode. He considered trying to rouse Samael in order to force him to open the golden doors. Yet this might prove to be an unwise action. His brother would be furious, once awareness returned to him. If Michael attempted to stimulate Samael's consciousness while the angels remained close by, the Lord of the First Essence would surely be even more infuriated. His pride would suffer greatly. Many of his followers and some adversaries would witness his demeaning experience of being heavily restrained. Michael was certain this indignity would prompt Samael to refuse to set Malkura and Uriel free.

The third archangel decided he should at least wait until the angelic crowd was gone. Therefore, he announced to the many angels who continued to stare at the lifeless archangels, "Go back to inner Chaos! There is no need for any of you to remain here. The fighting is over and we must now attend to the wounded. Decisions also have to be made on what should happen next. We archangels will inform you when we have agreed upon them."

Azazel stepped forward and questioned, "What of the injured angels who fought with Lord Samael? Shall we carry them to the inner realms of the Abyss? Kokabel and Semyaza are numbered among them." He moved even closer and with a sneer added, "Or must your decree of banishment continue to be upheld?"

Ignoring Azazel's contemptuous tone, Michael ordered, "I want *everyone* to move inwards! Those who are uninjured must bring all of the wounded to where healing will be administered. Go now!"

The seventh cast angel did not move. He persisted, "And Lord Samael and Lord Seriel? What is to become of them?"

Azazel turned to those who had fought with him and they echoed this questioning thought.

Becoming annoyed with the angel's disregard for his archangel authority, Michael demanded, "No more questions, Azazel! You have been vanquished and must obey my commands. These archangel brothers will not be harmed and will be reunited with you, eventually. Be gone!" He moved his crystal sword slowly in a wide arc, which encompassed Azazel and many of the crowd. This action indicated he would use the weapon, if his order was ignored. The threat quickly dispersed the onlookers. Some of the angels took flight toward the inner realms while others went to aid their injured colleagues.

Azazel strode away, but returned soon afterwards, carrying Kokabel. There were a number of deep, essence-leaking cuts on her limbs, and her thoughts were stilled. As he made ready to take his sister inwards, he declared, "Lord Samael will be furious when he discovers the ignoble manner in which you have bound him. You will surely come to regret having stripped him of his dignity." Then he flew upwards with his angelic burden.

Bethnael soon found Raphael, who was a short distance away, overseeing the moving of some injured angels. They both flew swiftly to Seriel. The fifth archangel sat down beside his sibling, positioning himself on the opposite side to where Gabriel was continuing to keep watch. He moved his hands along the extent of the deep wound and a mist of blue energy exuded from his palms. It settled on the total length and width of the gash. As it joined with Seriel's innate yellow, the vaporous power solidified and turned green. It formed a type of etheric seal over the injury and stemmed the flow of Seriel's essence. Looking up at Gabriel, Raphael informed:

"The wounds caused by the light wands are more serious than those received from other weapons. They burn deep into our etheric bodies and stimulate the loss of essence. It will take a duration for Seriel to heal. Did Michael strike this blow to our brother?"

"No, I did." Gabriel looked both embarrassed and deeply troubled. "I was attempting to distract him while Michael overcame Samael. In my haste, I did not give full thought to my action. The wands are extremely sensitive to our desires and motivations and I aimed mine carelessly." As though unable to continue to look upon the terrible wound, he turned his gaze away and added, "Seriel came to my aid when the daemons attacked me and I repay him with this great harm. Do you think he will ever forgive me?"

Raphael assured him, "Seriel is not Samael. Our seventh-born brother does not harbor the need to take revenge. Resentment does not grow within him. I am certain he will understand, if you express your sorrow." He stood up and quickly sealed both Mikael's and Metatron's minor wounds. Then, giving his attention back to Gabriel, he continued, "Now, I must hasten with our brother to the Source. It may be that either it or the Christ Soul will wish to meld with Seriel and give him healing." Raphael motioned Bethnael to give assistance and together they lifted up the inert archangel. The two flew with Seriel toward the Source.

Gabriel got up and walked over to Michael. He asked, "Is Samael showing signs of recovering?"

"Not yet, and I am wondering how we can persuade him to release our siblings when he does."

"Surely he will do that? The fighting is over." Gabriel reasoned. "Of what use would it be to keep them from us now that he is confined?"

"Perchance to bargain for his freedom?" Michael bent down and picked up the two sheathed wands. He handed Samael's to Metatron and Seriel's to Mikael. "Take these weapons to inner Chaos and guard them well. Wait for me at the meeting place." Mikael was immediately aloft, but Michael grasped Metatron's arm and questioned, "Is the wand's energy impacting on you? It is very strong."

The pure essence angel looked at the weapon as he held it. He waited for a short while and then observed, "I feel nothing from this wand. Should I?"

"For me it was quite overpowering, but perhaps it only affects archangels adversely or otherwise. Even so, do not take it from its holder." He removed his hand from Metatron's arm and instructed, "Go with Mikael! I will be with you once Samael has opened the entrance to his home."

Metatron flew upwards to join his brother, who was waiting for him, and together they sped away. Michael and Gabriel were now alone with their sibling. They stood looking down at him and watching for his first signs of movement.

Before too long his body began to jerk violently. Incomprehensible thoughts also came haltingly from his consciousness as awareness started to return. His two brothers stepped back a pace, uncertain what would happen next. Samael's eyelids fluttered and then he opened his eyes. His bewildered gaze looked all around and came to rest on Michael and Gabriel. Pure anger replaced puzzlement as memory flooded back into him. He attempted to sit up and discovered he was restrained. Twisting himself in a wild frenzy, Samael tried to free his arms from the rope. It held him fast and his rage escalated. His thoughts charged into Michael and Gabriel:

"You dare to *bind* me? Set me free! I will wreak havoc upon you for treating me thus!"

Michael moved forwards and, stooping down, grabbed Samael by the shoulders. As his brother continued to writhe about, he applied his strength. He forced him to be still and exclaimed, "Stop! I have restrained you with good cause. You cannot break free from the rope, therefore, cease to fight against it."

In answer, Samael willed pain into his brother's hands and arms. However, this did not make Michael release his hold, it made him more determined to maintain it. To the first archangel's surprise, his sibling then willed pain back into Samael through his shoulders. He declared:

"I am just as able as you to inflict suffering. Do not engage in a test of wills with me!"

Changing tactics, Samael jeered, "Your puny bindings cannot hold me. They are etheric matter and I can totally manipulate that medium. I will merely destroy the restraints with my thoughts and they will be no more. Behold!" He stared intently at the rope around his body. Yet nothing happened to it. He moved his attention to his tied ankles and glared at them. Again, his efforts brought no reward. Samael thought-screamed, "This is not possible! I have moved a mighty crystalline building with my thoughts. Your bindings cannot withstand my intent!"

Michael put forward, "Perhaps we can only move or remove that which was created by us. I formed the restraints, therefore, you cannot destroy them."

Ever quick to argue, Samael replied, "That is not so! I created the door of Uriel's home, yet he can maneuver it."

"Then maybe it is possible when we wish another to have command over our creation. Since that is not about to happen here, accept this fact, you are presently bound." Michael removed his hands from his sibling's shoulders because Samael had stopped struggling. Instead, he was looking to both sides of himself and asked:

"Where is Seriel? He will not allow you to treat me in this manner."

"Seriel was injured. Raphael has taken him to our parent," explained the third archangel.

Samael looked furious as he questioned, "Is he seriously wounded? Who dared to do this? Was it you, Michael?"

Gabriel announced, "I am the one who dealt him a blow from my light wand."

Evil thought-laughter emerged from the first archangel. He questioned, "What irony is this? *You* caused harm to our brother? Are you not the same archangel who considered my actions malevolent and worthy of banishment? What judgment will you bring upon yourself, Gabriel?"

Unable to challenge this reasoning, Gabriel moved away from Samael, who turned his attention back to Michael. He asked disdainfully:

"What do you propose to do with me? Will you call another council to deliberate on punishment?"

"No, we will take you to our parent and act upon its directive, but presently you will remain here." Michael pulled Samael up into a sitting position and continued, "You must release our siblings from your home. If, as you told us, you left them there for their protection, they can now leave. There is no longer any danger from the fighting. I trust you do not require the aid of your light wand to open the entrance doors?"

Samael's thoughts were suddenly stilled. He seemed intent on something. Then he raged, "Where is my crystal? It is gone! Return it to me *now*!"

Michael informed him, "Your wand has been taken to inner Chaos. I shall consult with the Source as to whether it should be destroyed or, eventually, given back to you."

"Bring it to me or I will not set Malkura and Uriel free!"

With a knowing smile, his third-born brother answered, "I presumed you would use their release as a bargaining tool. Setting them free is not open for negotiation, Samael. If you refuse, Gabriel and I will rend great holes in your abode with our wands. Then our siblings can emerge."

Not lost for an answer, the Lord of Lightning-Swiftness replied, "It well may be a crystal cannot blast another crystal. My home is built entirely of etheric minerals."

"That is possible, but no more speculation. Come, Gabriel! Let us mount an assault on Samael's crystalline abode." Michael stood up as the fourth archangel approached him. The two brothers walked away from their seated sibling.

Samael performed an ungainly shuffling motion in order to turn himself in their direction. He thought-yelled at their retreating forms, "What if Malkura and Uriel are close to the wall that you target? They could be injured by the penetrating light beam!"

This was a possibility which Michael had already considered and he trusted it would also occur to Samael. Therefore, he was ready with this answer: "Then that is a risk which we must take, if you refuse to open the doors. Should our sister and brother be injured, I, Gabriel and you must take responsibility for whatever befalls them." He stopped walking and, turning back for an instant, questioned, "Surely that will not concern you, Samael? You have previously harmed two of your siblings and not felt remorse."

The first archangel knew he was being manipulated, but his love of Malkura and closeness to Uriel would not allow him to place them in possible danger. He ordered, "Do not go further! Come back to me and I will agree."

Michael walked quickly toward him with Gabriel following closely behind. "You agree to open the door?" asked the third archangel as he reached his brother.

"I do, but only if you grant me one request."

"Bargaining, again, Samael?" Michael moved as though ready to retrace his steps. "There can be no negotiation!"

A distraught expression appeared on Samael's face as he pleaded, "I beg you, Michael, listen to me! I cannot bear the thought of Malkura seeing me so demeaned. I will instruct the door to open, if you will promise me she will not observe me bound."

Michael quickly answered, "I cannot release you, Samael. I do not trust you. I understand your distress, but I will not remove the bindings."

Gabriel offered, "What if I go to the entrance? Once I am there, Samael can open the doors with his thoughts and I will look for our siblings inside. When you know I have access to the home, Michael, you can immediately take

Samael to inner Chaos. In that way, Malkura will not see him."

With genuine gratitude, Samael put forward, "I thank you, Gabriel! I am in agreement with this plan."

Michael nodded his consent and the fourth archangel ran toward the abode, which was just beyond the range of their etheric vision. On arriving, his announcement: "I am in front of the entrance," was received by both brothers. Michael prompted:

"Now, Samael, show me you can be noble."

The first archangel concentrated briefly and then declared, "It is done!" In the same instant, Gabriel's confirmation: "The doors have opened," reached them.

Michael helped Samael to stand and, holding onto his brother, he asked his crystal sword to take them to the meeting place.

With the exception of Mikael and Metatron, no one else was close by when the two archangels arrived. This fact cheered Samael because his pride was suffering great humiliation. Michael remained beside him and explained:

"I will unbind your arms and wings now that you have done what I asked of you. However, I will restrict your hands." He untied the knots and unwound the rope from Samael. Michael allowed his brother the need to stretch his arms and wings. Next, he caused the rope to shrink in length and then wrapped it around Samael's wrists, as he held his sibling's hands behind his back. As Michael knotted the ends, the first archangel continued to open and close his wings. Uncertain whether this indicated a contemplation of flight, he warned Samael, "If you attempt to fly, I *will* strike you with my crystal!"

His brother smiled wickedly at him and replied, "Flying with bound ankles and wrists might prove difficult, but I always enjoy a challenge." Samael stilled his thoughts and Michael wondered if he would have to use his crystal sword.

Finally, the movement of wings ceased and his brother drew them tightly closed. He continued to smile as he observed:

"Of course, now that I am within inner Chaos, I can revert to my auric self. Your restraints will be useless then. Shall we see what happens?"

"If you so choose, but my crystal will blast you into many pieces, which I can then target with greater force, one-by-one. When I am done, it is certain, Lord Samael will be no more!"

The first archangel attempted to sit down, but due to his bound ankles, this proved to be an extremely awkward task. After toppling down and then righting himself, he replied, "You are a worthy match for me, dear brother. You could always find ways around whatever I put forward."

Michael suddenly noticed that neither of his angels were holding the sheathed crystals. He asked, "Where are the wands I gave into your keeping?"

It was Metatron who answered him. "When we arrived here, the Christ Soul came and told us we were to take them to our parent. We did, and the Source directed us to place them at the edge of itself. Once we had put the wands there, they were enveloped in Source consciousness and were no longer visible. I do not know what it has done to them."

"Probably crushed them!" declared Samael. Looking at Metatron, he asked, "Is that *my* light wand of which you tell?"

"Yes, my lord, and the other belonged to Lord Seriel."

Samael gave a cruel smile and remarked, "Just one more item for me to add to the accounting I will take against all those who have opposed me."

This threat evoked no response. Instead, Mikael informed his essence lord, "The Christ Soul also asked me to deliver a message to you, Lord Michael. He wishes to thought exchange with you. The Lord of the Second Essence is but a short distance from here, helping to heal the wounded. Metatron and I will guard Lord Samael while you are gone."

With a curt: "Do not attempt to escape, Samael!" Michael walked away from his seated brother and the angels. He soon came upon the rows of injured souls who were being watched over by the Christ Soul's and Raphael's angels. These wounded individuals exhibited deep cuts, bites and lacerations which had required seals to stop the loss of essence. Most were now lying or sitting while they waited for their etheric bodies to repair themselves. Only a few had not yet received contact with the securing blue vapor which would keep their essence safe. Michael also noted there were a number of angels, who had sprung from the Shekinah, administering and helping where they could. He felt certain his sister would want to assist in this process, once she returned to the inner realms.

The third archangel moved among the gathered beings, looking for the Christ Soul. Eventually, he found him a distance away from the main grouping. He appeared to be resting, but Michael quickly realized that was not his intent. All around him lay angels who had suffered wounds from the light wands or were missing wings and limbs. Tendrils of the Christ Soul's consciousness were wrapped around these maimed beings. Michael recognized his brother's action as being the same one the Source had used to heal Gabriel. As he walked by each melded angel, he suddenly discovered Seriel lying within an enveloping thread of his sibling's auric self.

Not certain whether his second-born sibling could thought exchange while otherwise busy, Michael stood watching Seriel. Unlike the other recuperating angels, the Lord of Sorcery had not reverted to his auric self and was not lying still. He appeared to be trying to break free from the consciousness which surrounded him. Seriel jerked his head from side to side and was pushing his tied hands against the tendril which embraced him. Michael speculated he might be recovering from the disabling effect of the crystal sword's beam. Samael's body had certainly jerked most violently as his awareness returned.

"Our brother does not wish to be given healing." This thought came from the Christ Soul.

"I was wondering whether you could communicate with me while your consciousness is occupied with another task," answered Michael. "Perhaps Seriel is just rousing from the immobility my crystal forced upon him?"

"No, that happened as soon as he was brought to me. He seemed to convulse into wakeful mode, and then was still for a short while. Yet once rested, he began to struggle in order to remove his awareness from mine. I cannot stimulate his damaged body to reconstitute its substance, if he refuses to remain melded with me. I will try, once more, to impress upon him the need to accept our blending."

"I was informed by my catalyst angel that you need to hold discourse with me. What do you wish to share?"

The Christ Soul appeared to be preoccupied with the unyielding Seriel, but then answered, "Our parent is about to create an astounding occurrence in the Abyss of Chaos, the like of which has never happened before. It is readying itself for this event and will need tremendous concentration and intent to accomplish the task. That is why I am presently giving healing to those who are severely injured. The Source must direct its full consciousness to what it hopes to achieve. It cannot be distracted by anything else."

Michael asked, "Do you know what it is planning to create?"

"It gave me little information," replied the Christ Soul. "I know it will forever change our existence within ALL THAT IS. The Source told me it is impelling all archangels and angels to move away from where this happening will take place. It will be some kind of violent upheaval which would destroy any who are caught within its extent. I believe it will be a barrier that separates outer Chaos from the central and inner realms."

This explanation brought a sudden memory back to Michael. He recalled the dream which had shown him the life force spiral. Within Gabriel's level, there was the section that appeared to resemble a gigantic hole. The third archangel felt certain this was connected to what the Christ Soul was expressing. Michael offered, "In one of my dreams, the Source showed me something I could not comprehend then. Now, I am sure it was indicative of this event."

The Christ Soul remarked, "Our parent gives to each of us some understanding of its thoughts and reasoning. Even Samael has shared a part of its desires."

Michael confided, "I can no longer feel akin to our first-born brother. He has grown so separate from us and I believe the Source requires me to forever strive against his wickedness." Looking down at Seriel, he added, "Samael has even influenced this brother to no longer think as we do."

Prompted by mention of the seventh archangel, the Christ Soul declared, "I have to end my attempts to meld with Seriel. His consciousness is powerful and will not maintain a blending with mine. Our brother's thoughts are filled with concerns about his light wand." The encompassing tendril loosened its hold on Seriel's form and retracted back into the Christ Soul's auric self.

Michael stooped down beside his seventh-born sibling and asked, "Why do you struggle against the Christ Soul? He is trying to help you heal."

Seriel attempted to sit up, even though he was obviously suffering great pain. He tried, but fell back with a look of agony contorting his face. He demanded of his brother, "Where is my crystal? Return it to my keeping!"

"Your light wand was given to our parent, as was Samael's," Michael explained. "I do not know what the Source will do with them."

Once more, the injured archangel endeavored to gain a seated position and Michael gave him help. However, having reached an upright state, Seriel shrugged himself free from his sibling's hands. He declared, "A light wand should never be separated from its keeper. Did you take mine, Michael, when you rendered my consciousness unable to function?"

"Yes, I did. I could not trust you or Samael to discontinue using your wands against us. Both of you have caused great injuries to the angels with your crystals' power."

"You had no right to take them," was Seriel's angry response.

Just then Gabriel, the Shekinah and Uriel flew down from above. They landed close to Michael and immediately circled around Seriel. Gabriel observed:

"It is good to see you alert, my brother. Now, I wish to apologize for injuring you so greatly. I knew you were about to go to Samael's aid and I had to stop you. I am not well familiar with the use of a light wand and did not realize my strong intent would be reflected in the beam's intensity."

Seriel answered, "I care naught about my wound. I only wish to retrieve my crystal wand."

The Shekinah knelt down next to the seventh archangel and, looking extremely upset, declared, "Oh, Seriel, that is a terrible injury!" She stretched out her hand and gently touched the green etheric seal. This caused her brother to flinch in pain, and a startled Malkura sat back on her heels. "I am sorry, dear brother, I did not mean to inflict more suffering."

Seriel gave her a wan smile and assured her, "I know that, and the pain is gone already."

Noticing the ropes around his wrists and ankles, the Shekinah looked up at Michael and asked, "Why is our brother bound?"

"I thought it necessary to prevent him from escaping, once his awareness returned to him. Samael is similarly restrained." The third archangel was annoyed by having to explain his actions.

"Surely it is not necessary?" questioned Malkura. "I am sure his wound would prevent him from flying or walking very far."

Grudgingly, Michael conceded, "I will untie his hands." He bent over Seriel and removed the rope from around his wrists. The Lord of the Seventh Essence made circling motions with his hands and wiggled his fingers. Then he placed his hands in his lap and, addressing his sister, offered:

"I thank you, my lady."

"Where is Samael?" asked Uriel.

Michael informed, "He is a short distance from here. My essence angels Mikael and Metatron are guarding him."

"I will go to him," answered Uriel. "Which direction shall I take?"

"If you will curb your impatience, brother, I will take you to him," Michael responded.

"Is Samael also wounded?" This questioning thought came from Malkura.

"He has no injuries." With undisguised distaste, Michael added, "He did not remain visible long enough for anyone to strike a blow against him. I was only able to overcome him with the courage of my angels and Gabriel."

"I will go with you to Samael," stated the Shekinah. She stood up ready to leave.

Michael drew her aside and shielding his thoughts from all of his siblings except Malkura, instructed, "That would not be advisable. Samael has already declared he does not want you to see him bound. It will incite his anger, if I take you to him. He might attempt to do something which would compel me to restrain him further. I think it would be best for you to wait until we know our parent's decision with regard to Samael's chastisement."

The Shekinah nodded reluctantly and agreed, "Very well, I am sure your suggestion is wise. If he is not injured, I can wait to see him. I will remain here with Seriel."

"Perhaps you can convince him to allow the Christ Soul to give him healing. Our second-born brother has tried, but Seriel refuses to accept his help." Michael moved back to Uriel and declared, "Let us go to Samael."

It was at that exact instant that an unknown and alarming sound began to reach the inner and etheric hearing of all the angelic horde. It started low and built gradually in volume until it filled each being's perception to the exception of anything else. The noise seemed to have a straining quality about it, as though great pressure was being applied in ever-increasing amounts. The whole of Chaos was beginning to vibrate with oscillating waves of sensation that caused each and every soul to feel unsteady in their stance or flight. They were buffeted by this unprecedented movement of the Abyss and they clung to one another for stability and courage.

Michael grabbed hold of Uriel to offer him support and Gabriel threw his arms around the Shekinah. However, Seriel sent this urgent thought to both of his siblings:

"Sit with me and we can brace ourselves against this unknown force!"

Both archangels obeyed him without question. They sat closely on either side of Seriel as, ignoring the pain from his wound, he encircled his arms around them. Holding on to each other, the three siblings steeled themselves for whatever was about to happen.

The daemons and demons were also subject to the effects of what was occurring. After escaping from the threat of Michael's crystal sword, they had hurried further outwards. Some were just considering moving back in the hope of harassing any angelic stragglers. As the noise and vibrations began, they all, without exception, ran, or flew, or rolled into the farthest depths of the Abyss. This new occurrence terrified them and they strove to be as far away from it as possible.

Those angels, who were close to what was taking place, also felt compelled to speedily retreat. Most flew toward the perceived safety of the Source. Yet there were a few ever-curious souls who overcame the sense of danger and waited close by in order to witness the phenomenon. Later, they would tell what they saw to any who would listen. Their tale would be retold, over and over, to all newly birthed angels throughout eternity.

As they watched, a great expanse of the central area of Chaos began to alter in appearance. Its substance appeared to repeatedly stretch in all directions and then buckle inwards. It was as though a mighty pair of hands was manipulating the very fiber of the Abyss. Pulling and pushing it with increasing and astounding power. Shaping it into a new form. With each alternative motion, the noise and vibration grew more intense until the nearby angels were pushed to the brink of madness. Just at the point when they knew they could bear no more, there came the most tremendous booming sound that would ever be heard throughout ALL THAT IS. Those who were not too frightened to look in the direction of the gigantic bang, saw the substance of Chaos exploding upwards and outwards. For an instant, the particles were all separated. Then they began to rejoin into huge, expanding spheres of dark matter. They were innumerable and ever-growing. Slowly, they drifted back into the bottomless chasm the explosion had created. They nestled side-by-side, underneath and above each other. And, thus, the Source had birthed new offspring into the Abyss of Chaos. It had brought forth myriad universes.

When the archangels had recovered from the soul-impacting blast, Michael stated to the Christ Soul:

"I believe our parent has created that of which you told me."

"I am certain it is so," responded the second archangel.

Michael released his hold on Uriel and prompted, "Come, brother! I will take you to Samael, and then I must go to the Source."

Chapter Twenty-Four

W hen Michael returned from the thought exchange with his parent, he explained to his siblings that something of great importance was about to happen. He requested Gabriel's help in carrying Seriel to a place nearby the Source. Michael also told the Shekinah to accompany them. Once the seventh and eighth archangels were settled at a short distance from their parent, he directed Gabriel to look for Raphael. The two brothers were to gather together as many angels as possible and bring them all to the same location. Meanwhile, Michael flew back to the Christ Soul and detailed everything the Source had shared with him. Due to being melded with a large number of injured angels, the second archangel would not be able to journey to the gathering. The Christ Soul showed no surprise at what Michael was telling him. He was aware that something of this nature would take place.

After sharing the information with his sibling, Michael walked quickly to where his angels were continuing to guard Samael. He instructed Mikael and Metatron to grasp hold of his brother by the arms and to pull him up into a standing position. Next he told his angels to maintain their grip on Samael as he untied the ropes from around the first archangel's ankles and wrists. Once again, Michael warned his sibling not to make any effort to escape. The group then moved toward the waiting crowd with Samael held tightly on either side by the two angels, while his third-born brother walked behind.

There was an ever-growing number of angels standing and sitting a short distance away from the consciousness boundary of the Source. There were some with minor cuts and abrasions from the recent battle, but many were unscathed due to not having taken part in the fighting. With the exception of Seriel, those with severe injuries were either with the Christ Soul or remaining in the rows of wounded souls. Michael waited for the return of Raphael and Gabriel with even more angels, and then he announced:

"Salutations to all! I have brought you together at the behest of our parent. As you may know, there was a mighty battle fought between myself and Lord Samael, together with Lord Gabriel and Lord Seriel. Many of you also stood beside us, and I thank those who gave their allegiance to me. After the affray ended, you must be aware that an unprecedented event took place within an area of the Abyss. I now wish to explain to you exactly what happened."

Thought-murmurs traveled throughout the gathering as angels nodded and expressed their agreement and feelings of expectation.

Michael continued, "We are all a part of a gigantic life force spiral that is continually expanding within the Abyss of Chaos. Our perception of this swirling existence is considered to be ALL THAT IS. Yet we know Chaos is both an integral part of this spiral and a totally separate matrix in which we are embedded. At the center of the life force spiral is our parent, the Source, who has created our souls and who constantly watches over us. This mighty being has given us free will with which we make the choices of how we will exist. When exercising this gift, there are a number of different interpretations being expressed. Lord Samael has chosen to use his free will to only satisfy his own desires. This has caused much upheaval and suffering to his siblings and even certain angels . . ."

"And, surely, it is the very nature of free will that allows it to be exercised in whatever manner a soul chooses?" interrupted Samael. "Otherwise, is it truly free will?"

A number of acquiescent thoughts rose from some of the angelic crowd. However, Michael ignored his brother's remark and continued:

"The Source is greatly troubled by its first-born son's behavior and has determined that others should not be subjected to it unless they choose to be. Until now we have always been able to travel to whatever area of the Abyss we wish to access. This is no longer possible. The inner realms and a part of the central section of ALL THAT IS are readily available, but there is a barrier preventing access to the outer realms. The extreme sound and vibrations we all experienced a short while ago was the Source manifesting this obstacle. Within the central area there is now a formidable and vast expanse of creations the Source has termed 'universes.' No soul can navigate its way directly through this obstruction in order to reach outer Chaos."

"So we are to be limited in our movement in the Abyss?" questioned Samael. "That would appear to be restricting our free will."

Michael answered, "Many souls have no desire to experience the outer realms. Now, if you will refrain from interrupting me, Samael, I shall explain the choices our parent is offering to you and any who choose to align themselves with you. Firstly, the Source is able to create a one-way portal through which you can pass to immediately access outer Chaos. Once there, you will not be able to travel inwards because of the barrier of universes. However, all of the Abyss beyond there will be yours to enjoy and rule. Our parent is giving that vast area to you to make of it what you will. The daemons are already there and can no longer harm those who choose not to pass through the portal. You will be free to hold sway over those creatures and any souls who wish to go with you. The Source will not interfere or influence your existence in any manner. Do you understand this first option?"

With a hint of boredom, Samael replied, "Of course, I do. And what, pray tell, is my second option?"

"To remain here with your siblings and parent. To forgo the notion that being birthed first you are more powerful and more important than any other. You must concede that the Source is the one from whom you will seek learning, advice and help. The use of a light wand cannot be yours. Our parent will destroy your three-pointed crystal and you must not choose another one to use as a powerful weapon. There is one additional requirement which I do not comprehend, but our parent has assured me that you will understand it. You must give due consideration to what the Source told you about the proliferation of your essence."

This final point brought thought-gasps and much discussion among the listening angels. All now looked toward Samael, eagerly awaiting his reply. He kept his thoughts silent for a short while which caused a buzz of speculation to begin to travel between the onlookers. Finally, he asked:

"And what of my light wand, if I choose to pass through the portal?"

"It will be returned to you later," Michael divulged.

"And what if I do not accept either option? Will the Source then give to me a third choice?" Samael looked around and beamed at the angelic assembly. "Perchance I will not accept one or the other option."

Michael walked toward his brother and declared, "Our parent is only offering two choices, but I am happy to give you a third. If you will not decide to either go to outer Chaos or remain with us, I will thrust you through the portal myself!"

Uriel and several angels moved swiftly toward the confronting siblings. Seriel also attempted to rise from his seated position, but Raphael and Gabriel firmly held his arms. The fifth archangel warned:

"If you stand up and walk, that will place stress upon the seal and it may break. Then your essence will begin to flow, once more. Be still, Seriel! We will not allow our brothers to exchange blows."

Samael stared at Michael and remarked, "I am tempted to choose the second option because then I could stay and match my skills against yours. As I have previously stated, you are a worthy opponent."

"Are you making that choice, brother?" asked Michael.

The first archangel paused, as though undecided. Then, shaking his head, he declared, "I think not. Having to consult with the Source and carry out its wishes would bring great boredom. I would rather enjoy the challenges of the unknown. The outer Abyss holds mysteries that intrigue my curious soul." Samael turned to the listening angels and exclaimed, "I am bound for a new adventure! Who will join me?"

There were numerous answering thought-shouts of "I will!" Chief among them came from Belial, Azazel, Shamshiel and Turel. Both Kokabel and Semyaza were not present. Being injured, they were resting within the rows of wounded angels. Uriel also answered in the affirmative and he quickly stood next to Samael.

Michael instructed, "All who wish to go with Lord Samael should take their leave of those they will see no more, once they have passed through the portal. Samael, you must now part company with our siblings." Then to his two angels, he added, "You can release your hold on my brother."

A large number of angels began to move among the crowd, embracing certain other angels and exchanging final thoughts. When these parting actions were done, those who were leaving stood in a group, waiting for Michael's next order. Meanwhile, once free from Mikael's and Metatron's grasp, Samael pulled Uriel into a close embrace and thought-whispered:

"I cannot allow you to come with me, dear brother. There may be many dangers and, thus, I will forever be concerned about your safety. I treasure the love and support you have given to me. The memory of your devotion will keep me strong."

A distraught Uriel answered, "I beg you, let me go through the portal with you! I have no desire to continue my existence without your companionship."

"No! I command you to stay here! If you truly love me, you *will* do my bidding. Remain safe and stalwart, sweet Uriel!" Samael released his tight hold on the sixth archangel and then walked in the direction of his other four siblings. Michael followed closely behind in the event his brother decided to take flight. Reaching the archangels, Samael offered to his fifth-born sibling: "I bid you to fare well!"

Raphael responded, "As I do to you, Samael. May you remain within the Source's keeping."

With a fleeting smile, Samael expressed, "That thought must no longer have meaning with regard to me." Then, addressing Gabriel, he put forward, "Now, you will be free from my annoyance and disruptive reasoning. Fare well, brother!"

"I also believe our divine parent will forever keep you safe and loved. May *you* fare well, Samael!" replied Gabriel.

Next, Samael stooped down to be on a level with Seriel. He placed a hand on his brother's shoulder and suggested, "You must rest so that your wound can heal. When you are recovered, I trust you will come to me?" Turning round to Michael, he questioned, "The portal will remain open for those who are too unfit to go with me now?"

"I am certain our parent will reopen it when those who which to pass through it are healed," replied the third archangel.

Bringing his gaze back to Seriel, Samael pressed, "What say you, my brother? Will you join me to explore outer Chaos?"

Seriel's expression was deeply troubled as he answered, "I have sworn my allegiance to you, thus, I must give you my support. When I am healed, I will follow you. Until then, may you remain safe and well!"

Finally, Samael turned his attention to the Shekinah who was sitting beside Seriel. Taking hold of her hands, he straightened up, bringing her into a standing position, too. He smiled down at her and, shielding his thoughts from all but his sister, asked, "And what of you, my lady? Will you accompany your wayward brother to his new realms?"

Tears began to brim in her eyes as she gave her equally shielded reply, "No, my lord, I cannot go with you."

"Ah, I forgot your promise to our parent. Perchance you will decide to forget it once you are without my loving presence. I know your love for me cannot be easily ignored."

Removing one of her hands from his, Malkura wiped away her tears and shared, "My sibling love for you is forever, as it is for all of my brothers. Yet my deeper emotion must be put aside. It has brought me too much pain. As I have previously told you, my lord, what was once between us has now ended."

A cold and disquieting expression appeared in Samael's purple eyes as he asked, "Am I foolish to love a sister who, in return, cannot love me despite my faults? I thought you were the epitome of unconditional love. I see that I was wrong."

"You have been cruel and selfish, Samael. How can I ever condone such disturbing qualities?"

Samael released her other hand and declared, "You slight me deeply by setting aside your love for me. Yet know this! No other archangel can complete you as I do. And I will allow no other brother to steal what we have shared. From the depths of the Abyss I shall be watching and *will* find a way of bringing you to me. And, if you give your love to another, you will find no joy, for I hereby lay a malediction upon any such union. Now, I take my leave of you, Lady Malkura, until our next meeting!" He walked quickly away from the Shekinah and moved toward the Source.

Taken by surprise, Michael had to almost run to catch up with him. As they strode along, Samael asked:

"Where is the Christ Soul? Does he not wish to bid me well in my new existence?"

"Our brother is preoccupied with healing many severely wounded angels," replied Michael. "He asked me to convey to you his eternal love and blessings."

"He is a brother with whom I have never felt an affinity. Yet he believes, as I do, in the duality of our souls. Thank him for his parting thoughts and tell him we may yet debate our shared conviction."

The two archangels arrived at the extremity of their parent's consciousness. To Samael its brilliance seemed even more apparent than when he had last held discourse with it. He declared:

"I am here, my surreptitious parent, but where is your portal to outer Chaos?"

"It is here, my son," replied the Source. Within the kaleidoscopic movement a pinpoint of darkness appeared close to where the two brothers were standing. It quickly pushed back the surrounding radiance as it expanded into a large, oval shape. Its size could easily accommodate an archangel's entrance into it, and its substance appeared to be the dark void of the Abyss. Yet there was a sense of great movement within it that was absent from the nothingness of Chaos.

Samael approached the portal. Then, turning to face the large, angelic gathering, he projected these thoughts so that each and every soul, who was present, received them: "To all of you who have fought beside me and will follow me through this portal, I give my gratitude and praise. You are noble beings and will reap the bounty of true self awareness. To all of you who have fought against me and have judged me to be evil, I give my contempt and degradation. You are ignoble beings and will suffer the deprivation of my wrath. The Lord of the First Essence will never forget what is done for or against him!"

Next, Samael brought his attention to Michael and asked, "Where is my light wand? You told me it would be given to me, if I chose to pass through the portal."

Michael explained, "The Source will not return it to you before you depart. Our parent does not trust you, Samael, and believes you would use the wand in some adverse manner. When Seriel comes to you, as I am certain he will, your wand will be given into his keeping before he steps through the portal. Our brother has also wounded many angels and must choose between existence in the outer Abyss or supplication to the Source."

"And what if I choose to ask my crystal to bring me back from outer Chaos?" taunted Samael.

Michael was happy to inform his brother, "Apparently, the barrier of universes will prevent that from happening. Now, are you ready to leave us?"

"Yes, when I have shared my last thoughts with you. Firstly, I wish to thank you for removing the binding restraints. I was spared the humiliation of Malkura seeing me confined in that manner. Now, to other matters." He stepped close to Michael and glared into his odami eyes. "You have always wished to be the leader of we archangels, even though you knew that was the right of the first-born son. Once I am gone, you will have your desire and can take charge of five siblings. Yet you will never hold sway over me nor Seriel. I care naught what you impose upon three of our brothers, but be mindful of how you behave toward the Shekinah and Uriel. Do not harm them in any manner and never forget they have my eternal love. You, my brother, will earn my everlasting rage, if you attempt to usurp my closeness with Uriel. Also, never allow him to pass through this portal. Finally, if you seek to win the affection of Malkura, I will bring damnation upon you!" Without waiting for Michael's reply, the first archangel swung away from his brother and jumped into the portal's void. Instantly, he was gone.

Recovering from Samael's outburst, the third archangel signaled the waiting group of angels to approach him. As they arrived, he motioned them, one-by-one, to step through the opening to the outer Abyss.

*   *   *

Seriel awoke from a troubled dream. He seemed to be drifting in and out of long sleeping periods which did not correspond with any resting phase. His chest wound was continually aching and intermittently ravaging his senses with jabbing spasms of unbearable pain. The most recent duration of sleep had brought him relief from the terrible agony. However, it plagued him with the dream horror of falling through a dark portal that opened up into nothingness. Once there, he floated aimlessly, and the awful loneliness of being the only soul in this desolate place caused him to wish to be no more. Waking brought the realization that he was neither in that void nor alone. Manah was sitting on a chair, engrossed in thought-painting a nearby wall with strokes of contrasting colors.

Looking around, Seriel remembered he was in the Shekinah's resting chamber. Raphael and Gabriel had carried him to this room on the direction of their sister after Samael and the angels were gone through the portal. Before his two brothers departed, Raphael untied the rope from around his ankles. Soon afterwards, Malkura asked Seriel whether the crystal capstone would follow her direction. Answering her that it would, he had wanted to ask why she needed to know this, but sleep claimed him even as the thought was forming. Beyond then, Seriel's consciousness wandered back and forth from dreams to wakefulness. Once, on opening his eyes, he saw Raphael sitting beside him. On another occasion, it was Samael who stood astride his body, but that was a dream. Most often, when waking, he found his sister watching over him.

Wanting to remain awake, the seventh archangel attempted to sit up. The noise of his movement attracted Manah's attention. She jumped up from the chair and quickly approached him. As she eased Seriel back into a lying down position, she scolded:

"No, no, my lord! You must remain completely flat. Lord Raphael believes you will heal more quickly, if you do not try to sit or stand."

He managed to give the angel a strained smile as he told her, "Perchance I do not wish to heal more quickly."

A small thought-giggle accompanied Manah's answer: "I can understand why you might wish to remain in my mistress's keeping. That would be much better than having to keep company with the wicked Lord Samael. I am hoping Lady Malkura will persuade you to not follow him to the outer Abyss."

"Where is my sister?" asked Seriel.

"She is with the Source, asking it for advice on how to speed your recovery. Should we hope our parent can give her no suggestions?"

"You are a mischievous angel, Manah, and you . . ." The throbbing torment suddenly enveloped his chest, once more, shattering his thoughts. Unable to cope with the pain, his consciousness quickly escaped into the nullification of sleep.

Later, when his dreams faded and he regained his waking state, Seriel discovered the Shekinah moving around him. She was intently placing small crystal clusters so that they encircled his resting form. Puzzled by her action, he asked:

"Why are you laying those minerals beside me, my lady?"

Startled, Malkura answered, "Oh! I thought you were sleeping. Do not concern yourself with what I am doing. It is something our parent offered as a method of enhancing the healing process. Continue to relax, Seriel. The resting phase will soon be upon us and that should give your etheric body a long duration in which to repair itself."

"There was a question I wanted to ask of you." Seriel tried to remember what it was, but his thoughts seemed distant and vague as a consequence of battling both pain and disturbing dreams. "I cannot recall what my query was, my consciousness is muddled."

The Shekinah sat down beside him within the circle of crystals. She laid a gentle hand on his forehead and offered, "You will remember when you are less troubled by the injury. Now, relax and allow sleep to comfort you." She brought her attention to the floor and it began to gently undulate. "As you once told me when I was in need of help, surrender to slumber and I will keep watch over you."

Seriel tried to remain awake because he wanted to share thoughts with his sister, but sleep conquered his desire. He moved into elusive dreams while the resting phase slowly passed. At one point, the seventh archangel was roused by a sharp stabbing pain in his chest. Opening his eyes, he saw the sleeping Shekinah lying a short distance away from him. He wished he could touch her, but she was just out of reach and, as he attempted to move, the painful spasm intensified. A number of the surrounding crystal clusters lay between him and his sister. Seriel wondered whether one of them might ease the intense cramping sensation. He grasped a purple cluster, drew it to himself and asked for the anguish to lessen. As the pain subsided, he returned to his dreaming thoughts.

When the resting phase ended, he awoke to find the floor was still and the surrounding crystals were gone. However, the purple cluster remained in his hand. He quickly noticed the Shekinah's catalyst angel, Ammashma, sitting on the same chair where Manah had previously sat. This first-cast angelic being was turned away from him and was busily braiding her long, maldor hair. Seriel remembered seeing her during the battle. She was fighting with another angel who was fairing badly from her fencing skills. He had thought about challenging her. She appeared to be a worthy match for his own developing interest in sword-play. However, as Seriel had watched her, she plunged her sword deep into her opponent's thigh and then flew away. He did not see her, again, until now.

Ammashma's stature was similar to that of her essence mistress, but their countenances differed. This catalyst angel's features were less perfect. Her blue eyes were not as striking as Malkura's and there was a quality of petulance about her mouth. Being a first casting, the color maldor was not only gracing her hair, but was also interspersed throughout her rulpiel body.

"Ammashma, where is your mistress?" Seriel slowly sat up, expecting the painful spasm to reoccur from his effort.

The catalyst angel moved around in the chair to face him and coldly answered, "Lady Malkura is with the Source."

The pain did not strike, again, and the dull ache had lessened. Feeling cheered by this realization, he asked, "Will she be returning soon? I need to exchange thoughts with her."

Seriel noticed there were a number of sealed wounds on this angel's arms. As he observed her, Ammashma manifested a length of narrow etheric material. She then bound and knotted it around the ends of her braided hair. Leaving the long plait resting against her chest, she turned away from him and merely offered, "She will come back when her discourse with our parent has ended."

Trying to ignore her rudeness, Seriel remarked, "I saw you fighting during the battle. You are skilled with the use of a sword."

Without altering her position, she told him, "I have no interest in your thoughts, my lord. I am only here because my mistress asked me to keep watch while she was gone."

Feeling his anger rising, Seriel retorted, "That well may be, but I am an archangel and angels should show respect when in our presence."

Ammashma spun round in the chair and declared, "Then behave in a manner that deserves respect! You did not warn Lord Gabriel of your first-born brother's treachery. Now, you have severely wounded a number of angels. Both you and Lord Samael are evil and should not be given the choice of staying or going to the outer Abyss. Regardless of your injury, *I* would banish you there without ever offering a reprieve!"

"Then perchance I should be grateful my siblings are less stern than yourself." Seriel suddenly felt the need to win this angel's approval. "Your mistress is a forgiving soul and has offered me sanctuary until my wound is healed. Can you not, at least, be civil to me?"

Standing up, Ammashma approached the seated archangel and exclaimed, "I love my mistress and wish only to see her happy. Lord Samael has brought her great sorrow and now you are distressing her in the same way. When you are gone to outer Chaos, I will encourage her to seek the companionship of either Lord Raphael or Lord Michael. They are the siblings with whom she is in accord. She should not be giving her affection to the lords of the first and seventh essences!" Looking away from him, her thoughts paused, and then she informed, "Lady Malkura is returning. I will go to meet her." The catalyst angel left the chamber without sharing anything more.

While Seriel was waiting for the Shekinah, he brought his attention to the chest wound and discovered the green seal was gone. Its absence revealed an ugly, yellowish-brown scar, which some would consider unsightly. Yet, unlike Samael, vanity was not a dominating quality of the seventh archangel. Therefore, its disfiguring effect did not trouble him. He attempted to get up from the floor.

Malkura entered the resting chamber just as Seriel was struggling to gain a standing position. She hurried over to him and grabbed his arm in order to help steady his balance. He managed to remain upright, after shifting his weight from one foot to the other and taking several unsteady steps. The Lord of the Seventh Essence gave an awkward thought-laugh as he stated:

"I seem to be a clumsy archangel. Brother Gabriel's attack was much more disabling than I realized."

"I think you should sit down, again. Can you walk to that chair?" The Shekinah indicated a nearby seat and tightened her hold on his arm.

Seriel moved toward the chair. With each step his gait grew stronger. However, on reaching it, he was grateful to be seated, once more. "Thank you, dear sister, for helping me now and for allowing me to recover in your home."

"I could not leave you out in Chaos. You gave me aid when I was in need and I have been given the opportunity to return your kindness." Malkura pulled another chair close to his, sat down and faced him. She was wearing a blue tunic-type garment with long flowing sleeves. Her hair was tied back with a color-matching length of material.

Uncertain what next to share, the seventh archangel asked, "Did Ammashma leave?"

"Yes, she went in search of Angel Mikael." Malkura smiled and expressed, "I believe she has a liking for him." She stopped, and then added, "I always seem to be sharing angel gossip with you. You must think I give all of my attention to such things?"

"I think your loving nature wants everyone to have a close companion, and I look upon that quality as an angelic attribute. However, your catalyst angel does not appear to be as loving as you. Ammashma was quick to share her feelings about me and Samael."

The Shekinah looked concerned as she remarked, "I was hoping you would remain asleep while I was gone. I know she holds a great dislike for both of you. I could not find Manah. That is why I asked Ammashma to watch over you while I carried the crystal clusters to the Source. I apologize for her bluntness."

"It is of no great concern. With regard to the clusters, I noticed they were gone. Why did you take them to our parent?"

"The Source instructed me to place crystals around you at the onset of the resting phase and to remove them at its end. Once collected, they had to be taken to our parent." Malkura shook her head as she observed, "I do not know why I had to give them to the Source. It merely told me they must not be used, again."

Seriel opened his hand and offered the purple cluster to her, explaining, "I was keeping this one while I slept. It seemed to ease the pain in my chest."

"You were gripping it so tightly that I did not want to wake you by trying to remove it." She took the cluster from him and placed it on the floor by her feet. "I can take it to the Source when I next go to hold discourse with it."

A silence fell between the siblings. Seriel knew this precious sojourn with Malkura would soon come to an end and he would be gone to the outer Abyss. There was so much he wanted to share with her, but he did not know how to broach the subject. Instead, he offered, "I have remembered the question I wanted to ask of you before I first fell asleep. Why did you want to know whether the capstone would follow your directive?"

Was it his imagination? Did the Shekinah look relieved as she answered, "I have wondered what was the nature of your forgotten question. My reason for asking was because I wished to request something of the capstone. I was unsure whether it would only respond to you."

"Before I gifted this home to you, I instructed both the entrance door and the capstone to only follow your directions."

"So what I have asked of it should be happening?"

"Indeed, it should. Can you not ascertain that it is doing your bidding?"

"No, I just have to trust that it is. Let me explain." She looked directly at him and asked, "Do you recall Samael telling us he had one more question for me and then he would release me?"

"I suspected it was an untruth, but I decided to behave as though I believed him," Seriel told her.

"Part of his statement was true. He did have a question for me." Her thoughts ceased, and then she continued, "Oh, I need to explain something else first. After you and Raphael left my home to gather the angels together for the meeting, Manah and I decided to stay for a short while longer."

"Yes, your angel told us this when she came to relate what had happened to you," agreed Seriel.

Continuing on, the Shekinah revealed, "We sat in one of the rooms below and shared our thoughts. Then, as we were leaving, Samael appeared before us, and you know what took place next. Now, Samael's question to me was about my thought exchange with Manah. He wanted to know exactly what I had told her . . ." The Shekinah paused, as though waiting for Seriel to interrupt.

This he quickly did with: "How could our brother know what was happening in your home?"

"We think alike, Seriel! That was my question to him." Malkura's expression changed to one of sadness. "He has a crystal with which he has secretly viewed me since the first banishment. It is similar in shape and size to the silver-sided one he wanted me to keep, but this one is darkly hued. When he looks into it, he can see me and what I am doing." She gave a little shudder and added, "It is a most unsettling feeling to know I am being watched in that manner. Even though I have loved Samael, I do not wish to be observed so closely. Therefore, I have asked the capstone to prevent him, or anyone, from watching me by any means while I am in my home. I can do nothing about our brother observing me when I am traveling about in Chaos, but I trust I am safe from his scrutiny here."

"I am certain you are." Seriel was stunned by what Malkura had revealed. There was something most troubling about Samael's secret action. As on several other occasions, he felt distressed about how much his brother had changed.

Another silence ensued. The Shekinah stared down at her hands while her sibling studied her saddened face. He knew he could not leave without expressing his feelings for her, but he was reluctant to begin. Finally, he asked, "Are you aware I severely injured several angels?"

Malkura looked up at him and replied, "Yes, Michael has told me that you did."

"Yet you have continued to show me kindness and loving care. Why?"

"You are my brother and I love you, as I love all of my siblings. Knowing that you wounded some of the angels has grieved me deeply, but I cannot turn away from you when you are in need of help." Malkura's gaze returned to her hands.

"You are truly an angelic soul, my lady. Neither Samael nor I are worthy of your love, whether it is given as a sibling or with much greater feeling." He leaned forwards and questioned, "Are you distraught now that Samael is gone?"

Continuing to look down, she answered, "I am both saddened and relieved. Having decided to put away my love for him, it was most painful to see him and be in his company. Now, I will not be reminded of his fall from grace. I can treasure memories of the once noble Lord Samael."

"And what of me? How will you remember Lord Seriel?"

Finally, she returned his gaze and he saw that her eyes were filled with tears. "If you go through the portal, I will think of you often. I will remember a brother who showed me great compassion when I was almost crazed with sadness. If you stay, I do not know what will transpire."

"I cannot stay. I have sworn my allegiance to Samael and our parent has asked me to keep watch over him."

"Then you must go." Tears began to course down her cheeks. "Oh, this bothersome fluid! Did you ask our parent what it is?" She dabbed her eyes with the wide cuff of one of her sleeves.

"The droplets are tears. The Source told me our eyes create them when we experience grief. I also learned that the aqueous objects, which Samael and I found, were our parent's tears. It shed them out of sorrow for its first-born son."

"That knowledge makes me feel even more saddened." The Shekinah sat gazing past her brother, lost in unhappy thoughts.

Once again, the sibling archangels sat in silence. Seriel knew he must declare his love for his sister. He might never have another opportunity to tell her. Taking hold of her hands, he asked:

"Do you recall when we last held each other's hands? You told me afterwards you had taken a notion to meld with me. I wish to know whether you desired our awareness blending because you felt gratitude toward me for the comfort I gave to you? Or was your wish prompted by a deeper feeling?"

Malkura closed her eyes and stilled her thoughts. Seriel waited for her reply, but none came. After a while, he pressed:

"I pray you, dear sister, look at me and answer my question. Do you hold an affection for me that is more than sibling love?"

The Shekinah opened her eyes and looked directly into his. There were no more tears, but utter sadness filled their green depths. She told him, "I have expected this question and I have dreaded it. I thought it was the one you wished to ask, yet could not remember. My answer may not please you, but it is all I can offer. I have loved unwisely once and, thus, cannot allow myself to cherish another brother who chooses strife and disruption over peace and harmony."

"I thank you for your honesty, my lady. May I be as forthright with you?"

A nod of agreement was her only response.

Continuing to grasp her hands, Seriel knew, at last, he could convey his feelings to her. "I have loved you both as a sibling, and so much more, from the instant of our birthing. You are more precious to me than I could ever express and I will never forsake my passion for you. It is eternal."

A rueful smile appeared, as Malkura remarked, "Manah told me that she and my angels knew it was so. Yet I was unaware. Why did you never tell me of your love?"

"I thought the depth of your devotion to Samael would last forever. I believed you both were inseparable."

"How wrong you were, Seriel."

"Indeed, I was." The seventh archangel released her hands, stood up and declared, "Now, I will take my leave of you. I wish to go to my home until I am ready to pass through the portal."

Arising from her chair, his sister observed, "Surely you are not yet strong enough to leave here? I would have you stay with me until you are fully recovered."

"I thank you for your concern, but I trust you will understand that I prefer to be alone. I must prepare myself to go to the outer Abyss." Seriel attempted to adopt a mode of efficiency in order to quell his churning emotions. "I will gift my home to Raphael. When I do, I will give him your emerald so that he can bring it to you. Also, I know you enjoy your discourses with our parent, thus, you may wish to move this abode closer to it. Just tell the capstone where you want the pyramid to be and it will quickly move it. Lastly, do you have a message that I can take to Samael? I know he will want to know whether you gave me such."

"He may not. Our parting was most unhappy. He was furious with me for not wishing to go with him." Malkura kept her thoughts to herself for a short while, then she suggested, "If he does ask you for a message, tell him his sister wishes him to fare well and that she hopes he will find his soul's destiny."

"I will also try to persuade him to not watch you through his crystal. Now, may you remain within our parent's loving care until, and if, we meet, again!"

"Dear Seriel, this parting is more upsetting than the one with Samael. Must you leave so soon?" She stepped close to him and lifted her arms, as if ready to embrace him.

Turning sharply away from her, he begged, "Please do not touch me, Malkura. If you do, you will destroy my resolve to go to our brother. I pray you, open the entrance door for me, but remain in this chamber. I cannot bear to delay my parting from you." Without looking back at the Shekinah, he began to walk slowly out of the room. As he moved along the corridors, his strength was quickly increasing. When he reached the open front entrance, he felt able to make the short flight to his home. Before he unfurled his wings, Seriel suddenly realized tears were streaming down his face.

Epilogue

When he was not sleeping, Samael frequently became engrossed in watching the Shekinah by means of the darkly hued mineral. In addition, he was obsessively making plans which would bring Malkura to him. Life without her loving presence was almost unbearable. Her refusal to go with him through the portal was haunting his dreaming and waking thoughts. He wished he had not become so enraged when she assured him she could never condone his cruel behavior toward his brothers. The first archangel had taken leave of his sister so abruptly and now he regretted that action. His final exchange of thoughts with her should have been less damning and more persuasive. The outer Abyss was a lonely place without her company. It felt as though his soul was becoming twisted and forced into a tortured existence.

Since returning to this area of Chaos, Samael was also using the remote viewing crystal as much to observe Michael as he was to view his sister. His third-born sibling appeared to be in preparation for some future event. He spent many of the waking phases either overseeing the manifestation of etheric weapons or encouraging angels to learn and master their fighting skills. When he was not preoccupied with these tasks, he held long sessions with the Source. Whatever was being planned would need close scrutiny.

Samael had come to look upon Michael as a hated adversary. He was convinced his third brother was the archangel for whom Malkura was developing a strong affection. When she told him she was beginning to live in closeness with siblings who did not bring her sadness, he was certain she held someone specific in mind. At first, he concluded it was Seriel. Knowing how much he loved the Shekinah, it seemed very possible she might begin to develop a fondness for the Lord of Sorcery. However, now that Seriel had joined him in banishment, that possibility no longer existed. Samael was certain his seventh-born brother would have never left Malkura, if she had disclosed a desire for closeness with him. Therefore, his jealousy turned to Michael.

The third archangel had been more than ready to do battle with him. Why? For no other reason than the issue of their sister. Why was he so outraged with Samael for wanting to keep the Shekinah in his home in order to exchange thoughts with her? Even Seriel did not consider that sufficient reason to fight against him. Malkura herself once asked him why he could not be more careful, like Michael. Obviously, even then she was holding admiration for her third sibling. That was before Samael took his revenge on Gabriel, therefore, her affection for Michael must be long standing. Perhaps it was the real reason she had turned away from her first-born brother? Expressing unhappiness at his treatment of Gabriel and Seriel might be her way of hiding the truth. Her feelings for Samael had waned as her love of Michael had grown.

Believing this, Samael began watching the Lord of the Third Essence through the dark crystal. He closely observed Michael and Malkura whenever they were together, but did not witness any intimacies between them that would verify his belief. There were occasions when Michael, or another brother, went to the Shekinah's abode. This caused Samael to become envious of all his siblings. They could enjoy Malkura's company in her own surroundings while he could not. His jealousy was heightened by his inability to know what was transpiring in her home. For some reason he was no longer able to view the interior of her pyramid. It was as though its inside was shielded from his crystal's power. Samael suspected Seriel might have knowledge of why this was happening, but he did not want to question him about it. In the event his brother was unaware of Samael's need for remote viewing, he would be alerting Seriel to it. When he had felt compelled to question Malkura about her discourse with Manah, he overlooked the resulting consequence. The Shekinah was horrified to learn that Samael was watching her, even when she was inside her home.

The first archangel did find some satisfaction in repossessing his light wand. Seriel brought it to him as soon as he arrived in the outer Abyss. Samael could move anywhere within his new realm via its power, but, as Michael had assured him, it could not take him inwards. When bored, he would repeatedly blast a daemon or two with his crystal. This gave him the idle pleasure of watching his prey explode into many pieces, which would then reform in readiness to be blasted, once again.

There was also another preoccupation which caught his quicksilver attention span. Samael's curiosity was stimulated by the chasm of universes. It was apparent that the spheres of dark matter were evolving. Yet he felt certain they were not merely a barrier to prevent his return to inner Chaos. His parent was far too devious and inventive to create such complex structures for the sole purpose of barricading him in his new home. He would observe them closely and look for opportunities to manipulate them to his own advantage. Such actions would greatly aggravate the Source and that, in turn, would give Samael tremendous satisfaction.

It was his right to exact some such compensation. Together with his burning jealousy, the first archangel was also harboring an ever-increasing sense of anger and resentment. He was the first-born son and should not be confined to any one section of the Abyss. It may have been his choice to pass through the portal, but the alternative was not viable for him. His parent made it appear as though he was being given choices, yet it had maneuvered him into doing what it wanted. Once again, its intent was hidden beneath the guise of free will.

Samael consoled himself by affirming that he would find ways to strike out at the Source. In some manner he would create pain and disruption for all the souls who would not follow his reasoning. In turn, their suffering would reflect back grief and despair to his parent. And for all those who would do his bidding, he would compel them to reject WHAT IS and embrace their duality. That would surely bring much disharmony and adversity throughout the life force spiral? He would wreak havoc and create chaos to show the Source his power was even greater than its own. Samael took great comfort from that thought as his existence in outer Chaos spread out before him.

$$* \quad * \quad *$$

The Shekinah was sitting on the floor of her chamber, waiting for the resting phase to begin. She was thinking about her first and seventh siblings as she held a small casket in her hands. Seriel had created this gift and Raphael brought it to her at his brother's request. This etheric object was a container for the emerald. It boasted her own innate color and was lined inside with a plush, darker rulpiel material. As she often did when holding it, the Shekinah moved her forefinger along the groove of the glyph that was etched on the lid. This action brought memories of Seriel lovingly tracing the symbols on her entrance door. Her brother held a passion for these expressions of their thoughts. She had questioned Raphael about this glyph and he explained what Seriel told him. It was a symbol within the angelic script that he was creating and which represented the beginning of her name.

Malkura opened the lid and looked at the green jewel cushioned inside. She touched it, but did not remove it from the box. As she closed the lid, she thought about how much this gift from Seriel portrayed her feelings toward Samael. Something exquisitely beautiful was resting within this closed case. It was safely hidden inside and could be looked at whenever she wished to be reminded of how perfect their love had once been. Yet it was a treasure that must remain confined and not allowed to blind her with its brilliance. Its container protected her from such overpowering beauty. The Shekinah smiled sadly as she reasoned how insightful her seventh-born brother was. He understood his sister's need to put away her love of Samael, but to not discard it completely.

Thoughts of Seriel were her frequent companions, even more so than those of Samael. She had thought about being present when he was ready to pass through the portal, but decided against going there. She could well imagine herself begging him not to go. Remembering his utterly distraught expression when he was taking his leave of her, he might have even agreed to stay. Malkura was torn between wishing he would remain, yet knowing she did not want to love another brother who might bring her great misery, again.

Once Seriel was gone, the Shekinah believed she would eventually find the peace she desired. She had not revealed her growing affection for him, therefore, he seemed to accept her presumed disinterest in his love for her. Yet as eternity moved on, she wished she could tell him what she did not share before. His sudden declaration of love caught her off guard, even though Manah had told her it was so. He was gone so quickly and she did not tell him what she would explain, if he ever stood before her in this room, once more.

Wiping away a tear, Malkura placed the casket on the floor next to herself. She lay down and waited for sleep to numb her regretful thoughts about the Lord of the Seventh Essence. Yet knowing Seriel loved her as more than a sibling, brought solace to her unhappy memories.

*   *   *

Standing close to the chasm of universes, Seriel was observing the spheres of dark matter. He came to this place frequently, partly because his curiosity was intrigued by the barrier of unique creations and also due to an inability to view his precious spiral. Watching these dark orbs expanding, brought pleasure to him. Their mystery dulled the ache of sadness which he was experiencing at the loss of his shimmering spheres. According to the angels, who had witnessed the birth of these universes, they were countless. However, only a certain number were visible to those who stood on either side of the wide chasm. Seriel had decided to give names to these spheres and one, in particular, was attracting his attention, more and more. Named Avia by the seventh archangel, this universe was not as large as some yet it was truly a place of becoming. Within its darkness, swirling gases had quickly manifested together with simple atoms. Now, those atoms were developing into greater complexity. Seriel felt certain Avia would soon be a significant part of ALL THAT IS.

The Lord of Sorcery drew his purple cloak closer to himself. There was a penetrating chill within this area of the Abyss which kept many away from observing the growing universes. Seriel had manifested this garment soon after arriving because he frequently spent a long duration here, gazing into the bottomless chasm. The cloak was long and wide so that he could wrap it completely around himself. It draped below and around the growth point of his wings, then extended up and over his shoulders, covering his arms and encircling the front of his body. A silver chain secured and held its two sides together at the base of his throat. Soon after he had created it, he noted with amusement that several other angels were copying his invention. Seriel's light wand was strapped to his right thigh, as it always was when he was not sleeping. Regaining his crystal's closeness was of great comfort to him.

Michael gave back his light wand just before he stepped into the portal. His brother also entrusted Samael's crystal wand to his keeping. Knowing how powerfully it had previously impacted on him, Seriel asked his own wand to protect him from the unbalancing vibrations while Samael's crystal was in his possession. This strategy worked admirably. He was completely unaware of its potency, which was a blessing because passing through the portal was a very disturbing experience. As he moved into its void, he underwent an extremely unsettling sensation. It was as though every single particle of his being was separated and isolated, then spun round and round for what seemed forever. Each particle was acutely aware and was desperate to rejoin with all the other particles, but was unable to come back together with them. When this trauma became beyond endurance, it was suddenly ended. There was an overpowering sense of his parent's divine love magnetizing each and every particle so that they rejoined and became whole, once more. Immediately, Seriel found himself standing in the outer Abyss.

Thoughts of his passage through the portal, brought other remembrances, too. Taking leave of his brothers was difficult and filled with sadness. Uriel had begged to go with him so that he could be reunited with Samael, but Michael ordered his sixth brother to remain. Seriel was desperately hoping his sister would not come to watch him leave. He did not believe he would be able to go, if she were standing close by. However, the Shekinah was not present to wish him to fare well and for that he was grateful.

His life within outer Chaos was slowly passing. Soon after his arrival, he created another pyramidal home for himself. Samael's earlier collecting of many minerals made it possible for Seriel to crown his building with a crystal capstone. When he was not observing the universes or exploring the outlying areas of the Abyss, the seventh archangel busied himself with creating a bounty of glyphs and symbols. Yet none of these interests could ever free him from thoughts of the Shekinah.

She filled his dreams and his waking musings. Her face was imprinted on his consciousness. He had no need of a darkly hued crystal in which to watch her, she was forever with him in his thoughts. Seriel had not yet broached the subject with Samael of his distant viewing obsession. He did not want to divulge that Malkura had informed him of it. He trusted another way of revealing his knowledge of the dark crystal would present itself. Seriel wondered why his brother would want to have such sharp reminders of what was now denied him. The seventh-born sibling much preferred to lose himself in fond memories and fantasies about what might have been.

His love for the Shekinah grew stronger as eternity moved on. Even though she apparently felt nothing more than sibling affection for him, he would never cease to adore her. He felt certain he would be contented forever just to be in her company and to see her happy, once more. And Seriel steadfastly cherished the hope he might, yet again, achieve this blessing. Before going through the portal, he had journeyed to his spiraling spheres for one last viewing. While there, an orb, which depicted a future possible happening, had greatly cheered him. In it he was, once again, within the inner realms of Chaos. The knowledge of that feasible event would nurture his soul's desire until it could become reality.

*   *   *

The Source sighed deeply within its slumbers as its dreams played on and on. It lovingly watched the developing outer realms of the Abyss of Chaos, and wept many tears for its two lost sons.

Printed in the United States
40352LVS00003B/51